A Book Of

SUPPLY CHAIN AND LOGISTICS MANAGEMENT

For

BBM Semester - VI

As Per New Syllabus w.e.f. 2015

Dr. Shaila Bootwala
M.Com., M.Phil, Ph.D. (Marketing)
Vice-Principal and Head, Dept. of Commerce
Abeda Inamdar Senior College
Pune

Raisa Sheikh
Co-ordinator – BBA
Abeda Inamdar Senior College, Pune

Asst. Prof. Fazil Mohammed Shareef
M.B.A.(Marketing) M.Com , NET

NIRALI PRAKASHAN™
ADVANCEMENT OF KNOWLEDGE

N3480

Supply Chain and Logistics Management (BBM - VI)   **ISBN 978-93-5164-850-5**

Second Edition   :   **January 2017**

©   :   **Authors**

Published By :   Polyplate

NIRALI PRAKASHAN

Abhyudaya Pragati, 1312, Shivaji Nagar,
Off J.M. Road, PUNE – 411005
Tel - (020) 25512336/37/39, Fax - (020) 25511379
Email : niralipune@pragationline.com

➢ DISTRIBUTION CENTRES

PUNE

Nirali Prakashan : 119, Budhwar Peth, Jogeshwari Mandir Lane, Pune 411002, Maharashtra
Tel : (020) 2445 2044, 66022708, Fax : (020) 2445 1538
Email : bookorder@pragationline.com, niralilocal@pragationline.com

Nirali Prakashan : S. No. 28/27, Dhyari, Near Pari Company, Pune 411041
Tel : (020) 24690204 Fax : (020) 24690316
Email : dhyari@pragationline.com, bookorder@pragationline.com

MUMBAI

Nirali Prakashan : 385, S.V.P. Road, Rasdhara Co-op. Hsg. Society Ltd.,
Girgaum, Mumbai 400004, Maharashtra
Tel : (022) 2385 6339 / 2386 9976, Fax : (022) 2386 9976
Email : niralimumbai@pragationline.com

➢ DISTRIBUTION BRANCHES

JALGAON

Nirali Prakashan : 34, V. V. Golani Market, Navi Peth, Jalgaon 425001,
Maharashtra, Tel : (0257) 222 0395, Mob : 94234 91860

KOLHAPUR

Nirali Prakashan : New Mahadvar Road, Kedar Plaza, 1st Floor Opp. IDBI Bank
Kolhapur 416 012, Maharashtra. Mob : 9850046155

NAGPUR

Pratibha Book Distributors : Above Maratha Mandir, Shop No. 3, First Floor,
Rani Jhanshi Square, Sitabuldi, Nagpur 440012, Maharashtra
Tel : (0712) 254 7129

DELHI

Nirali Prakashan : 4593/21, Basement, Aggarwal Lane 15, Ansari Road, Daryaganj
Near Times of India Building, New Delhi 110002 Mob : 08505972553

BENGALURU

Pragati Book House : House No. 1, Sanjeevappa Lane, Avenue Road Cross,
Opp. Rice Church, Bengaluru – 560002.
Tel : (080) 64513344, 64513355,Mob : 9880582331, 9845021552
Email:bharatsavla@yahoo.com

CHENNAI

Pragati Books : 9/1, Montieth Road, Behind Taas Mahal, Egmore,
Chennai 600008 Tamil Nadu, Tel : (044) 6518 3535,
Mob : 94440 01782 / 98450 21552 / 98805 82331,
Email : bharatsavla@yahoo.com

niralipune@pragationline.com | www.pragationline.com

Also find us on 🇫 www.facebook.com/niralibooks

Dedication ...

Dr. Shaila Bootwala, Dr. Anwar Shaikh, Mr. Vijay Naidu, Mr. Parvez Billimoria, and Nisar Sagar who have been a constant source of inspiration and guidance for me.

Thanks to Mr. Zahid Shaikh (of Sea Reach Global) for his support and help in editing some of the chapters on Logistics management. Also thanks to Mr. Jignesh Furia of Nirali publications for giving the opportunity to write this book. Thanks to the editing team of Nirali Publication and Ms. Supriya Singh.

I would like to dedicate this book to My Mothers Zeenat Shaikh (Jennifer Ann Miller) and Mrs. Dawn Hopson (Dawn Miller).

Asst. Prof. Raisa Shaikh

I would like to dedicate this book to my mentors and my siblings.

Mentors: Dr. Shaila Bootwala and Dr. M.D. Lawrence who have been a constant source of inspiration and guidance for me.

Siblings: My brothers Aslam, Omar, Adil and my darling sister Sumaiya for always being there whenever I needed their support.

Asst. Prof. Mohd. Fazil Shareef

Preface ...

With Globalisation and technological advancements, the role of supply chain and logistics management have transformed from a mere process of inventory, warehouse, transportation and distribution management to the role of strategic decision making and global collaborations. The modern supply chain management is driven by information technology and is more customers centric.

This book introduces students with the basic concepts of supply chain, Distribution and logistics management and gradually gives an insight to the concepts of Marketing and its importance in physical distribution. Concepts of International Logistics management, Role of Information Technology, the key issues in International markets and management have been covered for the students studying international business.

Special care has been taken while writing this book, keeping in mind the syllabus and the understanding level of students with language barriers.

Special Thanks to Mr. Zahid Shaikh (of Sea Reach Global) for his support and help in editing some of the chapters on Logistics and International Freight management. Also thanks to Mr.Jignesh Furia of Nirali publications for giving the opportunity to write this book. Thanks to the editing team of Nirali Publication and Ms. Supriya Singh, Mr. Akbar Shaikh, Miss Chaitali Takle, Prasad Chintakindi.

Prof. Dr. Shaila Bootwala
Asst. Prof. Mohd. Fazil Shareef

Syllabus ...

1. **Basic Concept about Distribution System**

   1.1 Basic concept of distribution system Logistics needs.

   1.2 Setting distribution objectives.

   1.3 Definition of physical distribution concept of distribution cost. Analysis of distribution cost. Element of total cost in physical distribution system.

   1.4 Developing channel design

2. **Channel Selection**

   Control System for efficiency. Productivity aspects of logistics management. Distribution and Customer satisfaction. Channel strategy decision. Channel management and Channel strategy.

3. **Selections of Channel Partner and Strategies of Channel of Distribution**

   - Objectives of Channel of distribution. Patterns of distribution.
   - Factors in the selection distribution channel.
   - Motivation of intermediaries Motivational tools and control areas.
   - Remuneration of the sales person.

4. **Logistics for Customer Satisfaction**

   Functional areas of logistics integration. Marketing and Physical Distribution.

5. **Physical Distribution Management**

   - Transportation
   - Modes of Transportation
   - Distribution analysis control and management. Standards of performance of distribution and analysis. Controlling the distributor and retailer.

Contents ...

Chapter 1...

Basic Concept about Distribution System

Contents ...

Learning Objectives ...

- To understand the Basic Concept of Distribution System

- To learn the Need of logistics

- To discuss the Steps for Setting Distribution Objectives

- To define Physical Distribution

- To explain the Concept of Distribution Cost and Analysis of Distribution Cost

- To study the Elements of Total Cost in Physical Distribution System

- To elaborate the Development of Channel Design

1.1 Introduction

Supply chains are the lifelines of most companies. Materials whether raw, semi finished or finished are procured from suppliers. Products are manufactured, stored and finally these finished goods are ready to be delivered to customers. Having a strong supply chain network is the key to success for any business engaged in production or customer services.

In earlier days companies depended solely on the historical sales forecasts for decision making in terms of production and shipments to customers. With a distinct change in the global economy, businesses are seeking different ways to survive steep competitions and adapt to the rapid technological advances and market conditions. Customer demand for supply of goods in the shortest period of time has posed a challenge to companies and therefore there are innumerable changes and developments resulting in various types of supply chains.

The elements of logistics and the supply chain have, of course, always been fundamental to the manufacturing, storage and movement of goods and products. It is only relatively recently, however, that they have come to be recognised as vital functions within the business and economic environment. The role of logistics has changed in that it now plays a major part in the success of many different operations and organisations. In essence, the underlying concepts and rationale for logistics are not new. They have evolved through several stages of development, but still use the basic ideas such as trade-off analysis, value chains and systems theory together with their associated techniques.

There are many terms which are used, often interchangeably. A widely accepted definition that uses some of these terms also helps to describe one of the key relationships. This is as follows:

Logistics = Materials Management + Distribution

An extension to this idea helps to illustrate that the supply chain covers an even broader scope of the business area. This includes the supply of raw materials and components as well as the delivery of products to the final customer. Thus:

Supply Chain = Suppliers + Logistics + Customers

Logistics and the supply chain are concerned with physical and information flows and storage from raw material through to the final distribution of the finished product. Thus, supply and materials management represents the storage and flows into and through the production process, while distribution represents the storage and flows from the final production point through to the customer or end user. Major emphasis is now placed on the importance of information as well as physical flows and storage, and an additional and very relevant factor is that of reverse logistics - the flow of used products and returnable packaging back through.

Logistics is the management of all activities which facilitate movement and the co- ordination of supply and demand in the creation of time and place utility. (Hesket, Glaskowsky and Ivie, 1973)

Logistics is the art and science of managing and controlling the flow of goods, energy, information and other resources. (Wikipedia, 2006)

Logistics management is the planning, implementation and control of the efficient, effective forward and reverse flow and storage of goods, services and related information between the point of origin and the point of consumption in order to meet customer requirements. (CSCMP, 2006)

Logistics is the positioning of resource at the right time, in the right place, at the right cost, at the right quality. (Chartered Institute of Logistics and Transport (UK), 2005)

1.2 Historical Perspective

There have been several distinct stages in the development of distribution and logistics.

1950s and early 1960s

In this period, distribution systems were unplanned and unformulated. Manufacturers manufactured, retailers retailed, and in some way or other the goods reached the shops. Distribution was broadly represented by the haulage industry and manufacturers' own-account fleets. There was little positive control and no real liaison between the various distribution-related functions.

1960s and early 1970s

In the 1960s and 1970s the concept of physical distribution was developed with the gradual realisation that the 'dark continent' was indeed a valid area for managerial involvement. This consisted of the recognition that there was a series of interrelated physical activities such as transport, storage, materials handling and packaging that could be linked together and managed more effectively. In particular, there was recognition of a relationship between the various functions, which enabled a systems approach and total cost perspective to be used. Under the auspices of a physical distribution manager, a number of distribution trade-offs could be planned and managed to provide both improved service and reduced cost. Initially the benefits were recognised by manufacturers who developed distribution operations to reflect the flow of their product through the supply chain.

1970s

This was an important decade in the development of the distribution concept. One major change was the recognition by some companies of the need to include distribution in the functional management structure of an organisation. The decade also saw a change in the structure and control of the distribution chain. There was a decline in the power of the manufacturers and suppliers, and a marked increase in that of the major retailers. The larger retail chains developed their own distribution structures, based initially on the concept of regional or local distribution depots to supply their stores.

1980s

Fairly rapid cost increases and the clearer definition of the true costs of distribution contributed to a significant increase in professionalism within distribution. With this professionalism came a move towards longer-term planning and attempts to identify and pursue cost-saving measures. These measures included centralised distribution, severe reductions in stock-holding and the use of the computer to provide improved information and control. The growth of the third-party distribution service industry was also of major significance, with these companies spearheading developments in information and equipment technology. The concept of and need for integrated logistics systems were recognised by forward-looking companies that participated in distribution activities.

Late 1980s and early 1990s

In the late 1980s and early 1990s, and linked very much to advances in information technology, organisations began to broaden their perspectives in terms of the functions that could be integrated. In short, this covered the combining of materials management (the inbound side) with physical distribution (the outbound side). The term 'logistics' was used to describe this concept (see Fig. 1.1). Once again this led to additional opportunities to improve customer service and reduce the associated costs. One major emphasis made during this period was that informational aspects were as important as physical aspects in securing an effective logistics strategy.

1990s

In the 1990s the process was developed even further to encompass not only the key functions within an organisation's own boundaries but also those functions outside that also contribute to the provision of a product to a final customer. This is known as supply chain management

2000 to 2010

Business organisations faced many challenges as they endeavoured to maintain or improve their position against their competitors, bring new products to market and increase the profitability of their operations. This led to the development of many new ideas for improvement, specifically recognised in the redefinition of business goals and the re-engineering of entire systems.

Logistics and the supply chain finally became recognised as an area that was the key to overall business success. Indeed, for many organisations, changes in logistics have provided the catalyst for major enhancements to their business. Leading organisations recognised that there was a positive 'value added' role that logistics could offer, rather than the traditional view that the various functions within logistics were merely a cost burden that had to be minimised regardless of any other implications.

2010 onwards

Companies are switching to technologies and software solutions for production and inventory replenishment planning. Bar codes are widely used for optimising inventory management. For example, a retail clerk scans a bar code at the cash register; the information about a purchase is automatically fed into the computer by special software which recalculates production and replenishment requirements. This updated information helps the production manager in deciding and optimising production and inventory levels.

RFID (Radio Frequency Identification Devices) is another technology being widely used these days. A RFID tag is attached to a product. These tags contain electronic chips which store information about the product. An RFID reader attached to a forklift identifies the product location stored on racks or stacks. These days automated forklifts with RFID readers identify as well pick the orders from the racks without any human intervention.

Collaborative Planning Forecasting and Replenishment (CPFR): It is a collaborative agreement between partners in a supply chain. The objective of CPFR is to jointly synchronise the activities of production replenishment and distribution. The end result is reduction in inventory cost and improves product availability across the supply chain.

More and more companies are now turning to Green Supply Chains, focusing more on sales returns management, better customer support services. Supply chains are now being subjected to Six Sigma and ISO 14001:2004 standards for quality management.

1.3 Distribution System

1.3.1 Basic Concept

The working of the economic system by which goods and services are supplied to consumers involves four basic market functions: production, distribution, exchange and consumption. Logistics assists in the efficient performance of each of these functions. Production transfers raw materials into finished goods (i.e. it creates form utility). In doing so, a long and intricate logistical chain is activated to bring the material together in the proper quality and quantity at the right time in support of the production process. The function of distribution, places raw materials in the hands of the producers, and finished goods in the hands of the consumers when and where wanted (i.e. it creates time and place utility). Transportation comes into play as a key element in this chain, but getting goods where and when involves much more than just the services of carrying products from here to there.

The manufacturers, customers and potential customers are dispersed geographically and therefore, if the manufacturer serves only the local market, he would be losing the potential for growth and profit. Physical distribution is therefore a vital function of production and marketing.

1.3.2 Definition of Physical Distribution

Physical distribution is the group of related activities interlinked with the supply of finished product from the production line to the end user or the consumers. The physical distribution system involves the marketing and sales channels of distribution, for example the retailer and or the wholesaler. It also involves important components like inventory, materials, packaging, order processing, transportation, warehousing, logistics and CRM. In short physical distribution is the movement of goods from the source of origin to the final end user.

A distribution channel may be defined as:

1. Handling, movement, and storage of goods from the point of origin to the point of consumption or use, via various channels of distribution.

2. Physical distribution is the art and science of determining requirements, acquiring them, distributing them and finally maintaining them in an operationally ready condition for their entire life.

According to **Philip Kotler** and **Gary Armstrong**: "It is the set of firms and individuals that take title, or assist in transferring title, to a good or service as it moves from the producer to the final consumer or industrial user."

The physical distribution system gathers a lot of attention from businesses and business owners because nearly half of the entire marketing budget of a product is taken up by the physical distribution system. As a result, these activities are often the focus of process improvement and cost-saving initiatives in many companies.

1.3.3 Physical Distribution Management

1. The term 'physical distribution management' is employed in manufacturing and commerce to describe the broad range of activities (like freight, warehousing, material handling, protective packing, inventory control, selection of site for various activities, marketing, forecasting) concerned with the efficient movement of finished products from the end of production line to the consumer and in some cases, includes the movement of raw materials from the sources of supply to the beginning of the production line.

2. 'Physical distribution management' is specifically concerned with the flow of goods through the economic system.

1.3.4 Importance of Physical Distribution

The importance of physical distribution to a company can vary and is typically associated with the type of product manufactured by the company. Strategically staging products in locations to support order shipments and coming up with a rapid and consistent manner to move the product enables companies to be successful in dynamic markets.

Physical distribution is managed with a systems approach and considers key interrelated functions to provide efficient movement of products. The functions are interrelated because any time a decision is made in one area it has an effect on the others. For example, a business that is providing custom handbags would consider shipping finished products via air freight versus rail or truck in order to expedite shipment time. The importance of this decision would offset the cost of inventory control, which could be much more costly. Managing physical distribution from a systems approach can provide benefit in controlling costs and meeting customer service demands.

Physical distribution is of great importance because of its various functions such as location analysis, transportation, material handling, warehousing, packing, order processing, packaging, inventory control, customer sales service. We will also study how distribution adds value to the marketing process and products in the below given sections.

By using the network of the channel partners the distribution function, adds value to the selling function by providing time, place and possession utilities to the customer. Time utility makes the product available 'when' a consumer desires it. Place utility makes the product available 'where' he desires it. Possession utility is given when the consumer buying the product gets the ownership transferred to him at a time and place suitable to him or her. For giving the possession utility the channels make the transaction easy by maintaining contacts with their upstream partners which could be the C&FA or even the firm. The downstream channels involved here are the distributors, wholesalers and the retailers. The transactions includes order taking, order communication, order processing, and delivery of the goods and collection of payments. While coordinating with the upstream partners, the downstream channel partners deal with these transactions.

Thus, the importance of Physical Distribution can be enumerated as given below:

1. Professional and effective distribution is important in terms of competitive advantage.
2. It is essential to have a good distribution system for achieving maximum customer value.
3. There is improvement in customer service.
4. The inability to provide the correct products at the correct place at the correct time may lead to loss in sales.

Besides that, the channel gives additional benefits of providing service that is connected to the product. For instance, if one were to buy a colour television, besides selling the TV to the consumer, the distributor provides the services of delivering it to the house of the buyer, assisting him in installing the set and run the programmes for him so that the TV instantly becomes useful to the purchaser.

Example of selling cars, washing machines and the like are all with the additional support which surpasses time, place and possession utilities.

In the case of industrial products, the service includes assistance in installation, running it and making the customer understand as to how he can run the equipment at peak capacity. It also includes giving direction on routine maintenance so that the machine does not stop working. This is also true for IT hardware.

In case of a software-seller who is allowed to sell IT software, he has to assist in running the software, parallel to the current legal software for the client to get used to the new software.

The importance given by the intermediaries is a direct result of the distribution strategy of the firm which is mainly directed by the customer service policy and the intensity of competition.

1.3.5 Functions of Physical Distribution

The **key functions** within the physical distribution system are

1. The **customer service** function is a tactical designed standard for consumer satisfaction that the business means to give to its customers. For example, a customer satisfaction approach for the handbag business stated above may be that 75 percent of all custom handbags that are delivered to the customer within 72 hours of ordering. An additional approach may consist of that 95 percent of custom handbags to be delivered to the customer within 96 hours of purchase. Once these customer service standards are fixed, the physical distribution system is then designed to achieve these goals.

2. **Order processing** is designed to take the customer orders and implement the specifics the client has purchased. The business is associated with this function because it directly connects to how the customer is serviced and achieving the customer service goals. If the order processing system is well-organised, then the company can avoid other costs in other functions, for example, transportation or inventory control. For instance, if the handbag business has a fault in the processing of a customer order, the company has to fall back on premium transportation modes, such as next day air or overnight, to meet the customer service standard set out, which will increase the transportation cost.

3. **Inventory control** is a main role player in the distribution system of a business. Costs consist of investment into current inventory, loss of demand for products, and depreciation. There are various kinds of inventory control systems that can be executed, such as first in-first out (or FIFO) and flow through, which are the different techniques used by companies to manage different products.

First in-first out, or **FIFO**, is a method in which the new products coming into the warehouse replace existing products of the same SKU(Stock Keeping Unit) so that merchandise is cycled and does not expire or become old as more recent production is available. **Flow through**, on the other hand, is product that does not get processed in the warehouse. It is offloaded from an inbound trailer, pushed across the warehouse and onto outbound trailers for departure without being stored in the warehouse.

1.3.6 Participants / Activities in the Physical Distribution Process

The primary participants of the physical distribution process are Producers, Wholesalers, Distributors, Retailers and End-users. However, the physical distribution process also involves management (planning, action and control) of the physical flows of raw materials and finished products from the point of origin to the points of use/consumption to meet the customer needs at a profit. It covers all the activities in the flow of goods between the producer and consumer.

In a distribution system, the following main interrelated activities affect customer service and the cost of providing the services.

1. **Order Receiving and Processing:** It involves all the activities right from receiving order, fulfillment of order and dispatch of order in a timely manner for effective customer service.

2. **Communication:** In a distribution system, many intermediaries are involved and hence a good communication system plays an important role. Proper information technology infrastructure and other medias are very important.

3. **Transportation:** The physical movement of goods right from getting the raw material to delivering the final product to the customer / end user needs a good selection of transportation system. Different modes of transport for inbound / outbound logistics can be either owned or outsourced to reliable service providers. Cost effectiveness of transportation can be analysed by the logistics managers.

4. **Distribution Inventory:** Distribution inventory includes all finished goods inventory. In terms of costs, it is one of the most important elements in a distribution system and accounts for about 25percent to 30percent of the cost of distribution. Inventories serve the time utility factor.

5. **Warehouses:** Warehouses are the storage area for inventories. A well managed warehouse system is based on the proper selection of site location, number of distribution centres, a good design layout, security for stored goods and provision for consolidation / break bulking of goods /packaging

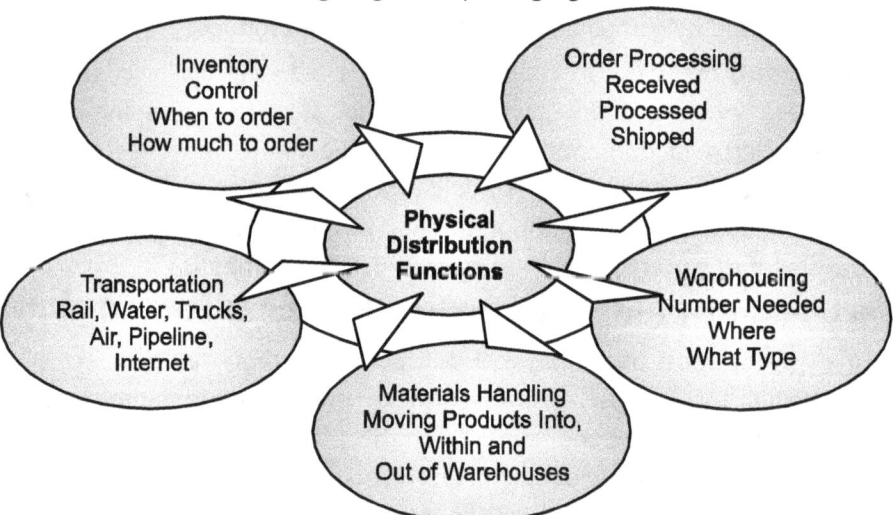

Fig. 1.1: Participants of a Physical Distribution System

6. **Materials Handling:** Materials handling is the movement and storage of goods inside the warehouse or a distribution centre. The cost of distribution can vary depending upon the type of equipments being used for materials handling. These equipments represent the cost element of a firm's capital.

7. **Protective Packaging:** Distribution inventories must be packed and protected and labelled for proper identification. They must be packed in such a way so as to fit them into proper storage spaces like racks / stacks etc and also they should be easy to be identified and loaded on the transportation systems when an order is received.

1.3.7 Setting Distribution Objectives

A distribution channel strategy enables you to sell to customers in geographical areas or market sectors that your direct sales team cannot reach. One can choose from a number of distribution channels, including wholesalers, retailers, distributors and the Internet. Each channel gives a different option for dealing with customers and prospects. However, to ensure that the distributors operate effectively, a strategy must incorporate the right level of control and support. The following is a gist of components for setting distribution objectives.

A firm's distribution objectives will ultimately be highly related—some will enhance each other while others will compete. For example, a more exclusive and higher service distribution will generally entail less intensity and lesser reach. Cost has to be traded off against speed of delivery and intensity (it is much more expensive to have a product available in convenience stores than in supermarkets, for example).

Narrow vs. wide reach: The extent to which a firm should seek narrow (exclusive) vs. wide (intense) distribution depends on a number of factors. One issue is the consumer's likelihood of switching and willingness to search. For example, most consumers will switch soft drink brands rather than walking from a vending machine to a convenience store several blocks away, so intensity of distribution is essential here. However, for sewing machines, consumers will expect to travel at least to a department or discount store, and premium brands may have more credibility if they are carried only in full service specialty stores.

Retailers involved in a more exclusive distribution arrangement are likely to be more "loyal"—that is, they will tend to recommend the product to the customer and thus sell large quantities,

Carry larger inventories and selections and Provide more services:

Distribution opportunities: Distribution provides numerous opportunities for the marketer that is generally connected to the other elements of the marketing mix. For instance, for a cost, the company can promote its objective by such activities as in-store demonstrations/samples and special placement. Placement is also an opportunity for promotion – for example, airlines understand that they, as "prestige accounts," can get great deals from soft drink makers who are keen to have their products offered on the airlines. In the same way, it may be useful to sell at low prices, certain premiums (for example, T-shirts or cups with the corporate logo.) It is even possible to have advertisements printed on the retailer's bags (for example, "got milk?")

Other opportunities involve "parallel" distribution (for example, having products sold both through traditional channels and through the Internet or factory outlet stores). Partnerships and joint promotions may involve distribution (for example McDonald's selling a branded product like Coke).

Deciding on a strategy: Considering the need for markets to be balanced, the same distribution strategy will probably not be successful for each company. Thus using advanced research tools and scanner information, one can judge how often different products are bought and items whose sales associate with each other. It is also useful to observe consumers using products and making purchase decisions.

On the basis of the following observations, one can make a distribution strategy and product placement.

- How much time is dedicated to choosing a product in a given category,
- How many products are compared,
- What different types of products are compared or are substitutes (for example, ice-creams vs. milk shakes in a mall),
- What are "complementing" products that may cue the purchase of others when placed nearby? Channel members – both wholesalers and retailers – may have important data, but their comments should be viewed with suspicion as they have their own agendas and may twist information.

Steps for Setting Distribution Objectives / Strategies

- **Reach:** If a strategy is to develop your business regionally or nationally, stress on the geographical regions you want to reach through a distribution channel and identify a network of distributors or retailers that give existing coverage of the territories. If a firm plans to export products, it must concentrate on established distributors who have comprehensive local market knowledge, consider marketing products on the Internet so that one can extend coverage to customers where there is no appropriate physical distribution network.
- **Cost:** Although a distribution strategy gives you a convenient platform for expansion, it is significant to compare the cost of dealing through indirect distribution channels with the cost of establishing your own network or direct sales operation. Without a distribution network, you will have to commit resources to order processing, stockholding, delivery, invoicing and customer service. Compare that with the lower margins you will make by giving distributors a discount for giving the same level of service and providing them with a program of marketing and training support.

- **Contribution:** In your strategy you should also consider the potential contribution of each distribution channel. Focus on working with distributors that give you access to an extra customer base, with no additional direct sales and marketing costs. Distributors also give you the local market knowledge, allowing you to set up your business in new markets without incurring heavy market entry costs.
- **Support:** Support and control are important factors in your distribution strategy. Appointing a manager to work with distributors allows you to observe their performance and identify their support requirements. Develop marketing support programs to meet the requirements of different channels. Options comprise funds for advertising or direct marketing campaigns or templates that allow partners to develop their own campaigns. If channel sales represent an important part of your business, develop advertising and marketing operations to drive business to your channel partners. The distributors' product and marketing knowledge will be improved by a training program and will allow them to deliver a higher standard of service to customers.
- **Customer Service:** It is significant to recognise the kinds of customers you wish to serve directly. Normally, these would be your largest customers or customers that demand levels of technical support beyond your partners' ability. Use channel partners to manage big number of smaller customers, cost effectively so that you can focus your resources on your important accounts.

1.4 Supply Chain

1.4.1 Introduction

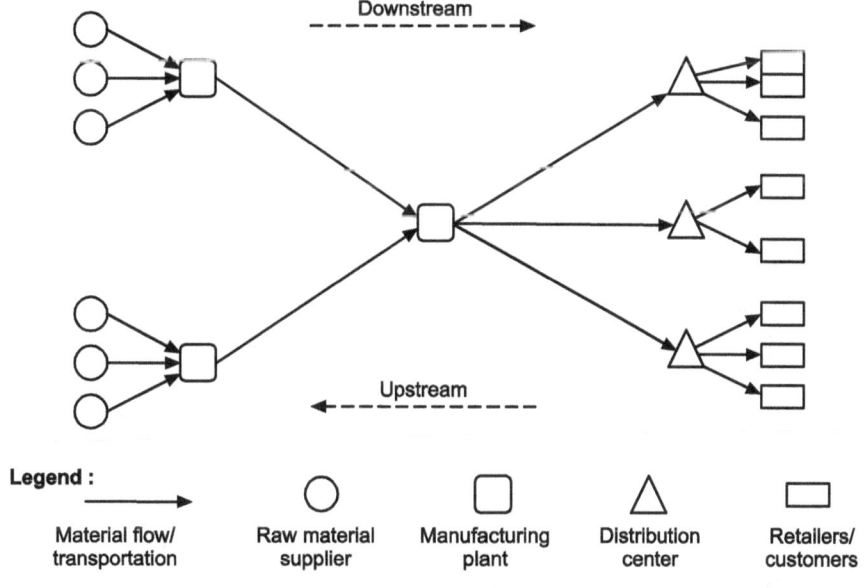

Fig. 1.2: A Simple Supply Chain

A supply chain is the network of organisations that are involved through upstream and downstream connections in the various processes and activities that generate value in the form of products and services in the hands of final customers. It is also known as a value chain.

It includes all parties involved directly or indirectly, in satisfying a customer's request. The supply chain consists of not only the manufacturer and suppliers, but also transporters, warehouses, retailers, and even customers themselves.

Within each organisation, such as a manufacturer, the supply chain consists of all functions engaged in accepting and filling a customer request. These functions include, but are not restricted to a new product development, marketing, operations, distribution, finance and customer service.

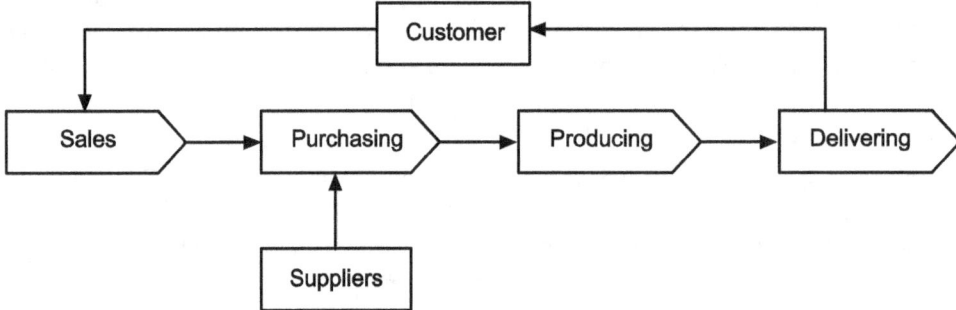

Fig. 1.3: A Conceptual Example of the Supply Chain Loop

Supply chain management is an application of an entire systems approach to supervise the complete flow of information, materials, and services from raw materials suppliers through industries and stores to the end customer. The connections are observed between the suppliers that give inputs, manufacturing and service support operations that change the inputs into products and services, and the distribution and local service contributors that confine the product. Localisation involves just the delivery of the product or some more involved process that modifies the product or service to the requirements of the local market.

1.4.2 Different Views of Supply Chain / Distribution Network

1. Process View

The processes in a supply chain are usually divided into a series of activities, each performed in the interface between two interrelated successive stages of a supply chain.

Supply chain consists of networks who are involved directly or indirectly, to fulfill customer requests. Supply chains consist of not only manufacturers and suppliers, but also transporters, retailers, warehouses and customers.

Supply Chain Stages

A typical supply chain includes a variety of components which include customers, retailers, distributors, manufacturer, supplier etc. Each stage of a supply chain is connected through the flow of product, information and funds.

Process view of supply chain is useful to make operational decisions as role of each member of supply chain is defined.

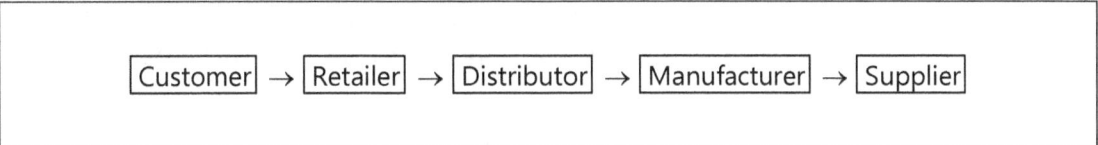

Fig. 1.4: Process view Supply Chain

(a) Customer: Customer places a requirement at a retail outlet or directly to the producer. The supply chain's goal is to convert customer requirement into customer order.

(b) Retailer: Retailer receives a customer requisition and information of what products the customers are buying. Here the main aim is to make a quick order entry and processes it efficiently through a well managed communication system.

(c) Distributor: The distribution channels enhance the supply chain network to make the products available to the customers in the shortest period of time.

(d) Manufacturer: Manufacturing facilities help to make the product according to order placed by customer. Manufacturers need to keep proper communications with the channel members to understand the exact requirements and products to be manufactured.

(e) Supplier: A supplier in a supply chain is an enterprise that contributes goods or services in a supply chain cycle. They supply raw materials or manufacture goods required as an input to other manufacturers.   For example a supplier or manufacturer of tyres supplies tyres to the manufacturer of cars.

2. The Push/Pull View

Today's supply chains have undergone significant changes and have become more customer demand-oriented. The channel members are forced to choose the approaches which will be beneficial to them and also which gives high profit returns. To recap, a supply chain is a basic network of suppliers and customers. Therefore, supply chain management by a particular business is the management of human resources, processes, materials and information within the supply chain which will give maximum returns on investment. A well managed supply chain ensures that all participants in a supply chain can benefit from improvements to the functioning of the supply chain as a whole.

A customer demand is also known as a Pull, while anticipating a customer demand based on sales forecast is known as a PUSH. It is important to understand from a whole supply chain viewpoint, whether a particular supply chain needs a push or pull strategy. It is usually difficult to estimate which kind of supply chain process is to be implemented and in general it depends on the perspective of the supply chain and its participant. Example of PULL process is, the demand for Samsung Smart phones is customer driven and hence the supply chains need to produce and keep sufficient stock of these smart phones. For the launch of new brands of smart phones with advance features, the company needs to use PUSH strategies through television advertisements and teaser advertisements on Youtube or social media sites.

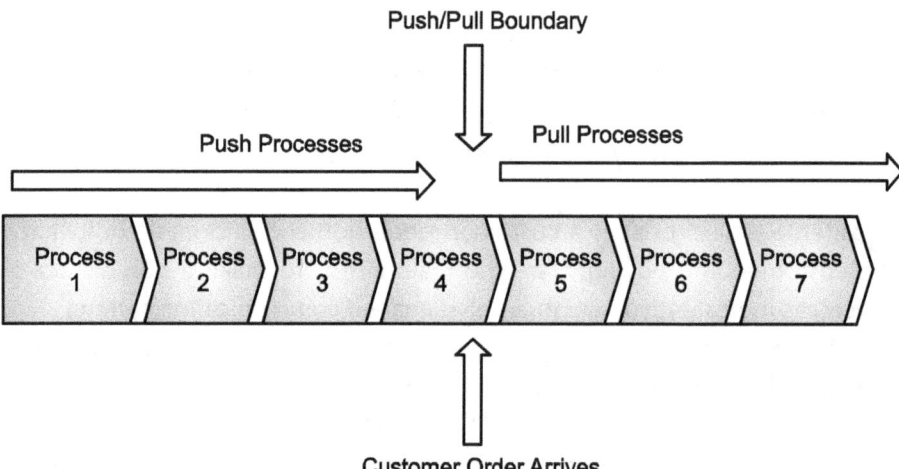

Fig. 1.5: Push/ Pull View of Supply Chain

What is a Push System?

Companies use a forecast approach for production and supply. This strategy or a process is called as "push system". Companies are confident and they are able to forecast that the goods will be sold soon and they may run into unexpected shortages. Decisions are taken at every reorders. The purchasing department makes an analysis of the quantity and frequency of purchases to be made. Forecasting in PUSH process is done at an aggregate level. The main disadvantage with PUSH system is that they are largely based on forecast, and it may go wrong. The other disadvantages includes missed sales, losing on customers to competitors, shortages, high carrying cost, emergency shipments, rescheduling of production etc.

What is a Pull System?

Pull systems use demand data for both stock replenishment and manufacturing. Only immediate customer requirements are taken into consideration. The Pull system is driven by the actual consumption recorded at the store as well as sales forecast.

In a Pull system, a slow moving item can be managed by a simple reorder point, but for large turnover items, minimum/maximum reorder policy can be used. Sophisticated software systems automate the demand-supply requirements providing an insight into customer demands and the required quantity of order replenishments. Many push systems put the majority of the inventory at the retail store.

Push-Pull System

Some companies are making use of the best features of both PUSH and PULL processes. The Push-Pull system is also known as lean inventory strategy or push-pull inventory control system. Forecasts in this case have to be reliable and accurate based on actual sales data. Inventory levels are adjusted as per requirements; therefore the main goal of push-pull is stabilisation of inventory levels by manufacturing or managing JIT (Just-in-time) inventories.

Managers need to plan and develop guidelines for meeting short and long-term production needs. For Push-Pull systems, sophisticated information systems and cloud based systems are being used.

Table 1.1: Characteristics of the Push and Pull Parts of the Supply Chain

	Push	**Pull**
Objective	Minimum Cost	Maximum Service Level
Complexity	High	Low
Focus	Resource Allocation	Responsiveness
Lead Time	Long	Short
Process	Supply Chain Planning	Order Fulfillment

3. **Cycle View of Supply Chain**

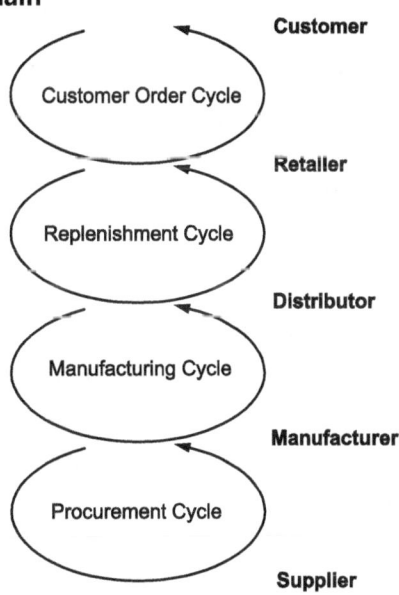

Fig. 1.6: Supply Chain Process Cycles

The processes in a supply chain are divided into a series of cycles, each performed at the interface between two successive stages of a supply chain. A typical supply chain includes a variety of stages including customers, retailers, distributors, manufacturers, and component suppliers. Each stage of a supply chain is connected through the flow of product, information and funds.

The cycle view of a supply chain is useful to make operational decisions as the role of each member of supply chain is defined.

1.4.3 Components of Supply Chain Management

A basic supply chain management system has five components:

1. The **plan**, which refers to the over-all strategy of the SCM programme including the development of SCM metrics to monitor; companies need a plan that is efficient in that it is cost effective, valuable to its customers, and provides high quality products or services.

2. The **source**, which refers to the suppliers who'll provide you with goods and services necessary for you to run your business; finding a reliable source to deliver the goods is challenging and takes time

3. The **make** or manufacturing component, which refers to the execution of processes needed to produce, test, and package your products or services; making the product requires testing, packaging and preparation before it can be delivered.

4. The **delivery**, which refers to the system for receiving orders from customers, developing a network of warehouses; getting the products to the customers; invoicing customers and receiving payment from them; and

5. The **return**, which is the system for processing customer returns and/or supporting customers facing problems with the products they received.

1.4.4 Participants in the Supply Chain

In its easiest form, a supply chain is composed of a firm and the suppliers and customers of that same firm. This is the basic group of participants that forms a simple supply chain. Extended supply chains enclose three additional kinds of participants. First there is the supplier's supplier or the final supplier at the start of an extended supply chain. Then there is the customer's customer or final customer at the end of an extended supply chain. In the end there is a complete category of firms that are service providers to other firms in the supply chain. These are firms who supply services in logistics, finance, marketing, and information technology.

In any given supply chain there are some group of firms who perform various functions. There are firms that are producers, distributors or wholesalers, retailers, and companies or individuals who are the customers, the ultimate consumers of a product. Supporting these companies there will be other companies that provide a range of needed services.

1. **Producers:** Producers or manufacturers are organisations that create a product. This includes those firms that are producers of raw materials and firms that are producers of finished goods. Producers of raw materials are organisations that mine for minerals, drill for oil and gas, and cut timber.

   It also consists of organisations that cultivate the land, raise animals, or catch seafood. Producers of finished goods use the raw materials and sub-assemblies prepared by other manufacturers to create their products. Producers can generate products that are indefinable such as music, entertainment, software, or designs. A product can also be a service such as trimming a lawn, maintaining an office, performing an operation, or teaching a skill. In many situations the producers of concrete, industrial products are moving to regions of the world where labour is inexpensive. Producers in the developed world of North America, Europe, and parts of Asia are producers of insubstantial objects and services.

2. **Distributors:** Distributors are firms that take inventory in bulk from producers and distribute a bundle of associated product lines to customers. Distributors are also known as wholesalers. They normally sell to other businesses and they sell products in big quantities than an individual consumer would normally purchase. Distributors protect the producers from variations in product demand by stocking inventory and doing much of the sales work to look for and provide service to customers. For the customer, distributors' fulfil the "Time and Place" function and they distribute products when and where the customer wants them.

   A distributor in general is an organisation that takes possession of important inventories of products that they purchase from producers and sell to consumers. On top of product promotion and sales the other functions that the distributor performs are inventory management, warehouse operations, and product transportation with customer support and post-sales service. A distributor can also be an organisation that only brokers a product between the producer and the customer and never takes possession of that product. This type of distributor mostly carries out the functions of product promotion and sales. In both these cases, as the requirements of customers evolve and the choice of available products changes, the distributor is the mediator that constantly tracks customer needs and matches them with products available.

3. **Retailers:** Retailers stock inventory and sell in smaller amounts to the general public. This organisation also closely follows the choices and demands of the customers that it sells to. It advertises to its customers and frequently uses some combination of price, product choice, service, and convenience to draw the attention of its customers for the product it sells. Discount department stores draw the attention of customers by using price and extensive product selection. Glamorous specialty stores provide an exclusive line of products and high levels of service. Fast food restaurants use convenience and low prices as their ultimate selling point.

4. **Customers:** Customers or consumers are part of an organisation that buys and uses a product. A customer organisation might buy a product so as to incorporate it into another product that they in turn sell to other customers, who are the end users of a product and who purchases the product in order to use it.

5. **Service Providers:** These are organisations that provide services to producers, distributors, retailers, and customers. Service providers have developed special skills that concentrate on a specific activity required by a supply chain. Due to this, they are able to perform these services more efficiently and at a superior price than producers, distributors, retailers, or consumers could do on their own.

Some common service providers in any supply chain are providers of transportation services and warehousing services. These are trucking firms and public warehouse firms and they are called as logistics providers. Financial service providers deliver services such as making loans, doing credit analysis, and collecting previous due statements.

These are banks, credit rating companies, and collection agencies. Some service providers deliver market research and advertising, while others provide product design, engineering services, legal services, and management advice. Still other service providers provide information technology and information collection services. All these service providers are incorporated to a greater or lesser level into the ongoing functions of the producers, distributors, retailers, and consumers in the supply chain.

Supply chains are composed of repetitive sets of participants that fall into one or more of these divisions. Over time the requirements of the supply chain as a complete unit remain quite stable. What changes is the combination of participants in the supply chain and the parts that each member plays. In some supply chains, there are few service providers because the other participants carry out these services on their own. In other supply chains efficient providers of specific services have developed other members to outsource work to these service providers rather than doing it themselves.

1.4.5 Elements of Supply Chain Management

To study the components of supply chain management, we first need to study the key elements of a supply chain:

1. **Production:** Production denotes the capacity of a supply chain to make and accumulate products. The facilities of production are factories and warehouses. Strategic decisions concerning the production focus on what customers' desire and the market demands. This first phase in developing supply chain dexterity takes into account how many products are to be produced, and what, if any, parts or components should be produced at which plants or outsourced to capable suppliers. These strategic decisions concerning production must also concentrate on capacity, quality and volume of goods, keeping in mind that customer demand and

satisfaction must be met. Operational decisions, then again, concentrate on setting up workloads, maintenance of equipment and meeting immediate client/market demands. Quality control and workload balancing are problems which need to be taken into consideration when making these decisions.

2. **Supply:** Next, an organisation must decide about what their facility or facilities are capable of producing, both inexpensively and efficiently, while maintaining the quality high. But most firms cannot provide excellent performance with the production of all components. Outsourcing is an excellent option to be taken into consideration for those products and components that cannot be produced efficiently by an organisation's facilities. Firms must cautiously select suppliers for raw materials. When choosing a supplier, a person's concentration should be on developing velocity, quality and flexibility while simultaneously decreasing costs or maintaining low cost levels. In brief, strategic decisions should be made to decide the core capabilities of a facility and outsourcing affiliations should develop from these decisions.

3. **Material Handling:** Material handling moves products before, after or between transportation and warehousing. Material handling activities usually take place within the premises of a warehouse. It is defined as activities, equipment, and procedures related to the moving, storing, protecting and controlling of materials in a system.

4. **Inventory Management:** Businesses supervise their everyday operations of manufacturing and marketing with the help of inventory. This could be in the form of raw materials, packing, materials, packing work-in-process on the production shop floor and finished goods.

5. **Order Processing:** A customer order is the message that sets the supply chain process in motion. Order processing starts with the receiving of a customer's order and ends with the final delivery of goods to him along with transfer of title. In other words, order processing is a set of activities for receiving, recording, assembling of products for dispatch to fill the customer order. The customer order cycle time is the total time consumed in order preparation and its transmittal, order receipt, order entry, order processing, warehouse picking and packing, preparation of invoices and shipping documents, transportation and delivery and unloading of goods at the customer's end.

6. **Warehousing:** Warehouses are the godowns for keeping and storing goods at various points along the distribution network to improve availability of material to customers and to reduce transportation costs. In this process of storage warehouses are required to perform many operations like receiving the incoming material; moving them in appropriate locations of storage areas; protecting and preserving them in a scientific and systematic manner for the maintenance of their original

value, quality and usefulness; gathering material as required by customers or for transfer to other locations; repacking the material; delivering the material to customers or dispatching for onward transportation; keeping records of material in stock.

7. **Transportation:** Transportation refers to the movement of goods, raw material and finished products between different facilities in a supply chain. In transportation the trade-off between awareness and competency is evident in the choice of transport mode. Quick modes of transport such as airways are very fast but also more costly. Slower modes such as ship and rail are very cost efficient but not as fast. Since transportation costs can be as much as a third of the operating cost of a supply chain, decisions made here are very important.

8. **Information:** Information is the foundation on which one has to make decisions concerning the other four supply chain drivers. It is the link between all of the activities and operations in a supply chain. To the point that this link is a strong one, the firms in a supply chain are capable enough to take good decisions for their own operations. This also has the tendency to maximise the profitability of the supply chain as a whole. That is the way how the stock markets or other free markets operate and supply chains have several similar dynamics as markets.

9. **Reverse Logistics:** Reverse logistics stands for all operations connected to the reuse of products and materials. It is "the process of planning, implementing, and controlling the efficient, cost effective flow of raw materials, in-process inventory, finished goods and connected data from the point of consumption to the point of origin for the purpose of recapturing its importance or removing the product. More accurately, reverse logistics is the procedure of moving products from their final destination for the purpose of capturing its importance, or removing the products. Remanufacturing and redoing activities are also included in the definition of reverse logistics." The reverse logistics process includes management and the sale of surplus plus returned tool and machines from the hardware leasing business.

1.5 Logistics

1.5.1 Introduction and Definition

The term 'Logistics' stems from the Greek word 'Logisticos' meaning 'the science of computing and calculating'. It was used first in the military. Webster defines logistics as 'the procurement, maintenance and transportation of military materials, facilities and personnel'. From military point of view, logistics refers to a supportive system which reflects the practical art of moving armies and materials engaged in combating the enemy to achieve the desired results.

Today, in the industrial and commercial world, logistics has acquired a wider meaning. The Council of Logistics Management (CLM) has defined it in 1991 as follows: Logistics is the process of planning, implementing and controlling of efficient, effective flow and storage of goods, services and related information from the point of origin to the point of consumption for the purpose of conforming to customer expectations.

Logistics is a part of the supply chain process that plans, implements, and controls the efficient, effective forward and reverse flow and storage of goods, services, and related information between the point of origin and the point of consumption in order to meet customers' requirements; in other words, describing the entire process of materials and products moving into, through, and out of the firm:

- **Inbound Logistics:** Inbound logistics covers the movement of material received from suppliers. Materials management describes the movement of materials and components within a firm.
- **Outbound Logistics:** Outbound logistics covers the movement of materials or finished goods from the manufacturing unit to a distribution centre or the end customer.
- **Reverse Logistics:** Reverse logistics represents all the operations that are connected to the reuse of products and materials. It is "the process of planning, implementing, and controlling the efficient, cost effective flow of raw materials, in-process inventory, finished goods and related information from the point of consumption to the point of origin for the purpose of recapturing value or proper disposal. More accurately, reverse logistics is the process of shifting the products from their usual final destination for the purpose of capturing value, or proper disposal. Remanufacturing and refurnishing activities also may be included in the definition of reverse logistics." The reverse logistics process includes the management and the sale of surplus as well as the returned equipment and machines from the hardware leasing business.

Business Implications: In today's marketplace, several retailers treat merchandise returns as individual, disjointed transactions. "The challenge for retailers and vendors is to process returns at a proficiency level that allows rapid, efficient and cost-effective collection and return of merchandise. Customer requirements facilitate demand for a high standard of service that includes precision and timeliness. It's the logistic firm's duty to shorten the connection from the return of origination to the time of resell." By following returns management best practices, retailers can attain a returns process that addresses both the operational and customer retention issues connected to merchandise returns. In additional, due to the link between reverse logistics and customer retention, it has become an important part within Service Lifecycle Management (SLM), a business strategy that aims to retain customers by co-ordinating a firm's services data together to attain greater efficiency in its operations.

Return of unsold goods: In some industries, goods are distributed to downstream members in the supply chain with the knowledge that the goods may be returned for credit if they are not sold. Newspapers and magazines serve as examples. This acts as an incentive for downstream members to carry more stock, because the risk of obsolescence is borne by the upstream supply chain members. On the other hand, there is also a different risk connected to this logistics concept. The downstream member in the supply chain may exploit the circumstances by ordering more stock than is needed and returning big volumes. In this way, the downstream partner is capable of offering high level of service without carrying the risks connected to large inventories. The supplier successfully finances the inventory for the downstream member. It is thus significant to analyse customers' account for hidden cost.

Reverse logistics is the process of managing the return of goods. Reverse logistics is also referred to as "aftermarket customer services". In other words, any time money is taken from a company's warranty reserve or service logistics budget one can speak of a reverse logistics operation.

1.5.2 Main Activities of a Logistics System

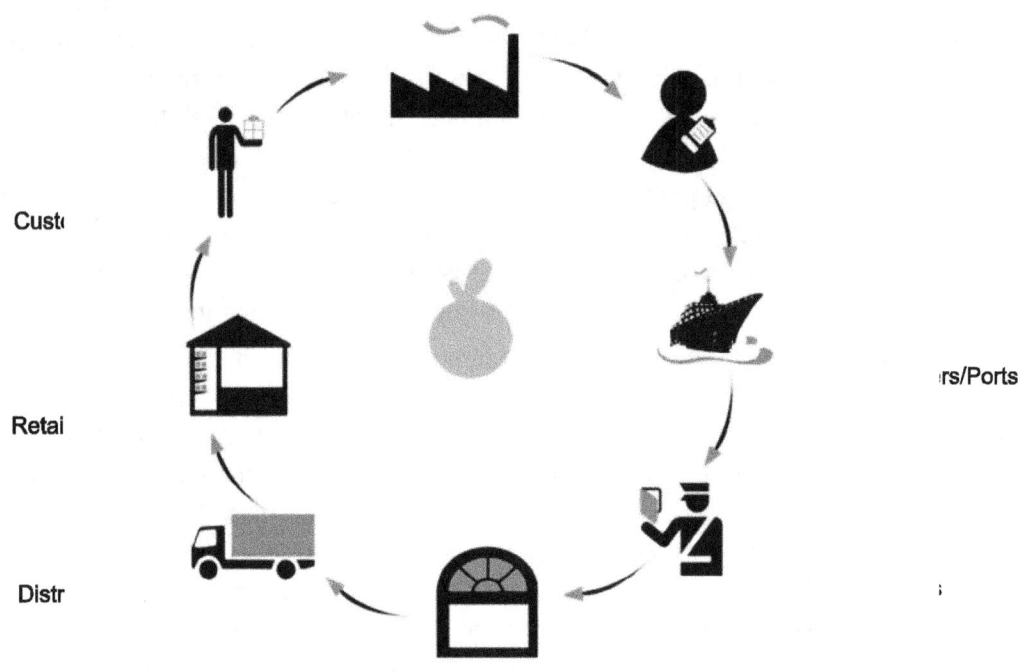

Cust

rs/Ports

Retai

Distr

Fig. 1.7: Main Activities of a Logistics System

1. Products are ordered, billed/invoiced, handled, packaged, packed, wrapped, bundled, sorted, crated, and braced.
2. Products are assembled and stored, warehoused, loaded, unloaded, shelved, displayed and cross-docked.
3. Products are shipped by air, railways, waterways, pipelines, and containers.
4. Products are exported, imported, documented, marked and consolidated.
5. Products are traced, tracked, recycled and disposed.
6. Customer's service standards of logistics are set (time, availability, errors etc.).

1.5.3 Logistics Needs

With globalisation and shortened product life cycles, the Indian industry is concentrating on re-engineering their supply chain and logistics activities to attain the competitive edge. Indian firms are increasingly incorporating their supply chains and outsourcing their logistics and supply chain management needs.

This has created a need for a variety of logistics and transportation solutions for the industry, ranging from solutions for multimodal transport, freight forwarding, material handling, warehousing, shipping, air cargo, packaging, inventory management and more significantly, in incorporating logistics and supply chains. A huge demand for logistics and transportation solutions and a developing infrastructure has made India – the logistics market of the 21st century and is been given unprecedented opportunities in the logistics business.

In the last ten years of the 21st century the Indian economy is zooming towards market orientation in which customers are considered as boss in almost all industrial segments. Logistics is additionally used as an effective weapon to combat competition, which leads a company towards non-price competition. Its dynamism has also become broader because of growth in the size and its multidimensional operations of business ventures. It is clear that the fragrance of logistics is pervading because of the increasing pressure on companies to reach the market at the most appropriate time and place at a least cost. In other words, it not only leads a company towards productivity and profitability by removal of wastage, restriction of cost and acceleration of sales but can also be used as an instrument of cost and acceleration of sales and as an instrument of core competency to offset competition. Therefore, it can be said, mere decrease in cost is not only the climax of logistics, but the real excitement is the improvement of productivity and profitability for core competency by providing superior customer service.

Logistics needs, to summarise is:

1. To make available the right quantity of right quality products at the right time and place in the right physical condition. In short, to ensure timely and intact delivery of goods and services to customers as per their requirements and specifications.

2. To offer the best possible customer service for core competency.
3. To minimise total logistical costs.
4. To maintain transparency in operations.

Operational Objectives

While achieving logistics missions of the enterprise, logistics managers are required to define operational objectives in more specific terms. Proper definition and communication of logistics operational objectives are a pre-requisite for the development, implementation, administration and control of logistics system design. Efficient performance of any logistics system needs careful consideration of following six 'R's about operational objectives of logistics manager.

1. **Right Response:** It refers to the ability to meet the service requirements of customers by means of quick response with positive attitude. Real time communication of information is the nucleus of the right response.

2. **Right Quality:** It includes consistency in the quality of the product which includes homogeneity in the features and their zero-defect delivery which means damage less delivery, right assortments and correct documentation.

3. **Right Quantity:** This objective deals with the maintenance of a minimum possible level of inventory required for a desired level of customer service. Any decrease in the inventory level for the same level of service results in a decrease in the inventory cost, which consequently achieves the logistics mission of minimum total logistics cost.

4. **Right Value:** Right value addition is due to the major contribution of logistics management system in creating time and place utilities. If a logistic system fails to meet its delivery commitment, the company will lose its customer immediately due to availability of a large number of alternative products in the market and then company will have to make further investment in finding a new customer. In short, if a product remains in the stock, its value will decrease and cost will increase. Logistics prevent this occurrence. Hence, it adds value by creating time and place utilities. Apart from this, the real value addition made by logistics is in terms of quality, quick response, better service and consistency and reliability of the total logistics system, which generate superior customer value.

5. **Right Costs Trade-offs:** This objective ensures the proper balance between total logistics cost and a desired level of customer service performance.

6. **Right Information:** It is the core logistics operational objective. Information regarding the requirement of goods is the primary aspect. Simultaneously, point-to-point information is one of the most important elements of customer service portfolio of recent times, enabling customers to meet their further delivery commitments or formulate their future sales and distribution strategies.

1.6 Distribution Cost

1.6.1 Concept of Distribution Cost

Distribution costs are generally defined as the costs incurred to deliver the product from the production unit to the end user. It is a broad terminology and it consists of several costs. Some of the costs are discussed below.

If the shipper is a distributor and it further sells to the retailer and the retailer sells to the end user then all the separate distribution costs at each stage would be incorporated in the total distribution cost. Furthermore, in some cases the manufacturer has a production unit at one place and the "product pick up place" by the forwarder at another place. The cost of moving the product from the place of production to the pickup point is also included in distribution cost. There are other kinds of costs as well that are included in the distributions costs. Handling cost of inventory at all points for instance production place, storehouse, sales point and packing costs are a part of distribution cost. Distribution managerial cost such as the salary expense of distribution manager and his/her office expenses are also part of distribution costs.

Freight cost is generally the most significant part of distribution costs. If the product is manufactured and sold in the same country then freight cost refers to the "trucking" or such transport fare to deliver the product. If the product is sold globally then it may include "air freight, Less than container load (LCL), Day-Definite LCL or Full container load (FCL)."

In case the product is transported by air the cost would be high and if it is transported through LCL the cost would be low but there is one further point to consider and that is, "transit time". The transit time for LCL is longer and the transit time for moving by air is smaller. Covering all aspects there is a need for comparative analysis between the product demand urgency and transport cost. If the product is required urgently and the shipper is losing sales revenue then it is best to decrease the transit time and increase the freight expense. For instance the sale loss is ₹ 10,000 and moving by air increase the freight to ₹ 20,000 then it is not advised to move by air. But it is suggested to move by air if the sale loss is ₹ 30,000.

1.6.2 Analysis of Distribution Cost

Distribution cost analysis is a part of cost accounting used as a review of costs connected to moving goods from production to retail outlets. Most firms use a supply chain for this activity, whether internal or external. Methods of distribution cost analysis are a cost-benefit analysis, activity based, or resource consumption style of cost accounting. Managerial accountants have the most responsibility to re-examine these costs and send a report to the upper management. Distribution systems can be very difficult; reviewing the linked costs may only happen a few times a year, though cost accounting often captures cost data.

1. **Cost-benefit analysis** is a typical form of review method in cost accounting. Managerial accountants list all the advantages — monetary and otherwise — the distribution system brings to the firm. Costs that are connected to paying for these benefits are also on the list. Distribution cost analysis begins with looking at whether the benefits outweigh the costs. In some cases, this is mostly a subjective look at costs and benefits, though more objective reviews can also arise.

2. **Activity based costing** is an in-depth review with regards to distribution cost analysis. Managerial accountants define each activity that makes an impact in the distribution system. All costs that are connected to each individual activity have their own places in the cost review. The reason for this process is to decide if the individual activity is too expensive with regards to the overall system. In most cases, managerial accountants cut down these costs in a per-product figure because this cost will probably be allocated to the products.

3. **The resource consumption method of cost accounting** is yet another available method for distribution cost analysis. Its aim is to define each resource used in a business process or activity and attach a cost for the use of the resource. Several difficult pieces may exist in a resource consumption accounting system. Cost drivers, value chain integration, and fundamental operations are all parts of the process that have an effect on the cost analysis stage. Finding ways to improve the entire distribution system financially and operationally can be due to resource consumption accounting.

   Not all methods of distribution cost analysis will work for a firm. Managerial accountants have a responsibility to find the best technique possible and execute it successfully. Changes may be required to stay current on new business activities. The final goal is to reduce the costs, become more efficient, and involve in competitive business behaviour.

4. **Total distribution cost (TDC)** analysis requires some assumptions. These include current observed rates and transit times for standard air freight, **full container load (FCL)**, and **less-than container load (LCL)** service.

5. **Cost Analysis in International Transportation / Shipping Industry**

Standard LCL service is the least expensive but slowest option with the lowest on-time delivery rate. An alternative is to purchase a dedicated twenty-foot container, which would be more expensive than LCL, but FCL service would shave approximately six days from transit time and be more reliable because it avoids consolidation/deconsolidation processes.

- Standard LCL would minimise transport-related costs, but would incur by far the highest inventory-related expenses due to long and highly variable transit times.

- Using full container load (FCL) rather than LCL reduces inventory-related costs, but to do so would spend more than the inventory-related savings on transport-related costs due to the wasted space in 20-ft. containers occupied by only 2,500 metric tons of freight.

- Switching to air freight to minimise inventory-related costs would incur the highest transport-related expenses, leading to the highest overall total distribution costs.

- Day-definite LCL could minimise total distribution costs (sum of transport and inventory related costs). Compared to LCL, the shipper would spend more on transportation to use day-definite LCL service, but would capture inventory related cost savings.

Shippers need to perform their own analysis with live data to reach an accurate conclusion, but even this simplified analysis demonstrates how many different factors affect each firm's total distribution cost calculation. Two of the most important are product unit value (value per kilogram) and inventory carrying cost (percentage of inventory value).

Logically, products with relatively high unit values or relatively high inventory carrying costs would be most likely to justify the higher cost of premium ocean service.

1.6.3 Analysis for Accounting

The accounting of selling and distribution overheads requires three types of analysis as given below:

1. According to nature or object of expenditure
2. By function or cost centre
3. By products or cost units

1. Analysis by Nature or Object of Expenses:

There are a number of basic or primary types in accordance with the nature or object of expenses for the purpose of analysis. Each expense is collected with reference to a standing order number or cost account number to which it belongs. The classification is generally done in a similar way as it is done in case of manufacturing overhead.

Following classifications may be adopted when such overheads are analysed by the nature or object of expenses:

(i) Remuneration

(ii) Supplies

(iii) Miscellaneous expenses

(iv) Services

(v) Fixed charges

(vi) Freight

(vii) Duty

(viii) Packing materials

(ix) Sales promotion

(x) Discount and allowances.

Like manufacturing expenses, selling and distribution overheads may also be fixed, variable and semi-variable. The salary of the sales executive in the head office is fixed, travelling allowance and salary of field salesmen are semi-variable and commission paid to the salesmen is variable.

2. Functional Analysis:

This analysis is also done in a similar way as departmentalisation and apportionment of manufacturing overhead is done to cost centres. The main operational functions with reference to selling overhead may further be classified in the following manner. Generally each of these functions that is., department or cost centre is put under the charge of one executive in order to have functional analysis and to make the executive responsible for the activities of his centre.

(a) Direct selling
(b) Advertising and sales promotion
(c) Transportation
(d) Warehouse and storage
(e) Credit and collection
(f) Financial
(g) General administration
(h) Warranty claims
(i) Miscellaneous.

The selling and distribution expenses analysed according to the various standing order numbers are further allocated to one or other functions to which they relate. Items which could not be allocated may be apportioned on suitable basis and where no suitable basis is available the apportionment may be done on arbitrary basis.

The analysis can further be extended to locations that is., to various territories, sales offices and to customers and salesmen etc. Like primary and secondary distribution summary in the case of manufacturing overhead, each item of selling and distribution is firstly analysed by functions and then by locations. Each function and location constitutes a cost centre for the purpose of accounting and control of selling and distribution overhead.

3. Analysis by Products or Groups of Products:

Selling and distribution expenses may also be analysed by products or groups of products. This is done in a similar way as absorption of manufacturing overhead to cost unit. But there are two differences between the two certain items of selling and distribution like packing, transport etc., may be directly allocated but no item of manufacturing overhead is directly allocated. Moreover, selling and distribution overhead is apportioned to cost of goods sold while manufacturing overhead is absorbed in the cost of production.

Analysis of these overheads may also be done by product groups. In order to do this the products must be grouped according to their common factors like price, methods of sales, salesmen and sales orders. For example, analysis can be made whether the goods were sold at wholesale price or at retail price.

From the above it is clear that analysis of selling and distribution overhead by products is nothing but an extension of analysis by functions. Such analysis virtually measures the effectiveness of such costs with regard to their application to the various products and is said to be analysis by manner of application.

This may be done either by channels of distribution or methods of sale or by customers. The channels of distribution for the purpose may be direct to customers, through retailers and through a chain of wholesalers and salesmen. Customers can be classified either according to the frequency of purchases made by them or according to their operations.

1.6.4 Methods to Apportion Indirect Functional Costs

Indirect functional costs can be apportioned by the following methods:

1. **A Rate per Article:** Under this method the total expenses are estimated and divided by some suitable basis over the various types of products sold. The total fixed expenditure allotted to each type of article is then divided by the estimated normal quantity of sales. This gives the rate per article. Advertisement, transportation and warehousing expenses may be apportioned by this method.

2. **A Percentage of Turnovers:** Where the selling price of each article is known, fixed selling expenses may be recovered as a percentage on the selling price. The percentage is ascertained from an analysis of the past accounts. This is suitable for apportionment of direct selling costs, general administration and finance cost and miscellaneous expenses.

3. **A Percentage of Cash Collected:** This is used for bad debts and for other credit collection expenses.

4. **A Percentage of Works Cost:** This method can be adopted where the business produces only one commodity. This method can also be used where various types of articles are produced, provided the selling expenses are small. This is often used for apportionment of fixed selling and distribution costs.

5. A percentage of stock of finished goods.

6. According to the number of orders.

7. According to the number of invoices.

8. A percentage of value added i.e. total sales values minus cost of materials.

The best method is to analyse each item of such expenses and allocate it to different products on the basis of services rendered.

1.6.5 Advantages Derived from Analysis

Following are the advantages which can be derived from the analysis of selling and distribution overhead by products, method of sales etc.

1. It is possible to calculate the profit or loss for each product, for each method of sales, and for each type of customer. Less profitable lines may either be brought on profitable lines by making efforts or dropped altogether.
2. There is a possibility of curtailing the excessive selling and distribution costs against a particular product or type of customer.
3. Taking into consideration the selling and distribution services, selling prices of different products may be adjusted.

1.6.6 Control of Selling and Distribution Overheads

The control of selling and distribution overheads is comparatively difficult because of certain special features of such costs which require a more detailed and exacting analysis. It is not possible to directly identify or link such costs with the cost of production as most of the expenses are incurred after the production is completed. The incidence of such overheads is dependent upon various factors such as distance of market, terms of sales, and extent of competition due to which it is not possible to fix standards.

1.6.7 Problems

The main problems which are in the control of selling and distribution overhead costs are as under:

1. No control over customers or competitors is possible.
2. Sales capacity of the organisations cannot be defined properly.
3. There is no direct supervision over the staff working outside and this requires the use of incentive schemes for remunerating such staff.
4. Individual business may establish market price without reference to cost of production.
5. It is difficult to obtain the market operation data.
6. It is difficult to determine the capacity of the market.
7. The difference of making or not making is not clear.
8. These expenses are of the nature of policy costs and as such are difficult to control.

Most of the items of the selling and distribution overheads are in the nature of policy costs and are uncontrollable at the lower levels of management.

1.6.8 Techniques

Following are the main techniques which may be used for exercising control over the selling and distribution overheads:

1. **Comparison with Past Results:** Each item of selling and distribution expenses is compared with that of a previous period. Such expenses may also be expressed as a percentage of sales or cost of production and then compared with the percentage of past period. This method is generally adopted in those concerns which cannot afford to introduce budgetary control and/or standard costing. Moreover, this is a rough method and has a little practical value in large concerns. As there are no suitable targets for measuring performance so no effective conclusions can be arrived at.

2. **Budgetary Control:** Under this method selling and distribution expenses are budgeted and compared with the actual expenses in order to ascertain the points of exception. Such budget system works in the similar manner as manufacturing overhead budget works. The whole of the expenses are classified into fixed, variable and semi-variable for the purpose of preparation of a budget.

3. **Standard Costing:** The set up of a system of standard costing for selling and distribution overheads is difficult as compared to manufacturing overhead. Moreover, it is simple to introduce a system of standard costing in case of distribution expenses as compared to selling expenses as distribution expenses can be directly related with sales. In those concerns, where standard costing system is in operation, standard cost per unit is calculated to have comparison with the actual and variance can be determined accordingly.

1.6.9 Analysis of Sales

Analysis of sales is the contributory factor to planning and control. Sales may be analysed in many ways and methods.

The purposes served by such an analysis are given below:

1. **By Salesmen:**

The turnover of each salesman is ascertained:

(a) So that actual sales may be compared with the budgeted sales or sales quotas in order to take corrective action wherever necessary,

(b) So that volume of sales may be compared with the selling costs in order to have control on the selling cots,

(c) To control and measure the relative efficiency of each salesman, and (d) to provide useful data for fixing up the sales commission and bonus payable to salesmen.

2. **By Sales Territories:**

The volume of sales is analysed according to the territories:

(a) So that sales forecast for each territory may be prepared,

(b) To prepare the budget of selling expenses,

(c) To compare the budget with the actual to measure and control the relative performance in respect of each territory,

(d) To control selling cost by co-relating with sales volume, and

(e) To assess the extent of penetration of competition in the field through market research of each territory.

3. **By Product or Product Lines:**

   Such analysis: is necessary to:

   (a) Ascertain the net profit for each product and compare with the past data for control purpose,

   (b) Plan production according to profitability that is., to decide upon the better product mix to strengthen or discard the weak lines etc.,

   (c) Ascertain the trend of sales of each product, and

   (d) Assist in the control of such costs by linking them with the sales volume for each product.

4. **By Customers:**

   Such analysis is useful to:

   (a) Ascertain the net profit by each type of customer,

   (b) Maintain a reasonable balance between different types of customers and the extent of discount allowed to each type of customers,

   (c) Ascertain customer wise potential in order to help the future sales drive or to know the effect of sales drive already undertaken, and

   (d) To determine the customer's preference in respect of quality and type of products.

5. **By Channels of Sales:**

   Such analysis may be done in order to:

   (a) Ascertain the profits of various channels e.g. wholesale, retail, etc., and

   (b) Assess the relative viability of each channel which ultimately helps in the future planning policy.

6. **By Unit Price:** Such analysis is done to:

   (a) Prepare a demand schedule in respect of each product,

   (b) Determine the optimum selling price of each product, and

   (c) Maximise profit by discriminating selling price in different markets or to different class of customers. This analysis gives information regarding price trends which ultimately is useful for formulating price policy.

7. **By Periods:** Comparison over a period of time will help to:

    (a) Reveal trends, periodic or cyclical movements, seasonal or fluctuating characteristics, and

    (b) Assist in the formulation of sales policy on a long-term basis.

8. **By Size or Order:** Such analysis will be useful to:

    (a) Compare the handling and transportation cost with the sales volume of various sizes, and

    (b) Decide upon the trade discount on quantity for the various sizes.

1.6.10 Overhead Costs Reports

No universal rules can be set for reports for overhead cost control which will be applicable under all circumstances and for all types of organisations. The needs of the organisation will determine the nature of reports to be prepared and submitted for overhead cost control, the preformed and the frequency of the preparation of such reports.

No final list for such reports/statements can be prepared but the following are the important reports which can be used for the purpose of exercising control over overhead costs:

1. **Idle Time Report:** This report is submitted daily to the foreman to have analysis of idle time. The works manager may have this report weekly according to the controllable and uncontrollable causes and cost of idle time. The main purpose of this report is to locate and control the causes and cost of idle time.

2. **Overtime Report:** This report is also submitted daily to the foreman and weekly to works manager to have an analysis of overtime according to causes and cost of overtime. The main purpose of this report is to locate causes of overtime and taking steps to minimise it.

3. **Plant Utilisation Report:** Plant utilisation report shows in respect of each plant or machine the capacity installed, the normal capacity, the utilised capacity and idle capacity classified by the reasons for under-utilisation of capacity. This report is submitted to the foreman daily and works manager weekly to analyse the idle capacity according to controllable and uncontrollable causes and cost of idle capacity. This report is prepared to locate and control the causes of idle capacity. Management may take steps to utilise the idle capacity in a way most profitable to the concern.

4. **Departmental Budget Reports:** These reports may be prepared separately for each of factory, administration, selling and distribution and research and development departments and submitted to the departmental heads monthly to compare the actual expenses with the budgeted allowances. The purpose of such reports is to control the expenses by analysing the expenses and to take remedial steps by the management for avoiding the recurrence of such variations.

5. **Departmental Operating Statements:** Such reports may be submitted to the top management monthly in order to have comparison of actual factory overhead costs with the standard costs for each production department and analysis of the variances. The main purpose of such report is to control factory overhead costs.

6. **Statement of Over or Under-Absorption of Overheads:** Such a statement is prepared to show the actual amount of overheads incurred and the amount of overhead charged and the difference being either the over- or under-absorption of overhead in respect of each department. A separate column may be provided for a supplementary rate to allocate or apportion the under- or over-absorbed overheads otherwise top management may indicate the manner in which the over- or under-absorption of overheads may be dispensed with.

7. **Comparative Profit and Loss Statement:** It shows the product-wise allocation of general and administrative expenses and selling and distribution cost and the amount of net profit on each product. This statement facilitates comparison between products which earn higher percentage of profit and those which can earn lower percentage of profit. This may facilitate management in respect of taking decision about increasing the production of one product and reducing or discarding the production of other product or products.

1.6.11 Element of Total Cost in Physical Distribution System

An integrated logistics system is an interface of procurement function, production function and physical distribution function of the total logistics function in order to achieve its basic mission of the best possible customer service at the least possible costs. The development of this integrated logistics system is distinguished by its attention to costs of both movement and demand-supply coordination. It brings synergy in business functions for economies of scale in logistics function. Thus, total cost analysis is essential in its design and acts as a key to manage it. The total cost refers to the sum total of the cost involved in various components of logistics function, namely:

(i)   Inventory cost;

(ii) Transportation cost;

(iii) Storage and warehousing cost;

(iv) Material handling and protective packaging cost;

(v)   Order processing cost;

(vi) Information cost;

(vii) Customer service cost; and

(viii) Production lot quantity cost.

Logistics costs are driven by activities that support the logistics process. Trade-offs are possible among the elements of logistics costs in order to minimise total costs given customer service level objectives. These elements are inter-related and various trade-offs exist. It is worth noting that some of these trade-offs are not realised in a continuous way. Consolidation of warehouses occurs at a discrete point in time and this will be different for various firms based on their decision to invest in new logistics systems. The primary goal of the firm in developing its logistics strategy is to provide customer service while reducing costs thereby increasing its profits and being competitive.

In this system approach, efforts are made to minimise the total cost of logistics rather than minimisation of the cost of individual component. Reduction in cost of one component of logistics leads to an increase in the cost of others. Thus, effective management and real cost saving can be accomplished by having an attempt to improve the efficiency of the total cost of integrated logistics system and not the separate cost of individual components. At the same time, efforts are also required to determine a trade-off between the total logistics costs and service standards required in order to meet the customer's expectations.

A firm could re-organise its logistics in many ways as a result of lower transportation costs. For one, it could reduce the number of warehouses and thereby increase the use of transportation services. Four factors influence the number of warehouses a firm chooses to maintain: cost of lost sales, inventory costs, warehousing costs, and transportation costs.

1. **Cost of Lost Sales:** The cost of lost sales is the most difficult to quantify. It would generally decrease with number of warehouses and would vary by industry, company, product, and customer. The remaining cost components are more consistent across firms and industries.

2. **Inventory Costs:** Inventory costs increase with the number of warehouses because firm maintain a safety stock of all (or most) products at each facility. More total space is required overall.

3. **Warehousing Costs:** More warehouses mean more space to be owned, leased or rented. Fixed costs across many facilities are larger than the marginal variable costs of fewer locations.

4. **Transportation Costs:** Transportation costs initially decline as the number of facilities increases due to proximity. Costs eventually increase for too many warehouses due to the combination of inbound and outbound transport costs.

A firm seeking to minimize total costs, the sum of the above components, could balance all cost components by solving a multi-facility location problem. As transportation costs decline possibly due to highway infrastructure investment, the minimum total cost will in general occur for fewer warehouses. The nature and timing of re-organisation will occur at different points for each firm. Sufficient potential gains will need to be realised before an investment hurdle rate is exceeded.

The logistics objective ensures a proper balance between total logistics cost and a desired level of customer service performance. For instance, addition of a new distribution warehouse increases the total logistics costs, which must be able to offer a more effective customer service as well as generate additional sales to meet additional logistics costs in the development of new facility. Hence, it brings out cost trade-offs between various elements of logistics cost.

1.6.12 Total- Cost Concept

The prime objective of a physical distribution system is to provide customer service and customer satisfaction. To achieve this, the total cost of distribution must be minimum. The interrelated channels affect each other, the total system cost and the service provided. Management must therefore carefully analyse the relationships between the networks and treat the system as a whole for effective distribution management.

Table 1.11: Cost Trade-off

	Rail (10 days)	**Air (1 day)**
Transportation cost	200	1000
In-transmit inventory-carrying cost ($ 10/day)	1000	100
Total	**1200**	**1100**

There are 2 related principles illustrated here:

1. **Cost trade-off.** The cost of transportation increased with the use of air transport, but the cost of carrying inventory decreased. There was a cost trade-off between the two;

2. **Total cost.** By considering all of the costs and not just any one cost, the total system cost is reduced. Note also that even though no cost is attributed to it, customer service is improved by reducing the transit time. The total cost should also reflect the effect of the decision on other departments, such as production and marketing.

The cost of distribution involving all the move-store activities of the product may be of the total cost. The cost of distribution should take into account not only the cost incurred on moving the product over different channels of distribution, but also on other activities. These activities have become inevitable the modern, customer oriented marketing approach.

A reduction in costs of distribution in one of the areas by itself may not give desired results. Other costs are also required to be controlled include:

1. **Inventory costs:** These are the costs which a locked up in inventory of goods, insurance, occupation of space, pilferage, losses, damage etc. The total inventory of any product amounts to almost 30 percent of the average level of inventory in the pipeline/stock.

2. **Warehousing costs:** The warehousing of materials steps up the cost of their supply o cost of distribution of finished product. Aiming at zero stock out or zero loss of production levels, it becomes essential to have adequate warehousing capacity and involve higher fixed and operating costs of warehouse in order to improve custom necessary to increase number of warehouses, which results in the decrease in the number of transport. As such management has to arrange the optimum number of warehouses.

3. **Production/Supply costs:** Production costs decrease with increase in volume production. If the same product is made at several plants, various other costs such as cost of transportation, transit times, warehouses and inventory costs are to be considered. Proper analysis has to be made of their effect on total cost of distribution.

4. **Channel of Distribution costs:** A critical assessment of the channels of distribution for examination of the use of or creation of adequate facilities for storage at the plant or field warehouses or with the distributor or stockiest.

   This will necessitate a total systems approach selection of channels of distribution.

5. **Communication and Data Processing Cost:** An effective distribution system requires continuous monitoring of order pricing, inventory control, accounts receivable, dispatches etc.

6. **Transportation costs:** The cost of transport varies generally with speed which the goods are transported. This affects transit inventory. As such best speed and inventory, cost of packaging also to be considered, while selecting particular mode of transport.

   An increased number of distribution points improves customer service but involves high costs. As such optimal number of distribution points which will keep the distribution cost minimum and improving customer service, desirable.

7. **Material Handling Costs:** A suitable material handling system should be designed to reduce the cost of material handling to a minimum. A total cost approach would require a consideration of not only the material handling system but also other relevant factors affecting the cost transport, customer satisfaction, inventory etc.

8. **Packaging costs**: Decision on packaging affected by mode of transport and material handling equipment. A total cost approach will make it necessary for us to select a packaging version which takes into account other distribution factors.

9. **Customer Service Costs:** All factors which affect customer service and volume of sales to be taken into consideration to evaluate the cost of distribution.

Before applying total cost approach, it is essential to examine various costs associated with distribution function, by studying the totals in depth before taking decisions. To make accounting easier, various costs are added as administrative heads. A firm seeking to minimise total costs, the sum of the above components, could balance all cost components by solving a multi-facility location problem.

The logistics objective ensures a proper balance between total logistics cost and a desired level of customer service performance. For example, addition of a new distribution warehouse increases the total logistics costs, which must be able to offer a more effective customer service as well as generate additional sales to meet additional logistics costs in the development of new facility. Hence, it brings out cost trade-offs between various elements of logistics cost.

1.7 Developing Channel Design

The process of developing an effective channel design can be broadly divided in two phases. In the first phase, a broad structure of supply chain network is visualised. This step includes the decision to be taken about whether the product can be sold directly or through some intermediate agent. In the second phase, the broad structure is broken into smaller activities to specify the location, capability of the channel member, capacity and demand allocation.

Whether a firm will be a one person operation or one that employs thousands of people and generates billions in sales, all are in business to serve the needs of markets. In order to do this, these firms must be assured that their products are distributed to their intended markets. Most producing and manufacturing firms are not in a favourable position to perform all the tasks that would be necessary to distribute their products directly to their final user markets. In many instances, it is the expertise and availability of other channel institutions that make it possible for a producer/manufacturer to even participate in a particular market. Other channel members can be useful to the producer in designing the product, packaging it, pricing it, promoting it, and distributing it through the most effective channels.

1.7.1 Factors influencing Channel Design

Managers have many factors to consider when choosing a product distribution channel. Channel choice may include questions like:

- To whom shall we sell this merchandise immediately?
- Who are our ultimate users and buyers?
- Are the customer needs met?
- What are the costs of meeting customer needs?
- Will the customer pick up the product personally or will the product be delivered to customer location?
- Will the product flow through different intermediate channels?

Other factors for considering channel or a network are:

1. Response time
2. Product variety
3. Product availability
4. Customer experience
5. Time to market
6. Order visibility
7. Returnability
8. Adaptability

The immediate and ultimate customers may be identical or quite separate, depending on the type of product, functions performed in the channel, and location in the channel. There is a need to know what the customer needs, where they buy, when they buy, why they buy from certain outlets, and how they buy. It is best that we first identify the traits of the ultimate user, since the results of this evaluation might determine the other channel institutions we would use to meet these needs. For example, the buying characteristics of the purchaser of a high-end electronics device might be as follows:

- Purchased only from a well-established, reputable dealer.
- Purchased only after considerable shopping to compare prices and merchandise characteristics.
- Purchaser willing to go to some inconvenience (time and distance) to locate the most acceptable brand.
- Purchased only after extended conversations involving all interested parties - including dealer, users, and purchasers.
- Purchase may be postponed.
- Purchased only from a dealer equipped to render prompt and reasonable product service.

Knowing the buying specifications of consumers, the channel planner can decide on the type or types of wholesaler and/or retailer through which a product should be sold. This requires that a manufacturer contemplating distribution through particular types of retailers becomes intimately familiar with the precise location and performance characteristics of those being considered.

In much the same way that buying specifications of ultimate users are determined, the manufacturers must also discover buying specifications of resellers. Of particular importance is the question, "From whom do my retail outlets prefer to buy?" The answer to this question determines the type of wholesaler - if any - that the manufacturer should use. Although many retailers prefer to buy directly from the manufacturers, this is not always the case. Often, the exchange requirements of manufacturers - for example, infrequent visits, large order requirements, and stringent credit terms - are the opposite of those desired by retailers. Such retailers would rather buy from local distributors who have lenient credit terms and offer a wide assortment of merchandise.

Channel choice is also greatly influenced by channel objectives. Channel objectives are based on the requirements of the purchasers and users, the overall marketing strategy, and the long-run goals of the corporation. In cases when a company is just getting started, or an older company is trying to carve out a new market niche, the channel objectives may be the dominant force on channel choice.

1.7.2 Categories of Channel Objectives

The following areas encompass the major categories of channel objectives:

- Growth in sales - by reaching new markets and/or increasing sales in existing markets.
- Maintenance or improvement of market share - educate or assist channel components in their efforts to increase the amount of product they handle.
- Achieve a pattern of distribution - structure the channel in order to achieve certain time, place, and form utilities.
- Create an efficient channel - improve channel performance by modifying various flow mechanisms.

After the distribution objectives are set, it is appropriate to determine the specific distribution tasks or functions to be performed in that channel system. The channel manager must be very specific in describing the tasks, and must define how these tasks will change depending upon the situation. An ability to do this requires the channel manager to evaluate all phases of the distribution network. Tasks must be identified fully, and costs must be assigned to these tasks.

There are six important distribution network systems or channel design.

1. Direct Shipping by the Manufacturer

In this option, the product is shipped directly from the manufacturer to the end customer, avoiding the retailer (who takes the order and initiates the delivery request). This option is also called as drop shipping. All inventories are stored at the manufacturer. The information flows from the customer, through the retailer, to the manufacturer, while the product is shipped directly from the manufacturer to customers as indicated in Fig. 4.1. In some instances like Dell, the manufacturer directly sells to the customer. Online retailers such as eBags and Nordstrom.com use drop shipping to deliver goods to the end consumer. eBags does not hold any inventory of bags and has them drop shipped directly from the manufacturer to the customer. Nordstrom carries some products in inventory while using the drop-ship model for slow moving footwear. W.W. Grainger also uses drop shipping to deliver slow moving items that are not carried in inventory.

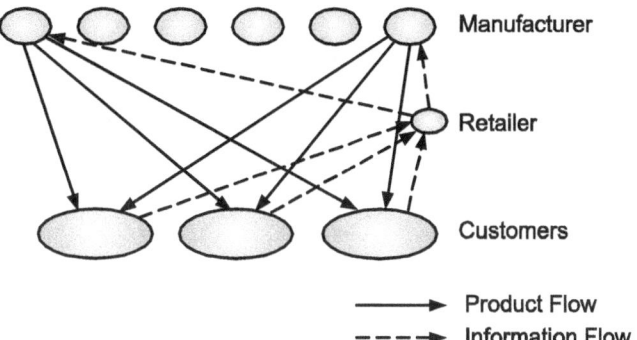

Fig. 1.8: Manufacturer Storage with Direct Shipping

2. Direct Shipping with In-transit Merge

Unlike pure drop shipping where each product in the order is straight away sent from each manufacturer to the end customer, in-transit join pieces of the order coming from various regions so that the customer gets a single delivery. The information and product flows for the in-transit merge network are as shown in Fig. 4.2. When a customer orders a personal computer from Dell along with a Sony monitor, the package carrier picks up the computer at the Dell factory, the monitor at the Sony factory and combines the two together at a hub before making a single delivery to the client.

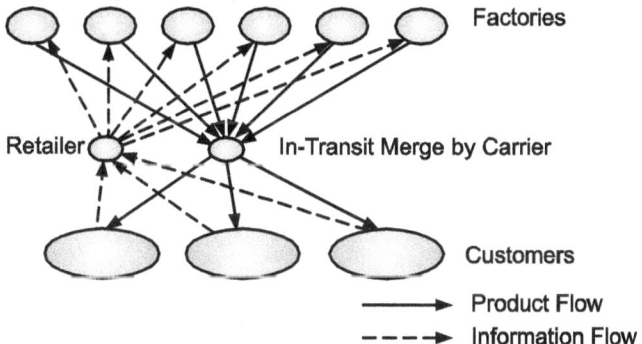

Fig. 1.9: In-Transit Merge Network

3. Distributor Storage with Carrier Delivery

Under this option, inventory is not held by manufacturers at the factories but is held by distributors /retailers in intermediate warehouses and package carriers are used to carry products from the transitional location to the final customer. Amazon.com as well as industrial distributors like W.W. Grainger uses this method together with drop shipping from a manufacturer. Information and product flows when using distributor storage with delivery by a package carrier are shown in Fig. 1.10.

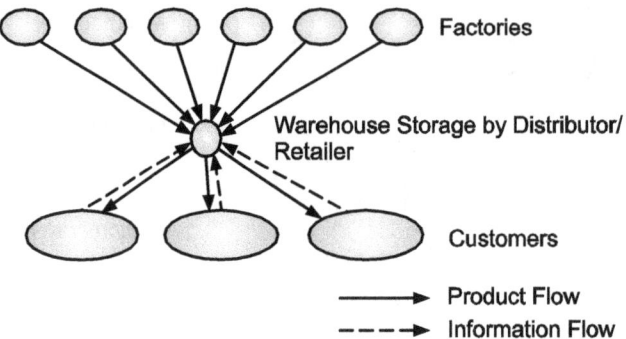

Fig. 1.10: Distributor Storage with Carrier Delivery

4. Manufacturer / Distributor with Customer Pickup

In this approach, inventory is stored at the manufacturer or distributor warehouse but customers place orders online or on the phone and then come to the allocated pickup points to collect their orders. Orders are transported from the storage site to the pickup points as required. Examples include 7dream.com operated by 7 Eleven Japan, which allows customers to pick up online orders at a designated store. An example is W. W. Grainger where customers can collect their orders at one of the Grainger retail outlets. In the case of 7dream.com, the order is delivered from a manufacturer or distributor warehouse to the pickup location. In the case of Grainger, some items are stored at the pickup location while others may come from a central location. The information and product flows in the network for 7-Eleven Japan are as shown in Fig. 1.11.

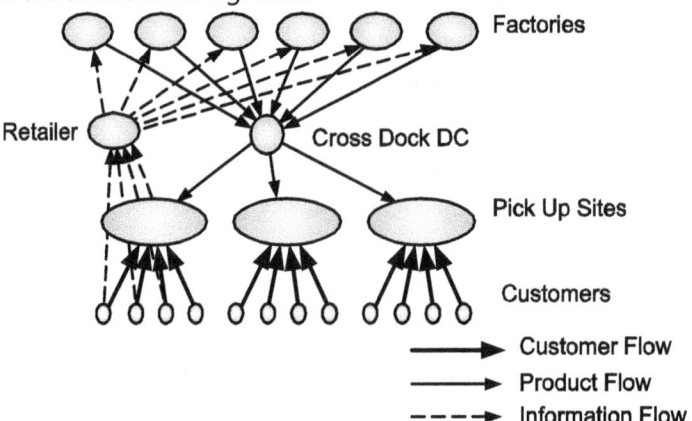

Fig. 1.11: Manufacturer or Distributor Storage with Consumer Pickup

5. Retail Storage with Customer Pickup

In this option, the inventory is stored locally at retail stores. Customers either walk into the retail store or place an order online or on the phone, and pick it up at the retail store. Examples of firms that offer numerous alternatives of order placement include Albertsons.com. Albertsons uses part of the facility as a grocery store and part of the facility as an online fulfillment centre. A business-to-business example is W. W. Grainger where customers can order online, by phone, or in person and pick up their order at one of the Grainger retail outlets. Alberston's stores its inventory at the pickup location itself. In the case of Grainger, some items are stored at the pickup location while others may come from a central location.

1.7.3 Online Sales and Distribution Network and its Impact on Customer Service

The Internet has affected the structure and performance of various distribution networks. Online sales affect various customer service elements.

1. **Impact on Response Time:** Physical products which cannot be downloaded, online sales take longer to fulfill a customer request than does a retail store because of the shipping time involved.

2. **Impact on Product Variety:** Companies engaged in online selling offer a larger variety of products. For example Naaptol sells a large variety of electronics and consumer products online.

3. **Impact on Product Availability:** By aggregating inventory, companies selling online are able to provide better product availability due to large inventories.

4. **Impact on Funds Transfer:** The internet and mobiles enhance the convenience and lower the cost of revenue collection.

5. **Impact on Cost:** Companies selling online can reduce the cost of facilities, transportations, and inventory.

Points to Remember

- The manufacturers, customers and potential customers are dispersed geographically and therefore, if the manufacturer serves only the local market, he would be losing the potential for growth and profit. Physical distribution is therefore a vital function of production and marketing

- According to Philip Kotler and Gary Armstrong: " Physical distribution is the set of firms and individuals that take title, or assist in transferring title, to a good or service as it moves from the producer to the final consumer or industrial user."

- Physical distribution is of great importance because of its various functions such as location analysis, transportation, material handling, warehousing, packing, order processing, packaging, inventory control, customer sales service.

- Companies use a forecast approach for production and supply. This strategy or a process is called as **"Push System"**.

- The **Pull System** is driven by the actual consumption recorded at the store as well as sales forecast.

- **Cycle View** of Supply Chain is useful to make operational decisions as role of each member of Supply Chain is defined.
- **Reverse Logistics** is the process of managing the return of goods. Reverse logistics is also referred to as "Aftermarket Customer Services".
- **Distribution Cost Analysis** is a part of cost accounting used as a review of costs associated with moving goods from production to retail outlets.
- **Cost-benefit Analysis** is a classic form of review method in cost accounting. Managerial accountants list all the benefits — monetary and otherwise — the distribution system brings to the company
- **Activity Based Costing** is a much more in-depth review in terms of distribution cost analysis. Managerial accountants define each activity that makes an impact in the distribution system
- **Total Distribution Cost (TDC)** analysis requires some assumptions. These include current observed rates and transit times for standard air freight, **full container load (FCL)**, and **less-than container load (LCL)** service.
- **The Internet** has affected the structure and performance of various distribution networks. Online sales affect various customer service elements.
- **Important factors for considering channel design are**: Response time, Product variety, Product availability, Customer experience, Time to market, Order visibility, Returnability, Adaptability

Questions for Discussion

1. Describe the basic concept of distribution system
2. What is the need of Logistics in distribution system?
3. Discuss the steps for setting distribution objectives.
4. Define physical distribution.
5. Explain the concept of distribution cost and analysis of distribution cost.
6. What are the elements of total cost in physical distribution system?
7. Elaborate the development of channel design.

■■■

Chapter 2...

Channel Selection

Contents ...

Learning Objectives ...

- To study the control system for efficiency
- To understand the importance and characteristics of an effective control system
- To enlist the factors influencing the control system
- To explain the responsibility centres for efficiency and performance
- To describe the controlling and measuring performances
- To know the productivity aspects of logistics management
- To elaborate on distribution and customer satisfaction
- To define the role of distribution in customer service and satisfaction
- To study channel strategy decision
- To summarise the process of channel management

2.1 Control System for Efficiency

Introduction

A control system or a management control system is a method or a tool designed to help managers make decisions which will increase the organisation's efficiency and performance. The performance of a physical distribution can be evaluated and controlled by implementing certain methods or tools which can gather and report data. A management control system (MCS) is a system which collects and uses the data to assess the performance of different organisational resources like human, physical, and financial and also the organisation altogether considering the organisational strategies. Ultimately, management control systems influence the behaviour of organisational resources to execute organisational strategies.

Management control systems include action and results control (**Merchant, 1998**). A tight control system can monitor individual behaviour more closely, resulting in a higher chance of motivating employees to act for the organisation's best interest. Then again, a loose control system may not be capable of observing individual behaviour closely and may cause a lower chance of having people act in the organisation's best interest. On the other hand, the execution and maintenance costs connected to the tight control system are usually high. Thus, when choosing control systems, top management generally analyses their associated benefits. For action control, systems are considered tight if there are frequent and comprehensive reviews, continuous direct supervision and important rewards or punishments given to the people affected. Thus, it is possible that employees will involve themselves in all of the actions important to the operation's success.

2.1.1 Importance of Management Control System (MCS)

The management control systems include the following areas of planning and control

(i)   Strategic planning

(ii) Management control

(iii) Task control

(iv) Strategic control

(v)   Operational control

The strategic planning and control handle issues relating to an organisation's basic goals and implementation followed by observing its progress. The management deals with proper allocation and effective utilisation of resources, sustenance in competition and transformation of the organisation's goals into reality. In operating the company, the operation controls deal with the factors of efficiency. Therefore, we can say that management control systems are the formal and informal systems which assist the management in driving the organisation towards its goals. They guide the employees effectively to achieve the organisation's objectives. Formal controls are given in writing by the management, whereas informal controls arise out of employees' behaviour.

2.1.2 Characteristics of Effective Control Systems

Effective control systems have certain characteristics. For a control system to be effective, it must be:

1. **Accurate:** Information on performance must be accurate. Assessing the accuracy of the information they get is one of the most significant control tasks that managers face.

2. **Timely:** To generate improvements, if action is to be taken in time, information must be collected, routed, and assessed quickly.

3. **Objective and Comprehensible:** The information in a control system should be comprehensible and be seen as objective by the people who use it. If a control system is difficult to understand then it will cause unnecessary mistakes and confusion among employees.

4. **Focused on Strategic Control Points:** The control system should be focused on those areas where deviations from the standards will probably take place or where deviations would cause the greatest harm.

5. **Economically Realistic:** The cost of executing a control system should be less than, or at most equal to, the benefits obtained from the control system.

6. **Organisationally Realistic:** The control system has to be in agreement with organisational realities and all standards for performance must be realistic.

7. **Co-ordinated with the Organisation's Work Flow:** Control information needs to be co-ordinated with the flow of work through the organisation for two reasons – (1) each step in the work process may affect the success or failure of the entire operation, and (2) the control information must get to all the people who need to receive it.

8. **Flexible:** Controls must have flexibility built into them so that the organisations can react quickly to overcome adverse changes or to take advantage of new opportunities.

9. **Prescriptive and Operational:** On detecting the deviation from standards, control systems should show what corrective action should be taken.

10. **Accepted by Organisation Members:** For a control system to be accepted by organisation members, the controls must be connected to meaningful and accepted goals.

2.1.3 Purposes of a Control System

The main purpose of a management control system is to help the management in co-ordinating the activities of the company and in guiding those activities towards attaining the company's overall purposes, goals and objectives.

The following functions are involved in the management control system –

(i)   Planning the activities of the company.

(ii)   Co-ordinating the activities of the company.

(iii) Communicating information to different levels of organisation structure.

(iv)   Assessing the data and deciding the course of action.

(v)   Influencing people to change their style of working.

(vi)   Control systems clearly communicate the organisation's goals.

(vii) It guarantees that every manager and employee understands the particular actions needed of him/her to attain organisational goals.

(viii) It also communicates the results of actions across the organisation.

(ix)   It guarantees that it adjusts to the changes in the environment.

The reason for management control system is to compare the original results with the set standards so as to guarantee that the work of each section of the company is pleasantly achieved with the work of the other sections. Therefore, management control systems bring about unity of purpose in an organisation. A company executes management control systems to guarantee that appropriate strategies are implemented to achieve its goals. They also guarantee that quick actions are taken in case of emergency. They also help the management in decision-making process.

2.1.4 Factors Influencing Control Systems

(i)   **Size and Spread of the Enterprise:** The size and spread of a big company is bound to be different compared with that of a small company. This would definitely determine the content and nature of the control system for each organisation.

(ii)   **Organisational Structure, Delegation and Decentralisation:** Laws and conventions rule organisational structure, and the extent of decentralisation and delegation in all ventures. For instance, the management philosophy of the State Bank of India will be different from that of the State Trading Corporation. Also, within a venture, the degree of decentralisation and delegation changes from one point of time to another to meet changed environmental challenges and the chances that these may present. All these influence management control systems practiced in organisations.

(iii) **Nature of Operations and Divisibility:** Nature of operations and their divisibility have an effect on management control systems. For instance, in the oil industry, for example, based on products sub-units cannot be formed. In many big trading firms, on the other hand, divisions can be formed on the basis of products. Again, in the paper industry, the different stages in pulp-making cannot be subdivided for the purposes of management control, though pulp-making all together can be considered as a division.

(iv) **Types of Responsibility Centres:** Different control systems are required for the different responsibility centres or sub-systems within an organisation. Whether the performance of a responsibility centre should be measured in terms of expenses or profitability or return on investment depends on the type of responsibility centre. For instance, a bank may implement different performance measures to measure performance of its different branches.

There are transactional differences between branches; some are deposit heavy or advance heavy, some are with or without safe deposit facilities or foreign exchange transactions. It is, thus, impossible to have profit as the only criteria for performance evaluation of all branches. Thus, control systems that have different criteria of performance should be used for different sub-units.

(v) **People and their Perceptions:** Perceptions of people in the organisation about the probable effects of the control system on their work life, job satisfaction, job security, promotion and general well-being could vary across organisations. These considerations will considerably influence the nature and content of the management control system required in the organisation and must be duly considered while designing management control systems.

2.1.5 Steps in setting up of a Control System

1. Specify the organisation's goals and objectives
2. Identify the key success factors of the organisation and actions which will focus and guide the crucial activities
3. Benchmark with other successful organisations
4. Establish responsibility centres by de-centralisation of the departments
5. Establish performance measures
6. Gather, analyse and interpret reports on financial and non-financial performances

2.1.6 Responsibility Centres for Efficiency and Performance

Any organisation headed by a manager who is accountable for the activities of that unit is known as a responsibility centre. The manager is accountable for the achievements of the tasks set in his unit. The tasks that are performed by different departments are divided into sub-tasks. In this regard, all departments in an organisation are responsibility centres. All responsibility centres use resources [inputs or costs] to generate something [output or revenues]. Normally responsibility is allotted to a revenue, expense, profit and/or investment centre. The decision will generally depend on the activity performed by the organisational unit and on the way in which inputs and outputs are measured by the organisational control system.

The organisational chart shows the sub-tasks being performed by different departments and also the tasks to be performed by each responsibility centre. The size of the responsibility centre is however, determined by the nature of the task, technology, people and the level in the organisation hierarchy. From the top management viewpoint, a division is a responsibility centre, from the divisional management's viewpoint; the market department of that division is a responsibility centre. And from the marketing manager's viewpoint, the sales, distribution, and advertising departments are responsibility centres.

Departments are de-centralised and responsibilities/tasks are delegated to managers/employees. Managers and departmental employees are evaluated for their performances. Different responsibility centres are set up for the purpose of control. They are as follows:

1. **Cost Centre:** Area for which cost data is accumulated such as an assembly department. The cost centre represents the organisational connection in which products/services are obtained that generate expenses with the assistance of which there can be a measured efficaciousness of the centres' activity. The cost centres are "subdivisions of the technical, productive, organisational and administrative frame of the enterprise in connection to which there is an organised analytical programming and monitoring of the production expenses." The cost centre can be an enterprise, a department, a section, a functional service which collects indirect expenses. If expense budgets are elaborated, then this can be also organised at a place of work.

2. **Expense Centre:** Area dominated by discretionary expenses such as legal or accounting. In expense centres, inputs [cost and expenses] are measured in monetary terms but outputs are not. Management will mainly focus on the control of the expenses or costs incurred by the responsibility centre. So budgets will be devised only for the input part of these centres' operations. Organisational units generally regarded as expense centres include administration service, and research departments.

3. **Revenue Centre:** Area primarily responsible for generating sales such as a sales office. The revenue centre represents the organisational connection in which the activity is appreciated as value according to the revenue obtained, such as the sales department within an organisation. The revenue is planned based on the achievements in the previous year and of their anticipation for the year on course. The management regularly analyses the revenue budget and that of anticipation, and intervenes in the case of deviations.

4. **Profit Centre:** Area responsible for controlling costs and generating revenues. The profit centre is the operational subdivision which performs its activity by attracting resources which generate revenue. The profit centre is the organisational centre within which profit can be calculated. There are subsystems, finite products or implemented services that are produced within profit centres which are sold outside and for which a selling price is calculated. If deviations emerge, particularly by not achieving the proposed profit, there are identified causes which led to this condition and measures are taken to improve the situation.

5. **Investment Centre:** Area responsible for income (revenues-expenses) in relation to its invested capital. The investment centre is the organisational connection in which there is emphasis on the relationship/difference between the revenue acquired from product sales and the investment made for all the resources required in production.

2.1.7 Performance Measures

A good performance measure will:

1. The goals of the organisation
2. Balance long-run and short-run concerns
3. Reflect the management of key decisions and activities
4. Be affected by actions of managers and employees
5. Be readily understood by managers and employees
6. Be used in evaluating and rewarding employees
7. Be reasonably objective and easily measured
8. Be used consistently and regularly

2.1.8 Controlling and Measuring Performances

The following costs measures are significant while assessing performances – controllable cost, uncontrollable cost and financial performance.

A. Financial Performance Measures

1. Controllable Cost

- Cost which is directly influenced by the manager of a responsibility centre during a specific time period.
- Absolute or total control is not needed in order for a cost to be classified as controllable.
- Key is to look for the managers who are in the best position to explain the results.

2. Uncontrollable Cost

- Any cost that cannot be affected by management of a responsibility centre within a given time span.

3. **Financial Performance**
    -   Principle of responsibility accounting says that it is just to assess managers only on the costs under their control.
    -   During evaluating the manager, uncontrollable costs should be ignored because nothing he or she does will have an effect on these costs.

B. Non-financial Performance Measures

-   **Control of Quality**: Quality requires meeting customers' needs and maintaining this level all through the production and sales process.

-   **Control of Cycle Time**: Cycle time is the time taken to complete a product or service summary measure of effectiveness and efficiency and a significant cost driver.

-   **Control of Productivity**: Relationship of outputs to inputs for material, labour and equipment.

Multiple productivity measures may include –

-   Labour cost as a percent of sales in rupees.
-   Sales per employee.
-   Machinery and equipment investments per employee.
-   Total labour cost per hour.

2.1.9 Control for Channel Efficiency

As part of the supply chain, manufacturing firms are increasingly placing greater emphasis on the management of their outsourced distribution channels. Channel conflicts can arise from either structural causes or attitudinal causes. The commonly used conflict resolution strategies are – negotiation and bargaining, problem-solving strategies, persuasion, political strategies, and co-optation. Apart from sales control, marketing communications control includes control of advertising, sales promotion, direct marketing, public relations, and brand management. Advertising effectiveness can be measured through copy testing or message testing and by monitoring recognition, recall, persuasion (attitude change), and purchase behaviour. The effectiveness of Internet advertising can be measured by considering four aspects – the purpose of the advertisement, the value of the intended outcome, the number of times the purpose was fulfilled, and the cost incurred on advertising. Effective channel management control is necessary to marketing planning.

Control for channel efficiency can be achieved through

1. Vertical integration of channels
2. Cost reduction
3. Cooperation
4. Protection

1. Vertical Integration of Channels

One way to control a channel of distribution is through vertical integration. A business must replace some or all of the marketing intermediaries down the line by taking over their activities. The range of intermediaries between producer and consumer includes wholesalers, retailers, agents and brokers. Some of their activities include representation, transportation, storage, customer service and advertising. Besides adding these jobs to an existing organisation, a business can achieve integration by merging with or acquiring the middlemen within the channel.

Types of Vertical Marketing Systems (VMS)

There are many ways by which a company can develop a vertical marketing system. The different integration approaches vary in terms of the level of investment, profitability, extent of control, the need to reduce risks, and the bargaining power of the other channel members. The commonly used types of vertical channel systems are the corporate system, administered type of system and the contractual system.

(a) Corporate VMS

In a corporate VMS, one company owns and operates the other channel members at different channel levels. A company develops a corporate VMS, when it intends to source nearly all of its internal requirements through the corporate VMS. A corporate system is preferable when the company is confident of protecting its key processes or trade secrets maintaining accuracy and high quality in the channel activities. When the manufacturer owns or performs operations at the wholesaler or retailer level, the vertical marketing system is said to be forward-integrated. When a retailer or wholesaler plans to operate or control the manufacturing aspects, a backward-integrated system develops.

(b) Administered VMS

Unlike corporate system, in the administered type of vertical marketing system, no channel member has complete control over other channel members. Managers of companies following the conventional distribution systems often attempt to first develop an administered system to compete against companies in corporate vertical marketing systems. The extent to which one channel member exerts an influence or control over others varies. In an administered VMS, the level of control is greater than in the conventional distribution system but less than that of a corporate system.

This type of vertical marketing system is widely prevalent in the retail sector because of the increase in the bargaining power of retailers over the last decade. Retailers have become more market and more corporate-oriented, with a centralised administration and distribution, increased product range and retail branding. The administered distribution systems are more long-term oriented due to the prevalence of a strong channel culture and possible competitive advantage for the dominant channel partner. In administered systems, price is not the sole criterion deciding the extent of inter-relationship between suppliers, manufacturers or retailers. The total relationship orientation on a long-term basis is considered. This type of system is widely prevalent in the grocery, apparel and furnishing sectors.

(c) Contractual VMS

This is another type of vertical marketing system in which an organisation enters into agreement or contract with other channel members to undertake different channel functions. Contractual systems consist of independent organisations that integrate their distribution operations through contracts. These organisations try to reap the advantages of a vertically integrated system while operating independently. The success of such inter-organisation contractual arrangements depends on the commitment and cooperation from different channel partners.

In a contractual VMS, the channel members must have a deep knowledge of the legal requirements since all the contractual agreements drafted are enforceable by law. Generally, companies that have high bargaining power or those functioning in highly volatile industries like information technology prefer to adopt a contractual system. All the members in the system must commit themselves, at least partially, to working as a team to achieve certain common goals. This is because organisations enter into such a system with different objectives like expanding the market demand for their products. This objective holds true for products in the maturity stage of the product lifecycle. Industry level promotion where companies not only promote their products but those of other channel members is one form of this approach. It is widely seen in the food products industry.

Retailer-sponsored Co-operative Organisations (RCOs) and Wholesaler-sponsored Volunteers

Organisations (WVOs) are two of the best-known forms of contractual vertical marketing systems. RCOs are formed when groups of independent retailers combine together and support a single wholesaler. The wholesaler caters to the different needs of the retailer groups and the retailers get benefits in the form of rebates or price discounts from the wholesaler.

2. Cost Reduction

Intermediaries add costs. After all, each must make money on the product or service. Just because intermediaries add costs, though, doesn't mean a business can automatically save through eliminating an intermediary. However, if a business does find that it can take over the activities of an intermediary and save controlling that part of the distribution channel might be advisable. The end consumer might enjoy a less expensive product, while the business gains expertise and control over the process. For instance, some businesses would rather sell directly to consumers via the Internet than go through a retailer.

3. Cooperation

Structuring the distribution channel so that all the intermediaries work as a unified system results in a vertical marketing system. One part of the system exerts control over the others, either through ownership of the rest, contracts or power and market influence. By controlling the system, a business can ensure cooperation among the intermediaries. Additionally, no one intermediary can put its own self-interest ahead of the good of the whole system. The resulting stability and cooperation benefits the business.

4. Protection

Without controlling the channels of distribution, a business owner has no way of knowing how any of the intermediaries will treat the product. A retailer intermediary, for instance, with an assortment of goods to sell, might not even properly display the product. Protecting a brand's image and its relationships with consumers also becomes easier to regulate if a business controls distribution.

2.2 Productivity Aspects of Logistics Management

The activities within a production unit or a distribution house have a significant effect on the efficiency of logistics management. Downtime due to equipment damage or a lack of productivity due to inefficient processes can have adverse effects. Numerous costs associated with downtime and inefficiency can lead to losses. These not only include upfront and visible costs, but also hidden costs, such as overtime, loss of revenue, emergency service calls and inefficient worker time, which can all lead to a very unsatisfied customer. An efficiently managed logistics system can increase the productivity and decrease the downtime, thereby increasing customer satisfaction.

A standard process within a warehouse or a manufacturing unit can be established to improve the productivity of a logistics management system. Below is a list of action items to be taken into consideration.

1. **Establish a Regular Maintenance Plan:** To prevent a downtime, machineries should be serviced regularly. A thorough inspection process of the machines guarantees that problems are identified earlier. Machineries which break down often can have a serious negative effect on productivity and has a bad effect on business.

2. **Replace out of Date Machinery:** Old machines slow the manufacturing process down. Installing new equipment is significant in improving productivity within your warehouse. A lot of times firms make the mistake of servicing machinery that needs to be changed even though buying replacement equipment would be less expensive in the end.

3. **Utilise New Technology:** New ways of handling and processing materials are being developed daily. Ensure you stay competitive through being constantly on the lookout for new and more productive materials handling equipment. You also must be ready to take the risk to use these technologies in your processes.

4. **Track Efficiency Levels:** Increasing efficiency doesn't start with purchasing a new forklift or building. You must analyse the state of your operations. If you aren't running at peak performance find out why this is. Efficiency is directly connected to profit, but waiting to see how your profits are behaving means you are too late to maximise efficiency.

5. **Improve Warehouse Layout:** It seems clear, but several warehouses can be improved by simple things such as warehouse layout. Several warehouses are given to maximise racking or pallet spaces. This severely impacts the flow through the warehouse and makes it ineffective. If aisles run the wrong way, product is placed in the wrong area and pick and replenishment slots are inefficient. Thus, the business needs to look at decreasing the travel time within the warehouse.

6. **Check Inventory:** Accuracy in inventory is important in measuring efficiency and reliability of any warehouse. Wrong inventory can result in missed sales and incorrect buying decisions, in addition to poor customer relations.

7. **Involve Employees:** Employees are regularly involved in the work and thus can provide insights on how to improve productivity. Start by asking an employee to identify a task they carry out every day, giving complete details on what is involved. Then ask them what they think could be improved upon.

8. **Improve Packing Operations:** Guarantee packers get complete orders; they should not be concerned with unfinished orders or should not look around the warehouse for missing items.

9. **Standardise the Process:** Create a centralised location. Manage loading and unloading and execute effective plans for decreasing time and inefficiency at each step within the process.

10. **Consider Different Software Options:** There are many software alternatives to assist you in tracking data better within your warehouse. This will allow you to make smarter decisions on your inventory. You will get more feedback enabling computers to track and perform calculations on the supplies in your warehouse.

2.3 Distribution and Customer Satisfaction

Customer satisfaction is the measure of a supply chain's effectiveness. It is the means by which firms in a supply chain try to distinguish their products, keep customers loyal, improve profits, and become the supplier of choice. In other words, it is an ongoing, escalating, process of adding value, meeting requirements, and exceeding expectations. The following section explains how all members of the supply chain can use the six keys to attain ultimate customer satisfaction.

Develop Objective Measures

Customer satisfaction is a scientific problem. Its formula is

Customer Satisfaction = Customer Perception of the Service – Customer Expectation of Service

The formula presupposes two critical points

- Customer satisfaction is based on customers' perceptions and expectations, not on a self-centred view of what the customer should want.
- The level of customer satisfaction will change as customers' expectations change.

Customer satisfaction needs the organisations in a supply chain to concentrate on the needs, expectations, and perceptions of those to whom they give products and services. Because the needs of customers change over time, firms cannot satisfy the customers with the same set of services and value-adds that worked yesterday. As customers revel in their patronage, they increasingly mix to please them.

The firms in a supply chain must know and be capable of recognising the special requirements of each level of their customer base. That is to say that they must understand the hierarchy of customer tiers.

In general terms, 'consumer service' is the service provided to the customer from the time of order placed till the product is delivered. Distribution plays an important role providing a good customer service.

Customer service in physical distribution function consists of providing products at the time and location corresponding to the customer needs. Improvement in customer service is possible when we talk of a service level. A customer service level is a measure of how well the customer service function is being performed. Customers would be cent-percent satisfied if a wide range of products were available at the right place and time in sufficient quantities to meet the needs and wants of all who were willing and able to buy. This is an ideal case indeed which is rate to a customer. However, high levels of customer satisfaction can be possible through a viable distribution system.

Distribution Factors for Customer Satisfaction include

- Time
- Dependability
- Communication
- Availability
- Convenience

2.3.1 Role of Distribution in Customer Service and Satisfaction

Customer satisfaction can be defined as the feeling a person experiences when an offering meets his or her expectations. There are two critical ways to improve customer satisfaction. The first is to establish appropriate expectations in the minds of customers. The second is to deliver on those expectations. Improving customer satisfaction is a goal sought by many businesses. In fact, some companies evaluate their salespeople based on how well they satisfy their customers; in other words, not only must the salespeople hit their sales targets, they have to do so in ways that satisfy customers. Teradata is one company that pays its salespeople bonuses if they meet their customer satisfaction goals.

We know that dissatisfied customers are likely to tell many more people about their negative experiences than satisfied customers are about good experiences. For example, telling a friend that a movie was average. Many companies believe that delighting customers by over-exceeding their expectations should result in both repeat business and positive word of mouth for a firm. Establishing appropriate expectations in the minds of customers is a function of the pre-purchase communications the seller has with them. If you set the expectations too low, people won't buy your offering. But if you set the expectations too high, you run the risk that your buyers will be dissatisfied. A common saying in business is "under-promise and over-deliver." In other words, set consumers' expectations a bit low, and then exceed those expectations in order to create delighted customers who are enthusiastic about your product. A seller hopes that enthusiastic customers will tell their friends about the seller's offering, spreading lots of positive word of mouth about it.

Another customer satisfaction strategy involves offering customers warranties and guarantees. Warranties serve as an agreement that the product will perform as promised or some form of restitution will be made to the customer. Customers who are risk-averse find warranties reassuring. Apart from this following are the various responsibilities handled by the distribution manager.

Distribution managers play an important role in the supply chain, concentrating on the flow of product rather than storage. Fulfilling customer orders correctly and quickly while attaining the least possible cost is a balancing act that distribution managers must play every day. They must synchronise people, processes, capacity and technology to attain customer satisfaction, meet internal goals, and give value-added services to the supply chain.

Managing the distribution system for maximum supply chain impact requires a lot of planning, co-ordination of fulfillment strategy with the implementation of distribution operations, analysis of key metrics, and information sharing. Additional ideas from this chapter include the following –

1. Distribution operations perform inventory handling, storage, and processing activities to streamline and place utility for the supply chain.
2. A number of supply chain challenges – balancing supply and demand, protecting against uncertainty, and promoting transportation economies, among others – can be addressed by distribution facilities.

3. Four main functions are performed by traditional distribution facilities – accumulation, sortation, allocation, and assortment.

4. Distribution operations are taking on value-adding roles – assembly, kitting, product postponement, sequencing, etc. to complement their basic functionality and to support evolving supply chain requirements.

5. Trade-offs must be made between space, equipment, and people – the main resources available to distribution managers.

6. It is important to match distribution procedures to the items being handled to safeguard product integrity, promote customer service and satisfaction, and give bigger control of the inventory.

7. Distribution network design issues involve centralisation/decentralisation of inventory the number and location of facilities, and facility ownership.

8. Effective facility planning – operational size, layout, and product placement – positively impacts labour productivity and response time.

9. Distribution execution includes five main processes connected to the handling and storage of product – receiving, put-away, order picking, replenishment, and shipping.

10. Fulfilment support functions provide co-ordination between key processes and across the supply chain, protect the organisation's inventory investment, and improve working conditions within the facility.

11. Distribution KPI's address asset utilisation, labour productivity, and cost efficiency of the operation, plus customer service quality issues and the final goal of perfect order fulfilment.

12. Warehouse management systems software solutions improve product movement and storage operations through efficient management of information and completion of distribution tasks.

13. Barcodes and radio frequency identification are the automatic identification tools of choice in distributing help, track, locate, and move product quickly with perfect accuracy rates to their consumers.

2.4 Channel Strategy Decision

A channel strategy is a vendor's plan for moving a product or a service through the chain of commerce to the end customer. Product manufacturers and service providers face a number of channel options. The simplest approach is the direct channel in which the vendor sells directly to the customer. The vendor may maintain its own sales force to close deals with customers or sell its products or services through an e-commerce website. Direct selling via catalogue represents another possibility, although this business has been largely subsumed by e-commerce. When devising a channel strategy, a vendor must make decisions about which channel or channels to use and the types of partners it will seek to cultivate.

The appropriate strategy can vary from one product or service to another. A vendor that builds a channel strategy around both direct and indirect sales channels must take care to avoid channel conflict. Channel partners will soon become disgruntled if a vendor's direct sales force competes with them for customer business. Thus, a channel strategy may involve market segmentation. For example, a vendor could target only large enterprises with its direct sales force, while reserving small and mid-sized businesses for its channel partners.

2.4.1 Types of Channel Strategy Decision

The major types of channels are conventional channels and vertical marketing systems (VMS). The conventional channel of distribution is a group of vertically connected self-governing organisations, each trying to watch out for itself, with limited concern for the total performance of the channel. The relations between the conventional channel participants are somewhat informal and the members are not synchronised closely. The focus of the channel organisation is on buyer-seller transaction rather than close collaboration throughout the distribution channel.

The second type of distribution channel is the vertical marketing system (VMS). Marketing executives in many companies realise the advantages to be gained by managing the channel as a synchronised or programmed system of participating organisations. Later on, we think about the influence of supply chain management approaches and the Internet on the operations of channels. These vertical marketing systems control the retailing sector and are important factors in the business and industrial products and services sectors.

A main characteristic of a vertical marketing system is the management of the distribution channel by one organisation. The programming and synchronisation of channel activities and functions are directed by the channel manager. Operating rules and guidelines show the functions and responsibilities of each member. The channel leader of the company assists and provides services to the participating organisations.

Three types of vertical marketing systems may be used – ownership, contractual and administered. Recently, a fourth form of vertical marketing system has developed in which the channel organisations form collaborative relations instead of being controlled by one organisation. We consider this as a relationship vertical marketing system.

1. **Ownership VMS:** Ownership of distribution channels from source of supply to end user involves a substantial capital investment by the channel co-ordinator. This kind of vertical marketing system also adapts to change compared to the other vertical marketing system forms. For these reasons a popular alternative may be to develop collaborative relationships with channel members (for example, supplier/manufacture alliances). Such arrangements have a tendency to decrease the coordinator's control over the channel but overcome the disadvantages of control through ownership. Nevertheless, in high competitive markets, the need for control of distribution may

make channel ownership more attractive. Globally, a lot of auto manufacturers are setting up their own retail outlets and buying out independent franchisees and distributors and regaining channel control to build an ownership vertical marketing system, substituting traditional channels.

2. **Contractual VMS:** The contractual form of the vertical marketing system may include different formal arrangements between channel participants including franchising and voluntary chains of independent retailers. Franchising is famous in fast foods, lodging, and several other retail lines. Traditional automobile dealerships are another example of a contractual vertical marketing system. Wholesaler-sponsored retail chains are encouraged by food and drug wholesalers to set up networks of independent retailers. Contractual programs can be started by manufacturers, wholesalers, and retailers. For example, the outstanding growth of Krispy Kreme doughnuts is biased in part on franchised stores in the United States which give a third of the company's income. Interestingly, Krispy Kreme's international growth is based on the franchised plan of its operation.

3. **Administered VMS:** The administered vertical marketing system exists because one of the channel members has the capacity to influence channel members. This influence may be due to financial strengths, brand image, specialised skills (for example, marketing, product innovation) and help and support to channel members. For example, for over a hundred years, DeBeers managed the worldwide distribution of rough diamonds through its marketing cartel acting as "buyer of last resort" to attain market stability and steady price appreciation for diamonds – by 1998 DeBeers had a diamond stockpile of $5 billion. On the other hand, DeBeers changed its strategy in 2000 to leverage its "Diamonds Are Forever" positioning concept with consumers and to brand diamonds—the company has moved down the value chain to take part in the finished jewellery market."

4. **Relationship VMS:** This kind of channel shares certain features of the administered vertical marketing system, but varies in that a single company does not exercise considerable control over other channel members. Instead, the relationship involves close collaboration and sharing of information, the relationship of vertical marketing system may be more logical in channels with only two or three levels. An example is the relationship between Radio Shack and Sprint (telephone services).

The economic performance of vertical marketing systems will probably be higher than that in conventional channels if the channel network is designed and managed correctly. On the other hand, the companies taking part in the channel should ensure concessions and be ready to work toward overall channel performance. There are rules to be followed, control is used in a variety of ways, and usually there is less flexibility with the members. Also, some of the needs of the total vertical marketing system may not be in the best interests of a specific participant. Nevertheless, competing in a conventional distribution channel against a vertical marketing system is a major competing challenge, so a channel member may find membership in a vertical marketing system to be advantageous.

The extraordinary story of Linux shows how informal relationship-building by parties at different stages in the value change can change an industry. The innovation feature describes how IBM and Intel, producing computer hardware and Dell, the leading reseller, have supported Linux's open-source software expansion. Commentators propose that industry's hostility toward the operating systems supremacy of Microsoft has encouraged much of the support given to Linux.

2.4.2 Selecting the Channel Strategy

The major channel-strategy decisions we have examined are summarised here (1) selects the kind(s) of channel to be used, (2) determines the desired intensity of distribution and (3) chooses the channel configuration. One of the first issues to be resolved is deciding whether to manage the channel, partner with members, or be a participant. This choice often rests on the bargaining power a company can exert in negotiating with other organisations in the channel system and the value (and costs) of performing the channel management role. The choices include deciding to manage or synchronise operations in the distribution channel, be a member of a vertically co-ordinated channel or becoming a member of a conventional channel system. In the choice of the channel strategy, the following factors are required to be evaluated.

1. **Market Access:** As stressed all through the chapter the market target decision needs to be synchronised with channel strategy, since the channel connects products and end users. The market target decision is not finalised until the channel strategy is selected. Information about the customers in the market target can assist in removing inappropriate channel –strategy options. Multiple market targets may need more than a single channel of distribution. One advantage of middlemen is that they have a set customer base. When this customer base matches the producer's choice of market target(s), market access is attained very quickly.

2. **Value-Added Competencies:** The channel that is chosen should offer the best combination of value-added competencies. To make this evaluation one needs to look at the competencies of each participant and the trade-offs regarding financial and flexibility and control considerations.

3. **Financial Considerations:** Two financial issues have an effect on the channel strategy. First, are the resources available for introducing the proposed strategy? For example, a small producer cannot afford to build a distribution network. Second, the revenue-cost impact of alternative channel strategies needs to be assessed. These analyses consist of cash flow, income, return on investment and operating capital needs.

4. **Flexibility and Control Considerations:** Management must decide how much flexibility it requires in the channel network and how much control it would like to have over other channel participants. An example of flexibility is how simply channel members can be added or removed. A conventional channel provides little chance for control by a member company yet there is a lot of flexibility in entering and exiting from the channel. The vertical marketing system offers more control than the conventional channel. Legal and regulatory constraints also have an effect on channel strategies in such areas as pricing, exclusive dealing, and allocation of market coverage.

Channel Strategy Illustration. Presume a producer of industrial controls for fluid processing (for example, valves, regulators) is thinking about channelling strategy options; using independent manufacturer's agents versus resting a firm's sales force to sell its products to industrial customers. The agents receive a commission of 8 percent on their dollar sales volume. Sales people will be paid an estimated $100,000 in annual salary and expenses. Salespeople should be recruited, trained, and supervised.

An illustrative channel strategy assessment is shown in the exhibit. The company sales force alternative is more costly than the use of independent sales agents. Presuming both alternatives generate contributions to profit, the trade-off of higher expenses needs to be assessed against flexibility and control considerations. One possibility that is frequently used by manufacturers seeking access to a new market is to primarily take help of the manufacturer's agents with a longer-term strategy of changing to a company sales force. This provides a chance to gain market knowledge while keeping selling expenses similar to the actual sales.

2.4.3 Strategies at Different Channel Level

We have looked at distribution mainly from the producer's point of view; wholesalers and retailers are also concerned with channel strategies, and some may use primary control over channel operations. For example, the retailer is a powerful force in its channels, as is Wal-Mart large food wholesalers and retailers are major factors in their channels distribution. Furthermore, decisions by wholesalers, distributors, brokers and retailers about which manufacturers' products to carry frequently have an effect on the performance of all channel participants.

Channel strategy can be examined from any level in the distribution network. The major distinction lies in the viewpoint used to develop the strategy. Intermediaries may have fewer options to consider than producers and, thus, less flexibility in channel strategy. However, their approach to channel strategy is often very active rather than passive.

2.4.4 Selection of Channel Strategy

The development of channel strategies requires decisions in three key areas:
*   Buyer Preferences
*   Relationship Orientation
*   Degree of Market Coverage

1. **Evaluation of Capabilities and Costs**
   - Product Considerations
   - Pricing Considerations
   - Marketing Communications Considerations
   - Evaluation of Availability

2. **Determining Channel Structure**
   - What channel structure is best for us to use?
   - Direct or Indirect Channels?
   - Single or Multiple Channels?
   - Vertical Marketing Systems?
   - Run a Trial Period
   - Set Performance Expectations
   - Create Communication Networks

Evaluating Channel Performance

   (i) **Financial Evaluation:** In the short run channel members will accept low levels of financial performance.

   (ii) **Evaluate Working Relationships:** In the long run channel members must have positive financial results to sustain channel relationships.

   (iii) **Evaluate Legal and Ethical Issues**
   - Are any laws being violated?
   - Are any exclusive territories set up?
   - Are any exclusive dealing arrangements being made?
   - Are resellers being bound to tying contracts?

   (iv) **Future Considerations for Channel Management.**

Firms must always ask, "How well can this channel be expected to perform in the future?"

Companies will be forced to alter their channels because of –
   - Changing consumer preferences
   - Intense competition
   - Innovation in information technology

Which Alternative Is Best?

   - There are trade-offs among the various objectives a company might try to accomplish with its distribution channel.
   - The decision depends on –
     o Which distribution objectives are considered most important.
     o Which are influenced by the business's competitive strategy and the other components of the marketing program.

- Consumer goods and services - Three basic strategies of retail coverage –
  - o Intensive Distribution
  - o Exclusive Distribution
  - o Selective Distribution

	Retail coverage	Major strength	Major weakness	Products most appropriate for
Intensive	Maximum	Maximises product availability	Lack of retailer support	Low-involvement consumer convenience goods.
Exclusive	Single	Matches retailer clientele with target market; facilitates close cooperation with retailer	Risk of relying on single retailer	High-involvement speciality or shopping goods
Selective	Limited	Provides adequate coverage but not at the expense of manufacturer-retailer cooperation	Difficult to implement given inter-store competition, especially where discounts may occur	Infrequently purchased shopping goods

- **Promotional Effort, Market Information, and Post-sale Service Objectives**
  - o The theory of transaction cost analysis (TCA) argues that when substantial transaction-specific assets are involved, the costs of using and administering independent channel members are likely to be higher than the costs of managing a company sales force and/or distribution centres.
- **Cost-effectiveness**
  - o Minimising physical distribution costs subject to the constraint of achieving some target level of product availability and customer service.
  - o Make-or-buy decisions
  - o Supply chain management
- **Flexibility**
  - o Generally, vertically integrated systems are difficult to alter quickly.
  - o Channels involving independent middlemen are often more flexible.

- **Multichannel Distribution**
  - o Companies are increasingly using multiple channels.
  - o Some use dual distribution systems.
  - o Hybrid system is a variation.
  - o Multichannel systems employ separate channels to reach different target segments.
  - o Members of a hybrid system perform complementary functions for the same customer segment.

3. **Channel Design for Global Markets**

   Market Entry Strategies
   - Exporting is simple because it involves the least commitment and risk.
   - Contractual entry modes are non-equity arrangements that involve the transfer of technology and/or skills to an entity in a foreign country.
   - Overseas direct investment can be implemented in two ways—through joint ventures or sole ownership.

   Channel Alternatives for Global Market
   - The use of domestic middlemen who provide marketing services from a domestic base.
   - The use of foreign middlemen.

   Channel Alternatives for Services
   - Ordinarily, the marketing of services does not require the same kind of distribution networks as does the marketing of tangible goods.
   - Marketing channels for services tend to be short—hence the emphasis on franchising.

4. **Vertical Marketing Systems**
   - Corporate VMSs
   - Contractual VMSs
   - Administered VMSs
   - Relational VMSs

5. **Sources of Channel Power**
   - Economic power
   - Coercive power
   - Expert power
   - Referent power
   - Legitimate power

The power of any firm within a distribution channel is inversely proportional to how dependent the other channel members are on that firm.

- Channel control strategies
- Pull strategy
- Push strategy
- Trade promotions

Manufacturers typically use a combination of incentives to gain reseller support and push their products through the channel.

- Most of these incentives constitute sales promotion activities
- Categories of sales promotion activities
- Consumer promotions

6. Trade Promotions

- Incentives to increase reseller purchases and inventories
- Incentives to increase personal selling effort
- Incentives to increase local promotional effort
- Incentives to improve customer service
- The changing role of incentives in relational distribution systems
- The importance of good distribution decisions in designing a marketing plan is simple: **Customers won't buy your goods or service unless it is conveniently available when and where they want to buy it.**
- Distribution channel decisions have a major economic impact because distribution costs often exceed the costs of producing a good or service.
- Channel design involves decisions about the appropriate types and numbers of middlemen to include in the distribution channel in order to link the marketing strategy for the good or service to the needs of the target customers.

Distribution channels can be designed to accomplish a number of objectives including

- Maximising the product's availability
- Satisfying customer service requirements
- Encouraging promotional effort
- Obtaining timely market information
- Minimizing distribution costs, and
- Maintaining flexibility

A manufacturer or service provider can attempt to gain the support and direct the efforts of its channel partners

- Through vertical integration
- By legal contracts
- By providing economic incentives, and/or
- By developing mutually beneficial relationships based on trust and the expectation of future benefits

2.5 CHANNEL MANAGEMENT AND CHANNEL STRATEGY

The present competitive market environment is characterised by customers seeking convenience and service while purchasing goods and distributors becoming more organised by providing specialised services. The ever growing customer expectations impose a special importance for effective channel management. Efficient channel management helps companies reduce costs, reach potential customers efficiently and earn profits. Intermediaries play a key role in providing convenience and service to customers. As distributors are becoming increasingly specialised, effective channel organisation and management becomes imperative.

Marketers should consider some important aspects for better channel management. Most importantly, the marketer has to select and recruit the right channel members. Subsequently, the focus has to be on motivating channel members and increasing the firm's profitability. Later, the company has to periodically evaluate the performance of channel members to ensure that they remain competitive in the market. Marketers are required to modify their channel arrangements, in line with the market changes.

2.5.1 The Process of Channel Management

Managing the process of channel management begins well before one chooses the selling options and, in most cases, should start even before the product is made. To properly manage the process, it's important to know the reason for using the steps so as to bring the sales partners into the loop regarding the marketing strategies and set benchmarks to measure the effectiveness of the efforts.

After designing a channel of networks, it must be managed efficiently for desired results, the final goal in channel management should be a "win-win'" for everybody including customers. Profit-making alone should not be the reason for the producer and his channel members, satisfying the target customers' requirements should be a priority. Thus, for efficiently managing the distribution channels, the following wing steps can be considered.

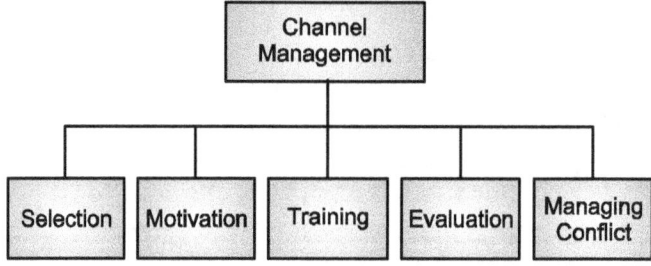

Fig. 2.1: Steps of Channel Management

2.5.2 Channel Selection and Management

Channel members play a major role in distribution of goods and services of the producers to the consumers. The principal functions that channel members undertake are transfer of ownership of goods, negotiation of titles to the goods and physical movement of products. Wholesalers, retailers, transporters, logistic services providers and distributor agents are channel members who perform some of these functions. The marketing managers are responsible for taking decisions on the nature and type of channel members to use, the channel design and the number and kind of channel members through whom the company should sell. A distribution channel is described in terms of the length, breadth, number, and types of channel members.

1. Unconventional Channels

Unconventional means not conventional, not traditional, and very different from the routine ones. Thus, unconventional marketing channels are the channels used for marketing or distribution which are not routinely used. The desire and need to market products differently yet effectively at times resulted in alliances with less than conventional marketing channels. Unconventional channels are tapped to sell products. For example, take a guerrilla marketing approach to particular projects to maximise efficiencies. But what exactly does the term 'guerrilla' marketing mean? It seems to mean different things to different people.

Guerrilla marketing is an unconventional system of promotions that relies on time, energy and imagination rather than a big marketing budget. Typically, guerrilla marketing campaigns are unexpected and unconventional; potentially interactive; and consumers are targeted in unexpected places. The objective of guerrilla marketing is to create a unique, engaging and thought-provoking concept to generate buzz, and consequently turn vital. The term was coined and defined by Jay Conrad Levinson in his book *Guerrilla Marketing*. People like and ascribe to the idea of unconventional approaches but there also are times when a big fat branding and marketing campaign will be the best way for a client to achieve their marketing objectives. We feel that way all the time but lack the resources to blow out a big time brand message so the company continues to grow using a myriad of what is considered to be affordable tactics and channels.

2. Channels for Consumer Goods and Industrial Goods

The long-term commitment of a business towards the market influences its choice of marketing channels. The design of a marketing channel is influenced by factors like technological advancement, changing demographics and competition. There are several dimensions for choosing a channel design, which include:

- Length of the channel – the number of intermediaries between the producer and the customers.
- Breadth of the channel – the number of outlets available to customers.
- Costs of selecting a particular channel.

A channel design decision is made considering the channel structure, channel intensity and the type of intermediaries used. While channel structure refers to the number of levels of channel intermediaries, channel intensity refers to the total number of channel intermediaries required at each level. The type of intermediaries at each level may include manufacturer's sales force, manufacturer's representatives or industrial distributors.

3. Channels for Services

A channel is a distinct way of distributing a product or a service from the producer to the end customer. The channel members are the participants forming the channel. In the case of goods distribution, a multi-tier or multi-level distribution structure including manufacturer, wholesaler, distributor, retailer and customer is quite common. In case of distribution of services, such an elaborate three or four-layered structure may be replaced by a simpler one or two-layered structure.

The following distribution channel members are prevalent in India.

(a) **Service Brokers:** A broker is a person or a company who brings buyers and sellers together and assists in the negotiations without getting involved in the financing or assuming any risk. Some examples of specialised brokers are –

- **Share Brokers:** They bring the share sellers and share buyers together. Sometimes they would advise their clients on the direction of movement of the share prices, long-term prospects, analysis, etc. However, their main business is to bring the buyer and seller together to transact the shares at mutually acceptable prices. With the direct online trading now prevalent through both National Stock Exchange (NSE) and Bombay Stock Exchange (BSE) such share dealings have become easier.

- **Real Estate Brokers:** In the absence of a broker, both the owner of the real estate and the prospective buyer of the property need to advertise. For individuals, this may turn out to be expensive. Brokers have on their list potential properties in major areas of the city and also know the prospective customers. Therefore, the broker can bring the two parties together and arrange for a site visit at no risk to either party, to let the clients decide on the suitability of the deal. Later, the broker helps both the parties to conclude the deal at mutually agreeable terms. In return, the broker gets one to three months rent as the charges for facilitating the transaction.

(b) **Service Agents:** Agents generally represent either the buyer or the seller on a more permanent basis than the brokers. They may have formal written agreements to ensure long-term continuity. Agents may represent more than one marketer of complementary goods or services to generate a viable business volume.

- **Shipping Agents and Travel Agents:** Generally, they represent one or more shipping line or airline for selling cargo space or passenger space. They co-ordinate between the shipper or traveller and the line that provides the service.

They have at their finger tips the timetables, days of docking, special cargo offers and can make special offers to a potential shipper with specialised cargo or for group travel bookings etc. The agent may be the only visible representative of the shipping company or airline.

- **Insurance Agents:** The life as well as non-life insurance is promoted by Life Insurance Corporation of India (Life) and General Insurance Corporation (Non-Life/General) through the use of agents. These active salespersons representing the corporations establish contacts with prospects that need to cover various risks. They convince them to buy the most suitable cover. Usually, corporations back these agents up through development officers. The agents get commission on the premium income received by the corporation.

- **Credit Card and Bank Loans Agents:** A number of financial institutions realise the need for appointing external agencies to enhance the level of business generated. These agents meet the potential clients, understand their needs, make competitive offers on behalf of the principals and finally help conclude the business transaction in return for commission.

(c) **Professional Service Agents:** A professional service agent is one where the knowledge base of the expert enables clients to seek solutions to their problems. The key to the marketing of such services is the credibility. Therefore, large accountancy, auditing, and consultancy firms tend to get substantial upmarket corporate business in these areas. In order to ensure the service effectiveness, professional service providers adopt the policy of global brand names with local partnerships.

Thus, auditing and accounting firms have chartered or certified public accountants based in the city of operation to run the local establishment by using their local business contacts for marketing. In this way, the entrepreneurial spirit remains vibrant for vigorous business growth. The organisations gain by having global presence and are able to secure business from clients from any location due to geographically wider presence.

(d) **Direct Marketing:** The innovation in telecom sector has enabled the marketer to find various means of directly getting in touch with the individual customers. These include telemarketing (showing the product or service on the television and asking the customers to call telephone numbers in their area to book the orders), direct e-mail and postal mailers to the select potential customers in the target market segments and personal contact selling.

(e) **Franchising:** Franchising is one of the major ways of distribution of services. The parties involved are the franchiser, the franchisee, and the customers. In India, franchising arrangement has been successful in the areas of photographic development and printing services (for example, Fotofast), restaurants and hotels (for example, Holiday Inn, McDonalds), tuition and coaching classes (for example, Jog Classes), health clubs and fitness centres, computer training institutes (for example, NIIT, Seed Infotech).

A franchiser licenses a trade or service mark to the franchisees in return for financial compensation. The franchiser usually specialises in a particular type of business model, which enables standardisation in the service delivery and promotion and leads to a high degree of customer satisfaction. The model of franchising has worked out well in the Indian markets. Some of the examples are –

(i) **Computer Training Institutes:** Companies such as NIIT pioneered this technique. They appointed a number of franchisees in all the major cities of India, including district towns and in some cases even taluka places. This enabled rapid development of computer education within the country.

The standardised requirements to set up such institutes are rented or owned premises at locations convenient for the students, use of state-of-the-art hardware and licensed software mostly provided by the franchiser at a price, employment of certified trainers and availability of infrastructure to represent the classroom layout.

The franchisee can charge authorised fees from the students and offer a well-designed standard course with educational material, including software supplied by the franchiser. The franchisee is authorised to conduct standard examinations and issue certificates of the franchiser, including that of the software supplier such as Microsoft.

This business model has developed to such an extent that franchisees started specialising the educational services as per the target market segments of home learners, children and housewives, students, companies and institutions for employee training.

(ii) **Photographic Services:** Chains of photographic services stores have been set up in all major cities and towns offering colour and black and white photo film development and printing, photo enlargement and printing, passport-size photographs, conversion from film to CDs, sale of photographic equipment and films etc.

The franchisee needs to own a shop and laboratory premises which are well located. They need to purchase, install and operate a franchiser-recommended standard automatic processing laboratory, shop decor, furniture, and equipment. In addition to it, chemicals, supplies and films have to be purchased from the franchiser.

In return, the franchisee gets benefited from the franchiser advertising, the use of the logo and the brand of the franchiser. The prices, delivery period, and quality of printing are standardised and are of high quality.

(iii) Coaching Classes: Trainers such as Career Forum offer training for competitive examinations such as MBA entrance tests, Graduate Registration Examination (GRE), and Test of English as Foreign Language (TOEFL).

The course contents, course material, and course methodology are standardised and ensure an excellent chance of securing high grades and admission. Thus, franchising is one of the most successful arrangements for services distribution.

4. Horizontal Marketing Channels:

A horizontal marketing system is an arrangement within a distribution channel in which two or more firms at the same channel level work towards a common goal. In this system, the two firms not related to each other come together with the objective of cashing in on a market opportunity. Most companies operate through a strategic alliance or a joint-venture. This type of an arrangement is formed because the organisations on their own do not have the resources, experience or the know-how to explore the marketing opportunity to their business advantage. Horizontal systems have become popular due to the fact that co-operating firms put to function, skills and resources that others do not have. Organisations have started making use of horizontal integration to gain advantages that are not possible in the vertical system.

Companies often join together to market an existing product, or create a new distribution venture to market a new product because they lack tangible and intangible resources, physical and capital resources, and an established brand name in order to reach customers effectively for ultimately a successful joint effort.

With the economy at a downturn, companies throughout many industries are finding it difficult to maintain the same profits that they experienced earlier. During tough economic times, rivalry between companies heavily increases; this means, companies need to work especially hard to remain competitive and visible in consumers' eyes. The importance of developing channels thus cannot be denied. A very powerful way of working together to combine financial, production and marketing resources to accomplish more than any one company could alone is called horizontal marketing system.

The success of a horizontally integrated system lies in the integration of four different functional areas - operational integration, intellectual integration, social integration and emotional integration among channel members. Operational integration deals with the standardisation of the production and distribution processes between the co-operating firms. Intellectual integration involves sharing information among the co-operating firms, about the requirements, leading to the development of customised processes. Horizontal arrangements have been successful in pharmaceutical and retail distribution segments.

5. Multi-Channel Marketing Systems

A multi-channel marketing system is a supplier's system which makes use of two or more channels to reach consumers with his product(s). It may create conflict between the supplier and his middlemen when inter-channel competition to sell the same product intensifies. When the channels are used for different products there are few problems.

(i)   Commonly, producers who use multi-channel marketing systems operate their own retail stores as well as sell through other wholesalers and retailers. Multi-channel retailers are also called Merchandising Conglomerates.

(ii)   Multi-channel marketing uses more than one purchasing passageway to give customers access to products and services. These different marketing channels could include websites, retail stores, mail order catalogues, direct mail and e-mail. Multi-channel marketing involves using two or more of these channels to provide increased benefits to both the company and its customers.

(iii)   The main benefit of multi-channel marketing for companies is often said to be the increased interaction with customers. Increased customer interaction increases opportunities for the promotion of products and services which increases potential profits. If a company can make sales through different channels such as through an e-commerce website as well as a brick and mortar store, the amount of sales potential is expanded

(iv)   Cross-channelling is an important consideration of multi-channel marketing. This offers customers much appreciated conveniences such as being able to check the availability of an item on the company's website before driving down to the local store to pick it up. In order to make the most of cross-channelling within multi-channel marketing, the customer base must be clearly understood in terms of what conveniences and information it expects. The success of multi-channel marketing often relies heavily on partner services. For example, a manufacturer of pharmaceuticals may have a repackaging and rebranding specialist to take their products from old or bulk packaging and repackage and re-label them. The re-packagers make sure both the packaging and the labelling are suitable for strong commercial distribution.

(v)   Retailers are another important part of multi-channel marketing. For instance, a mail order catalogue could contain a coupon that must be redeemed at the company's brick and mortar retail store. The coupon offer from the mail order channel drives traffic to the retail store channel. Once those customers are in the store, sales people would be prepared to present other great offers to keep increasing sales.

(vi) Another type of partner often involved in multi-channel marketing approaches is a consultant. Consultants analyse what channels would be best for a certain company. They are experts on marketing channels and could include creative directors from advertising agencies, e-commerce sales strategists from e-mail websites and merchandise analysts from retail stores. Multi-channel marketing consultants should understand consumer trends and how they affect the different buying channels such as store, website, mail, e-mail and telephone.

Although multi-channel marketing is the current trend, it is not an entirely new concept. Multi-channel has roots in the age-old "media mix" idea, which essentially said that buyers were reached at different times in different ways, and that the most successful marketing programmes contained an appropriate mix of media for the targeted audience. The theory was that effective use of multiple media helped a selling organisation become top-of-mind when the buyer was ready to make a purchasing decision.

New methods of marketing are emerging that seek to more effectively use prospect and customer data to filter target lists, construct personalisation rules and produce and execute marketing campaigns across and among the full range of media channels available. The most successful campaigns reach consumers in a sequenced and consistent manner. This creates an indirect benefit of enforcing and enhancing corporate branding. Therefore, organisations that can harness the power of other marketing channels and produce more personalised communications could put themselves in a good position to capture market share from those that don't.

There are two critical components to effective multi-channel marketing –

1. Creating relevant offers via personalisation
2. Co-ordination and management of multiple marketing channels

In a multi-channel marketing context, personalisation means using what is known about the recipient to create the offer, customise the messaging and deliver it to them in the format requested. For channels other than telemarketing, this can include personalised greetings, relevant messages based on demographics and compelling graphics.

The other critical element lies in the design and execution of campaigns that coordinate among the full breadth of channels available to reach prospective buyers. Much like personalisation, this requires strategic and tactical planning. When marketers can sequence communications and "hit" prospective customers with consistent communications through various media channels, the effectiveness of campaigns increases greatly.

Many executives fear that one channel will take business away from another. The Web site will steal from the catalogue, for example. The truth is that customers who interact with a company over multiple channels are more loyal and profitable than single-channel customers. To become a successful multi-channel marketer, one first needs to understand the customers and their preferences, then communicate effectively through the desired channels.

Channel Selection Process

Companies need to concentrate on strengthening core competencies and outsource other activities, for succeeding in the market place. With a careful selection of channel members, the distribution channel function can be outsourced. This is very important for any company as the channel members represent the company in the market. Replacing existing channel members is difficult. Therefore, firms have to be cautious while recruiting, to ensure that an ideal channel member can be selected. An ideal channel member will be the one who will serve the right customer at the right time with the right attitude. Hence, a careful recruiting and selection procedure is essential for selecting channel members suiting the company's requirements.

Once companies appreciate the significance of recruitment and selection of proper channel members, they should consider the following guidelines for effective recruitment.

- To assess the exact role to be played by the channel members or the nature of the job they have to perform.
- To analyse the qualifications of the channel member in terms of the firm's requirements.
- The authority to be delegated to channel members.
- Changes that may occur in the future with regard to the role played by channel members.
- Recruiting a channel member should be a continuous process as channel members may leave the organisation or the organisation might feel the need to change existing channel members.

There can be various reasons emphasising the need for continuous recruitment of channel members. For example, a revision in the company's product policy may call for new types of channel members. Change in customers' tastes and preferences will also influence the company to look for the new channel members if the existing channel members are unable to cater to the changed conditions.

Recruiting Manufacturers

Like manufacturers recruit channel members, retailers also choose the right kind of manufacturer for maximising their sales.

Screening

Screening involves elimination of applicants not matching the set criteria. The guidelines used for screening channel members are as follows –

- Screening based on the market segments the channel members will have to serve.
- The second is to assess the channel member's capability to serve the market.
- Compatibility of service with the product's stage in the product lifecycle. As distribution requirements change during the different stages of the product

lifecycle, it is essential to select channel members who best suit these requirements. For instance, if a new type of industrial equipment is launched, it needs highly specialised distributors during the initial stage of the product lifecycle. These distributors should be able to explain the technical features to customers. Once the product reaches the maturity stage, specialised distributors may not be required for demonstrating technical details to customers, as they are well aware of the product and its usage.

- Generally, manufacturers prefer channel members who are successful in the market. However, successful channel members carry a large number of products and may not have space for more products. However, this does not mean manufacturers need to settle for sub-standard channel members. Instead, they should select appropriate channel members who can invest sufficient time for effective distribution and improve sales. This carries a lot of importance in the present environment where customers look for convenience and service while making purchase decisions.

- Another important criterion for screening channel members is support required. The company can extend financial and strategic support during the initial stages of the relationship, if channel members need such support provided the accrued benefits of extending such support offset the costs involved. Otherwise, the company should eliminate such applicants.

Criteria for Selection of Channel Members

After screening, the firm will be left with a small list of potential channel members for selection. The company has to spot from this list, the most suitable channel members who best fit its requirements. Sales, product, experience, administrative and risk factors are some of the factors for selecting channel partners.

1. **Sales Factors:** While selecting channel members, the primary factor of consideration is the member's ability to sell the company's products in the market. The channel member's knowledge and expertise of the market are also important preconditions for selection.

2. **Product Factors:** Product factors include the channel member's expertise and knowledge of the products to be handled. The channel partner's abilities to handle products effectively and provide the necessary after sales services to customers are primary factors that determine the selection of a channel member.

3. **Experience Factors:** It is equally important to evaluate the distributor on his past experience. Assessing the type of customers handled and industries served in the past and their satisfaction levels will provide a good insight and help selection of channel members.

4. **Administrative Factors:** Administrative factors such as the amount of work being handled by the channel member and the distributor's pricing patterns have to be considered for evaluating channel members.

5. **Risk Factors:** Assessment of risk factors involve evaluation of the potential of channel member's past performance, the channel member's commitment to the organisation's progress and costs incurred in selecting a member.

The recruitment process includes placing advertisements in the press of getting the sales people to visit the markets and speak to the promising candidates. Sometimes, existing channel partners also give good references of prospective candidates in other towns.

Given below are two examples from the consumer products industry on the guidelines which are assessed before appointing channel members – C&FA and a distributor.

Example 1: A Carrying and Forwarding Agent (C&FA)

The main requirement of a C&FA should be that he is a transporter with good warehousing facilities. The C&FA is usually chosen to work in areas or a state in which he is placed.

The responsibilities of a C&FA include receipt of goods, storage and care, order receipts from sales people, order processing, dispatch with correct documentation, record keeping, sales and stock reports, collection of sales proceeds from distributors and managing secondary transport for dispatches. The criteria for selection of a C&FA are summarised at Table 2.1 below.

Table 2.1: Parameters for Selecting C&FA

Parameter of Selection	Criteria for Selection
Location of the party	In or close to a main market of the company
Location of the warehouse	Close to the major market Outside octroi limits Should have good road/transport access Labour availability Utilities support Connected by phone
Past experience	As a C&FA for a similar company As a transporter should have access to a good warehouse
History of past experience	Should have handled similar but non-competing companies Ability to maintain confidentiality of transactions

contd. ...

Financial strength	To handle all operating expenses till reimbursement
	Insurance
IT capability	Adequate own hardware
	Trained staff to handle simple programmes and reporting formats
Flexibility	In operating hours daily
	To handle peak loads
Transportation facilities	Reliability
	Consistency in source of vehicles
	Additional volumes to be handled at short notice
Attitude, commitment	To be of the highest order/positive
	Willing to expand the business
	Disciplined

Example 2: A Distributor

A distributor is also called as a redistribution stockist. He purchases the company products from the company and sells it to all the wholesalers, retailers and establishments from where the final consumers buy it or where it may get consumed. The distributor 'invests' in the product and guarantees that it reaches closest to the point where the end user purchases the product and thus has got a major responsibility within the distribution network. He is thus selected based on a bigger number of parameters as can be seen in table 2.2 below.

Table 2.2: Parameters for Selecting a Distributor

Parameter of Selection	Criteria for Selection
Size of the channel partner	Current business portfolio
	Financial strength/asset ownership including personal assets of partners
Own sales force	Number of sales people
	Qualifications, background, experience
Current business	Products handled, volume handled
	Should be of similar products but non-competitive
	Product quality, compatibility and complimentary
Reputation	Leadership in the market
	Integrity, fairness in dealings

contd. ...

Market coverage	Territory/intensity, regularity, reliability, relationship, productivity, beat plan adherence
	Value of institutional business handled if any
Credit extended in the market	Percentage of outlets
	Percentage of current business
	Bad debts if any
Stock distribution	Ready stocks or order booking
Infrastructure availability	Warehouse, distribution vans, hardware/personal computers/ connectivity
Sales performance	On current business, awards, prizes, certificates won, performance
Management of business	Educational background, qualifications of partners, direct involvement in business
Market working	Efforts on merchandising displays
Handling sales promotions	Past experience
Inventory management	Adherence to stock norms recommended by the company

For companies like FMCG and pharmaceuticals only some of the channel partners like C&FA's and distribution can be recruited. The other channel members like wholesalers, retailers and chemists already exist in the market and automatically become part of the network. The effort is only in persuading them to stock and sell the company products.

A distribution channel encompasses several relationships that assist channel members in carrying out various channel functions. Suppliers tie up with various intermediaries in the distribution channel as they help suppliers or manufacturers achieve the objectives of making products available to end customer cost effectively. An analysis of the performance of channel partners by suppliers becomes necessary to evaluate the channel's effectiveness, while designing or structuring a distribution channel. A distribution channel can be assessed in terms of Key Performance Areas (KPAs) such as channel effectiveness, channel efficiency, channel productivity, channel equity and channel profitability.

2.5.3 Channel Motivation and Management

'Channel motivation' is almost the same as motivation of the human resources of a business marketer. Higher the motivation, higher would be the level of satisfaction and better would be the performance, which would, consecutively, increase the motivation farther. This 'virtual' cycle is an age-old truth known to many business marketers. The reverse that is, lower motivation would lead to lower performance, is also an acknowledged truth.

No business marketer can thrive with demotivated channel members. Both, monetary and non-monetary motivation could help. There should always be a balance between monetary and non-monetary motivators. A number of studies done by the author bring out that honest, fair and transparent policies and practices over time turn out to be the best motivators for channel members. The firms connected to the house of Tatas, like Tata Steel, Tata Motors, and Larsen & Toubro and many more, have maintained very high motivation levels and morale because of the honest and transparent policies towards channel members. These firms may not pay high commissions or organise very fanciful dealer meets, but the channel members respect their honesty and transparency. In addition to the monetary rewards through commissions and discounts, a business marketer can develop many non-monetary reward and recognition procedures and systems for the channels, imagination, creativity and innovativeness in these would pay rich dividends. These need not be 'run of the mill' kind of rewards and recognitions, but they should be done on a sustained basis. An age-old saying in India is that 'channel members are hungry for recognition'. Small and big recognitions and rewards go a long way in keeping the morale, motivation and excitement high. Involving 'family members' of the channel members in functions and ceremonies, could work wonders. Examples of motivators are –

- **Rewards and Recognition**
  - Annual Dealers' Conference
    - Recognition of best performers across various product categories
    - Recognition of best sales, service and parts personnel at dealerships
    - Publication in 'in-house' magazines of the achievements of a channel member or his team, or even of some family member

- **Engagements**
  - Dealers councils and meetings
    - Regular forum for dealers to interact with senior management about larger issues in their regions and to seek solutions

Motivating channel members takes many different forms so as to fulfil the different requirements at each level in the channel. As wholesalers can purchase products from a number of sources, profitability is the main motivation for product selection. Presuming the profit motivation has been satisfied, the wholesaler becomes concerned with the marketing programs the manufacturer offers to assist in selling the products to retailers. Wholesalers will consider the credit alternatives and the terms of payment when assessing the profit potential of doing business with a particular supplier. Retailers are generally first concerned with the maintenance or product supply and availability. When consumers cannot find the products they want at one retailer, they will frequently search for another that has what they are looking for. Retailers do not like losing customers. The second interest of a retailer is how much profit the product carries. The only way for a retailer to remain in business is to be profitable. The main motivational considerations for wholesalers, retailer and product users are listed in Table 2.3 in their general order of importance.

Table 2.3: Motivational Considerations for Channel Members

For Wholesalers	For Retailers	For Product Users
Profit	Product availability	Product utility
Credit and terms	Profit	Value received
Marketing programs	Credit and terms	Credit and terms
Competitiveness	Marketing programs	Retailer service
Policies	Competitiveness	Product information
Training	Training	Guarantees
Legal and regulatory	Legal and regulatory	Legal and regulatory

Organising to Motivate Channel Members

1. **Recruit the Top Producers:** Motivating channel members should begin at the time when a manufacturer or marketer is recruiting intermediaries for channel participation. Choosing the most desirable and productive wholesalers and/or retailers in the start is significant for the motivation of all channel members. The best channel intermediaries will be keen to work together and are encouraged by the relationship with other top firms in the marketing channel. The main development goal is to encourage the top producing intermediaries to become a part of your channel organisation. Enticements that will attract the top producing channel members are things such as good profits, selective distribution, high-quality products and guarantees, advertising and promotional support in the channel, good communications, training, credit programs, and many other services provided by the manufacturer.

2. **Set Qualification Standards:** The other side of the question concerning the motivation of channel members is in qualifying the right intermediary members to make it possible. The manufacturer or marketing firm should be attractive to the intermediaries, yet it also must set selection criteria or qualifications for the intermediaries. The organisation of channel compatibility must begin with a list of selection criteria so as to provide a base for channel member compatibility. The marketing channel members that are chosen must have all the basic criteria for best performance. Selection criteria are established and applied so as to allow the manufacturer to form a compatible and effective system of marketing channel

intermediaries. These selection criteria should include consideration of the following points – (1) financial strength, (2) management ability, (3) market coverage, (4) product line compatibility, (5) channel competitiveness (6) channel member compatibility, and (7) customer services capabilities.

Locating the top producers, how do manufacturers and marketers find wholesalers or retailers that probably have the desired qualifications? There are many areas from which recommendations may come. Those that have been found to be the most reliable are – (1) the manufacturer's sales force, (2) other channel members, (3) market research agencies, (4) trade sources, and (5) other non-competing channel members.

2.5.4 Channel Training and Management

For effective performance training is a necessary input. Depending on the nature and features of the product, training of middlemen may be needed for selling and servicing. When the product is technically difficult, it may be desirable for middlemen personnel to be trained both in selling and servicing. The training inputs may consist of a manual for middlemen, salespersons and special classroom training courses. Furthermore, suitable motivational methods such as high margins, commission on productivity, sales contests, allowances on displaying and advertising can stimulate the interest of the channel members and assist in gaining their co-operation for efficient working. Motivational meetings with distributors and jointly planning the sales and distribution goals, inventory management, advertising programmes and middlemen training requirements will bring about smooth associations, and co-operation.

The main purpose here is to improve the performance of the dealers, their salesmen and service people. Sharpening of their sales skills and product knowledge and service capability is the particular objective. It is the dealers who have to sense, serve and satisfy the needs of the customers. Customers visiting the store turn to the dealer for information and guidance. Unless the salesperson is correctly equipped, such guidance cannot be made available. So, training the dealer/his sales staff becomes important. The firm equips them with the required knowledge, skills, techniques and altitudes. Any progressive company will, thus, make dealer training an important part of its channel management endeavour.

2.5.5 Channel Evaluation and Management

On a regular basis, business marketers are required to develop robust procedures to assess the performance of the channel members. To conduct an objective and useful evaluation of the performance, they should develop a set of performance measurement criteria. Depending upon the nature of the products and markets, the frequency of evaluation could be quarterly, half yearly or even yearly. The performance criteria could consist of the following list:

- Achievement of targets: sales, profits, market shares, inquiry generation and so on
- Development of new customers
- Successful introduction of new products
- Frequency of customer contacts
- Involvement in image building activities
- Participation in the promotional activities
- Feedback from the customers on channel service and behaviour
- Efficient and innovative ways to serve the customers at lower costs

On the other hand, care should be taken to guarantee that the evaluation does not become an activity that penalises the channel for its failures. The objective should be to develop the capabilities of the channel members. The evaluation should assist in recognising the strengths and the weaknesses of the channel member in an objective way. These should then be used to reward the channel and assist it in overcoming its weaknesses.

The development of annual and quarterly performance targets should be a joint venture. This should start by reviewing the past performance and analysing the future 'market scenarios, including the competitive and regulatory environment.

While assessing the performance, the marketer must keep in mind that the channel is an autonomous entity and due respect must be shown to its status. Being the 'principals', same marketers may presume the role of a boss who can scold the subordinates. At times, the power by good quality of being a marketer, can also lead to arrogant behaviour. Such behaviour patterns must be avoided as these could harm long-term cordial relations and channel loyalty. In an ever increasing competitive scenario, earning and maintaining channel loyalty has become very significant. L&T's switchgear division is very proud of its loyal channel comprising around 600 stockists. Despite the attractive incentives provided by the new multi-national companies entering the Indian markets, none of the channel members become part of the competitors' channel.

Performance evaluation/appraisal of a marketing channel can take place based on various perspectives. The evaluation assesses the marketing channel's financial performance and looks into societal contributions made by individual members of the channel. From the societal perspective, the performance of marketing channels can be assessed by measurement of overall channel performance in terms of the channel's efficiency, effectiveness and equity. To evaluate at a micro-level, an individual channel member's financial performance is determined by studying the channel tasks performed by the member. Channel effectiveness is another parameter that measures channel performance and its ability to satisfy customer needs. It focuses on issues like lot size, delivery time, location convenience and assortment breadth.

Channel equity refers to the distribution of opportunities available to all customers in evaluation of the marketing channels of a region. The primary purpose of distribution is to get the company products within arm's reach of desire. Any channel evaluation system has to keep this in mind and find out how well the distribution channel is serving this primary purpose.

The criteria for evaluation of the channel members vary with their categories and are as follows:

Table 2.4: Criteria for Evaluation

Criteria for evaluation	Popular performance measures
Sales target achievement	• Primary sales • Secondary sales • Achievement of sales target • Sales growth by period • Market share achieved
Inventory management	• Average level of inventory maintained • Inventory turnover (inventory to sales ratio) • Inventory of slow moving stocks • Storage quality
Selling resources	• Number of sales people • Target achievement by each sales person
Market coverage	• Calls per day • Productive calls per day • Extension of credit • Support to new product launches • Support to promotions
Back office support	• Use of PCs • Trained manpower • Reports, records

(a) Channel Performance at a Macro Level

A marketing channel's performance is measured in terms of its ability to meet the manufacturer's business objectives. Performance at macro-level is evaluated in terms of contributions made by the marketing channel to the society. Major elements that will decide the success of an intermediary are channel efficiency, productivity, effectiveness, equity and profitability.

Channel efficiency is a channel performance dimension that determines the ability of intermediaries to perform necessary channel functions with minimal costs. Productivity deals with the extent to which the total channel investment in the form of inputs have been optimised to yield maximum outputs. Productivity and efficiency deal with maximising outputs for a given level of inputs while keeping down costs irrespective of problems faced during the distribution process. The channel's performance is also measured by the intermediary's assistance to suppliers in meeting their objectives. The intermediary's contribution towards the supplier's efficiency and productivity is determined by the extent of contribution to the suppliers' profit and sales.

(b) Channel Performance at a Micro Level

Channel performance at micro-level involves a closer look at the performance of individual intermediaries of a marketing channel. Each intermediary should help the manufacturer achieve the objectives of goal attainment, pattern maintenance, integration and adaptation.

Goal attainment refers to achieving the firm's goals by maximising outputs given the cost constraints and company-specific obstacles.

Pattern maintenance involves co-ordination of processes and functions among organisational units to help the smooth functioning of system.

Integration indicates the co-ordination among the components of a channel or an organisation to meet common objectives and maintain the single unit entity. Adaptation is the modification of resources required to meet system objectives.

An organisation must be able to achieve all four objectives to facilitate smooth functioning of the system.

2.5.6 Managing Conflict

Channel members from the same marketing channel system. Conflict always has negative connotations and is driven more by feelings than facts. A situation of conflict arises, when in a social system like marketing channel, if one entity in the relationship is behaving in a certain way that will directly affect the performance of the other entity or come in the way of its goals.

Sources of Conflict: There are many reasons why conflicts arise in distribution channels. Learning about conflicts is important in conflict analysis.

- **Faulty channel design:** The primary reason for arising of channel conflicts is faulty channel design.
- **Attitudinal differences:** The different sources of conflicts can be classified into those arising from attitudinal differences and those arising from structural differences

among channel members. Attitudinal differences arise from differences in perception, channel roles and channel communications. Conflicts can also arise on account of unexpected changes in the competitive environment, consumers and markets, differences in economic and ideological objectives among channel members.

- **Structural differences**: Structural differences arise mainly due to goal divergence or incompatibility among channel members, tendency towards autonomy and greater control by channel members and competition for scarce channel resources (financial, technological support), especially from manufacturers in multi-channel systems.

- **Goal incompatibility:** Channel conflicts may arise due to incompatibility of goals and objectives among channel members. Differences in policies and procedures of a channel member may be problematic and impede the progress of other channel members. This divergence of goals may lead to one channel member acting in a way that is detrimental to goal achievement for another channel member. This may occur without the former being aware of its impact on the latter. Goal conflicts in an agency relationship can be reduced by designing contracts that ensure mutual benefit for both the principal and agent. The contract must consider the functions and structure of ownership arrangements within the channel and the compensation/incentives on achieving required performance levels for channel members as a part of the agency relationship. Thus, the solution to reducing conflicts in an agency relationship is to ensure that the agent's goals align with the principal's goals.

- **Differing Perceptions of Reality:** This is another prominent source of conflicts in distribution channels. It is perception of reality that enables channel members to anticipate future events and their consequences. This, in turn, induces channel members to develop alternative courses of action and estimate the probable results. The perception of reality also has an influence on the goals and values of channel members. However, perceptions of reality can be different.

    Different perceptions of channel members may be due to one channel member wrongly perceiving the role of another channel member regarding marketing channel functions and flows.

- **Lack of proper communication** flow among channel members. This affects the way reality is perceived by them. Information influencing the decision-making process affects the behaviour of channel members. Thus, conflicts arise among channel members, when channel members have different approaches to interpreting information, decisions made and goals set.

- **Clashes over Domains:** Conflicts in marketing channels arise from the domain definition and the extent to which other channel members accept it. The domain of channel members consists of product range, population and territories served and functions to be performed. Differences in domain automatically give rise to conflicts among channel members.

- **Product Range:** Handling a large number of products results in reduction in loyalty among channel members. Distributors cannot show the same level of loyalty towards the products of all manufacturers. This variation in loyalty gives rise to conflict of interest between manufacturers and distributors.

- **Population and Territory Coverage:** Conflict over customer accounts and territory coverage are unavoidable when there are many channel members serving a particular consumer segment. Channel members may cater to certain accounts and other channel members may compete for the same accounts. Hence, manufacturers or suppliers must specify territories for channel members. The same is true in franchising, where market territory expansion is a major source of conflicts. The franchiser's strategy of market penetration with the help of new franchisees may reduce the sales of existing franchisees. This is because a franchisee attracts customers from beyond the assigned territories too. With an entry of new franchisee in the region, customers beyond the actual territory may shift to the new franchisee due to proximity of location. Hence, even though the franchiser does not infringe the contract, franchisees may become dissatisfied.

- **External changes:** Market channel strategies adopted by channel members also contribute to channel conflicts.

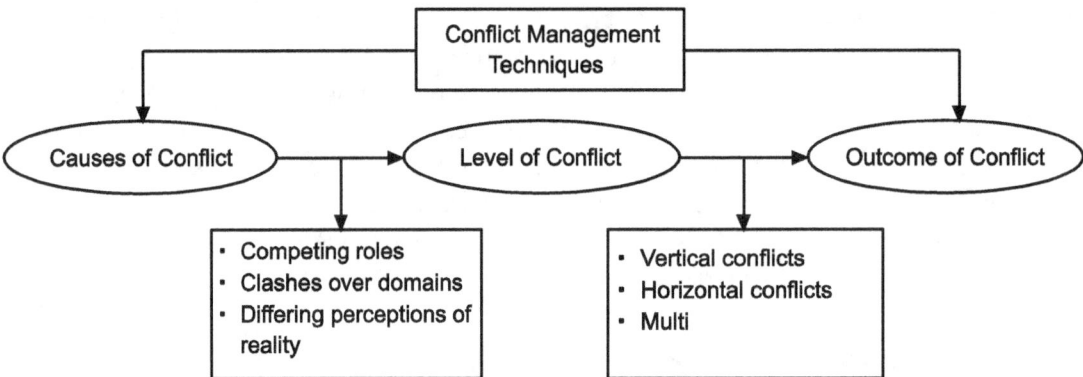

Fig. 2.2: Channel Conflict Model

Performance of Channel Functions: Sometimes, channel members may feel that they are being asked to perform functions incompatible with their organisational goals. This happens when channel members prefer to perform only channel functions that help them achieve individual goals. As these goals are not common to all channel members, it gives rise to functional conflicts. For instance, manufacturers have a strategic outlook towards marketing their products, while marketing channels focus on operational aspects. To avoid inconvenience of operations, retailers may not train their personnel to identify whether a product returned is genuinely faulty, and then refund customers. Due to this, manufacturers will encounter losses when many products are returned and marketing channels have to be given replacement. Thus, difference in roles among channel members causes conflict.

Types of Conflicts

Channel conflicts can be categorised into different types depending on timing and levels of the channel. They are pre-contractual and post-contractual conflicts, vertical, horizontal and multi-channel conflicts.

Pre-contractual and Post-contractual Conflicts

Channel conflicts may occur at two different points of time in the channel relationship. It could be before a relationship develops or after it commences between channel members. These conflicts arise whenever channel members enter into new relationships.

- Pre-contractual conflicts arise when the principal decides to offer a contract to an agent. The major issues are whether a particular agent has the characteristics a principal wants and what strategy should the principal employ to find this out. These problems occur during recruitment of new salespeople or marketing personnel, selection of dealers for their distribution channels and choosing advertising agencies.
- Post-contractual conflicts happen after the relationship between channel members begins. The causes are generally unforeseen events, which must be identified and dealt with immediately. One major issue that appears in post-contractual conflicts is the method of evaluation of channels, so that their actions confine to the principal's goals. For instance, differences may arise between the principal and channels while designing compensation programmes.

Channel Level Conflicts

Conflicts can take place at different levels of the marketing channel system – between manufacturer and retailer, wholesaler and retailers, between two wholesalers or retailers at the same level and so on. Channel level conflicts are classified as vertical, horizontal and multi-level channel conflicts.

(i) **Vertical Channel Conflicts:** Vertical channel conflicts arise between channel members operating at different levels within the same channel structure. Conflicts between manufacturer and distributors, when the manufacturer tries to enforce pricing and service policies on the distributor, is a type of vertical channel conflict.

(ii) **Horizontal Channel Conflicts:** Horizontal type of channel conflicts arises between channel members operating at the same level within the channel structure. For example, a conflict between two franchisees over clash of domains is an example of horizontal channel conflict.

(iii) **Multi-Channel Conflicts:** Multi-channel conflict occurs when the manufacturer establishes two or more channels catering to the same market. For example, conflicts arise between the manufacturer and wholesalers, when the manufacturer tries to bypass wholesalers by resorting to newer channels like the internet marketing or direct mail.

Conflicts are generally perceived as dysfunctional. However, a complete elimination of conflict among channel members is not recommended because channel members may become complacent in developing mutually beneficial relationships with other channel members and will not compete effectively. Innovation may also be lost. Hence, a certain level of conflict is required as a constructive mechanism in channel relationships.

Techniques to Resolve Channel Conflicts

Conflicts between two channel members can be resolved either by one channel member modifying/changing its organisational goals or by conceding some amount of autonomy/ resources to the other channel member. Conflict resolution processes can be made into effect through mutual agreement or by the use of channel power.

Conflict resolution mechanisms can be divided into two categories – in the first (systematic mechanism), the conflict resolution mechanism is based on the policies that channel leaders implement to resolve channel conflicts in a streamlined manner. These conflict resolution mechanisms are aimed at increasing the level of understanding among various channel members. Some systematic mechanisms include joint memberships in trade organisations, exchange of personnel between two or more channels, distributor councils and various programmes such as co-optation. The second category of conflict resolution mechanism is based on behavioural and attitudinal responses channel leaders offering to solve conflicts in a distribution channel. These responses of channel members are problem-solving, persuasion, bargaining and political strategies.

Some strategies implemented under both categories are:

1. **Negotiation (Bargaining):** Negotiation or bargaining is used by channel members as a tool for resolving conflicts. Negotiations usually take place over price, cash credit, discounts, delivery, inventory levels and other elements in the marketing mix. In negotiations, goal differences are considered as fixed and conflict resolution mechanisms do not mean development of common goals. The outcome of negotiations varies depending on the number of channel members and the extent of balance of power among them.

During negotiations, channel members participate in low risk behaviour, where information exchange is kept to the minimal to reduce the financial, social and physical costs incurred. Sometimes channel members, during negotiation, behave rigidly. Threats, promises and conditional commitments are common features of negotiation process.

The negotiation process is very important especially in marketing channels, because its efficiency has a direct impact on the selling and purchasing costs among channel members. Some differences commonly experienced during negotiations are –

2. **Initial Bids:** During bargaining, channel members with greater power than their partners make more demanding initial bids. Similarly, weak bargainers put forward less demanding bids or conditions.

3. **Extent of Flexibility:** Channel members with greater power do not yield much from their initial bargaining conditions compared to channel members who have less power.

4. **Time of Negotiation:** More powerful channel members are able to obtain an acceptable agreement faster than less powerful channel members.

5. **Communication Content:** Channel members with greater power frequently make use of commanding language and actions during negotiations with other channel members.

6. **Negotiation Outcome:** Channel members with more power reach agreements that give them a larger share of total profits of the channel group.

7. **Persuasive Mechanism:** Persuasive conflict resolution is another method used by channel leaders to resolve conflicts. The objective is to move both parties (channel members) towards a common set of goals. In this method, each channel member tries to influence and change the view of other channel member with regard to the conflicting issues. The basic approach used in persuasive conflict resolution mechanism is to highlight the importance of mutually beneficial common goals over individual goals and also reduce differences present in individual goals of each channel member. However, in this method, channel members involve in high risk behaviour by sharing important information to arrive at a common goal. This is in contrast to the low-risk behaviour observed during negotiations. This type of conflict resolution mechanism is often exercised between franchisers and franchisees. For instance, franchisers may have to persuade franchisees to maintain product quality levels consistently across franchises to project a uniform business image.

Problem-Solving Strategies

This method is also used as a conflict resolution mechanism to settle conflicts among distribution channels. Here, both parties share common objectives, but differ on the decision making criteria. Open transfer of information about goals and objectives takes place and both parties try to sort out differences by exploring alternative solutions. Unlike in negotiations, co-operation and co-ordination exist among channel members. Channel members are ready to modify certain conditions to arrive at a mutually acceptable solution.

1. **Political Strategies**

This is another conflict resolution tool, similar to bargaining. In this case, channel members that have disagreed over each other's objectives agree to a third party becoming involved. This party acts as an ally to the channel members. This method is resorted to only when all other interpersonal methods of solving conflicts fail to work. Political-based conflict resolution strategies make the use of diplomacy, mediators and arbitrators to solve conflicts.

- **Diplomacy:** It is an approach where each side deputes a person or group to meet its counterparts to resolve the conflict.

- **Mediation:** In this case, a third party tries to settle conflicts between channel members, either by urging them to continue negotiations till a solution is reached or takes into consideration recommendations made by the mediator.

- **Arbitration:** In arbitration, the two parties present their agreements to one or more arbitrators, referees or a private judge and accept the verdict delivered. Usually, channel members have a clause in their contracts stipulating the use of arbitration in case of conflicts between them. There are many arbitration centres all over the world, where organisations can take their disputes.

- **Co-optation:** Co-optation is an information intensive mechanism, which involves free information transfer between aggrieved parties. Co-optation is a mechanism where a new member from outside the organisation is appointed and is involved in the decisions and policies of top management. A channel member makes an effort to win the support of other channel members by including them in its advisory council or board of directors.

  Co-optation allows the concept of sharing responsibility so that channel members from different levels can become prominent in the entire distribution system and are committed to the programmes and policies of one another. In this method, one channel member may have to make concessions on its policies and plans to seek the support of the newly elected member from other channel organisations. Co-optation reduces conflicts as long as the channel member treats the new individual member seriously and listens to them. This mechanism is risky because of the physical, economic and financial cost involved.

Exchange of personnel between two or more channels is also viewed as an effective conflict resolving mechanism. This enables participants to visit each other's facilities and facilitates better understanding of each other's point of view. Another frequently used method is the encouragement of joint membership in and between trade organisations. For example, if manufacturers and retailers are associated with each other's trade associations, they become aware of each other's limitations and problems, apart from approach to business. In addition to these strategies, channel members can reduce the frequency and intensity of conflict by adopting following practices during routine channel functions.

2. Personal Relationships

Channel members must develop personal relationships to reduce the intensity of conflicts and discuss various conflict issues rationally.

- **Error Clarification:** Whenever a channel member errs, it must be brought to the notice of the other channel partner, so that new problems due to lack of awareness of the reciprocating firm do not arise.

- **Distribution Indicators:** Channel members must develop distribution indicators for giving an alert to those affected. The indicators can be inventory levels, value of sales or order volumes.

- **Meetings:** The sales personnel of manufacturers must be frequently in contact with sales personnel of other channel intermediaries so that they can share views and prevent arising of conflicts.

- **Appreciate each Channel Member's Requirements:** By visiting the manufacturer's plant and observing activities like ordering procedures and quality management activities, the channel member can gain a clear picture of potential difficulties in getting a product delivered on time. Likewise, by making joint visits to trade fairs and sharing information, both parties can enjoy a harmonious working relationship.

- **Communication:** The communication process within the channel structure and between channel members should be streamlined. This can be ensured by continuous sharing of information through networks. It is generally observed that attitudinal differences occur due to improper communication and information processing among channel members. Hence, by designing communication programmes that increase exchange of information about goals, expectations and future plans among channel members, the quantum of conflict will be considerably reduced.

Points to Remember

- A management control system (MCS) is a system which collects and uses the data to assess the performance of different organisational resources like human, physical, and financial and also the organisation altogether considering the organisational strategies.
- Characteristics of effective control systems
  1. Accurate
  2. Timely
  3. Objective and Comprehensible
  4. Focused on Strategic Control Points
  5. Economically Realistic
  6. Organisationally Realistic
  7. Co-ordinated with the Organisation's Work Flow
  8. Flexible
  9. Prescriptive and Operational
  10. Accepted by Organisation Members
- Factors Influencing Control Systems
  1. Size and Spread of the Enterprise
  2. Organisational Structure, Delegation and Decentralisation
  3. Nature of Operations and Divisibility
  4. Types of Responsibility Centres
  5. People and their Perceptions
- Cost Centre is the area for which cost data is accumulated such as an assembly department.
- Expense Centre is the area dominated by discretionary expenses such as legal or accounting.
- Revenue Centre is the area primarily responsible for generating sales such as a sales office.
- Profit Centre is the area responsible for controlling costs and generating revenues.

- Investment Centre is the area responsible for income (revenues-expenses) in relation to its invested capital.

- In a corporate VMS, one company owns and operates the other channel members at different channel levels

- In the administered type of vertical marketing system, no channel member has complete control over other channel members.

- Contractual systems consist of independent organisations that integrate their distribution operations through contracts.

- 'Consumer service' is the service provided to the customer from the time of order placed till the product is delivered.

- Ownership of distribution channels from source of supply to end user involves a substantial capital investment by the channel co-ordinator. This kind of vertical marketing system also adapts to change compared to the other vertical marketing system forms.

- The contractual form of the vertical marketing system may include different formal arrangements between channel participants including franchising and voluntary chains of independent retailers.

- The administered vertical marketing system exists because one of the channel members has the capacity to influence channel members.

- Relationship VMS shares certain features of the administered vertical marketing system, but varies in that a single company does not exercise considerable control over other channel members.

- A broker is a person or a company who brings buyers and sellers together and assists in the negotiations without getting involved in the financing or assuming any risk.

- Agents generally represent either the buyer or the seller on a more permanent basis than the brokers.

- A professional service agent is one where the knowledge base of the expert enables clients to seek solutions to their problems.

- Criteria for Selection of Channel Members
  1. Sales Factors
  2. Product Factors
  3. Experience Factors
  4. Administrative Factors
  5. Risk Factors

Questions for Discussion

1. What is control system of efficiency?
2. Explain the importance of effective control system.
3. List the characteristics of effective control system.
4. Elaborate on the factors influencing the control system.
5. Write a short note on the responsibility centres for efficiency and performance.
6. State the controlling and measuring performances.
7. Summarise the productivity aspects of logistics management.
8. Define distribution and customer satisfaction.
9. Describe the role of distribution in customer service and satisfaction.
10. Summarise the process of channel management.

Chapter 3...

Selection of Channel Partner and Strategies of Channel of Distribution

Contents ...

Learning Objectives ...

- To Understand the Meaning and Objectives of Channel of Distribution
- To Study the various Patterns of Distribution
- To Explain the Factors in the Selection Distribution Channel
- To Learn the Motivational Tools and Control Areas in Channel Management
- To Elaborate the Remuneration of the Sales Person

3.1 Channels of Distribution

3.1.1 Introduction

Chain of intermediaries, each passing the product down the chain to the next organisation, before it finally reaches the consumer or end-user, is known as the 'distribution chain' or the 'distribution channel.' The distribution channel is a process of transferring the products or services from producer to customer or end-user. Channels of distribution are nothing but marketing channels.

The most important aim of these channels is delivery. Physical distribution is the only process through which public and private goods and services are made accessible for use or consumption. Procedures of such goods and services are able of generate only the form or structural utility related to their products and services. The production organisation is done in such a skilful way that the products they produce can not only be seen, analysed but also sold in the market. They are called mediators, because they link the production branch and the consumption branch and provide arrangement of a wide variety of distribution-oriented institutions and agencies. The roles of mediators are as follows –

- Mediators improve the efficiency of the process.
- They help in the appropriate planning of the routes of the transactions.
- They help in the searching process.
- They assist in the sorting process.

3.1.2 Definition

A channel, as explained above is a passageway that allows the happening of certain processes. Marketing, on the other hand, is an exchange process. The term "channels of distribution" represents a system that contributes to the exchange process by covering the distance between the producer and the consumer.

1. **William J. Stanton**, *"A channel of distribution or a marketing channel is a path traced in the direct or indirect transfer of the title to a product as it moves from a product to ultimate consumers or industrial users."*

2. **Beckman**, *"The course taken in the transfer of the title to a commodity constitutes its channel of distribution. It is the route taken by the title to a product in its passage from its first owner, an agricultural producer or a manufacturer, as the case may be, to the last owner, the ultimate consumer or the business user."*

3. A channel of distribution or marketing channel is a structure of intra-company organisation, units and intra-company agents and dealers, wholesalers and retailers, through which, a commodity product or service is marketed.

4. Channels of distribution are defined as set of pathways, a product or service follows after production, reaching to the final end-user for its consumption through the purchasing process.

5. Channels of distribution are defined as a group of exchange relationships, which create customer value in acquiring, consuming, and disposing of products and services.

From the above definitions, it can be concluded that channels of distribution are important ingredients of the distribution as a process of taking the product or service from its production centre to the consumption centre. In this process, marketing channels provide sufficient value to the customers and provide a competitive advantage to the producer.

3.1.3 Objectives of Channels of Distribution

A marketing distribution channel is a well-knit network of organisations that are interconnected with their efforts to provide sellers a means of infusing the market with products and for the buyers a way of purchasing those goods, doing all this as efficiently and profitably as possible.

The distribution channels are designed to achieve the following objectives –

1. **Increase in the Availability of Products:** The first objective is to make the product available to the customer. The availability has two aspects to itself – the level of coverage desired in terms of appropriate number of retail outlets and secondly, positioning of the product within the store. Product availability is an important factor for convenience goods, where the customer does not invest his time and energy to wait for a particular brand. However, for exclusive and important products instant availability is of less importance.

2. **Meeting Customers' Service Requirements:** To meet the growing service requirements and to create differentiation over competitors, distribution channels become critical. Service requirements include – order cycle time (the time period it takes to process the order), dependability (uniformity and consistency of delivery), communication between seller and buyer (to brush off the problems instinctively), convenience (to accommodate special needs if any, of the customers), and post-sale services (installation, help lines, user training, repair, and spare parts availability).

3. **Ensure Promotional Support:** Promotional support means support from the distribution channel members for the product, which includes in-store displays, use of local media, and cooperation in special promotional events. This type of support is especially important in highly competitive markets, along with expensive and complex consumer durable goods.

4. **Obtaining Market Information:** As the intermediaries are in direct contact with the customers in the market, they are the best source of getting first hand information with regard to trends in sales, inventory analysis, and moves of the competitors and customers' reactions.

5. **Increase Cost-Effectiveness:** Costs that are incurred in achieving the firm's channel objectives should be less when compared to the gains we derive from it. There is usually a trade-off between the cost of channel, associated with physical distribution activities like transportation and storage of inventory.

6. **Maintain Flexibility:** The channel must be flexible. A flexible channel is a channel where it is easier to switch the channel structure or to add a new type of middleman without an increase in the cost and without getting into a legal conflict with existing channel members.

3.2 Patterns of Distribution

Though the patterns of distribution are changing and new patterns are developing day by day, international marketers need to have a general awareness about the traditional distribution system. The traditional distribution system will not change overnight and its mortal remains will remain for years and years to come. Almost every international firm is forced by the structure of the market to use some middlemen in the arrangement of distribution. It is very easy to think that, since the structural arrangements of foreign and domestic distribution seem to be the same, the foreign channels will also be similar to the domestic channels. However this is untrue. It is only when the variety of details of actual distribution patterns are understood, the intricacy of the task of distribution can be appreciated.

The following description will convey about the variety of distribution pattern.

1. **General patterns:** Generalising the internal distribution channel patterns of various countries is as difficult as generalising the behavioural patterns of people. In spite of the clearly seen similarities, marketing channels are not the same across the globe. The existing marketing methods taken for granted in the United States are rare in many countries.

2. **Middlemen services:** The service rendered by the people in trade varies sharply at the retail and wholesale levels from country to country. In Muscat for example the basic reason of trading system is to handle the physical distribution of goods available. Whilst on the other hand when the profit margin is low and there is a battle for customer preference the wholesalers and retailers try to offer extra services to make their goods more and more alluring to consumers. In the event of lack of motivation in middlemen for promoting or selling goods the manufacturer must provide adequate incentive to the middlemen or undertake the promotion and selling effort himself.

3. **Line breadth:** Every nation has a different pattern concerning the amplitude/breadth of the line by wholesalers and retailers. The distribution system of some countries seems to be characterised by intermediaries that perform or can get everything. Every intermediary seems to be a specialist dealing in very narrow lines only. Government regulations in some countries limit the amplitude of the line that can be carried by intermediaries, and licensing requirements to handle certain goods are not uncommon.

4. **Costs and margins:** The levels of costs and intermediate margins vary widely from country to country depending on the level of competition, services, effectiveness or

ineffectiveness of scale, and geographic factors and turnover business-related market size, purchasing power, tradition and other basic determinants. In India, competition in large cities is so intense that the costs are low with thin margins in rural areas, but lack of capital has allowed some traders with capital to obtain monopolies with high prices and resulting wide margins.

5. **Channel length:** Some correlation can be found between the stage of economic development and the length of the distribution channels. In each country, the channels are likely to be shorter for industrial products and high priced consumer goods than for cheap products. It is observed that there is an inverse relationship between the channel length and the size of the purchase. Combination retailers-wholesalers and semi-wholesalers exist in many countries by adding one or two links to the length of the distribution chain. In China, for example the traditional distribution system for over-the-counter drugs consists of major local wholesalers divided into three levels. First level wholesalers supply drug in major cities such as Beijing and Shanghai. The second level serves medium-sized cities and the third level distributes to countries and cities with 100,000 people or less. It may be profitable for a company to sell directly to the two top-level wholesalers and have them sell to the third level, which is so small that it would not be profitable for the company to look for.

3.3 Factors in the Selection of Distribution Channel

There are a number of factors which are objective and subjective in nature and vary from company to company which influence the choice or selection of channel of distribution. However there are some factors which stand out in influencing the selection of channel of distribution.

They may be described as under –
(a) Factors Relating to Product Characteristics
(b) Factors Relating to Company's Characteristics
(c) Factors Relating to Market or Consumer's Characteristics
(d) Factors Relating to Middlemen Considerations
(e) Factors Relating to Environmental Characteristics
Let us explorer each of these in detail.

3.3.1 Factors Relating to Product Characteristics

Product manufactured by a company is one of the most important factors in the selection of the channel of distribution.

Characteristics of a product are as follows –

1. **Industrial/Consumer goods:** When the product is an industrial product, direct channel of distribution is best as the number of customers is relatively small and so is their need for personal attention. However, in case of a FMCG or consumer goods, indirect channel of distribution, such as wholesalers, retailers is more suitable.

2. **Perishability factor:** Perishable goods means those goods that have a very short shelf life, such as vegetables, milk, butter, sea foods, bakery products, fruits etc. These perishable goods require direct selling as they must reach the consumers as early as possible because of their perishable nature.

3. **Unit Value factor:** When the per unit value of a product is high, it is economical to choose a direct channel of distribution like a company's own sales force rather than a team of middlemen. In contradiction, if the per unit value is low and the total amount involved is small, it is better to choose an indirect channel of distribution, that is, through middlemen.

4. **Obsolescence factor:** The world is changing day by day. People, preferences, likes and dislikes, change on a daily basis. When the degree of obsolescence is high in products like garments, shoes, mobiles and electronic gadgets it is desirable to sell directly to retailers who specialise in the respective areas.

5. **Weight and Technicality factor:** When the products are huge in size or bulky or are technically complicated, it is better to choose direct channel of distribution rather than the indirect one.

6. **Standardised Products:** When we talk about standardising the product we mean that each unit is similar in shape, size, weight, colour and quality etc. Once the products are standardised it is ideal to choose indirect channel of distribution. On the other hand, if the product is not standardised and is produced on order, it is best to have a direct channel of distribution.

7. **Frequency of Purchase:** Products that are purchased frequently and regularly need a direct channel of distribution so that the cost and burden of distribution is reduced for such products.

8. **Newness and Market Acceptance:** For new products with low degree of market acceptance, there is a need for persistent selling efforts. Therefore indirect channels may be used by appointing middlemen as sole agents. This will ensure channel loyalty and forceful selling by intermediaries.

9. **Seasonality factor:** When the product is subject to variations due to seasonal changes, such as woollen textiles in India, it is best to appoint sole selling agents who will undertake the sale of production by booking orders from retailers and dispatch goods as soon as they are ready.

10. **Product breadth factor:** When the company is manufacturing a large variety of products, it has greater ability to deal directly with customers as the breadth of the product line enhances its capability to secure the sale. Hence, direct channel is the best choice.

3.3.2 Factors Relating to Company's Characteristics

The choice of distribution channel is also influenced by company's characteristics such as to its size, reputation, financial position, current marketing policies, past channel experience, and product-mix etc.

Some of the main factors relating to the company characteristic are –

1. **Financial Strength:** The financial strength of the firm also determines the channel of distribution. An organisation which is financially sound may opt for direct selling. On the contrary, an organisation which is financially weak has to depend on intermediaries and, hence, has to select indirect channel of distribution, such as wholesalers, retailers, with strong financial background.

2. **Size of the Company:** A large-sized firm producing a wide range of products would prefer to have a direct channel for selling its products. On the other hand, a small-sized firm would prefer indirect selling by appointing some intermediaries like wholesalers, retailers etc.

3. **Marketing Policies:** The marketing policies formulated by a company play a very significant role in influencing channel choice. The policies pertinent to channel decision may relate to delivery, advertising, after sale service and pricing etc. For example, a company which has a policy of prompt delivery of goods to ultimate consumers may prefer direct selling and thus avoid appointing intermediaries and will adopt a speedy transportation system.

4. **Product-Mix:** The wider is the company's product-mix, the greater will be its strength to deal with its customer directly. Similarly, uniformity in the company's product-mix ensures greater homogeneity or uniformity and similarity in its marketing channels.

5. **Past Channel Experience:** Past channel experience of the company also affects the selection of channel of distribution. For example, in case of an established firm, its past good experience of working with certain kind of intermediaries will affect the choice of intermediary and the firm is likely to opt for the same channel and vice-versa.

6. **Reputation:** It is said that reputation travels faster than the man. It is true in the case of firms also who wish to choose channel of distribution. In case of firms with outstanding reputation like Tata Steel, Hero Honda, Hindustan Unilever etc., indirect channel of distribution (wholesalers, retailers etc.) is more appropriate and profitable.

3.3.3 Factors Relating to Market or Consumer's Characteristics

The consumer and market characteristics that influence the channel choice significantly may be summarised as under –

1. **Consumers' Buying Behaviour:** Consumers' buying behaviour also affects the channel decision. If the consumer expects credit facilities or desires personal services

of the salesman or wants to make all purchases at one place, the channel of distribution may be short or long depending on the ability of the firm for providing these facilities. If the producer can afford these facilities, the channel will be shorter otherwise longer.

2. **Location of the Market:** When the customers are spread over a wide geographical area, the long channel of distribution is most suitable. On the other hand, if the customer is concentrated and localised, direct selling would be beneficial.

3. **Number of Customer:** The number of customers also affects the channel decision. For example, if the number of customers is relatively large, the channel of distribution may be indirect and long, such as wholesalers, retailers etc. On the other hand, if the number of customers is small or limited, direct selling may be useful.

4. **Size of Orders:** Size of orders of the customers also affects the channel decision considerably. Where customers purchase the product in bulk, direct selling may be preferred. On the other hand, where customers purchase the product in small quantities, frequently and regularly, such as cigarettes, matchsticks etc., long channel (wholesalers, retailers etc.) of distribution may be preferred.

3.3.4 Factors Relating to Middlemen Considerations

The choice of the channel of distribution is also influenced by the middlemen consideration. They may include the following –

1. **Sales Volume Potential:** In selecting channel of distribution, the firm should consider the ability of the middlemen to ensure a targeted sales volume. The sales volume potential of the channel may be projected through market surveys. Though, it should be kept in mind that no single channel is capable for achieving the targeted sales potential. Two or more channels may be required for this purpose.

2. **Availability of Intermediary:** Availability of the right type of intermediary is also a significant consideration in making channel decision. In this connection, the company should make efforts to select aggressive oriented intermediary. In case they are not available, it is better to wait for some time and then select. In such cases, the company should manage its own channel so long as the right type of middlemen is not available.

3. **Middlemen's Attitude:** The attitude of the middlemen towards the policies of the firm also affects the channel decision. For instance, if the firm follows the resale price maintenance policy, then the choice is limited. On the other hand, if the company allows the middlemen to adopt their own price policy, the choice is quite wide. Quite a large number of middlemen would be interested in selling company's products.

4. **Services Provided by Middlemen:** If the nature of product is such that requires after-sales services, repair services etc., such as automobiles, cars, scooters etc., only those intermediaries should be appointed who can provide such services, otherwise the company should adopt direct selling channel.

5. **Cost of Channel:** Another factor considered is the cost involved in the distribution. Direct selling is generally costlier and thus distribution arranged through intermediaries is more economical. In this reference, it must be kept in mind that the channel which ensures efficient distribution at the least expenses and which secures the desired volume of sales should be chosen.

3.3.5 Factors Relating to Environmental Characteristics

The environmental factors include competitor's channels, economic conditions, legal restrictions, fiscal structure etc, as given below, affect significantly the channel choice.

1. **Economic Condition:** When economic conditions are favourable such as inflation, it is better to opt for indirect channel of distribution because there is an all-round mood of expectancy; market tendencies are bullish and favourable. On the other hand, if the market is depressed (such as deflation), shorter channels may be beneficial.

2. **Legal Restrictions:** The legislative and other restrictions imposed by the government are extremely formidable and give final shape to the channel selection. For example, in India, M.R.T.P. Act, 1969 prevents channel arrangements that tend to considerably reduce competition, create monopoly and are otherwise prejudicial to public interest. With these objectives at the backdrop, it prevents exclusive distributorship, territorial restrictions, resale price maintenance etc.

3. **Competitors' Channel:** This also affects the channel choice decision. Mostly, in practice, similar types of channels of distribution used by the competitors are preferred.

4. **Fiscal Structure:** Fiscal structure of a country also affects the channel selection decision. For example, in India, Sales Tax rates vary from State to State and form a considerable part of the final price payable by a consumer. As a result, it becomes an important factor in evolving channel arrangements. Differences in the sales tax rates in two different states would not only bring about difference in the price payable by a consumer but also in the distribution channel selected.

3.4 Motivation of Intermediaries

It is often necessary to motivate the members of distribution channel. This is due to differing needs of the intermediaries and producers. These needs do not coincide with one another (for example, a manufacturer can find the exclusive distribution of their products at high prices, while a retailer may want to use penetration strategy to pursue the market through budget pricing of a wide range of goods). The situation is further complicated by the fact that intermediaries and producers often have different perceptions of their own role in the distribution chain. Doyle suggests two levels of motivation – promotional and partnership.

1. **Promotional channel motivators (PCM):** Promotional channel motivators or PCM are usually short-term incentives to support the supplier's goods; for example, a trade discount may be given to encourage the channel member to place voluminous orders or a cash discount may be given to encourage prompt payment and an increase in his profit margin.

2. **Partnership motivators (PM):** Partnership motivators or PM on the other hand, tries to build a longer-term relationship between channel member and suppliers; for example, the supplier may share important information about the market or provide direct training to the sales team of his distributor at no extra cost.

Evaluating the Effectiveness of the Strategies

It is important that the effectiveness of the strategies to be evaluated in order to determine the future course of action as to which strategy to retain and which one to be discarded. Various indicators may be used to determine the effectiveness of the strategies. Sales volumes generated through the use of a particular strategy, is a good indicator that may tell the effectiveness of the strategy. Strategies that are effective should result in higher sales and greater value of sales. Yet another indicator could be the cost of maintaining the strategies. A strategy may result in higher sales and better revenue but the cost of maintaining the strategy may be so high that it becomes unjustifiable to retain the strategy.

3.4.1 Motivational Tools and Control Areas

1. **Enhancing Profit Opportunities**

   Companies may motivate the intermediaries by enhancing their profit opportunities. This may be achieved through strategies such as easier terms of credit, extensive advertising and promotion etc. These strategies will make it easier for the intermediaries to sell the products thereby encouraging the intermediaries to buy more of the company products.

Advantages

- It boosts profit-making opportunities not only for the intermediaries but also for the company. When the intermediaries sell more and more, the company's profit also increases. Another advantage in implementing this strategy is that it strengthens the bond between the company and the intermediaries giving birth to a loyalty factor.

Disadvantages

- This strategy increases the advertising and promotion cost for the company.

2. **Encourage Greater Participation of Dealership in Decision-making**

   The manufacturing company should create a sense of partnership between themselves and the intermediary. This can be accomplished by giving the intermediaries an opportunity to contribute in the decisions of the company that may have a direct impact on the distribution of the products. These decisions may revolve around pricing, advertising, promotion and delivery of goods.

Advantages

- Greater amount of involvement of the intermediaries in the company's decision-making process will create a sense of ownership within the intermediaries thereby motivating them to do what is in the best interest of the company. Another advantage is that since the intermediaries are closer to the final consumer they may have a better understanding of the needs and preferences of the consumer and therefore their involvement in decision making can be extremely fruitful.

Disadvantages

- It may lead to exposure of company's activities to the competitor though the company wants to involve the intermediaries in decision-making; the fact that these intermediaries are already in a strong relationship with the competitors cannot be overlooked. Hence the company must take into consideration that there is a possibility that some dealers may have an orientation towards competitors. Another disadvantage is that this strategy gives the dealers substantial amount of power over the distribution of the product.

3. Developing an Attractive Incentive System

The third strategy that can be used to motivate the intermediaries is to develop an attractive incentive system. These incentives may include trade discounts, cash discount, provision for training and development and equipment handling. These incentives will encourage the intermediaries to give preference for the company's products over those of the competitors.

Advantage

- Incentive system uses a partnership approach rather than coercive/forceful approach to selling. This improves the relationship between the intermediaries and the company.

Disadvantage

- It increases cost for the organisation since additional incentives need to be given. Another disadvantage is that it gives considerable power to the intermediaries to influence product distribution.

4. Frequent and Timely Delivery

The timeliness of the delivery matters a lot when it comes to distribution of goods. Producers must make sure that intermediaries get goods in time and when the customers need them. Companies can motivate the intermediaries by making the frequency and timeliness better.

Advantage

- It not only enhances the intermediary's experience but it will also enhance the satisfaction of the end consumer.

5. Strict Sales Quota

Developing strict sales quota is a strategy that has been used as a strategy for motivating intermediaries to sell more of the company goods. The producer sets a quota for each distributor in order to persuade them to increase their sales.

Advantage
- The power to influence the supply chain remains with the producers. Another advantage is that this strategy does not involve extra cost.

Disadvantage
- It involves use of coercive power instead of creating partnership.

According to the marketing guru, Philip Kotler, with constant training, supervision and encouragement producers can draw on the following types of power to draw cooperation –

- **Coercive power**. Manufacturer threatens to withdraw a resource or terminate a relationship if intermediaries fail to cooperate. Produces resentment.
- **Reward power**. Manufacturer offers intermediaries extra benefits for performing specific acts.
- **Legitimate power**. Manufacturer requests a behaviour that is warranted by the contract.
- **Expert power**. Manufacturer has special knowledge that the intermediaries value.
- **Referent power**. Intermediaries are proud to be identified with the manufacturer.

3.5 Remuneration of the Sales Person

For such a target-driven role, pay packages tend to be result-oriented and usually include lots of incentives. It's important that the managers spend time investigating the right combination of basic pay and incentives, to attract, retain and motivate the appropriate candidates and be clear about what is offered from the onset.

The typical pay structure for a salesperson is composed of a fairly low basic salary with an additional amount of commission. However, at most levels of seniority, salespeople are amongst the best-paid employees in business, so think about the level you're planning to recruit at and budget accordingly.

3.5.1 Some Basic Sales Salary Terms

Before we talk about how a sales person gets paid, let's cover a few basic terms that one should know.

1. **Base Salary** refers to a salary that the sales person will receive irrespective of the sales he does. This part of the salary is not based on your sales performance. Just showing up on job will earn you a base salary, but only getting a base salary will not be able to keep your job for long.

2. **Quota** is yet another word used for a goal the sales person must achieve. A quota is the total rupee value, or a number of items a sales person is supposed to sell in a given span of time. This period of time is usually one year or it may be broken down into monthly targets.

3. **Commission** has a variety of definitions. In sales, commission means the amount of money a sales person earns based on making a sale. This is generally calculated as a percentage of the sale value or an amount based on the number of units the sales person sells.

4. **On Target Earnings (OTE)** is what a sales person can expect to make if he/she achieves 100% of his/her quota. This is a combination of the sales person base salary plus the commission or bonus.

5. **A Spiff** is a type of extra income a sales person gets for selling something very specific. This is usually used to force a certain item for sale. If a mobile store wants to get rid of old handset models they might offer an extra spiff for every handset the sales person sells. A spiff is above and beyond what a sales person would normally earn for making the same sale.

3.5.2 Common Pay Structures for Salespeople

There are various methods to pay the salespeople; however, here are some of the important methods used for remunerating the salesmen –

1. Salary basis
2. Commission basis
3. Salary and commission basis
4. Pooled commission
5. Profit sharing

1. **Salary Basis**

   Under this method, salespeople are paid a fixed salary regardless of the number of sales affected by them. This is the most common method adopted by several organisations. The sales person is given a salary scale with pre-decided annual increments.

   This technique is simple in operation and involves lower administrative cost. Salespeople are guaranteed a fixed amount at the end of each month, providing a sense of job security. This method may reduce the sales volume generated by salespeople and is useful to gain their trust, loyalty and increased morale. Further the chance of misunderstandings between the employer and employees is minimised.

   Despite the many advantages, this method also suffers from certain drawbacks. It offers no incentive for efficient salesperson. He gets nothing extra, even if he achieves more sales targets. This technique does not distinguish between the inefficient and efficient salespeople. This system makes the salesperson inactive and less entrepreneurial.

2. **Commission Basis**

   Under this method, salespeople are paid a fixed percentage of sales as commission. With the increase of sales, commission increases and with the decrease, it falls. The first method is based strictly on time and this method is based on piecework system, that is, payment will be made according to the volume of sales made by a salesperson. The commission rates are usually predetermined.

This method can be used successfully by the new companies. It provides efficient salespeople. The more you sell, the more you get. The volume of sales can be increased. This system ensures services of salesperson that cannot be hired permanently.

This has lower administrative expenses. Salesperson's efficiency is clearly distinguished. This method ensures more flexibility compared to base salary. The system also has certain drawbacks. It does not ensure job security to salespeople as it operates strictly on the principle "more sales more commissions and no sales no commission". This leads to uncertainty in income.

The salespeople often adopt reprehensible means to increase sales to earn more commission. This system is not suitable for depression and periods of sudden changes in demand. In order to increase sales and earn more, the salesperson can sell goods on credit. Credit sales can lead to bad debt and recovery can become difficult.

3. **Salary and Commission Basis**

   Salary and Commission Basis is a combination of the first two methods. The salesperson gets a fixed salary and a fixed percentage of sales is also guaranteed. This provides greater incentive and greater pay to the seller. This method aims to eliminate the limitations of the first two methods.

   The salary provides a sense of security, while the commission provides incentives for higher sales. This method is increasingly gaining recognition and immense popularity these days. This mode of payment distinguishes efficient salesperson from the inefficient ones and makes them loyal towards the organisation.

4. **Pooled Commission**

   This system is designed to eliminate the disharmony that arises because of the distribution of territories and areas of efficient salespeople. In some areas, goods are sold very easily, without any special efforts while it is not easy to sell in other regions.

   Each salesperson likes to have that area where sales can be easily affected. But a company cannot assign such areas to all the salespersons. Thus salespersons operating in difficult areas in a particular region pool in their commission and distribute equally among themselves.

5. **Profit Sharing**

   Some organisations provide some of the benefits to vendors along with salary and commission. It is an additional plan to the aforementioned methods. It is useful to increase the morale of the salespeople and improvement in meeting sales targets.

Points to Remember

- A channel of distribution or a marketing channel is a path traced in the direct or indirect transfer of the title to a product as it moves from a product to ultimate consumers or industrial users.
- Objectives of Channels of Distribution
  1. Increase in the availability of products
  2. Meeting customers' service requirements
  3. Ensure promotional support
  4. Obtaining market information
  5. Increase cost-effectiveness
  6. Maintain flexibility
- Patterns of Distribution
  1. General patterns
  2. Middlemen services
  3. Line breadth
  4. Costs and margins
  5. Channel length
- Factors in the Selection of Distribution Channel
  1. Factors relating to product characteristics –
     (a) Industrial/Consumer goods
     (b) Perishability factor
     (c) Unit Value factor
     (d) Obsolescence factor
     (e) Weight and Technicality factor
     (f) Standardized products
     (g) Frequency of purchase
     (h) Newness and market acceptance
     (i) Seasonality factor
     (j) Product breadth factor
  2. Factors relating to company's characteristics –
     (a) Financial strength
     (b) Size of the company
     (c) Marketing policies
     (d) Product mix
     (e) Past channel experience
     (f) Reputation

3. Factors relating to market or consumer's characteristics –
    (a) Consumers' buying behaviour
    (b) Location of the market
    (c) Number of customer
    (d) Size of orders
4. Factors relating to middlemen considerations –
    (a) Sales volume potential
    (b) Availability of intermediary
    (c) Middlemen's attitude
    (d) Services provided by middlemen
    (e) Cost of channel
5. Factors relating to environmental characteristics –
    (a) Economic condition
    (b) Legal restrictions
    (c) Competitors' channel
    (d) Fiscal structure
- Common pay structures for salespeople
  1. Salary basis
  2. Commission basis
  3. Salary and commission basis
  4. Pooled commission
  5. Profit sharing

Questions for Discussion

1. Describe the meaning and objectives of channel of distribution.
2. What are the various patterns of distribution?
3. Explain the factors in the selection distribution channel.
4. Discuss the motivational tools and control areas in channel management.
5. Elaborate the remuneration of the sales person.

■■■

Chapter 4...

Logistics for Customer Satisfaction

Contents ...

Learning Objectives ...

- To understand the basics of logistics for achieving customer satisfaction
- To study the functional areas of logistics integration
- To learn the meaning, importance and participants of physical distribution
- To explain the different types of marketing channels

4.1 Logistics

4.1.1 Introduction

In today's competitive environment, the pursuit of customer satisfaction highly depends on the organisation's overall service quality. Customer satisfaction and the service provided are the key elements of logistics. Satisfaction of customers' expectations regarding service quality affects business performance and encourages customer loyalty. Thus, customer satisfaction is the ultimate assessment of the quality of a service provided. Service quality and customer satisfaction are generally recognised as the major decisive factors in maintaining long-term and successful business relationships. Therefore the quality of logistics service and customer satisfaction is especially important in the current business environment, as the relationship between the service provider and the client is usually long-term and for the relationship to be long- term, a logistics service provider has to provide a service in line with the customers' expectations, leading to the appropriate level of customer satisfaction. Logistics service quality is the comparison between the customers' expectations with the customers' perception of the quality of service provided.

Therefore, logistics companies must ensure every customer service related aspect, no matter what it entails – acceptance of orders, their execution or the solution of problems. A client of a logistics company must be sure that the chosen company understands his needs.

4.1.2 Definition

The term 'Logistics' stems from the Greek word 'Logisticos' meaning 'the science of computing and calculating'. It was used first in military. Webster defines logistics as 'the procurement, maintenance and transportation of military materials, facilities and personnel'. From a military point of view, logistics refers to a supportive system that reflects the practical art of moving armies and materials engaged in combating the enemy to achieve the desired results.

Today, in the industrial and commercial world, logistics has acquired a wider meaning. The Council of Logistics Management (CLM) has defined it in 1991 as follows: **Logistics is the process of planning, implementing and controlling of efficient, effective flow and storage of goods, services and related information from the point of origin to the point of consumption, for conforming to customer expectations.**

- Part of the supply chain process that plans, implements, and controls the efficient, effective forward and reverse flow and storage of goods, services, and related information between the point of origin and the point of consumption in order to meet customers' requirements.

- Describing the entire process of materials and products moving into, through, and out of firm, inbound logistics covers the movement of material received from suppliers. Materials management describes the movement of materials and components within a firm. Physical distribution refers to the movement of goods outward from the end of the assembly line to the customer. Finally, supply-chain management is somewhat larger than logistics, and it links logistics more directly with the users' total communications network and with the firm's engineering staff.

- Process of moving and handling goods and materials, from the beginning to the end of the production, sale process and waste disposal, to satisfy customers and add business competitiveness.

- Process of anticipating customer needs and wants; acquiring the capital, materials, people, technologies, and information necessary to meet those needs and wants; optimising the goods- or service-producing network to fulfil customer requests; and utilising the network to fulfil customer requests in a timely way.

- Customer-oriented operation management.

4.1.3 Significance of Logistics Management

With globalisation and shortened product lifecycles, the Indian industry is focusing to re-engineer their supply chain and logistics activities to achieve the competitive edge. Indian companies are increasingly integrating their supply chains and outsourcing their logistics and supply chain management requirements.

This has created the need for a range of Logistics and transportation solutions for the industry, ranging from solutions for multimodal transport, freight forwarding, material handling, warehousing, shipping, air cargo, packaging, inventory management and more importantly, in integrating logistics and supply chains, etc. to name a few. A potentially huge demand for logistics and transportation solutions and a developing infrastructure has made India – the logistics market of the twenty-first century and thrown open unprecedented opportunities in the logistics business.

It is the gift of the beginning of the last decade of the twenty-first century that the Indian economy is zooming of towards market orientation in which customers are considered as the 'boss' in almost all industrial sectors. Logistics may be further used as an effective weapon to combat competition, which leads a firm towards non-price competition. Its dynamism has also become wider due to expansion in the size and its multidimensional operations of corporate enterprises. It is clear that the fragrance of logistics has been pervading due to mounting pressure on firms to reach the market at the most opportune time and place at a least cost. In other words, it not only leads a firm towards productivity and profitability by elimination of wastage, curtailment of cost and acceleration of sales but can also be used as an instrument of core competency to offset competition. Thus, it can be said, mere reduction of cost is not only the climax of logistics, but the real excitement is the enhancement of productivity and profitability for core competency by providing superior customer service.

4.1.4 Objectives of Logistics

The major objectives of logistics are as follows –

(i)   To make available the right quantity of right quality products at the right time and place in the right physical condition. In short, to ensure timely and intact delivery of goods and services to customers as per their requirements and specifications.

(ii)   To offer the best possible customer service for core competency.

(iii)   To minimise total logistical costs.

(iv)   To maintain transparency in operations.

Operational Objectives

While achieving logistics missions of the enterprise, logistics managers are required to define operational objectives in terms that are more specific. Proper definition and communication of logistics operational objectives are a pre-requisite for the development, implementation, administration and control of logistics system design. Efficient performance of any logistics system needs careful consideration of the following six 'R's about operational objectives of logistics manager.

1.   Right Response.
2.   Right Value.
3.   Right Quality.
4.   Right Cost Trade-offs.
5.   Right Quantity.
6.   Right Information.

1.   **Right Response:** It refers to the ability to meet the service requirements of customers by means of quick response with positive attitude. Real time communication of information is the nucleus of the right response.

2.   **Right Quality:** It includes consistency in the quality of the product, which includes homogeneity in the features, and their zero-defect delivery, which means damage-less delivery, right assortments and correct documentation.

3.   **Right Quantity:** This objective deals with the maintenance of a minimum possible level of inventory required for a desired level of customer service. Any decrease in

the inventory level for the same level of service results in a decrease in the inventory cost, which consequently achieves the logistics mission of minimum total logistics cost.

4. **Right Value:** Right value addition is due to the major contribution of logistics management system in creating time and place utilities. If a logistic system fails to meet its delivery commitment, the company will lose its customer immediately due to availability of a large number of alternative products in the market and then company will have to make further investment in finding a new customer. In short, if a product remains in the stock, its value will decrease and cost will increase. Logistics prevent this occurrence. Hence, it adds value by creating time and place utilities. Apart from this, the real value addition made by logistics is in terms of quality, quick response, better service, consistency, and reliability of the total logistics system, which generate superior customer value.

5. **Right Costs Trade-offs:** This objective ensures the proper balance between total logistics cost and a desired level of customer service performance.

6. **Right Information:** It is the core logistics operational objective. Information regarding the requirement of goods is the primary aspect. Simultaneously, point-to-point information is one of the most important elements of customer service portfolio of recent times, enabling customers to meet their further delivery commitments or formulate their future sales and distribution strategies.

4.1.5 Components of Logistics Management

A large number of individual activities are required to perform in the logistics management system in order to achieve its operational objectives. These individual activities largely attributed as its components and can be grouped broadly into three categories, namely, generic, primary and supportive components.

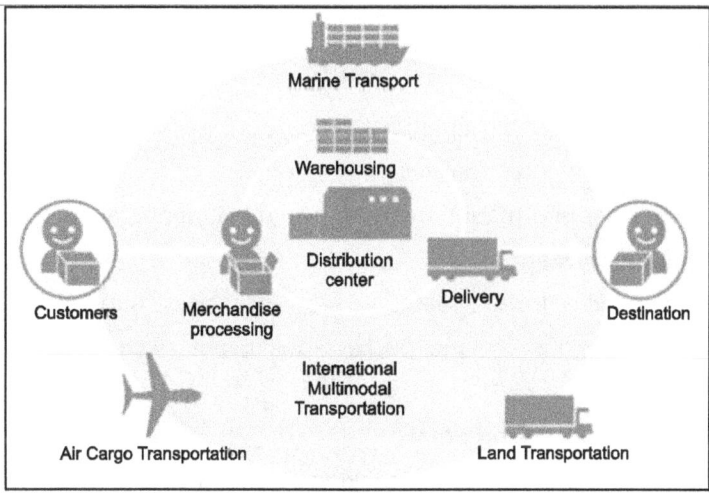

Fig. 4.1

(A) Generic Components

It includes:

(i) **Customer Service:** It brings about an interface of logistics with marketing that determines

- Customer service requirements for products and/or competitive advantage;
- Corporate vision towards service goals;
- Service expectations of customers and their response;
- Development of customer service standard;
- Logistics cost-service trade-off;
- Infrastructural requirements; and
- Development of evaluation and appraisal mechanism.

(B) Primary Components

These include:

(ii) **Network Design**

- Number, size and location of facility network required to perform logistics operations;
- Relationships among locational facilities;
- Their costs and customer service capabilities; and
- Infrastructure of each facility centre.

(iii) **Transportation**

- Requirement, availability and regularity of the transport service;
- Modes of transport and co-ordination between them;
- Transport cost, freight and tariff;
- Fleet management;
- Transit insurance and claim processing;
- Time, speed and intact delivery; and
- Point-to-point information pertaining to movement status.

(iv) **Inventory Management**

- Stocking policies for raw materials, work-in-process and finished goods;
- Zero-inventory, just-in-time, push-or-pull inventory strategies;
- Inventory cost;
- Product mix at stocking points;
- Number, location and size of stocking points; and
- Approach towards safety stock, recorder point and lot size.

(v) Order Processing

- Order receiving and recording;
- Speedy order processing and transmission;
- Ordering and back-order systems;
- Warehouse picking and packing;
- Dispatch scheduling;
- Point-to-point information pertaining to order status;
- Accurate, legal and required documentation; and
- Order processing cost.

(C) Supportive components

These include:L

(vi) Storage and Warehousing

- Warehouse location and configuration;
- Infrastructural facilities;
- Operational mechanism;
- Space determination;
- Goods placement;
- Up-to-date recording of goods' stock position;
- Protecting and preserving the physical attributes of goods;
- Proper loading and unloading system;
- Marshalling goods for dispatches; and
- Warehousing cost.

(vii) Materials Handling

- Safe, smooth and speedy placing and positioning of goods to facilitate their movement and storage;
- Material handling equipment selection and replacement policies;
- Storage and retrieval frequency of goods;
- Material handling equipment and operating costs; and
- Usual life and resale or scrap value of equipment.

(viii) Protective Packaging

- Protection from loss and damage;
- Design of package required for handling and storage;
- Market value of the package;
- Reuse of packages;
- Scrap value of the packages; and
- Packaging cost.

(ix) Procurement

- Make-or-buy decision;
- Vendor selection and management;
- Quality specification;
- Supply schedule;
- Vendor service capability;
- Vendor-company relationship;
- Vendor training and development; and
- Procurement cost.

(x) Information

- Information requirement for logistics system;
- Sources of data and their reliability;
- DBMS for processing, analysis and storage;
- Formats for information presentation to facilitate decision-making;
- Computer infrastructure (hardware, software and connectivity); and
- Information cost.

(xi) Forecasting

- Nature and trend of demand;
- Elements of forecast;
- Forecast technique and system; and
- Administration and error.

One can also derivate the closely linked components of the logistics system as

1. **Logistics services** support the movement of materials and products from inputs through production to consumers, as well as associated waste disposal and reverse flows. They include activities undertaken in-house by the users of the services (for example, storage or inventory control at a manufacturer's plant) and the operations of external service providers. They comprise physical and non-physical activities (for example, transport, storage and supply chain design, selection of contractors, freightage negotiations respectively). Most activities of logistics services are bi-directional.

2. **Information systems** include modeling and management of decision-making and more important issues are tracking and tracing. It provides essential data and consultation in each step of the interaction among logistics services and the target stations.

3. **Infrastructure** comprises human resources, financial resources, packaging materials, warehouses, transport and communications. Most fixed capital is for building those infrastructures. They are concrete foundations and basements within logistics systems.

4.1.6 Important Activities of Logistics

1. **Demand Forecasting/Planning:** Procurement, plant and warehouse site selection, return goods handling, traffic and transportation management, customer demand.

2. **Order Processing:** Products are ordered, billed/invoiced, handled, packaged, packed, wrapped, bundled, sorted, crated, and braced.

3. **Materials Handling and Inventory Management, Warehousing and Storage:** Products are assembled, packed, stored, warehoused, loaded, unloaded, shelved, displayed and cross-docked. Products are shipped by air, railways, waterways, pipelines, and containers. Products are exported, imported, documented, marked and consolidated. Products are traced, tracked, recycled and disposed.

4. **Logistics Communications:** Customer service standards are set (time, availability, errors etc.).

5. **Customer support:** Customer services, parts and services support, customer loyalty, reverse logistics.

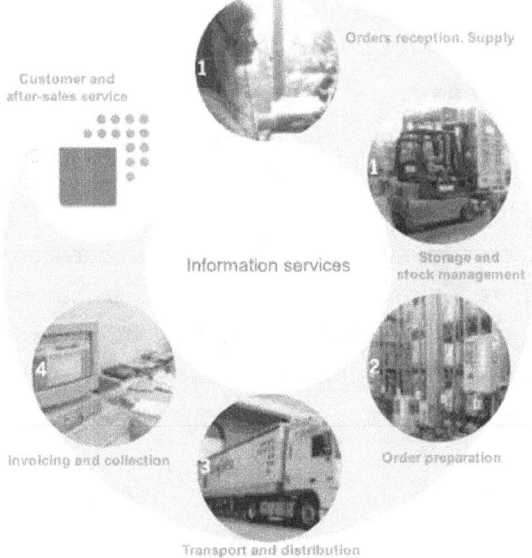

Fig. 4.2

4.1.7 Key Issues and Challenges for Logistics

For effective logistics, there are several key issues and challenges faced by the organisation or the supply chain. The movement of product, movement of information, time, service, costs and integration can be challenging when they are unplanned or designed wrongly.

1. **Transport of products**

   Logistics is sometimes confused with transportation by many companies. Actually, there is more to logistics than just transportation. *The Council of Logistics Management (CLM) has defined it in 1991 as* **"Logistics is the process of planning, implementing and controlling of efficient, effective flow and storage of goods, services and related information from the point of origin to the point of consumption for the purpose of conforming to customer expectations".**

   - The movement of products should complement the company decision strategies.
   - If cost reduction is the main objective, then the focus should be on strategies for cost tradeoffs
   - If customer service is the main objective, then products must emphasise on timely delivery and customer satisfaction.
   - There should be optimal inventory and supply pipeline to ensure it meets the customer demand.
   - The movement may be extremely broad in geographical scope. Raw materials and completed units can move between and among all regions of the world. While other departments in the company may focus on select geographical regions for sourcing, manufacturing or sales, logistics must deal with all of these.

2. **Transfer of Information**

   - Information about the raw materials and products must be detailed. In addition, there should be a proper track of orders received, products delivered and the balance stock.
   - Timely and accurate information must flow between the company and its suppliers, carriers, forwarders, warehouses and customers.
   - It must also move internally among purchasing, customer service, logistics, manufacturing, sales, marketing and accounting.
   - Information technology is a requirement for logistics and the organisation's capabilities.

3. **Quick Response/Time**

   - With expansions of a firm to the global market, it should have the ability to respond to the global marketplace dynamics must be quick.

- Raw materials, intermediate products, etc must be ordered and arrive completely, accurately and quickly.
- Orders must be filled completely, accurately and quickly.
- The delivery time or the lead-time must be based on customer service, competitiveness and value-added services.
- If the company responds to its customers sluggishly, then the customers will shift to those who can give better prompt services. The customers do not tolerate back orders.

4. **Service**

Service is the understanding of the customer requirements. Service means timely delivery, the company's credentials, and the company's culture. Logistics is the link to all these elements. When the scope is wide geographically, the suppliers, the manufacturing unit, warehousing and customer relations become very crucial. The movement of products within this value chain has a major impact on the effectiveness of Logistics.

5. **Cost/Budgets**

- Cost is the key measure by which logistics effectiveness is often measured.
- Purchase of raw materials, freight charges, labour, warehousing facility charges, inventory-holding costs are all the items reflected on the Balance Sheets. Therefore, cost tradeoff is important in logistics management.
- Cost control, cost reductions, and cost management is important for corporate profitability. Funds and budgetary control is the responsibility of all the managers for profitability.
- Cost has a relation to service. Service defined against costs or costs against service develops into operating costs and budgets. The company must make sure that the cost can be managed; otherwise, costs can go out of control and incur losses to the company.
- For global logistics, there may be issues of currency conversions and fluctuation in the exchange rates. Airfreight is quoted in the currency of the origin country. Ocean terminal and other accessorial origin charges are also in origin country currency. Warehouses in other countries will invoice in origin currencies. Currency conversion and dynamics can create unfavourable or favourable cost variances that have nothing to do with logistics performance.

6. **Logistics Integration**

- Logistics is a process; therefore, for effective logistics it is relevant that every element of the organisation or every element of the functional areas of logistics do its part. It necessitates integration of internal functional departments as well as external integration.

- The suppliers, the transportation carriers, warehouses must understand the company's objective clearly. The company must share the logistics vision and plan with them. This sharing and understanding will better enable them to co-operate. They may be able to offer ideas and gain sharing to further improve the logistics effectiveness and the key issues with it.

- Integration with customers or distributors is also important. Every employee of a company must be focused on satisfying customers. Meeting with key distributors is very good. This shows how much we value them and want to work with them. This is a competitive advantage. Partnerships and alliances can be developed or enhanced.

7. The External Issues

External issues involve the transportation carrier who brings material from the supplier to the manufacturing unit, who moves it from the plant to a distribution centre or who takes it to the customer. External can also involve a rented warehouse.

8. The Global Logistics

A company engaged in imports, and exports, and when we talk about logistics, there are numerous other factors to be considered. For example, people working in Asia, Europe, America or the Middle East have different time zones. It means that there must be a good understanding of plans and strategies by each element. In addition, there are cultural factors. Different cultures view and understand businesses differently. These understandings and their complexities can compound if the strategies and plans for doing business are not the result of collaborative effort with input by all groups. Different global areas must work together; share the product information efficiently for doing a profitable international business.

4.1.8 Logistics for Customer Satisfaction

The term logistics is frequently misinterpreted to mean transportation. But the fact is, the scope of logistics goes well beyond transportation. Logistics forms the system that ensures the delivery of the product in the entire supply chain. This involves packaging, transportation, storage and handling methods, and flow of information. The impact of logistics in the ability of a company to satisfy its customers cannot be overstated. All other efforts at modernisation within a company would not bear fruit until the logistics system is properly designed to assist the smooth and efficient flow of products in the system.

The topic of logistics is comparatively new in India. There have been some firms that have done work in this area, but a large number of firms are only now beginning to realise the significance of designing and managing the entire supply chain. With India joining the global marketplace, the role of logistics assumes greater significance.

The industrial policies in India have encouraged manufacturers to establish plants in remote, backward areas due to inexpensive land and tax benefits. This poses some serious logistical problems. Apart from a poor road and transportation network, the existing communications system in India leaves a lot to be preferred by any international standard. It is in this perspective that logistics has to be considered in India.

The Value of Logistics

Material handling and storage are typically labeled as "non-value adding" activities. While one can understand the motivation behind such labeling as one aimed at waste reduction, it can lead to wrong assumption that all material handling and storage can be avoided. While manufacturing processes provide "form utility", logistics-related activities provide "time and place" utility to a product. The challenge is to provide the time and place utility at a competitive cost. If a company can achieve this goal, it will gain a significant competitive advantage in the marketplace.

Pull vs. Push Systems

There are two basic approaches of bringing the product to its final destination, that is, the customer. In a push system (See Fig. 4.3), products are pushed from the manufacturing plants to distribution points based on a sales forecast. The second approach is the pull system (See Fig. 4.4) which requires that the product be pulled from the plants based on actual demand.

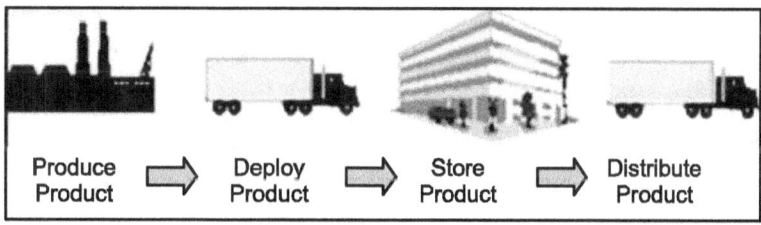

Produce Product ⟹ Deploy Product ⟹ Store Product ⟹ Distribute Product

Fig. 4.3: Push system

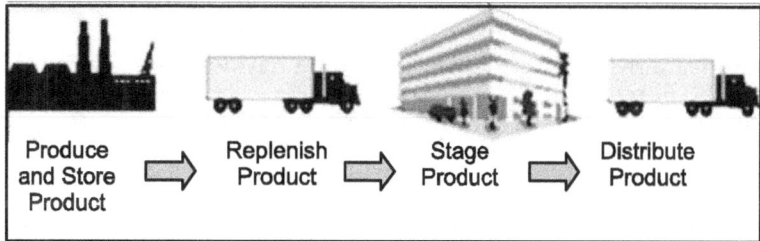

Produce and Store Product ⟹ Replenish Product ⟹ Stage Product ⟹ Distribute Product

Fig. 4.4: Pull system

In a push system, since all the products are deployed based on the sales forecast for each region, an inaccurate sales forecast incurs several severe penalties that include –

- Increased safety stock
- Larger distribution centers/godowns
- Higher stock transfer rates

The pre-order deployment of product increases safety stock. Since there is greater uncertainty associated with forecasts, which are often little better than educated guesses, the system must provide for variations in the demand in a particular region serviced by the particular godown. In addition, the system must provide for errors in the overall forecast for the country as a whole. These concerns lead to the carrying of larger safety stocks, which necessitate larger godowns.

The irony in the concept of safety stocks is that although sufficient stocks may exist in the system, the product mix demanded in a particular region may not exist in the regional godown. This necessitates inter-godown transfer of goods. The result is an increase in the transportation costs system-wide, in addition to handling and shipping costs, information costs, product loss and damage, and poor customer service. The more points of distribution in the system, the greater the penalties incurred for unpredictable order fluctuations.

The goal of any logistics system is to maintain or improve customer service. In the push mode of operation, the penalties of higher safety stock, larger godowns, and inter-godown transfer are not the only penalties. Stock rotation becomes more difficult to maintain. Handling of all products at each godown involves unloading, staging, storing, picking, staging and loading for shipment. All these activities involve an element of cost. In addition, there is a potential for product damage each time a product is handled.

There are some positive aspects of a push system as well. These are –

- Small plant warehouses
- Potential for higher customer service
- Lower transportation costs

Since the majority of the product is stored at the godowns, the plant needs to maintain a low inventory of finished goods. This allows the plant to utilise its space for production and eliminate the need for a full warehouse staff. If the forecast is accurate, the push system provides the potential for higher customer service by having the product ready for delivery directly to the customer/retailer. Finally, by having the products deployed in the godowns, the plants have the capability of shipping full truckloads and thereby reducing the system-wide transportation costs.

A push system works best when sales are consistent, the product variety is small, and there are a few regional distribution points.

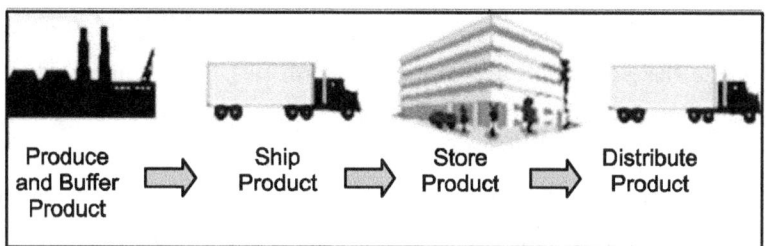

Produce and Buffer Product ⇨ Ship Product ⇨ Store Product ⇨ Distribute Product

Fig. 4.5: Push/Pull Systems

4.1.9 Reverse Logistics

Reverse logistics stands for all operations connected to the reuse of products and materials. It is "the process of planning, implementing, and controlling the efficient, cost-effective flow of raw materials, in-process inventory, finished goods and connected data from the point of consumption to the point of origin for the purpose of recapturing its importance or removing the product. More accurately, reverse logistics is the procedure of moving products from their final destination for the purpose of capturing its importance, or removing the products. Remanufacturing and redoing activities are also included in the definition of reverse logistics." The reverse logistics process includes management and the sale of surplus plus returned tool and machines from the hardware leasing business.

Business Implications: In today's marketplace, many retailers treat merchandise returns as individual, disorganised transactions. "The challenge for retailers and vendors is to process returns at a specialised level that enables fast, competent and cost-effective collection and return of merchandise. Customer needs facilitate demand for a high standard of service that consists of precision and timeliness. It is the logistic company's duty to curtail the connection from the point of return of origination to the time of resell. By following returns management best practices, retailers can attain a returns process that addresses both the operational and customer maintenance problems connected with merchandise returns. Additionally, due to the relation between reverse logistics and customer retention, it has become a key constituent within **Service Lifecycle Management** (SLM), a **business strategy** aimed at maintaining customers by bundling even more co-ordination of a firm's services data as one to attain greater effectiveness in its operations.

Return of unsold goods: In particular, industries, goods are distributed to downstream members in the supply chain with the knowledge that the goods might be given back for credit if they are not sold. Newspapers and magazines serve as examples. This acts as an inducement for downstream members to bring in more stock, because the upstream supply chain members tolerate the risk of elimination. On the other hand, there is also a distinct risk connected to this logistics concept. The downstream member in the supply chain might exploit the circumstances by ordering more stock than is needed and returning large volumes. Like this, the downstream partner is capable of providing high level of service without carrying the risks connected with large inventories. The supplier efficiently finances the inventory for the downstream member. It is thus important to analyse customers' account for hidden cost.

Reverse logistics is the procedure of supervising the return of goods. Reverse logistics is also referred to as "Aftermarket Customer Services". In other words, any time money is taken from a firm's warranty reserve or service logistics budget one can speak of a reverse logistics operation.

4.1.10 Achieving Tradeoff between Customer Service and Cost

An incorporated logistics system is a boundary of procurement function, production function and physical distribution function of the total logistics function to attain its basic mission of the best possible customer service at the smallest amount of costs. The development of this incorporated logistics system is notable by its awareness to costs of both movement and demand-supply co-ordination. It brings synergy in business functions for economies of scale in logistics function. Therefore, total cost analysis is important in its design and acts as a key to supervise it. The total cost refers to the sum total of the cost engaged in different constituents of logistics function, namely:

(i)   Inventory cost;

(ii)   Transportation cost;

(iii)   Storage and warehousing cost;

(iv)   Material handling and protective packaging cost;

(v)   Order processing cost;

(vi)   Information cost;

(vii) Customer service cost; and

(viii) Production lot quantity cost.

Logistics costs are motivated by activities that support the logistics process. Trade-offs are possible among the parts of logistics costs to reduce the total costs of given customer service level objectives. These parts are inter-related and different trade-offs exist. It is important to note that some of these trade-offs are not realised in a continuous manner. Consolidation of warehouses happens at a distinct point at a particular time and this will be different for different companies based on their decision to invest in new logistics systems. The major goal of the company in building its logistics strategy is to give customer service while decreasing the costs thereby increasing its profits and being competitive.

In this system approach, efforts are made to reduce the total cost of logistics rather than reducing the cost of individual component. Reduction in cost of one component of logistics brings about an increase in the cost of others. Thus, effective management and real cost saving can be achieved by trying to improve the efficiency of the total cost of integrated logistics system and not the divided cost of individual components. Simultaneously, efforts are also required to settle on a trade-off between the total logistics costs and service standards needed to meet the customer's expectations.

A company could reorganise its logistics in numerous ways because of lower transportation costs. For one, it could decrease the number of warehouses and thereby increase the use of transportation facilities. Four factors influence the number of warehouses. A company that opts to maintain – cost of misplaced sales, inventory costs, warehousing costs, and transportation costs.

1. **Cost of Lost Sales:** The cost of lost sales is hard to measure. It usually declines with the number of warehouses and differs by industry, company, product, and customer. The remaining cost constituents are more reliable across companies and industries.

2. **Inventory Costs:** Inventory costs rise with the number of warehouses because companies maintain a safety stock of all products at each centre. Overall more space is required.

3. **Warehousing Costs:** More warehouses mean more space to be owned, leased or rented. Fixed costs across many facilities are bigger than the marginal changeable costs of smaller number of locations.

4. **Transportation Costs:** Transportation costs at first reduce as the number of facilities increases due to its closeness. Costs in time increases for too many warehouses, because of the combination of inbound and outbound transport costs.

A company seeking to reduce total costs, the sum of the above constituents, could balance all cost components by solving a multi-facility location problem. As transportation costs decline however, possibly due to highway infrastructure investment, the minimum total cost will in general occur for fewer warehouses. The nature and timing of reorganisation will occur at different points for each firm. Sufficient potential gains will need to be realised before an investment hurdle rate is exceeded.

The logistics objective ensures a proper balance between total logistics cost and a desired level of customer service performance. For instance, addition of a new distribution warehouse raises the total logistics costs, which provides a more effective customer service and produces additional sales to meet additional logistics costs in the development of a new facility. Hence, it leads to cost trade-offs between different elements of logistics cost.

4.2 Logistics Integration

4.2.1 Definition

An integrated logistics system is an interface of procurement function, production function and physical distribution function of the total logistics function in order to achieve its basic mission of the best possible customer service at the least possible costs. The development of this integrated logistics system is distinguished by its attention to costs of both movement and demand-supply coordination. It brings synergy in business functions for economies of scale in logistics function. Thus, total cost analysis is essential in its design and acts as a key to manage it. The total cost refers to the sum total of the cost involved in various components of logistics function.

4.2.2 Concept of Integration in Logistics Operation

1. **Internal Integration**
   - First Stage of Internal Integration - Materials management and physical distribution management
   - Second Stage of Internal Integration - Logistics management

2. **External Integration**
   - Supply chain management
   - Functions in coordinated fashion
   - One operational command - Performance in isolation loses sight of overall picture.

4.2.3 Key Elements of Effective Integrated Logistics

- Shippers
- Suppliers
- Carriers (railroad, air, water, pipeline)
- Warehouse providers
- Freight forwarders
- Terminal operators (ports)
- Government (regulator of logistics)

4.2.4 Objectives of Logistics Integration

- Rapid response
- Minimum variance
- Minimum inventory
- Movement consolidation
- Lifecycle support

4.2.5 Importance of Integrated Logistics

- Scope is wide spread – functions of logistics are spread across various stages of value chain in the organisation
- Provides interface between marketing and customers, marketing and operations, operations and supplier
- Provides competitive edge to business in the current environment
- Handles flow of information, materials and recovery cycle
- Tackles cost reduction

4.2.6 Planning for Logistics Integration

1. **Logistics Processes**
   - Supply chain segmentation
   - Logistics network planning
   - Logistics management and organisation
   - Manufacturing and materials management

2. **Procurement and Inventory Decisions**
   - Basic inventory planning and management
   - Inventory and supply chain
   - Purchasing and supply management

3. **Warehousing and Storage**
   - Warehousing options
   - Storage and handling systems (palletised)
   - Storage and handling systems (non-palletised)
   - Order picking and replenishment plan
   - Receiving and dispatch management plan
   - Warehouse management and information plan

4. **Freight Transport/Transportation Planning**
   - Rail and intermodal transport
   - Road freight transport: Vehicle selection
   - Road freight transport: Vehicle costing
   - Road freight transport: Planning and resourcing
   - Sea transport
   - Air transport

5. **Operational Management**
   - Cost and performance monitoring
   - Benchmarking
   - Information and communication technology
   - Outsourcing: Services and decision criteria, selection, management
   - Outsourcing management
   - Security and safety in distribution
   - Reverse logistics management

4.2.7 Functional Areas of Logistics Integration

1. **Procurement/Purchasing**

   Procurement is a key activity in the supply chain. It deals with the sourcing activities, negotiation of contracts and well-planned selection of goods and services that are usually of importance to an organisation. It is essential that the goods, services or works are appropriate and that they are procured at the best possible cost to meet the objectives of an organisation which is in terms of quality and quantity, time, and location.

Another term used synonymously in procurement management is purchasing. Purchasing is an integral part of an organisation since it plays a vital role for revenue generations and cost reductions. Purchasing and procurement are both being used interchangeably but actually, procurement is the process of acquiring goods or services from an external source or a supplier, while purchasing is the process of how goods and services are ordered.

Some definitions of procurement are –

- *According to the Merriam Webster Dictionary*: *"Procurement is the act or process of procuring; especially, the obtaining of military supplies by a government".*
- *"Procurement is the acquisition of goods, services or works from an external source".*
- *Procurement is the act of obtaining or buying goods and services. The process includes preparation and processing of a demand as well as the end receipt and approval of payment.*

Procurement serves basic three areas of supply requisitions –

(a) Internal customer: Internal purchase requirements like stationery, office equipments, and other supplies of an organisation may be raised for conducting day-to-day activities. These requirements are sent to competent vendors for purchasing. This kind of purchase is are more dependent on quotations and cost effectiveness.

(b) Procurements in response to emergencies: Procurements carried in response to political emergencies, natural calamities humanitarian causes have special needs. For political emergencies like wars and civil attacks, government needs to keep supplies of arms and ammunitions. Government agencies that are authorised will send purchase requisition to its supplier or may release an "invitation to tender" for competitive bidding.

(c) Optimisation of stocks for productions: The workers of a production unit raise a purchase requisition in order to maintain optimal stock levels for the smooth operations of the production process. These requirements are further processed by the purchase department. Purchase officer plays a key role in such type of procurement.

In strategic procurement, it is important that the procurement activity meets the objectives of an organisation. It is important that the goods, services or works are as per the standard requirements and that they are procured at the best possible cost to meet the needs of the purchaser in terms of quality, quantity, time and location.

The main objectives of procurements management include –

- **Support operational requirements:** To understand the business requirements for procurement, and keeping optimal levels of inventory.
- **Planning and co-ordinating:** To plan and co-ordinate the purchasing needs with all the procurement teams in order to reduce administration and increase cost reductions.
- **To achieve maximum integration with the other departments of the firm.**
- **Strategic sourcing:** To be able to identify the most reliable suppliers through "tendering" (pre-qualifying suppliers and retaining only those that are capable of meeting the organisation's requirements sourcing).
- **Purchasing:** To make purchases as per the organisation's policies and procedures. All purchases must follow the approved procurement processes. Purchases must be made with the objective of cost reductions.
- **Quality:** To procure quality materials and services cost effectively from reliable vendors and suppliers. Review of specifications or statement of work. Review the requirements for the material or service being provided.
- **Delivery time:** Ensure timely delivery through the selection of capable and efficient suppliers.
- **New and cheaper supplies:** Identify the availability of new products and monitor trends in market prices though market research.

Procurement Process

(a) Expression of Interest (EOI)

Expression of interest is the practice of seeking an indication of interest from suppliers and service providers who are competent to undertake work. The objective of the **EOI** process is to identify and pre-register organisations that are interested in entering into the contract and have the expertise and financial capacity.

The EOI is the first stage of a multi-stage tender process. It helps to –

- To gather the information of potential suppliers and service providers for a single contract.
- To establish a panel of suppliers and service providers for several contracts for work-in-progress.
- It helps to identify the applicants with the best proposals.

EOIs enable the competency of applicants to be assessed in relation to several evaluation criteria drafted by the strategic purchasing management team. It helps in evaluation of suitability and helps to recommend and short-list the most suitable applicants to be invited to provide priced tenders or detailed proposals in the next stage.

(b) ITT (Invitation to Tender)

Qualified suppliers or contractors are invited to submit sealed bids for the purpose of procurements. The "tender notice" clearly defines the goods or services required by the organisation and the time frame. It is also known as RFT (Request for Tender).

(c) ITB (Invitation to Bid)/Restricted Tendering

ITB is an oral or written invitation to prospective suppliers to submit a bid on materials or services. Invitation to bid (ITB) is sent only to selected contractors, sellers, or vendors who have been pre-qualified through the initial screening process. It is also called as Restricted Bidding or **RFB** (Request to Bid)

Prequalification of Bidders

Screening of potential contractors, suppliers, or vendors on the basis of factors such as –

- Experience
- Financial ability
- Managerial ability
- Reputation
- Work history to develop a list of qualified bidders who will receive the invitation-to-bid (ITB) documents.

(d) RFP (Requests for Proposals)

RFPs are publicly advertised and suppliers respond with a detailed proposal, not with only a price quotation but also with service specifications, roles and responsibilities, delivery schedule etc.

A purchaser advises the potential suppliers with the following criteria –

- Statement and scope of work
- Specifications
- Schedules or timelines
- Contract type
- Data requirements
- Terms and conditions
- Description of goods and/or services to be procured
- General criteria used in evaluation procedure
- Special contractual requirements
- Technical goals
- Instructions for preparation of technical, management, and/or cost proposals

(e) RFQ (Requests for Quotation)

Request for quotation (**RFQ**) is a document that an organisation submits to one or more potential suppliers to obtain price or quotes for the goods or services.

(f) Contract Negotiation And Award

A contract defines the rights and obligations of both parties once the contract is awarded. A contract is finalised when an offer is made, negotiated and accepted.

Contract Negotiation: Contracts are negotiated with potential suppliers, which can be in terms of costs, quality, and delivery schedule. Penalties are also described in the contract in case of any deviations from the terms mentioned in the contract.

Contract Award: Contracts are awarded to suppliers after negotiations by mutually signing a "contract document". A formal agreement, including specified conditions of contract with all relevant information is included in the agreement and the party, which has made the successful offer signs it. Contracts are awarded by writing a letter of acceptance, paying advance money for the goods, services or works provided, issuing a purchase order etc.

E-Tendering

E-Tendering is an internet-based process in which the entire tendering process right from advertisement to finalisation of tenders are carried online. The advantage of e-tendering is there is speedy exchange of information, reduction in the use of papers and improved efficiency in the administration.

A tender notice is advertised on an online web portal of a private or a government organisation. These opportunities are generally an open tender, through which a large number of suppliers are able to register and submit their interest. An e-procurement system manages tenders through a web site. This can be accessed anywhere globally and has greatly improved the accessibility of tenders.

Suppliers and buyers communicate via an email, website or through more advanced EDI (Electronic Data Interface) software system. Some business intelligence software and e-procurement systems automate the supplier selection process. Public sector organisations use e-procurement for contracts to get benefits such as increased effectiveness and cost savings, transparency and fair means of supplier selection.

2. Production/Facilities

Production

Production refers to the capacity of a supply chain to make and store products. The facilities of production are factories and warehouses. Strategic decisions regarding production focus on what customers want and the market demands. This first stage in developing supply chain agility takes into consideration what and how many products to produce, and what, if any, parts or components should be produced at which plants or outsourced to capable suppliers. These strategic decisions regarding production must also focus on capacity, quality and volume of goods, keeping in mind that customer demand and satisfaction must be met. Operational decisions, on the other hand, focus on scheduling workloads, maintenance of equipment and meeting immediate client/market demands. Quality control and workload balancing are issues that need to be considered when making these decisions.

Supply

Next, an organisation must determine what their facility or facilities are able to produce, both economically and efficiently, while keeping the quality high. However, most companies cannot provide excellent performance with the manufacture of all components. Outsourcing is an excellent alternative to be considered for those products and components that cannot be produced effectively by an organisation's facilities. Companies must carefully select suppliers for raw materials. When choosing a supplier, focus should be on developing velocity, quality and flexibility while at the same time reducing costs or maintaining low cost levels. In short, strategic decisions should be made to determine the core capabilities of a facility and outsourcing partnerships should grow from these decisions.

3. Supplier Management

Supplier management is a management system that facilitates close cooperation between the suppliers and the procurement department or an organisation. It combines the procurement value through efficient management during the sourcing cycle, promotes cost reductions and controls any risk factors.

It continuously optimises supplier's performance by centralising sourcing, contract management, performance evaluation and implements refined strategy to improve procurement efficiency and results. Collaboration and communication between suppliers increase overall production efficiency and reduce development costs. The suppliers are assigned responsibilities with clear guidelines and standard requirement, allowing multiple suppliers to work together and this enables cooperation on production development and manufacturing. It helps streamline the sourcing and product cycles through improved supplier communication and collaboration, resulting in higher production efficiency and lower production error.

Supplier Selection

With increasing challenges due to customer demands, the procurement activity has become a complex process. Therefore, the need for procuring goods and services from competent and reliable suppliers has become a very important factor in supply chain management. Supplier assessment and evaluation therefore is an important process in procurement management.

Supplier selection and evaluation is required to identify qualified and eligible suppliers. It also helps in collecting information and developing a database from a pool of eligible suppliers. Having a good base of competent suppliers ensures the supplies are procured efficiently, the delivery lead-time is reduced, and the cost of procurement is substantial and as per the company's cost goal.

Supplier Evaluation Criteria

The procurement department team drafts the various eligibility criteria for selection of competent suppliers. In general, the following aspects are crucial in the selection of suppliers.

- **Product quality:** Materials to be supplied by the supplier must correspond to the buyer's requirement. Preferences are usually given to those suppliers who have certified ISO 9001 quality management system.

- **Good market credentials:** A stringent reference check and customers feedback is undertaken to evaluate the supplier's credentials.

- **Financial stability:** Financial stability can be measured by financial ratios from suppliers yearly, quarterly, annually by requesting them to submit these financial reports.

- **Contractual and standard compliance:** Contract terms are analysed and evaluated from amongst the number of proposals submitted by different suppliers. Terms that fall in line with the buyer's needs are shortlisted.

- **Pricing:** When the procurement is based on cost effectiveness and is more focused on cost reductions, pricing becomes an important factor for supplier selection.

- **Production capacity:** For the procurement of finished goods or raw materials that are input for the production process, or for the imports and exports businesses, the production capacity of the supplier is of high importance, to maintain a smooth flow and optimum levels of supplies.

- **Product liability insurance:** In case of product damage, pilferages and non-compliance, the supplier has to ensure that he is able to provide compensations and that the loss is forfeited.

- **Experience:** Besides market credentials and expertise, experience of the supplier in a particular area of sourcing is important for the supplier selection process. Experienced suppliers are largely preferred for procurements in which the investment of money is huge. Government and large private organisations where the sourcing requirement is on a long-term basis and quantity required is huge, experience of the supplier plays an important role.

- **Product receipt quality:** Upon receipt of the products, the inspection team performs a quality check and specifications as per the specifications documents. This information can be obtained from the supplier history, which aids in the evaluation of a supplier. Product quality of supplier is also evaluated from the samples received.

- **Technical compliance:** With globalisation of procurements, technical expertise of the supplier is largely considered as important criteria for the selection of suppliers. Use of technology, advanced machineries, can shorten the lead production and delivery time. Technical compliance criteria are highlighted in tender documents along with its detailed description.

- **Production duration and delivery performance:** The total time taken for production is critical when products are to be supplied in specific quantities and they have to be delivered within the specified time. From the supplier history, an organisation can evaluate the delivery performance and production compliance.
- **Geographic location:** Suppliers who are closely located to the buyer's factory locations, warehouses or retail outlets would be preferred more than those suppliers who are located out of their business limits.

Secondary review of selected suppliers

- Based on the analysis and evaluation of suppliers, the most qualified suppliers are selected, this leads to further discussions and negotiations.
- Product samples are sent for testing and evaluation and the report and the sample forwarded to the purchase officer or the manager.

Final Review of Selected Suppliers

After evaluating the report and on-site inspections, a conclusion is drawn about the most eligible supplier to be awarded with the contract. For the purpose of risk-management, a list of other supplier as alternative suppliers is made. In case of production disruption with the primary supplier, it ensures that the production has minimum impact on unforeseeable circumstances.

4. Material Handling

Material handling moves products before, after or between transportation and warehousing. Material handling activities usually take place within the premises of a warehouse. It is defined as activities, equipment, and procedures related to the moving, storing, protecting and controlling of materials in a system.

In a warehouse, the material is handled at various stages. When the material is received in the warehouse, it is unloaded from the vehicle and kept on the unloading docks. From there, the material is moved to an incoming material area where the material is unpacked, inspected, and sorted. The material is then moved to the storage areas and put away in appropriate storage locations. The material is stored in a way to minimise damage and deterioration during storage. When the material in store is required to be delivered to customers, the material is picked up from their storage locations as per the customer orders. The materials so collected are taken to order assembly area, where the materials collected as per order requirement are packed. The packed material is moved first to the dispatch area and then to the loading docks. Finally, the material is loaded on the vehicles for transportation to the customers.

Material handling operations are concerned with the four dimensions of material handling – movement, time, quantity, and space.

Material handling involves movement of material that includes horizontal movement from one place to another and vertical movement of lifting and lowering. It is desirable to complete a material handling task in as short a time as possible. Time dimension also covers scheduling of use of material handling equipment and activities to ensure timely completion of material handling tasks with minimum equipment. Then material handling is concerned with the quantity of material handled and stocked that is measured in weight, volume, or number of pieces. Material handling is also concerned with efficient use of space. The amount of space used for storing and handling material is the fourth dimension of material handling. Description of any material handling system needs to cover description of these four dimensions as well.

Transport equipments (conveyors, cranes, and industrial trucks), positioning equipments, unit load formation equipment, storage equipments (S/R machines of an AS/RS, or storage carousels), identification and control equipments are available for use in material handling systems.

Packaging of products is done to protect and preserve the products and improve stability during handling and storage in the warehouse and during transportation.

5. Inventory Management

Inventory, is a list of goods and materials stored for future use, mainly in the production process or those goods and materials themselves, held available in stock by a business. Thus, today's inventory is tomorrow's production. **The raw materials, work-in-process goods, and completely finished goods are considered a portion of a business's assets that is ready or will be ready for sale.** The turnover of inventory represents one of the primary sources of revenue generation and subsequent earnings for the company/business. **Therefore, inventories are materials or resources of any kind having some economic value, either awaiting conversion or use in future.**

Inventory is the total amount of goods or materials stored in a factory at any given time. Stores holding inventories must know the accurate number of items on their shelves and storage areas in order to place orders or manage losses. Factory managers should know the number of product units available for customer orders. Restaurants should order more food than their existing supplies and menu needs. All such businesses rely on an inventory count to give answers.

Inventory and its Control

The inventory control is fundamentally based on cost-study, as there are several costs associated with inventory.

Inventory control is concerned with minimising the total cost of inventory. The three main factors in inventory control decision-making process are –

- The cost of holding the stock (for example, based on the interest rate).
- The cost of placing an order (for example, for raw material stocks) or the set-up cost of production.
- The cost of shortage, that is, what is lost if the stock is insufficient to meet all demand.

The third element is the most difficult to measure and is often handled by establishing a "service level" policy, for example, certain percentage of demand will be met from stock immediately.

The ABC Classification: The ABC classification system is to group items according to annual sales volume, in an attempt to identify the small number of items that will account for most of the sales volume and that are the most important ones to control for effective inventory management.

Reorder Point: The inventory level R in which an order is placed, where, R = D.L, D = demand rate (demand rate period day, week, etc.), and L = lead-time.

Safety Stock: Remaining inventory between the times that an order is placed and when new stock is received. If there are not enough inventories then a shortage may occur.

Safety stock is a hedge against running out of inventory. It is an extra inventory to take care on unexpected events. It is often called buffer stock. The absence of inventory is called a shortage.

Types of Inventory

(a) **Raw material inventory:** These inventory items are used in the manufacturer's conversion method to manufacture components, sub-assemblies or finished products. These are raw materials, other supplies, parts, and components that enter into the product during the production process and generally form part of the product.

(b) **Work-in-process inventory:** This inventory is made up of all the materials, components, assemblies, and subassemblies that are in process of being processed or are waiting to be processed within the system. This usually includes raw material that has been released for initial processing and material that has been entirely processed and is waiting final inspection and acceptance before inclusion in finished goods. In short, these are raw materials and other supplies, parts and components that enter the product during the production process and generally form part of the product.

(c) **Finished goods inventory:** These are completed, finished products ready for customer order, that is, sale. Hence, finished goods inventory is the collection of finished goods. These products have been inspected and have passed last inspection needs so that they can be transferred out of WIP and into finished goods inventory.

(d) **Transit inventory:** It results from the need, to transport items or materials from one location to another and from the fact that there is some transportation time involved in getting from one location to another. Sometimes, this is referred to as pipeline or movement inventory.

(e) **Buffer inventory:** Inventory is at times used to guard the product from the uncertainties of supply, demand, unpredictable events such as poor delivery, reliability or poor quality of a supplier's products. These inventory cushions are regularly referred to as safety stock or buffer inventory. It is an amount held on hand that is over and above that presently required to meet demand. Usually, the higher the level of buffer inventory, the better the company's customer service.

(f) **Anticipation inventory:** At times, firms, in anticipation of a possible future event, will acquire and hold inventory that is in excess of their existing need. Events may include anything, a price increase, an impending labour strike, etc. This approach is normally used by retailers, who regularly build up inventory months before the demand for their products will be unusually high (for example, seasons , new year).This process is also called "smoothing" as it smoothes the peaks and valleys in demand, allowing the firm to maintain a constant level of output and a stable workforce. For manufacturers, it avoids layoff costs associated with production cutbacks or worse, the idling or shutting down of facilities, excessive overtime (hiring, training etc.) for increased production time when demands picks up.

(g) **Decoupling inventory:** Not often, one will be able to witness a production facility, where every machine in the process, produces at precisely the same speed. It may so happen that one particular machine processes parts several times faster than the machines in front of or behind it. Yet, at a single glance, it appears that all machines are running smoothly at the same time. It could also be possible, that one notices several machines under repair or undergoing some form of preventive maintenance. Even so, this does not seem to interrupt the flow of WIP through the system. The reason for this is the existence of an inventory of parts between machines, a decoupling inventory that serves as a shock absorber and cushioning the system against production irregularities. As such, it decouples or disengages the plant's dependence upon the requirements of the system.

(h) **Cycle inventory:** Economic order quantity (EOQ) is an effort to balance inventory holding or carrying costs with the costs incurred from ordering or setting up machine. When large quantities are ordered or produced, inventory holding or carrying costs are increased, but ordering costs decreases. Conversely, when lot sizes decrease, inventory holding or carrying costs decrease, but the set-up or ordering cost increases since more orders are required to meet demand. When these two costs are equal, the total cost is minimised. Cycle inventory results from ordering in batches or lot sizes rather than ordering material strictly as needed. Therefore, they are also called as lot-size inventories.

(i) **MRO goods inventory:** Maintenance, repairs, and operating supplies or MRO goods are items that are used to support and maintain the production process and its infrastructure. These goods are normally an outcome of the consumption of the production process; however, they are not directly related to the finished product. For example, oils, lubricants, coolants, janitorial supplies, uniforms, gloves, packing material, tools, nuts, bolts, screws, shim stock, and key stock. Office supplies, such as staples, pens and pencils, copier paper and toner are considered part of MRO goods inventory.

(j) **JIT inventory:** JIT or Just in Time inventory is very popular these days. It is a system is in which the supplies, materials or goods are produced or procured based on demand. Joint collaboration between the suppliers, manufacturers and distributors or retailers put an effort not only in cutting the inventory holding cost but also strive to meet the customer demands.

(k) **Zero inventory:** Zero inventory is a system in which a company keeps very little or no inventory in storage. Zero inventories are the goal of just-in-time inventory management and the two terms are used interchangeably. Placing an order of exactly what it needs to sell and receive in a stipulated period helps in cost reductions in supply chains.

Stock Classification

(a) HML classification (High, Medium and Low)

In this type of classification, unit value is an important criteria and it is not based on the annual consumption value. The items of inventory should be listed in the descending order of unit value and it is up to the management to fix limits for three categories.

For example,

All items of unit price above ₹ 10000: H category

Unit price between ₹ 1000 to ₹ 10000: M category

Unit price below ₹ 1000: L category

(b) VED classification (Vital Essential Desirable classification)

In VED classification, analysis is done to determine critical items and its effect on production and other services. This method is generally used for classification of spare parts. If a part is vital it is given V classification, if it is essential, then it is given E classification, and if it is just desirable, the part is given D classification. For V items, a large stock of inventory is generally maintained while for D items, minimum stock is enough.

(c) SDE classification (Scarce Difficult Easy)

In the SDE analysis, classification of items is based on its availability. This system is useful in cases of scarcity of supply.

In SDE analysis, S refers to 'scarce' items, generally imported, and those that are in short supply. D refers to 'difficult' items that are available locally but are difficult items to procure. Goods are procured from distant places or for which reliable suppliers are difficult to find fall into D category. E refers to items which are 'easy' to obtain and which are accessible in the local market.

(d) GOLF classification (Government Ordinary Local Foreign)

The transactions with the government involve a long procedure and payment, in advance or against delivery. Ordinarily, moderate lead times – Local – instant purchase on cash; Foreign – lot of documentations and clearance from DGFT (Directorate General of Foreign Trade).

(e) FSN Classification (Fast Moving, Slow Moving)

FSN classification is based on frequency of issues and uses. To carry out an FSN analysis, whichever is later, the date of receipt or the last date of issue is considered to decide the number of months, which have lapsed since the last transaction. The items are usually grouped in periods of 12 months.

Fast Moving (F) = Items that are frequently issued/used.

Slow Moving (S) = Items that are issued/used less for a certain period.

Non-Moving (N) = Items that are not issued/used for more than certain duration.

FSN classification helps to establish and organise proper warehouse layout by locating all the fast moving items near the dispatch area to reduce the handling efforts. Management can also focus on the non-moving items to make decisions as to whether they are in needs in the future or they can be disposed. This helps to improve organisation's capital utilisation and cash flow.

(f) SOS Classification (Seasonal, Off Seasonal)

Seasonal items that are available only for a limited period should be stocked for meeting the needs of the full year, for example, fruits and vegetables.

Off seasonal items are those available throughout the year. For example, back-to-school and summer items are examples of these clearance products.

(g) XYZ Analysis

XYZ analysis classifies items into X, Y, Z categories by consumption rate of high, medium, low respectively. The grouping of ABC and XYZ analysis gives a stock strategy matrix that is frequently used in inventory optimisation.

(h) Stock on Hold, Scrap and Obsolete

In warehouse operations, for easiness of identification, inventory is also classified as –

- **Stock on Hold:** Inventory that is frozen or blocked and cannot be released for sale or consumption.

- **Scrap and Obsolete:** Scrap category is categorised by materials that are rejected, damaged, not usable or those that have crossed the shelf life, and expiry date.

(i) Harmonised System Nomenclature

The Harmonised Commodity Description and Coding System generally referred to as "Harmonised System" or simply "HS" is a multipurpose international product classification of traded products developed by the World Customs Organisation (WCO). It came into effect in 1988 and it consists of over 5000 commodity groups. Each group is given an identification code of six digits. HS code is used by about 200 countries for imports and exports.

Example 1: An example of a product classified according to its form would be **Rice**. The classification will also change depending on whether the rice is with husk, semi milled or milled. Rice is classified under the Header 1006 Rice. Rice with husk (paddy or rough) will be coded as 100610 and Rice which is semi milled or wholly milled (polished or unpolished) will be coded as 100620

Example 2: HS Code 01 Live animals (Chapter 01)

0104	Live sheep and goats
010410	Live sheep
010420	Live goats

Applications of HS Codes

1. Collection of internal taxes
2. Transport tariffs and statistics
3. Monitoring of controlled goods (for example, wastes, narcotics, chemical weapons, ozone layer depleting substances, endangered species)
4. Areas of custom controls and procedures, consisting of risk assessment, information technology and compliance.

6. Order Processing

A customer order is the message that sets the supply chain process in motion. Order processing starts with the receiving of a customer's order and ends with the final delivery of goods to him along with transfer of title. In other words, order processing is a set of activities for receiving, recording, assembling of products for dispatch to fill the customer order. The customer order cycle time is the total time consumed in order preparation and its transmittal, order receipt, order entry, order processing, warehouse picking and packing, preparation of invoices and shipping documents, transportation and delivery and unloading of goods at the customer's end. Order processing is key to achievement of logistics and supply chain objective in terms of achievement of required level of customer service, reduction in order cycle time, point-to-point information apart from fulfillment of legal formalities for movement and transfer of title.

7. Warehousing

Warehousing function is very critical as it acts as a node in linking the material flows between the supplier and customer. Warehousing gives time and place utility for raw materials, industrial goods, and finished products, enabling organisations to use customer support as a vibrant and value-adding competitive tool.

Definition and Importance

Robert Hughes has defined warehouse as *"Warehousing is a set of activities that are involved in receiving and storing of goods and preparing them for reshipment."*

Warehouses are the godowns for keeping and storing goods at various points along the distribution network to improve availability of material to customers and to reduce transportation costs. In this process of storage, warehouses are required to perform many operations like receiving the incoming material; moving them, putting in appropriate locations of storage areas; protecting and preserving them in a scientific and systematic manner for the maintenance of their original value, quality and usefulness; gathering material as required by customers or for transfer to other locations; repacking the material; delivering the material to customers or dispatching for onward transportation; keeping records of material in stock.

Warehouses perform two important roles

(a) **Central Location:** A warehouse gives a central location for receiving, storing and distributing products. As each inbound batch arrives, liability for the goods shifts to the warehouse personnel. Products are checked against delivery challans, examinations and sampling is done, it is then arranged and dispatched to their temporary storage location.

(b) **Value Added Operations:** Warehousing raises the utility value of goods by giving a way to have the exact products available at the right place in the right time. Consolidation of orders, packaging, product mixing and cross-docking in the warehouse also gives importance to the overall logistics system.

Process and Function of Warehouse

(a) **Preparing a Receiving Report**: On receipt of the goods or even services from a supplier, it is important that the shipment is checked to ensure that the correct quantity and quality was received. A receiving report must be instantly completed which indicates that –

- The date the material was received or service was performed; whether the delivery was on time.
- The quantity of material received and whether any discrepancies exist when compared with the packing list.
- Whether the quality of the material meets specifications.
- The names of the personnel who performed these checks.

This receiving report can be of great help to the bookkeeper in maintaining accurate records, and when paying the bills.

(b) **Inspection of Goods:** At the time of receiving goods, inspection may include close inspection and functionality testing of the acquired items, or may include counting units received and performing a surface inspection to evaluate whether any damage may have taken place in transit.

Goods may be subject to –

- 100 percent inspection.
- Sampling – various types of sampling may be used (for example, single, double, or sequential).
- No inspection (for example, if a supplier is certified through the technique below) under Clause B-5, Certificate of Conformance.

(c) **Valuation of Goods:** When the vendor sends the invoice for a particular delivery, the value invoiced is considered as a latest price than the one fixed in the purchase order when it was formed, **possibly** a few months ago. Usually, people receive the invoice after the goods. As a result, the value of the delivery is not known at the time of goods receipt. In this case, the value estimate is based on the purchase order. The value of the goods receipt is measured based on the amount received and the net order price.

(d) **Storage of Goods:** Correct and secure storage is of the important functions of a warehouse. **Non-perishable** items are consolidated, repackaged and dispatched from the central storage warehouse. Vegetables and fruits need cold storage warehouses.

(e) **Order Processing:** Order processing is the term usually used to describe the procedure or the workflow **connected** with picking, packing and delivery of goods to the shipping carrier.

(f) Receipt of Orders

- **Order generation:** To receive an order from a customer or a channel member order.
- **Order entry:** Checking accuracy of order received, availability of requested items, billing.

(g) Order Picking

- Order picking can be done manually, automated or by robots/RFID methods.
- Order picking is an important aspect within any warehouse. It forms as much as 55% of operation costs within any distribution centre, compared to shipping, storage and receiving stages and has a direct impact on customer satisfaction levels.

(h) Inspection of Goods before Delivery

- Checking the selected items against purchase order.
- Checking for the quality and quantity of items.

(i) Dispatch and Shipments

- Preparation of bills of lading/waybill.
- Loading goods on trucks/goods carriers/containers.

(j) Updating Records of Inventory: Once the goods have been loaded, inventory database must be updated for efficient inventory management. It can be done manually for small stores or automatically by a software system.

Important Factors for the Efficient Management of a Warehouse

(a) Inventory accuracy: Maintaining accurate information about the stock is very crucial. Different methods of inventory counting are applied. Inventories can be calculated using EOQs (Economic Order Quantity) or ABC Analysis for storing optimal levels of inventory.

(b) Inventory location: Storing goods and stocks with proper arrangements and in a well-organised manner helps to locate the stock easily when an order needs to be picked.

(c) Space utilisation/warehouse layout: Utilising warehouse space for optimal usage which is easy for unloading, storing and loading for dispatch needs proper planning of a warehouse.

(d) Picking optimisation: Order picking is one of the important tasks of warehousing. Orders can be manually picked in a small warehouse. In case of a huge production facility, automation plays an important role. To meet the challenges, forklifts, conveyors, barcodes and RFIDs are being used.

(e) **Order processing and dispatch:** Once the order is received goods are picked from their storage locations and ready for dispatch. The order is documented and the goods are loaded. For internal or interstate transportation three important documents are necessary.

- The Bill of Lading/B/L or BoL
- Freight Bill
- Terms of Sale (FOB Free on Board or C&F, that is, Cost and Freight).

(f) **Warehouse security:** Security from theft, pilferages, fire-breakouts, and roof leakages and goods damages are special areas where warehouses need to address. Losses and damages can incur additional cost.

(g) **Globalisation:** With globalisation and increase in consumer markets, warehouses need to be automated and the dispatch of goods has to be efficient and prompt. This is achieved with skilled manpower, automations in the warehouse, and use of information technology.

(h) **E-commerce:** With the advent of E-commerce, more and more customers tend to make purchases online. The delivery time demanded is also very short, hence, the need for break-bulk and consolidation warehouses.

Warehouse Planning and Ideal Layout

Planning a warehouse is very important for proper storage and materials handling. While planning a warehouse, the following factors are to be considered –

- Plan for good space utilisation
- Use maximum height of the building
- Minimise aisle space
- Use an effective storage plan
- Plan for efficient materials handling flow
- Use efficient materials-handling equipment
- The throughput of the pallets should be considered
- Plan for productivity
- Specify the umbrella
- Use one-story facilities
- Move goods in a straight line
- Future-proof the design

Ideal Layout Plan

Layout of a warehouse depends on the projected material handling system and needs development of a floor plan to facilitate product flow. It is hard to simplify the warehouse layouts since they are developed to fit specific needs.

Following points need to be considered while planning a warehouse layout –

- Concrete materials
- Earthwork
- Site utilities
- Roofing

- **Roofing**

Columnar trusses on RCC columns to support pre-painted polyester coated sheets/GI/galvalume. Fibre glass (Translucent) for about 2% of the roofing area for natural light.

Pre-engineered steel structures with pre-painted polyester coated sheets with turbo ventilators, translucent; should be used in warehouses.

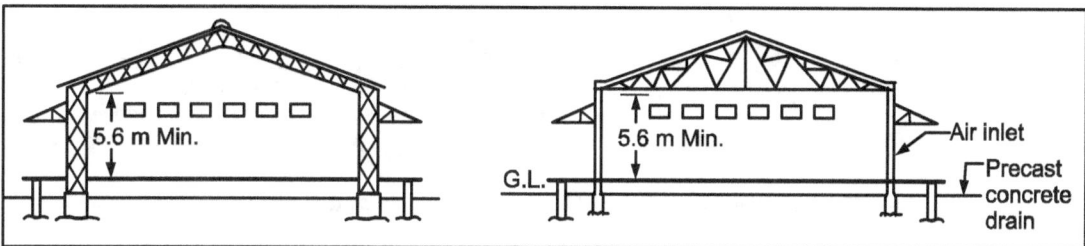

| Steel Frame Trusses (Span 21.5 mm) Cable Roof | Conventional Structural Steel or Tubular Trusses (Span 21.5 m) |

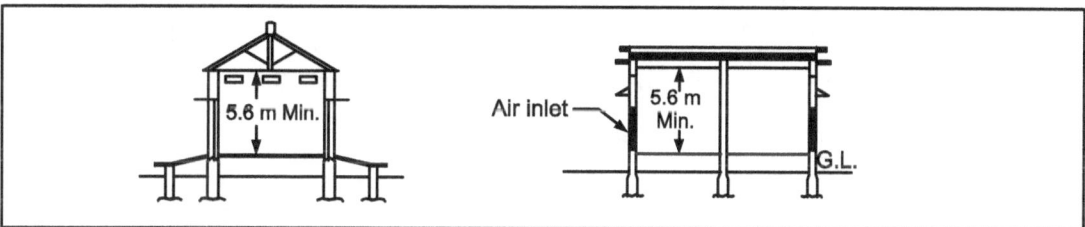

| Timber Trusses (Span 8 m) | RCC Flat Roof (Span or each bay 6 m) |

Fig. 4.6: Different types of Warehouse Roofing

- **Flooring:** Flooring should be damp proof, rigid, durable and free from cracks.
- **Fire protection:** Use of suitable fire safety and protection systems.
- **Pilferage/theft protection.**
- **Use of pallets and other materials handling equipments.**

If pallets are to be used, then the first step is to decide the pallet size.

The most common pallet sizes are 40 X 48 inches and 32 X 40 inches.

The packages to be kept on the pallet and the associated patterns will settle on, to a certain extent, the size of pallet best suited to the function. Regardless of the size ultimately selected, management must adopt one size for the total operation.

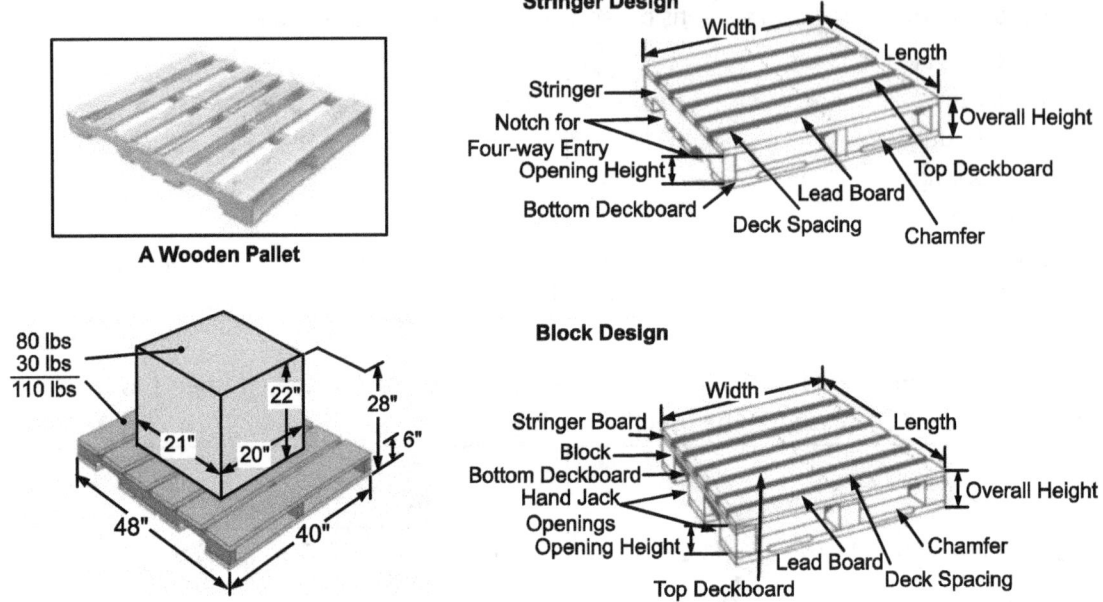

Fig. 4.7: Wooden Pallet Dimensions and Load Bearing

Table 4.1

Sr. No.	Type of Aisle / Pallet	Accessibility
1.	Standard Aisle Pallet Racking	100% access to every pallet
2.	Standard Aisle Double Deep	FILO (First In Last Out)
3.	Narrow Aisle Pallet Racking	100% access to every pallet
4.	Push Back	FILO (First In Last Out)
5.	Drive In	FILO (First In Last Out)
6.	Mobile	100% access to every pallet
7.	Pallet Live	FILO (First In Last Out)

The Warehouse Buildings

1. **Office building:** Office space must be provided as per the requirement of the office staff and customers along with all the facilities of toilets, drinking water etc.

2. **Security measures for the site perimeter:** Warehouses have external walls and fences. Even if there is a physical fence, there are practically infinite ways of entering a premise that makes perimeter security extremely difficult. However, by combining entry detections systems, CCTVs, and security systems the ideal "immediate support" is achieved.

3. **Controlling the access to the road:** For the purpose of discovering unregistered cars, recording the time of arrival and departure, shortening the admission process after getting out of the car, etc., recognition systems that screen car number plates are becoming more common.

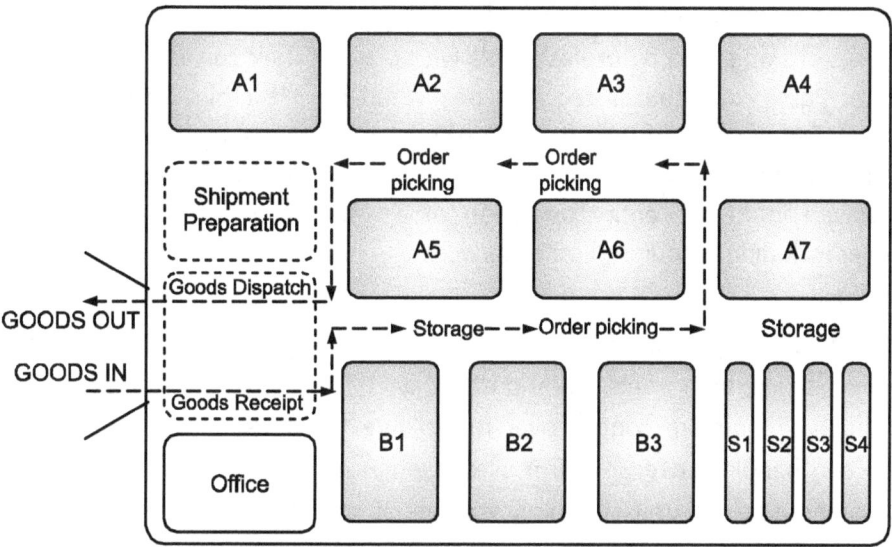

Fig. 4.8: Ideal Layout for A,B,C Category of Goods

A1 – A7: "A" Category of goods B1 – B3 – "B" Category of goods S1 – S4 - "C" Category of goods

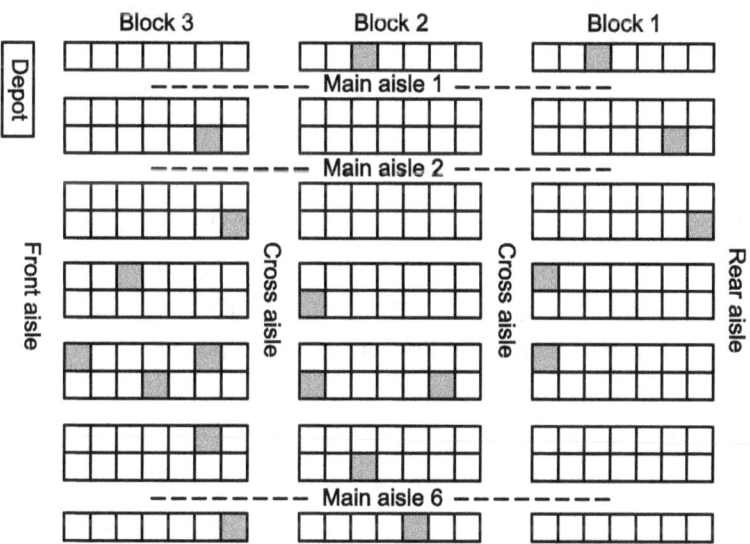

Fig. 4.9: Ideal Warehouse Design for Efficient Order Picking

Different Types of Warehouses

(a) Public Warehouse

A public warehouse is a storage location where any firm can store their goods. The warehouse owner is responsible for fulfilling the obligations arising from the placing of goods under the customs warehouse procedure.

Public warehouses are operated by professionals who provide their services to the large number of firms. Public warehouses can also be owned by 3PL (Third Party Logistics service providers). Fee is charged for providing warehouse services. A firm may choose the warehousing, keeping in view the location and freight rates. There is no fixed investment involved in it. The entire operation of a warehouse is managed by the warehouse owner including labour and other services.

(b) Private Warehouse

A private warehouse is operated by the organisation engaged in production or a distribution channel member. The warehouse may be owned or leased by the organisation and has complete control over its activities. It is used when a firm has special storage and handling needs. A firm uses it when it product is moving to large areas. These warehouses are used for high volume of goods. The major benefits of private warehousing include control, flexibility, cost, and other intangible benefits.

(c) Bonded Warehouse

Bonded warehouses are licensed by the government to store goods prior to payment of taxes, customs duties, octroi charges etc. Government wields very tight control over all actions in and out of the warehouse facility. In bonded warehouses ad-valorem are applicable, that is, the charges include the cost of overheads of supervision charges, insurance premium and different kind of mixed expenditure.

(d) Government Warehouse

Warehouses fully owned by government and leased to public on certain terms and conditions. The government warehouse facilitates storage and handling, import-export warehousing facility, clearing and forwarding facility, etc. Government warehouse includes food grain warehouses, industrial warehousing, custom bonded warehouses, container freight stations, inland clearance depots and air cargo complexes.

(e) Cold Storage Warehouse

Cold storage warehouses are provided for perishable goods like fruits, vegetables, milk and milk products. Cold storage preserves agricultural products and refrigeration helps in eliminating sprouting, rotting and insect damage. Several perishable products require a storage temperature with a negative cold temperature as low as -25°C.

(f) Consolidation Warehouse

Consolidation warehouses join the logistical flow of many small shipments to a particular market area. A single company uses consolidation warehousing, or many companies may join together and use a for-hire consolidation service.

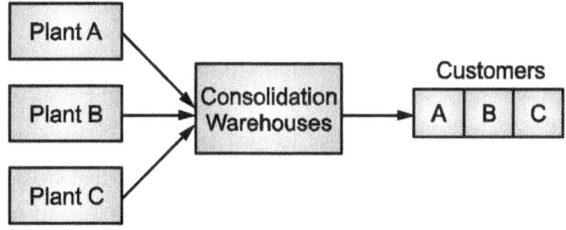

Fig. 4.10: A Consolidated Warehouse

(g) Break Bulk Warehouses

- Break bulk warehouse operations are same as consolidation except that no storage is performed. A break bulk operation obtains combined customer orders from producers and transports them to individual customers.
- The break bulk warehouse splits individual orders and organises it for local delivery. Because the long-distance transportation movement is a big shipment, transport costs are lesser and there is less trouble in tracking.

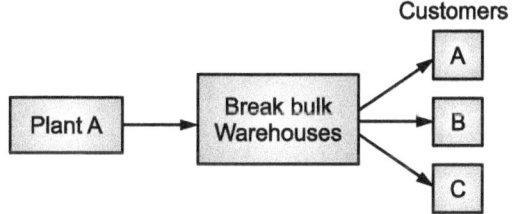

Fig. 4.11: A Break Bulk Warehouse

(h) Special Economic Zone or Free Zone

A special economic zone is not a building, but a location. This location is a geographical location that has been created for receiving goods for shipments. These areas are called as bonded logistics parks. These parks are economical and cost effective.

(i) Warehouses for Reverse Logistics

More and more organisations are focusing on the management of Returns of Goods or Reverse Logistics. A dedicated service for storage of returned goods demands for a warehouse specially used for reverse logistics process. A warehouse facility is equipped with the entire infrastructure for managing receiving goods returns and dispatching to the source of origin.

Warehousing in International Logistics

Warehousing plays an important role in international supply chain and logistics. Order picking consumes about 55% of warehousing activity. Warehousing is an important activity in international logistics. The location of the warehouse and order picking efficiency play an important role.

(a) Cross-docking

In cross-docking, materials are unloaded from inbound transport system like a truck, railroad or semi-trailer. These materials are then directly loaded into outbound trucks, trailers, or rail without any or little storage in between. The warehouse just acts as a platform for unloading and loading of materials. Cross-docking may also be used for changing the transportation system, or for sorting of materials which are meant to be shipped to different destinations, or to consolidate materials from different origins into containers or other transport system.

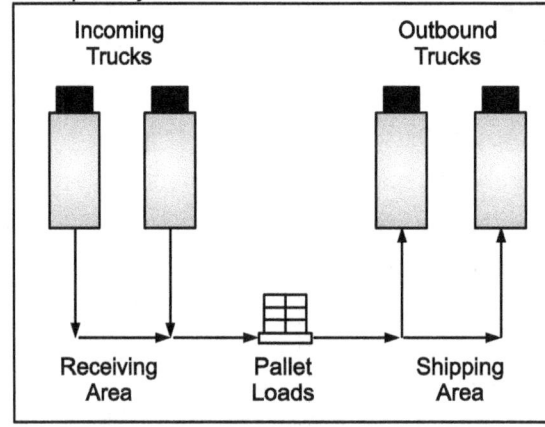

(a) Cross-Docking

(b) Cross-Docking

Fig. 4.12

(b) Marshalling

Marshalling is defined as bringing goods for dispatch at a dockyard or a shipyard. Goods are first brought to a marshalling yard that is a place where goods trains and other loads (such as wagons coming in from nearby goods shed) are received, sorted out according to a plan, and dispatched via another means of transport like a goods train.

Containerisation is a system of intermodal (different modes of transportation) freight transport using shipping containers. The containers have standardised dimensions like 20 feet long × 8 feet wide × 8 feet 6 inches high or 9 feet 6 inches high for high cube containers. Once the containers are loaded with goods, they are transported by means of container carriers.

Equipment	Interior Dimension	Door Opening	Tare Weight	Cubic Capacity	Payload
 20" Dry Container	L : 5.919 m 19' 5" W : 2.34 m 7' 8" H : 2.380 m 7' 9.5"	W : 2.286 m 7' 6" H : 2.278 m 7' 5.5"	1.900 kg 2.189 lbs	33.0 cbm 1,116 cft	122,100 kg 148,721 lbs
 40" Dry Container	L : 12.051 m 39' 6.5" W : 2.34 m 7' 8" H : 2.380 m 7' 9.5"	W : 2.286 m 7' 6" H : 2.278 m 7' 5.5"	3,084 kg 6,799 lbs	67.3 cbm 2,377 cft	27,397 kg 60,401 lbs
 40" HQ Container	L : 12.056 m 39' 6.5" W : 2.347 m 7' 8.25" H : 2.380 m 8' 9.5"	W : 2.286 m 7' 6" H : 2.278 m 7' 5.5"	2,900 kg 6,393 lbs	75.0 cbm 2.684 cft	29,600 kg 61,256 lbs
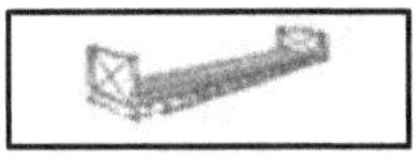 20" Flat Rack Container	L : 5.702 m 18' 8.5" W : 2.438 m 8' H : 2.327 m 7' 7.5"		2,330 kg 5,137 lbs		25,220 kg 55,600 lbs
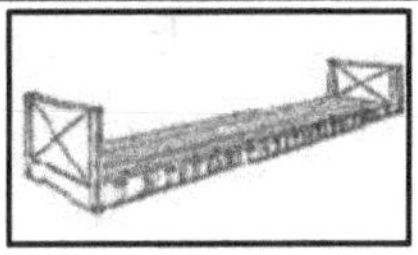 40" Flat Rack Container	L : 11.820 m 38' 9.25" W : 2.148 m 7' H : 2.095 m 6' 10.5"		5,260 kg 11,596 lbs		28,390 kg 62,590 lbs

Fig. 4.13: Different Types of Containers and their Payloads

Put Away

Put away is an internal logistics process from receipt of goods up to when it is stocked in its final destination within a warehouse. The processes include inspection, break bulk, determining the appropriate destination, preparing the destination location, transporting the items, and physically stocking them in an area where it is ready to be dispatched.

4.2.8 Factors affecting the Evaluation and Growth of Integrated Logistics

- Growth of the consumer awareness and the marketing concept
- Introduction of the computer
- Globalisation of business and the development of world trade blocks
- Growth of JIT manufacturing, supply management, transportation and electronic data interchange (EDI) in the 1980s and 1990s

4.2.9 3PL and 4PL Logistics

3PL or a third party logistics company is a company that works with the shipping companies in order to manage another company's logistics operations department. 3PL companies are dedicated service providers or companies that take outsourced work of another company for its logistical needs.

3PL third party logistics providers provide integrating operations like inventory management, packaging, warehousing, cross-docking, transportation services and freight forwarding. These services are customised as per the customer's specific needs.

Types of 3PL Providers

1. **Standard 3PL:** These companies pick orders, pack, perform warehousing and distribution functions
2. **Service Developer 3PL:** These companies provide value added services such as shipment tracking, tracing, cross-docking and specific packaging.
3. **Customer Adapter 3PL:** These 3PLs take over the operations of a firm's logistics upon a customer's request.
4. **Customer Developer 3PL:** The 3PL integrates itself with the company, and finally takes over the entire logistics operation.

4PL provider is an integrator that collaborates resources, capabilities and technologies to run complete supply chain solutions. 4PL or fourth party logistics company takes over the logistics section of a business. This could be the entire process, or a part of a business that is crucial to the business, for example, a mobile phone importer. The main function is to import mobiles; however, they need to have accessories and spare parts for these mobiles. A 4PL would manage the total logistic operations for the spare parts business also.

Functions provided by a 4PL company

- Procurement
- Storage
- Distribution
- Processes

The important difference between 3PLs and 4PLs is the 3PL targets an activity or a logistical function, whereas the 4PL manages the entire logistics process. A 4PL may also manage the 3PL.

4.3 Marketing & Physical Distribution

The working of the economic system, by which goods and services are supplied to consumers, involves four basic market functions **– production, distribution, exchange and consumption**. Logistics assists in the efficient performance of each of these functions. The role of the production is such that it transfers raw materials into finished goods (it creates form utility). While doing so, in support of the production process, a long and an intricate logistical chain is activated to bring the material together in a proper quality and quantity, and at the right time. The function of distribution places raw material in the hands of the producers and finished goods in the hands of the consumers, when and where needed (that is, it creates time and place utility). Transportation plays a significant part in this chain, but getting goods where and when involves much more than just the services of carrying products from here to there.

4.3.1 Definition of Physical Distribution

Effective physical distribution involves addressing the issues of inventory, transportation, warehousing, storage, and communication. It thus, bridges the gap between the consumer demand and the producer supply, although the consumer can include both, the individual user of a product and the user of raw materials or finished goods produced by someone else.

Physical distribution is concerned with the set of activities consisting of efficient movement of finished goods from the end of the production process to the consumer. It is an element of a larger process known as "distribution," which includes wholesale, retail marketing, and the physical movement of products. Physical distribution takes place within various wholesaling and retailing distribution channels. Some of the important decision areas of physical distribution are customer service, inventory control, materials handling, protective packaging, order procession, transportation, warehouse site selection, and warehousing.

Physical distribution is defined as –

1. Handling, movement, and storage of goods from the point of its origin till the point of its consumption or use via various channels of distribution.

2. Physical distribution is the art and science of determining requirements, acquiring them, distributing them and finally maintaining them in an operationally ready condition for their entire life.

Physical Distribution Management

1. The term 'physical distribution management' is employed in manufacturing and commerce to describe the broad range of activities like freight, warehousing, material handling, protective packing, inventory control, selection of site for various activities, marketing, forecasting, concerned with the efficient movement of finished products from the end of production line till the consumer, and in some cases, includes the movement of raw materials from the sources of supply till the beginning of the production line.

2. 'Physical distribution management' is specifically concerned with the flow of goods through the economic system.

4.3.2 Importance of Physical Distribution

Physical distribution is of great importance because of its various functions such as location analysis, transportation, material handling, warehousing, packing, order processing, packaging, inventory control, and customer sales service.

The physical distribution purpose, with the help of various networks of channel partners, adds value to the selling function by providing time, place, and possession utilities to the consumer. Time utility is making the product available 'when' a consumer needs it. Making the product accessible 'where' he desires is called as "place utility". It is possession utility, when the consumer buying the product, gets the rights transferred to him at a time and place suitable to him. The channels, for providing the possession utility, shorten the transaction by maintaining contacts with their upstream partners like Carry and Forwarding Agents (C&FA) or even the company. Upstream channel members are closer to the producer and the downstream channel members are closer to the consumers. The distributors, wholesalers, and the retailers are the downstream channels involved here. The transactions concerned here could be of order taking, order communication, order processing, delivery of goods, and collection of payments. The downstream channel partners, in co-ordination with the upstream partners take care of these transactions.

The importance of physical distribution can be studied as follows –

1. **Minimisation of distribution costs:** A thorough study of transportation and storage costs can be done using the efficient structure of physical distribution. This lessens the distribution cost without adversely affecting the level of customer service and satisfaction.

2. **Better customer service:** Efficiently done physical distribution offer customers the service they look forward to, that is, having the products accessible to the customer's demand or desire. For example, quick services such as installation, repair, and spare parts from the supplier can produce accelerated sales and profits.

3. **Increase in sales volume:** The main aim of physical distribution is to expand sales volume through different inventory management techniques. It proves profitable to both, the consumer as well as the manufacturers. On assurance of regular supply, the consumers can store lesser amount of goods. However, at the same time, because of low inventory and distribution costs, the manufacturers produce more with an equal amount of finance.

4. **Stabilisation of prices:** Efficient physical distribution systems, through coordinating demand and supply, help in stabilising the prices of products in the market. If the demand exceeds supply, additional supplies can be released from the warehouses. Conversely, if supply exceeds, the produced goods can be kept in the warehouses with the intention of controlling the fall in prices.

5. **Effective product planning:** The existing physical distribution system, like the type and nature of transportation and storage services need to be thought about while deciding on a product. This aids in effective product planning.

6. **Size of inventory:** If the existing transport facilities are efficient enough, the size of inventory can be kept small. In contrast, if the storage and transport facilities are ineffective, the size of the inventory can be large to store stocks of raw material for ensuring continuous and smooth flow of production.

7. **Channel of distribution:** The existing physical distribution system affects the channel of distribution. In case the product demands storage, it should be sold through wholesalers who possess their own storage amenities. If the firm decides to run its own warehouses, the places of their location should be verified.

4.3.3 Participants in Physical Distribution Process

In order to introduce their products to public some businesses need "mediators". Market intermediaries, are parts of the supply chain connecting the manufacturer and the ultimate consumer. These "mediators" or "middlemen" keep the distribution channel open and flowing. They generate time, place and possession profits for manufacturers by ensuring market coverage, reducing market coverage cost, rising availability of cash flow through financing and credit, providing storage space, ensuring availability of products regularly, linking the manufacturer with the customer, and growing customer ease.

1. **Wholesalers:** Basically, wholesalers are businessmen who independently own businesses. These intermediaries purchase goods from manufacturers and take title

to the goods. Then, they resell those goods to retailers or organisations. Full-service wholesalers provide services like storage, order processing, and delivery. They actively participate in promotional support and normally, although they handle products from quite a few producers they specialise only in a specific product. Limited-service wholesalers, as compared, offer few services and often serve as drop shippers, wherein the retailer passes the customer's order information to the wholesaler, who then packages the product and ships it straight to the customer.

2. **Distributors:** Distributors are chosen by manufacturers who buy product for resale. They are like retailers, similar to wholesalers and are privately owned by operated companies. These mediators usually work with several businesses and cover a particular geographic area or market sector. They execute several functions like selling, delivery, extending credit, and maintaining inventory. Though the main role of a distributor is quick access to goods and after-sales service, they typically focus on a narrower product choice to make sure better product knowledge and customer service.

3. **Retailers:** Retailers work directly with the customer. Intermediaries who work with wholesalers and distributors often provide services in one location, of various products manufactured by various producers. Customers compare and pick up items of their choice even if they are related but are not manufactured by the same producer, such as jam and cheese. Purchasing grains directly from a manufacturer would be lengthy and costly for a customer, but doing the same from a local retail "mediator" would prove easy, quick and convenient.

4. **Agents and Brokers:** Agents and brokers trade their products or product services for a commission or a percentage of the sales price or product revenue. These mediators have legal right to act on behalf of the manufacturer or producer. Agents as well as brokers, execute less service than wholesalers and distributors. They never take title to the products they manage. Bringing the buyers and sellers together is the primary function of the agents and brokers. For example, real estate agents and insurance agents who sell items, do not own them, instead they get a commission for putting buyers and sellers together. Agent intermediaries, also act as manufacturer's representatives who sell various non-competing goods and organise for their delivery to customers in a specific geographic area.

4.4 Marketing Channels

Chain of intermediaries, each passing the product down the chain to the next organisation, before it finally reaches the consumer or end-user, is known as the 'distribution chain' or the 'distribution channel.' The distribution channel is a process of transferring the products or services from producer to customer or end-user. Channels of distribution are nothing but marketing channels.

The most important aim of these channels is delivery. Physical distribution is the only process through which public and private goods and services are made accessible for use or consumption. Procedures of such goods and services are able of generate only the form or structural utility related to their products and services. The production organisation is done in such a skilful way that the products they produce can not only be seen, analysed but also sold in the market. They are called mediators, because they link the production branch and the consumption branch and provide arrangement of a wide variety of distribution oriented institutions and agencies. The roles of mediators are as follows –

- Mediators improve the efficiency of the process.
- They help in the appropriate planning of the routes of the transactions.
- They help in the searching process.
- They assist in the sorting process.

4.4.1 Definitions of Marketing Channel

A channel, as explained above is a passageway that allows the happening of certain processes. Marketing, on the other hand, is an exchange process. The term "marketing channel", represents a system that contributes to the exchange process by covering the distance between the producer and the consumer.

1. **William J. Stanton**, *"A channel of distribution or a marketing channel is a path traced in the direct or indirect transfer of the title to a product as it moves from a product to ultimate consumers or industrial users."*

2. **Beckman**, *"The course taken in the transfer of the title to a commodity constitutes its channel of distribution. It is the route taken by the title to a product in its passage from its first owner, an agricultural producer or a manufacturer, as the case may be, to the last owner, the ultimate consumer or the business user."*

3. A channel of distribution or marketing channel is a structure of intra-company organisation, units and intra-company agents and dealers, wholesalers and retailers, through which, a commodity product or service is marketed.

4. **Stern and El-Ansary,** *"Marketing channels are defined us sets of interdependent organisations involved in the process of making a product or service available for use or consumption."*

5. Marketing channels are defined as set of pathways, a product or service follows production, reaching to the final end-user for its consumption through the purchasing process.

6. Marketing channels are defined as a group of exchange relationships, which create customer value in acquiring, consuming, and disposing of products and services.

7. **American Management Association** *"Marketing channels are defined as an organised network of agencies and institutions, which in combination, perform all the activities required to link producers with users to accomplish the marketing task."*

From the above definitions, it can be concluded that marketing channels are important ingredients of the distribution as a process of taking the product or service from its production centre to the consumption centre. In this process, marketing channels provide sufficient value to the customers and provide a competitive advantage to the producer.

4.4.2 Importance of Marketing Channels

In light of the competitive markets characterised by the diminishing lines of product differentiation and heavy competition in all business sectors, one of the most important factors that decides business success or failure is market penetration. This has really extended the role of marketing channels from just serving the markets to making the markets, by converting potential markets into profitable orders. The following points elaborate the importance of marketing channels by virtue of their responsibilities.

1. The foremost role of a marketing channel is to bridge the gap between the production and the consumption process. These gaps are classified as time gaps, space gaps, quantity gaps, and variety gaps.

2. Marketing channels ensure the smooth flow of products from the producer to the end-user, as they bridge the gaps.

3. Marketing channels reduce the amount of time and expenditure of the manufacturer, by reducing the number of contact points between the point of production and the point of consumption.

4. They help the manufacturers, by providing them with updates of customer requirements from time to time.

5. They also participate actively in product promotion through efficient product displays and other techniques like discounts, promotional schemes, and so on.

6. The marketing channels often influence other marketing decisions. The types of product, nature of its demand, etc. govern the pattern of marketing channel adopted by the firm. Similarly, decisions on sales force, its type, size, etc. depend on the nature and size of the adopted marketing channel. The adopted channel's pattern influences the pattern of the sales person's operations and has a sizeable impact on the size and complexity of the marketing department of the firm. Marketing channel decisions usually bind the firm with long-term commitments.

4.4.3 Different Forms of Channels

Since the channel arrangement that exists is wide, it is difficult to generalise the structure of channels across all industries. However, distribution channels are usually of two types –

(A) Direct marketing channel or zero level channel.

(B) Indirect marketing channel.

(A) Direct Marketing Channel or Zero Level Channel

This distribution system transfers goods from the producer directly to the consumer. It has no mediators.

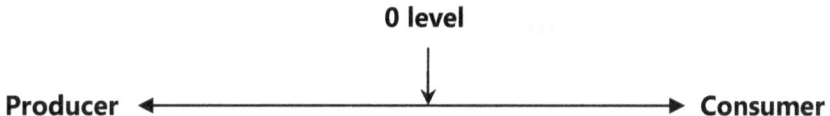

(B) Indirect Marketing Channel

This can be further divided into following four categories

1. **One level channel:** This type of channel has only one mediator between the producer and the consumer. The mediator can be a retailer or a distributor.

If the mediator is a distributor, this type of channel is used in particular products like sewing machine, toaster, cupboard or medicinal products.

2. **Two level channel:** This type of channel has two mediators, that is, wholesaler or distributor and retailer.

3. **Three level channel:** This type of channel has three mediators, that is, distributor, wholesaler and retailer. This method is also used for convenience products.

4. **Four level channel:** This type of channel has four mediators, that is, agent, distributor, wholesaler, and retailer. It is same as the former two. This type of channel is used for consumer durable products also.

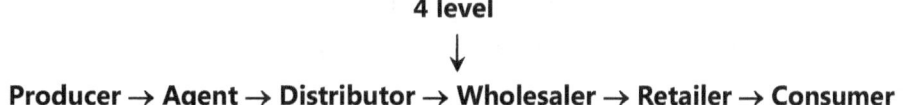

There is no watertight classification of channels. Some different types of channels are also likely. Different types of distribution or marketing channels rely on the nature of the product and services.

4.4.4 Unconventional Channels

Unconventional means are not conventional or traditional. They are very different from the routine ones. Hence, unconventional marketing channels are the channels used for marketing or distribution that are not routinely used. The desire and need to market products differently yet effectively, results in alliances with less than conventional marketing channels. Unconventional channels are tapped to sell products. For example, guerrilla-marketing approach can be used for particular projects, to maximise efficiency.

The definition of guerrilla marketing is, 'an unconventional system of promotions that relies on time, energy, and imagination rather than a big marketing budget'. Typically, guerrilla marketing campaigns are unexpected and unconventional, potentially interactive, and consumers are targeted in unexpected places. The objective of guerrilla marketing is to create a unique, engaging, and thought-provoking concept to generate a buzz that would consequently turn viral. The term was coined and defined by **Jay Conrad Levinson** in his book **Guerrilla Marketing**. People like and ascribe to the idea of unconventional approaches, but there are times, where a big fat branding and marketing campaign is required to achieve certain marketing goals. The company, since it lacks the resources to blow out a big- time brand message, continues to grow using tactics and channels that are affordable.

Unconventional Marketing Tactics

Marketing demands a big deal of creative skills and innovative ideas to develop activities and programmes that would capture the attention of the consumers. Marketing, being competitive in nature, marketers in many companies try non-traditional and exceptional forms and means of marketing approaches. These unconventional marketing strategies are known as **guerrilla marketing**. Guerrilla marketing refers to exceptional and unusual methods used for performing marketing activities with an aim of attaining maximum outputs from minimum resources and expenses.

This being unconventional forms of marketing, it makes good use of creativity and innovative breakthroughs in providing public awareness about the products and services. Guerrilla marketing benefits small businesses especially those whose resources are not readily accessible.

Various Types of Unconventional Marketing

A number of unconventional marketing techniques are effective and creative making it an option for many marketers. Guerrilla marketing relies on time, energy, and creativity instead of vast marketing budget. Such techniques are interactive and take place at unusual places.

1. **Undercover marketing**: As the term implies, it involves promotional approach that is subtle where customers are not aware that they are being targeted or being marketed upon. It is also called as buzz marketing or stealth marketing.

2. **Buzz marketing:** It is basically word-of-mouth marketing. Here, the users interact with potential consumers and highlight the product value and profits. It creates anticipation and excitement among customers about a product or service being marketed. It is often referred to as a marketing hype.

3. **Experiential marketing:** This type of unconventional marketing appeals to the emotions. An emotional attachment is developed with a certain brand, product, person, or idea.

4. **Viral marketing**: Being closely associated with buzz and stealth marketing, it makes use of social networking sites for generating brand awareness and other marketing goals like sales generation. It is undertaken through self-replicating viral approaches like by word-of-mouth or the use of internet. Video clips, e-books, interactive flash games, and even text messages are examples of viral advertisement.

5. **Ambient media marketing:** It is effective for brand name recall and is generally conducted along with conventional means of advertising. Messages or captions on the handles of supermarket carts, slogans on grocery bags, huge images on the sides of buildings, and similar conceptual ambient techniques are examples of this type of marketing.

Other examples of unconventional marketing can be grassroots marketing, wild posting campaigns, astro-turfing, and presence marketing.

Principles of Unconventional Marketing

The following are the principles of unconventional marketing –

1. Though guerrilla marketing is beneficial for small businesses, it has been largely adopted by big business entrepreneurs. It consists of minimum usage of resources and maximum usage of creativity and psychology. The basic investment here is the time, energy, and marketing creativity or imagination. Profit generated and not the sales are the main basis for the measure of business success.

2. While growing the network, target on referrals, create more interaction with existing customers, and larger transactions instead of focusing in achieving new prospects.

Co-operation and not competition is a big thing with other businesses. Being creative and imaginative in nature, it should use a blend of marketing techniques in the promotion of a product or service. Online approach is an efficient tool to empower the business.

Pros and Cons of Unconventional Marketing

Unconventional marketing gives a lot of profit to the marketers as well as the users. It is not only cost-effective form of advertisement but also focused on profits. Collaboration and co-ordination are highlighted to maximise marketing efforts. Profit generation is the major focus, as it is concentrated on the target market. Its quality of being unique and rare, attracts customers more than traditional means since anything new and creative arouses interest.

Mostly, guerrilla marketing is valuable for both, small sized as well as medium sized businesses. Hence, the cons are more of challenges. Marketers must have a deep sense of time and maximised force with unique imaginations, not to forget the fact that it works best when collaborated with other marketing activities.

4.4.5 Channels for Consumer Goods and Industrial Goods

A long-term commitment of a business towards the market influences its choice of marketing channels. The design of a marketing channel is influenced by factors like technological advancement, changing demographics, and competition. There are several dimensions for choosing a channel design, which include –

- Length of the channel – the number of mediators between the producer and the customers.
- Breadth of the channel – the number of outlets available for customers.
- Costs of selecting a particular channel.

A channel design decision is made considering the channel structure, channel intensity, and the type of intermediaries used. While channel structure refers to the number of levels of channel intermediaries, channel intensity refers to the total number of channel intermediaries required at each level. The type of intermediaries at each level may include manufacturer's sales force, manufacturer's representatives or industrial distributors.

A channel structure adopted by a company depends on the number of intermediaries it uses to distribute its products to end users. These intermediaries constitute different channel levels.

The length of a channel is different for consumer markets and industrial markets. The possible channel levels are zero level, one level, two level, and three level.

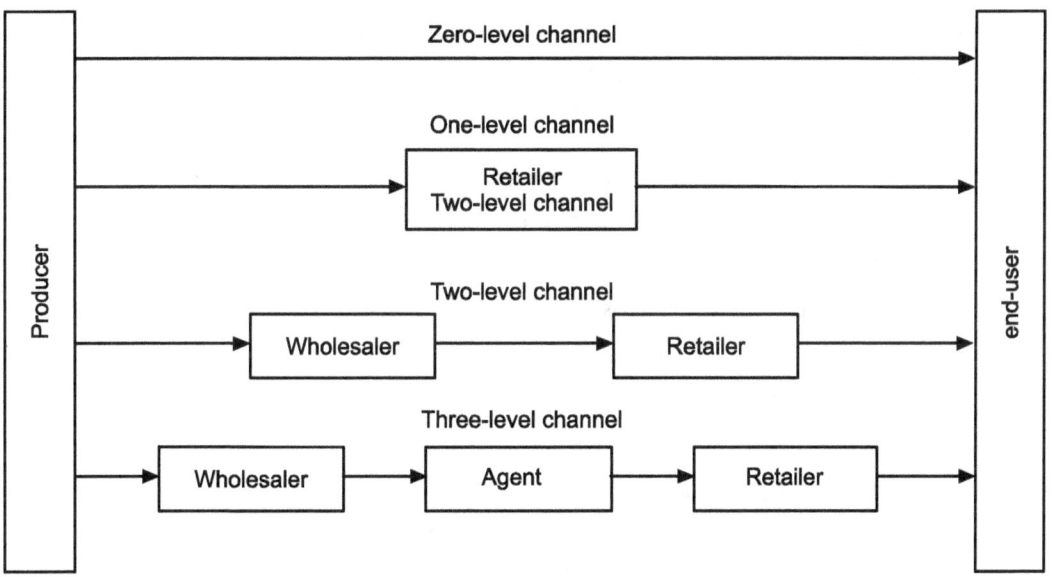

Fig. 4.14: Channel Levels in Consumer Markets

Consumer Channels

Manufacturers may reach out to consumers either directly, that is, without any means of distribution channels, or by using one or more means of distribution channel members.

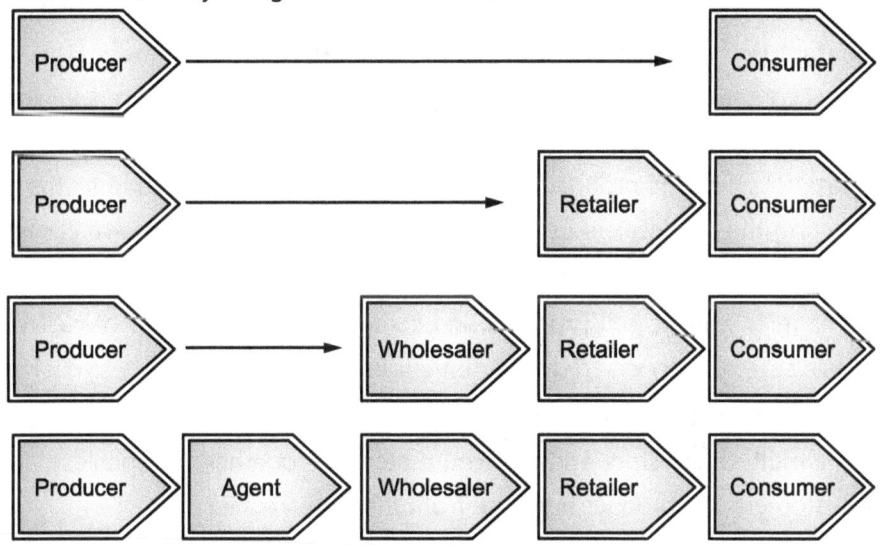

Fig. 4.15: Distribution Channels for Consumer Goods

1. **Manufacturer to consumer:** Direct marketing is personal selling, direct mail, telephone selling, and internet. Lakme cosmetics, Tupperware, Aqua Guard, and Flipkart are examples of companies engaged primarily in direct marketing.

The company interacts with the customers directly via salespersons, mail, telephone or internet and generate sales. The manufacturers directly send the products to customers.

2. **Manufacturer to retailer to consumer:** Retailers have grown in size. Growth in retailer size means that it has become cost-effective for manufacturers to provide directly to retailers rather than through wholesalers. Due to their huge buying capabilities, supermarket chains and corporate retailers apply considerable power over manufacturers. **Wal-Mart** uses its enormous retail sales to compel manufacturers to supply goods at regular intervals directly to their store at concessional price.

3. **Manufacturer to wholesaler to retailer to consumer:** The use of wholesalers makes economic sense for small retailers with limited order quantities. Wholesalers after buying in bulk from producers, sell smaller quantities to various retailers. However, in some markets, large retailers have the control to buy directly from manufacturers and thus cutting down the wholesalers. These big retailers are also capable of selling products at cheaper rate to consumers, than retailers who buy from the wholesaler. Wholesalers rule where retail oligopolies or monopolies are not dominant.

4. **Manufacturer to agent to wholesaler to retailer to consumers:** This channel is used by companies when it enters foreign markets. It does not have sufficient sales to warrant the setting up of a sales and distribution infrastructure; hence, it delegates the task of selling its product to an agent who does not take title to the goods. By contacting the wholesalers in the foreign market, the agents receive commission on sales.

Since companies want to sell products and cater to a larger number of customers, they increasingly use several channels to distribute their products.

A company's product may be found at many places, an exclusive store, in a company-owned store, a multi-brand store and a discount store all together. Companies have realised that not all customers of a product purchase from the same retailer.

Industrial Channels

Industrial channels are generally shorter than consumer channels. Direct selling is common due to closer relationship amongst the manufacturer and the customer, and due to the nature of product sold.

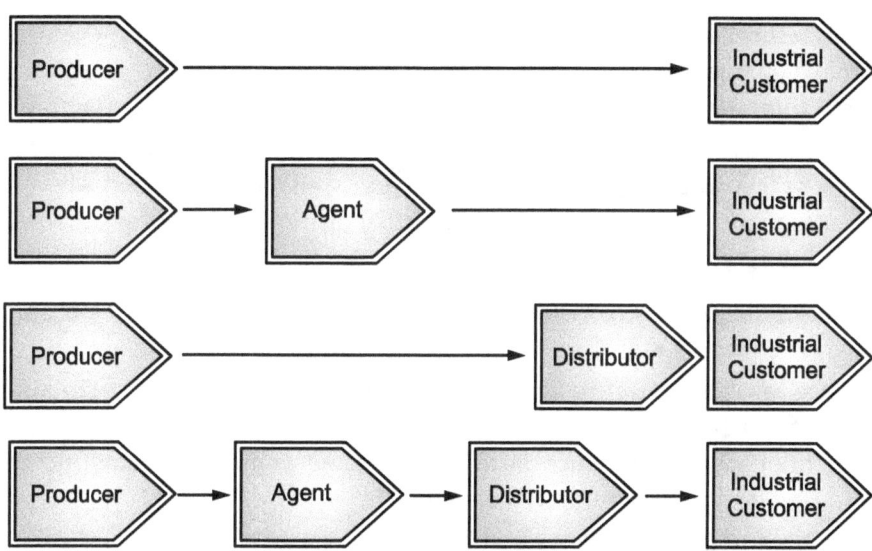

Fig. 4.16: Distribution Channels for Industrial Goods

1. **Manufacturer to Industrial Customers: This is a regular and common channel for costly** industrial products like heavy equipments and machines. Since the product affects the operations of the buyer, there needs to be close relationship between the manufacturer and the customer. The seller has to partake in various activities like installation, commissioning, quality control, and maintenance jointly with the buyer. The seller is also in charge for many aspects of the operations of the product long after the product is sold. The nature of the product demands a progressing relationship between the seller and the buyer. The large size of the order makes direct selling and distribution economical.

2. **Manufacturer to Agent to Industrial Customer:** A company that sells industrial products can utilise the services of an agent who sells a variety of products from several producers on a commission basis. Such arrangement spreads selling costs and is profitable to companies with no resources, to set up their own sales and distribution operation. This arrangement permits the seller to reach more number of customers without investing in a sales team. However, the company does not have much authority over the agent, who does not give the same amount of time and attention as a company's dedicated sales team.

3. **Manufacturer to Distributor to Industrial Customer:** Distributors are used for less costly and more regularly bought products. The company has both internal as well as field sales staff. Internal staff takes care of the customer, distributor generated enquiries, order placing, order follow-up, and checking inventory levels. Outside sales staff is quite proactive to discover new customers, get product specifications, distribute catalogues, and collect market information. They address their problems and keep them motivated to sell the company's products by visiting distributors. Distributors facilitate customers to purchase small quantities locally.

4. **Manufacturer to Agent to Distributor to Industrial Customers:** The manufacturer appoints an agent, as it is less expensive, instead of a dedicated sales force, to serve distributors.

    The agent sells the product of a number of suppliers to an industrial distributor, who further sells it to the business user. This type of channel is needed when consumers demand goods rapidly and when an industrial distributor can offer storage facilities.

4.4.6 Channels for Services

A channel is a distinct way of distributing a product or a service from the producer to the end customer. The channel members are the participants forming the channel.

In the case of goods distribution, a multi-tier or multi-level distribution structure including manufacturer, wholesaler, distributor, retailer, and customer is quite common. In case of distribution of services, such an elaborate three or four-layered structure may be replaced by a simpler one or two-layered structure.

The following distribution channel members are prevalent in India.

1. **Service Brokers**

    A broker is a person or a company who brings buyers and sellers together and assists in the negotiations without getting involved in the financing or assuming any risk. Some examples of specialised brokers are –

    *   **Share brokers:** They bring the share sellers and share buyers together. Sometimes they would advise their clients on the direction of movement of the share prices, long-term prospects, analysis, etc. However, their main business is to bring the buyer and seller together to transact the shares at mutually acceptable prices. With the direct online trading, now prevalent through both National Stock Exchange (NSE) and Bombay Stock Exchange (BSE) such share dealings have become easier.

    *   **Real estate brokers:** In the absence of a broker, both the owner of the real estate and the prospective buyer of the property need to advertise. For individuals, this may turn out to be expensive. Brokers have on their list potential properties in major areas of the city and also know the prospective customers. Therefore, the broker can bring the two parties together and arrange for a site visit at no risk to either party, to let the clients decide on the suitability of the deal. Later, the broker helps both the parties to conclude the deal at mutually agreeable terms. In return, the broker gets one to three months rent as the charges for facilitating the transaction.

2. **Service Agents**

    Agents, generally represent either the buyer or the seller on a more permanent basis than the brokers. They may have formal written agreements to ensure long-term continuity. Agents may represent more than one marketer of complementary goods or services to generate viable business volume.

    *   **Shipping agents and travel agents:** Generally, they represent one or more shipping lines or airlines for selling cargo space or passenger space. They co-ordinate between

the shipper or traveller and the line that provides the service. They have at their fingertips the timetables, days of docking, special cargo offers, and can make special offers to a potential shipper with specialised cargo or for group travel bookings, etc. The agent may be the only visible representative of the shipping company or airline.

- **Insurance agents:** The life as well as non-life insurance is promoted by Life Insurance Corporation of India (Life) and General Insurance Corporation (Non-Life/General) through the use of agents. These active salespersons representing the corporations, establish contacts with the prospects who need to cover various risks. They convince them to buy the most suitable cover. Usually, corporations back these agents up through development officers. The agents get commission on the premium income received by the corporation.

- **Credit card and bank loans agents:** A number of financial institutions realise the need for appointing external agencies to enhance the level of business generated. These agents meet the potential clients, understand their needs, make competitive offers on behalf of the principals, and finally help conclude the business transaction in return for commission.

3. **Professional Service Agents**

A professional service agent is one, where, the knowledge base of the expert enables clients to seek solutions to their problems. The key to the marketing of such services is the credibility. Therefore, large accountancy, auditing, and consultancy firms tend to get substantial up-market corporate business in these areas. In order to ensure the service effectiveness, professional service providers adopt the policy of global brand names with local partnerships.

Thus, auditing and accounting firms have chartered or certified public accountants based in the city of operation to run the local establishment by using their local business contacts for marketing. In this way, the entrepreneurial spirit remains vibrant for vigorous business growth. The organisation gains by having global presence and are able to secure businesses from clients of several locations due to geographically wider presence.

4. **Direct Marketing**

The innovation in telecom sector has enabled the marketer to find various means of directly getting in touch with the individual customers. These include telemarketing (showing the product or service on the television and asking the customers to call telephone numbers in their area to book the orders), direct e-mail, and postal mailers to the select potential customers in the target market segments and personal contact selling.

5. **Franchising**

Franchising is one of the major ways of distribution of services. The parties involved are the franchiser, the franchisee, and the customers. In India, franchising arrangement has been successful in the areas of photographic development and printing services (for example, Fotofast), restaurants and hotels (for example, KFC, Hyatt), tuition and coaching classes (for example, Chate Classes), health clubs and fitness centres, and computer training institutes (for example, NIIT, SEED Infotech).

A franchiser, licenses a trade or service mark to the franchisees in return for financial compensation. The franchiser usually specialises in a particular type of business model, which enables standardisation in the service delivery and promotion and leads to a high degree of customer satisfaction. The model of franchising has worked out well in the Indian markets. Some of the examples are –

(i) **Computer training institutes:** Companies such as NIIT pioneered this technique. They appointed a number of franchisees in all the major cities of India, including district towns and in some cases even taluka places. This helped in rapid development of computer education within the country.

   The standardised requirements to set up such institutes are rented or owned premises at locations convenient for the students, use of state-of-the-art hardware and licensed software mostly provided by the franchiser at a price, employment of certified trainers, and availability of infrastructure to represent the classroom layout.

   The franchisee can charge authorised fees from the students and offer a well-designed standard course along with educational material, including software supplied by the franchiser. The franchisee is authorised to conduct standard examinations and issue certificates of the franchiser, including that of the software supplier such as Microsoft. This business model has developed to such an extent that franchisees started specialising the educational services as per the target market segments of home learners, children and housewives, students, companies, and institutions for employee training.

(ii) **Photographic services:** Chains of photographic services stores have been set up in all major cities and towns offering colour, black and white photo film development and printing, photo enlargement and printing, passport-size photographs, conversion from film to CDs, sale of photographic equipment, and films, etc.

   The franchisee needs to own a shop and laboratory premises that are well located. They need to purchase, install and operate a franchiser-recommended standard automatic processing laboratory, shop decor, furniture, and equipment. In addition to it, chemicals, supplies and films have to be purchased from the franchiser.

   In return, the franchisee gets benefited from the franchiser advertising, the use of logo, and the brand of the franchiser. The prices, delivery period, and quality of printing are standardised and are of higher quality.

(iii) **Coaching classes:** Trainers such as Career Forum, offer training for competitive examinations such as MBA entrance tests, graduate registration examination (GRE), and test of English as a foreign language (TOEFL).

The course contents, course material, and course methodology are standardised and ensure an excellent chance of securing high grades and admission. Thus, franchising is one of the most successful arrangements for service distribution.

4.4.7 Importance of Physical Distribution in Customer Satisfaction

Physical distribution is the process of making the movement of the product to the consumers. It encompasses all the activities involved in the physical flow of products from producers to consumers. Physical distribution makes the product available at the right place and at the right time, thereby maximising the company's chance to sell the product and strengthen its competitive position. The products have to be carried to places of consumption; they have to be stored; and they have to be distributed. The product has to be marketed over an extensive marketing territory. It has to be transported through long distances, stored for a considerable length of time before being consumed.

Physical distribution largely determines the customer service level. Inefficient physical distribution leads to loss of customers and markets. There are some products that are subject to the seasonality factor – either production is continuous but demand is seasonal, or demand is continuous but production is seasonal. In all such cases, physical distribution acquires additional importance.

Physical distribution activities determine how quickly inventory moves from the production line to retail stores or to the distribution centers. Although each step in the physical distribution pipeline is important on its own, the process as a whole relates closely to customer satisfaction. Therefore, it is important to not only include physical distribution in customer service programs but also measure how effective the process is at satisfying your customers.

Set Customer Service Goals

- Analyse the key element of physical distribution that affects your customers the most.
- Set and prioritise customer service goals that relate directly to these identified aspects.
- Focus on these three most important elements – timeliness of delivery, order cycle time and merchandise availability.
- Accuracy of orders to be filled, product quality and optimal inventory are also important factors to be considered.
- Common customer service goals that relate to these aspects include the variety and assortment of merchandise, percentage of items unavailable or out of stock and the percentage of returns due to damaged or defective merchandise.
- Set plans for returns of goods.

4.4.8 Technologies used in Physical Distribution and International Logistics

Automated Materials Handling Systems

Equipments used for movement of products and goods and for the purpose of packaging, storage or shipment are known as Materials Handling Systems. Pallets, shelves, racks, carts etc. are used for storage and handling of goods. Forklifts, industrial trucks, conveyors are used for the movement of materials. Automation of materials handling equipments has improved the order picking time and so it has helped in expediting order processing.

Some examples of automated materials handling systems are –

- RFID (Radio Frequency Identification Devices) Tags for order picking by voice or by handheld scanners
- Forklifts with RFID mounted readers for order picking
- Automated conveyor belts for movement of products
- Materials handling robots which pick, move or pack products
- High speed sorters
- Robotic palletisers

E-COMMERCE: B2B (Business to Business), B2C (Business to Customer), C2C (Customer to Customer), G2B (Government to Business) and G2C (Government to Customer) provide value added services to customers. The most important aspect of E-commerce is 24 × 7 accessibility, low price of products, high quality of goods and value added services like door-to-door delivery system, online payment system or cash on delivery (COD) system. The purchasing attitude of the customer has greatly increased because of portals like Flipkart, Jabong, and Naaptol. Customers can place orders comfortably from their homes, and get deliveries at their doorsteps. E-commerce today has expanded to online service like online travel bookings, hotel reservations, cabs and taxi services, online educational admissions, and online movie ticket bookings. Confirmations can be directly received in the customers' mailboxes or mobile devices.

EDI (Electronic Data Interchange)

In a supply chain, partners, that is, the suppliers, vendors and manufacturers need to exchange business documents like RFQs (Requests for Quotations), invoice, bills, and tenders etc. The EDI system is useful in exchanging these commercial documents from one computer to another in a standard electronic format. Businesses benefit due to the EDI system with cost reductions, quicker order processing, reduction of errors and improved business relationships.

ERP (Enterprise Resource Planning) is a widely used computer system for management of all the processes and functions of a business enterprise. Following are some applications used for supply chain management –

- **SAP** (*System Application Products in Data Processing*): SAP modules specially designed for different processes of supply chain management are being globally used to meet customer demands of quality products, timely delivery, and better payment options. Some of the modules of SAP include –

(a) SAP PP – Production Planning

(b) SAP MM – Materials Management

(c) SAP SD – Sales and Distribution

(d) SAP WM – Warehouse Management

(e) SAP SRM – Supplier Relations Management

(f) SAP CRM – Customer Relationship Management

(g) SAP Logistics Information System

- **ORACLE ERP:** Oracle is one of world's leading enterprise software companies. Oracle has developed a high portfolio for itself by developing highly sophisticated software applications for almost every industry, any business size and almost every budget. Their core business applications include CRM (Customer Relations Management), SCM (Supply Chain Management), Transportation Management, Human Resource Management, Finance Management etc.
- **Microsoft Dynamics:** It is a business solution from Microsoft that aids in real time Customer Relationship Management, Sales Management, Supply Chain Management and Business Intelligence with reporting tool. Microsoft Dynamics can be combined with Office Suite, Skype and Yammer to connect instantly to your team from anywhere and to any device.

Global Sourcing Websites

In international business and organisations involved in centralised procurements global sourcing through websites provides a platform for a developing a strong database of verified suppliers, vendors, customers and products. It provides a competitive advantage for organisations who seek economies of scale through corporate-wide standardisation and benchmarking.

According to **Monczka, Trent, and Handfield, 2005, Purchasing and Supply Management, 3rd edition**, **Global Sourcing** can be defined as –

"Proactively integrating and coordinating common items and materials, processes, designs, technologies, and suppliers across worldwide purchasing, engineering, and operating locations"

Advantages of Global Sourcing

Some advantages of global sourcing include

- Increase supply capacity
- Develop a large database of supplier/vendor sources to compete challenges
- Gain knowledge of potential local and international markets
- Gain access to resources and skills from alternate choice of availability

Online Shipment Tracking System

A **Shipment Tracking Management System** helps you track consignments and shipments once the order has been processed. Customers, traders, business enterprises, importers and exporters can track their shipments through online tracking systems. Shipments can be tracked using their consignment numbers, booking numbers, bill of lading number, container numbers, waybill numbers etc. For example, DHL Express tracking systems help to track a parcel, track a package, track shipments and check shipment delivery status online. The DHL Express SMS system allows mobile phone users to track the progress of single shipments. The customer needs to simply text the waybill number and the response is sent with the status within seconds. DHL eTrack can track multiple shipments at any one time and functions on any email-enabled device like a PC, mobile phone or handheld device.

Delivery Drones

Delivery drones are unmanned aerial vehicles (UAV) used for the logistics service of medicines, foods, packages and other goods. It is also known as a "Parcelocopter" since it is used for delivery of parcels. Ambulance drones are being used for transport of defibrillator machines that are used on patients with cardiac arrests. 'Tacocopters' were used by the company TACO for the delivery of food products; however the **Federal Aviation Administration** (FAA) put a legal binding on TACO Company. Amazon's prime air drone and Dominoes' 'Domicopter' will be wandering streets at an altitude of 400 km, less than 100 mph as per the FAA regulations to reach its target within 30 minutes. The 'Domicopter' will deliver its pizza hot on arrival with its special packaging system. However, delivery systems using drones need a pilot certification and have to abide by the regulations of government and security agencies.

Fig. 4.17

A Dominoes Delivery Drone carrying Pizza

Cloud Based Supply Chains

A cloud based supply chain solution allows users anywhere in the world, with the proper permissions, to collaborate with other users since they are working off the same server and data set. Users find transparent and visible data that is, what one person saves, the others can see and what others save the initial user can see. New cloud computing technologies scale the value chains across the users. SCM applications delivered via software as a service (SaaS) models, Oracle SCM Cloud etc. enable data and analytics, mobility and social media functions. They reduce costs, increase efficiency and allow users to proactively monitor warehouse and inventory operations, and the flow of materials is efficiently streamlined.

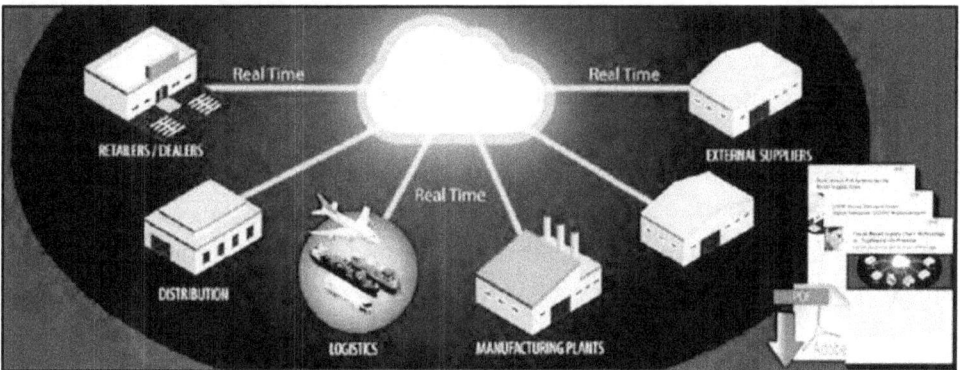

Fig. 4.18: A Typical Cloud-based Supply Chain

Points to Remember

- Logistics is the process of planning, implementing and controlling of efficient, effective flow and storage of goods, services and related information from the point of origin to the point of consumption, for conforming to customer expectations.
- Important Activities of Logistics
  1. Demand Forecasting
  2. Order Processing
  3. Materials Handling
  4. Logistics Communications
  5. Customer support
- Challenges for Logistics
  1. Transport of products
  2. Transfer of Information
  3. Quick Response
  4. Service
  5. Cost
  6. Logistics Integration
  7. The External Issues
  8. The Global Logistics
- Reverse logistics stands for all operations connected to the reuse of products and materials. It is "the process of planning, implementing, and controlling the efficient,

cost-effective flow of raw materials, in-process inventory, finished goods and connected data from the point of consumption to the point of origin for the purpose of recapturing its importance or removing the product.

- An integrated logistics system is an interface of procurement function, production function and physical distribution function of the total logistics function in order to achieve its basic mission of the best possible customer service at the least possible costs.
- Procurement is a key activity in the supply chain. It deals with the sourcing activities, negotiation of contracts and well-planned selection of goods and services that are usually of importance to an organisation.
- Production refers to the capacity of a supply chain to make and store products.
- Supplier management is a management system that facilitates close cooperation between the suppliers and the procurement department or an organisation.
- Material handling moves products before, after or between transportation and warehousing.
- Inventory, is a list of goods and materials stored for future use, mainly in the production process or those goods and materials themselves, held available in stock by a business. Thus, today's inventory is tomorrow's production.
- Order processing starts with the receiving of a customer's order and ends with the final delivery of goods to him along with transfer of title.
- Warehousing function is very critical as it acts as a node in linking the material flows between the supplier and customer.

Questions for Discussion

1. Discuss the significance of logistics for achieving customer satisfaction.
2. What are the various components and activities of logistics?
3. Describe the functional areas of logistics integration.
4. Define physical distribution and explain the importance and participants of physical distribution.
5. Explain the different types of marketing channels.

■■■

Chapter **5**...

Physical Distribution Management

Contents ...

Learning Objectives ...

- To study the meaning and importance of transportation
- To understand the various modes of transportation
- To explain distribution analysis control and management
- To learn the controlling of the distributor and retailer

5.1 Transportation

5.1.1 Introduction

Transportation refers to the movement of goods, raw material and finished products between different facilities in a supply chain. In transportation, the trade-off between awareness and competency is evident in the choice of transport mode. Quick modes of transport such as airways are very fast but also more costly. Slower modes such as ship and rail are very cost-efficient but not as fast. Since transportation costs can be as much as one third of the total operating cost of a supply chain, decisions made here are very important.

The mode of transport used in a distribution channel has a major impact on the performance and customer service. It directly affects transportation time and the cost incurred. The longer the time taken to transport the goods from the production unit to the end customer, the higher is the cost involved in materials-in-transit and materials handling. The performance and service provided to customer reduces if the speed of transportation reduces. However, at the same time if the speed of transportation is increased, the total cost is also increased. One solution to this problem is that the stock must be maintained nearer to the customers by assigning a channel member nearer to the end users.

Transportation serves three important aspects in a supply chain:

- Time benefit
- Place utility
- Cost benefits

5.1.2 Role and Importance of Transportation

Transportation as the means to carry people and goods from one place to another has become very important in each stage of human civilisation. The situation of the world would be very different if the present means of transportation were not developed. Transportation has contributed much to the development of economic, social, political and cultural fields. Faster industrialisation is impossible without the development of transportation. It is especially necessary to promote transport system for the proper development of agricultural sector and rural areas. Development of transportation facilitates mass production and distribution.

One or another means of transport is essential for mass production, whether it is to purchase and bring raw materials or to distribute finished goods. Transportation expands old markets and creates new ones resulting in increased demand for goods and hence production is increased. The contribution of transportation is very important to transport commodities to every corner of the world in the least possible time. Non- development of transportation would result in the market being limited in local areas and production would be limited to meet local needs only. This situation would not help the economy of the country and it would remain in an undeveloped condition.

Different industries that produce perishable goods such as fisheries, poultry firms, horticulture, dairy etc. rely heavily on transportation to carry the perishable goods to consumers living in distant places in time.

The role and contribution of transportation is of immense value in marketing. The functions of transport in marketing can be discussed as follows:

1. **Physical Supply of Products:** As seen above, transportation is indispensable in the carriage of necessary raw materials to the factory for production of goods and supply of finished goods to consumers. By creating a place and time utility of goods, it significantly increases the aggregate sales of goods. The fact that transportation helps in carrying goods to the scattered consumers in different places, narrows the gap between producers and consumers and helps to distribute goods to the consumers at a minimum cost and time.

2. **Specialisation:** Transportation brings about division of labour and specialisation on geographical or regional basis. Localisation of industries is affected by transportation costs. Production of goods may be undertaken at such places where the environment is ideal for minimisation of production costs. Maximum utilisation of local resources is both economically and socially necessary.

3. **Mobility of Labour and Capital:** Transportation provides mobility to labour and capital. If more labour force is available at any place, transportation economically encourages labour and capital to be used and invested in more sectors that are productive.

4. **Stabilisation in Price:** Transportation helps to bring stability in the price of different products by establishing coordination between demand and supply. It also facilitates the supply of necessary goods regularly to the consumers. Moreover the consumers get the necessary goods at lower prices as competition among producers is encouraged, thus making mass production at lower costs possible.

5. **Other Importance:** Transportation has also social, political and cultural importance. By narrowing geographical distances, it establishes utility. National integration is brought about by this consolidation of social and cultural utility. Transportation

nurtures and establishes relationships with foreign countries. Moreover, it also helps widen knowledge and skills in different sectors. All these aspects of transportation help establish social utility, uniformity and integrity, and strengthen the national security.

5.1.3 Strategic Planning for Transportation

Strategic transportation decisions are based on meeting the customer demands and inventory or stock holding. Although air transport is the fastest way to deliver a product to the customer, it is much costlier than shipments by boats or rail. On the other hand, using sea or rail for shipments would incur inventory-holding costs and therefore a higher level of inventory has to be maintained to meet the quick demands of the customer. Since 30% of the cost of a product is incurred by transportation, therefore use of appropriate and efficient modes of transport is a critical strategic decision. Transportation is an important strategic decision-making component since it serves time, place and cost benefits. Transportation provides a base for normal inventory cycle build-up, lead-time for stock replenishment, and sales expected in the territory.

Strategic Decisions for Transportation include:

- **Facility:** The type of facilities including plant layout, warehousing facility, cross-docking or break bulking
- **Inventory :** Inventory aggregation leads to economies of scale
- **Transportation:** Choice of transportation mode will give cost and time utility benefits

5.1.4 Transportation Management

A transportation management system is an organised system that may use information technology for the effective transportation operations. Transportation system is an important component of the supply chain.

Transport management can be achieved by planning for the following aspects of supply chain and logistics functions.

1. **Cross-Docking:** Cross-docking is a logistics practice where the goods are unloaded from an incoming transport system like a truck or semi-trailer and then directly loading these goods onto outbound transport system with very little or nil storage. This is done for changing the type of transportation or loading for the purpose of dispatch to a different geographic location.

   Cross-docking is useful where deliveries are time bound. In this method, scheduling of truck/ transportation arrivals/departures is very crucial.

2. **Distributor Storage with Carrier Delivery:** Package carriers or delivery vans are employed for the transportation of goods directly from the manufacturers to the

customer or the retailer. The retailer does not hold any product inventory, but it forms a link for the order placement between the customer and the manufacturer. The retailer receives demands and orders from the customer and passes that information to the manufacturer.

3. **Drop-Shipping:** The technique by which the retailer does not keep goods in stock but instead transfers customer orders and shipment details to the manufacturer, another retailer, or a wholesaler, who then ships the goods directly to the customer, is known as drop-shipping. In retail businesses, the majority of retailers make their profit on the difference between the wholesale and retail price. However, some retailers earn a commission, which is actually an agreed percentage of the sales, paid by the wholesaler to the retailer.

Advantages of drop-shipping for high-value and low unpredictable demand items

1. The demands of all the customers for a specific product are met directly through the manufacturer. The finished goods inventory is stored at the manufacturing unit's warehouse or storage area. The inventory of finished goods is aggregated over different consumers.
2. Manufacturers can customise the products as per the customer's demand and order placement.
3. A product mix can be provided at lower costs.

Disadvantage of Drop-Shipping

1. Direct shipment increases the burden of storage on the manufacturer
2. Manufacturers and retailers must have a robust information system to have effective communication
3. Returns of goods are difficult to handle
4. Responsiveness to order placement is longer, hence the shipment also takes a longer duration
5. Direct shipment increases freight costs

5.1.5 Transportation Network

A transportation network is the route and intermediate location designs for the purpose of efficient transportation and break bulking of products. The products are dispatched from the manufacturing units to pre-determined locations, which are transported through the routes as planned. These locations and routes are designed to reduce the cost using the economies of scale in transportation. Typical distribution channel uses transportation networks that combine several of these basic network types.

There are three types of network designs:

1. **Point-to-Point:** In a point-to-point network, the product is transported from manufacturer to a customer directly using a singly transportation system.

2. **Hub and Spoke:** A hub is a central distribution node, which can be a warehouse, a distribution centre, cross-dock warehouse, trans-shipment etc. The different nodes or the spokes are connected to the hubs. Hub and spoke distribution network is an integrated logistics system for economising the costs. Hub and spoke distribution centres receive products from different sources, consolidate the products, and send them directly to final destinations.

3. **Milk Route / Milk Run:** Milk Route or Milk Run gets its name from the dairy industry, which uses this method very commonly for their milk distribution. In this transportation network, one transport van or a vehicle moves from one point to another along a loop or in a circular route. It covers multiple locations where smaller materials are to be collected and/or delivered. For example, a customer needs a certain product every week. Instead of every supplier delivering the products every day, one vehicle collects the product from different locations/suppliers and delivers it to the customer to meet his daily requirement. In this way, one singly vehicle load fulfils the requirements of the customer from each supplier.

Routing and Scheduling of Transportation

Transportation costs along with the inventory holding costs can burden the organisation financially. Besides, timely delivery of products to the end customer results in greater customer satisfaction. Therefore, routing and scheduling of transportation is a key factor of transportation management.

Three basic methods are adopted for the efficient management of transportation:

1. **Clustering:** Assignment of trucks to demand points
2. **Routing**: Sequencing demand points; trucks use these sequences to visit demand points
3. **Scheduling:** Exact time of visits/loading and unloading

Network Model Building Block – Node

1. **Supply Node:** The source of commodities, for example, the raw material suppliers, vendors and those who are involved in consolidation or break bulking and packing of intermediate or finished products

2. **Trans-shipment Node:** These nodes are intermediaries like the distribution centre pools or cross-docks

3. **Demand Node:** These are the sink nodes or the destination nodes or places where commodities are finally delivered for consumption.

Network Model Building Block – Arc

The ARC model connects two nodes. It is mostly designed for the activities of procurement of raw materials, handling distribution centres, warehousing, production process and trans-shipments.

Network Design Considerations:

- **Plant Locations**: Which location arrangement best meets our current and future demands in terms of procurement and distribution?
- **Plant Missions:** How do various structures and tiers affect our logistics network?
- **Supplier** locations and supplier missions.
- **Cost** of procurements, funds for procurement activity
- **Production Costs:** What effects do changes in freight volumes and shipping patterns have?
- How do new relations affect our service level and total costs?
- **Production Capacities:** How can we improve capacity exploitation for transports in various regions?
- **Freights:** Freights for replenishment of distribution centre/outbound dispatch/ inbound freight.
- **The Type of Tariff applicable** like door-delivery/direct delivery/delivery through distribution centres/retail outlets.

5.1.6 Transportation Costs

The main objective of logistics is a proper balance between total logistics cost and customer service and customer satisfaction. For example addition of a new channel member increases the total logistics cost, but the channel member is expected to offer effective customer support and increase the sales volume to compensate with the increase of transportation/logistics costs.

(A) Cost related to Transportation

1. **Vehicle**: Purchase or Rental
2. **Fixed Operating Cost:** Labour, Airport Terminal Gate Charges, Drivers Salaries or Wages
3. **Trip Related:** Cost of Fuel/Labour/Taxes
4. **Quantity** : Quantity of goods being loaded: Loading/Unloading Cost
5. **Overhead Cost:** Cost of Planning and Management of Route, Overheads for Operations etc.

(B) Costs Associated With International Logistics/Transportation

In international shipments, the type of shipping terms affects the freight charges. The shipping terms or the **INCOTERMS** are as below:

Shipment freight terms for cost planning:

1. **LTL** (Less than Truck Load): The cost would be much cheaper, since the truck can be shared with other consignees.
2. **FTL** (Full Truck Load): It is cost effective for carrying goods in bulk.

3. **LCL** (Less than Container Load): Container loads can be shared with other shipments.

4. **FCL** (Full Container Load): Full containers are cost effective for bulk imports or exports.

5. **Free on Board** (**FOB**): The exporter delivers the goods at the specified location (and on board the vessel). "**FOB JNPT**" means that the exporter delivers the goods to the Jawaharlal Nehru Port, India, and pays for the cargo to be loaded and secured on the ship. This term also declares that where the responsibility of shipper ends and that of buyer starts.

6. **Carriage and Freight** (or "Cost and Freight")(C&F, CFR, CNF): Insurance is payable by the importer, and the exporter pays all expenses incurred in transporting the cargo from its place of origin to the port/airport and ocean freight/air freight to the port/airport of destination.

7. **CIF (**Cost Insurance and Freight): Cost of transportation in this case also includes insurance charges.

8. **DD** (Door-to-Door delivery): The quoted price of DD service includes shipping, handling, import and customs duties and delivered up to the destination port or address of the buyer.

9. **DDP** (Delivery Duty paid): The seller is responsible for all the expenses incurred for a shipment.

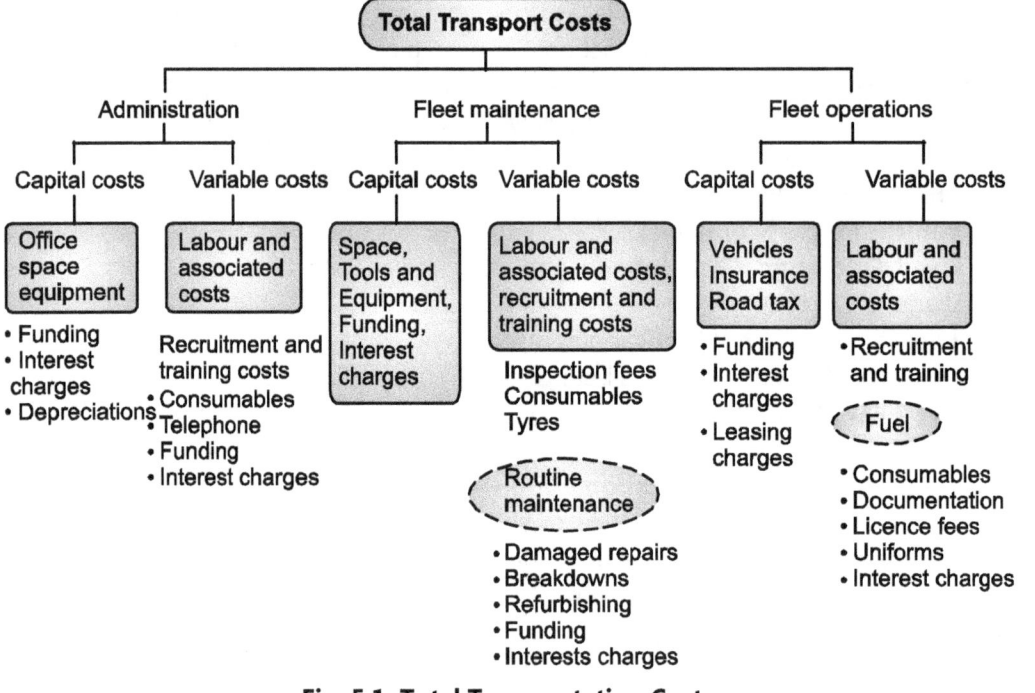

Fig. 5.1: Total Transportation Costs

5.2 Modes of Transportation

There are three basic modes of transport that a company can choose from:

1. **Domestic:** Includes Roadways, Railways, and Inland Waterways.
2. **International:** Airways, Seaway, Oil Pipelines
3. **Multimodal:** Transports using multiple modes like Roadways and Seaway in a combination.

5.2.1 Domestic Transportation

Road Transport: India being a developing country with its huge agricultural and manufacturing activities, road transport is widely used. Road transports are suitable for carrying goods within the country or intra-state transport. It is especially useful for countries that are landlocked. Road transports provide door delivery services for domestic and as an intermodal transport for international shipments. Some types are trucks, tempos, and flat racks.

1. **Trucks** are a relatively quick and very flexible mode of transport. Trucks can go almost anywhere. The cost of this mode is prone to fluctuations though, as the cost of fuel fluctuates and the condition of roads varies.

   Truck Load

   LTL (Less than Truck Load): LTL shipping is much more cost effective when compared to other available shipping options. The main advantage in using an LTL carrier is having items transported for a fraction of the cost of hiring an entire truck and trailer for one shipment. Since the carrier is moving multiple shipments from multiple shippers, the freight carrier pools all the shipments into a single truck. The concept is now like cost sharing with friends, where each shipper pays a fraction of the cost of the truck. LTL loads typically have more destinations or pick-up locations to accommodate the different needs of the various shipments on board.

   FTL (Full Truck Load): FTL or "full truck load" means that the load will fill up the entire truck. Shippers that accommodate full truckloads cater to those customers who typically ship in bulk. The large amount of goods being shipped offsets the cost of a larger truck. The larger FTL loads usually contain a shipment for one company and one destination.

   Flat Racks: Flat racks consist of a floor structure with a high loading capacity composed of a steel frame and a softwood floor and two end walls. Flat racks are used for carrying odd shaped and oversize loads such as boilers, steel coils, cars, heavy vehicles, timber etc.

2. **Railways**: Railways are important transport systems that carry goods, postal couriers, letters etc. Railways also transport imports and exports between two country borders.

Railways are cost effective but can be slow. Essential commodities like coal, automobiles, agricultural products, chemicals are transported via a railway system (goods train). Many companies like ACC have their mines and factories closely linked with the government railways for their distribution networks.

3. **Inland Waterways:** Inland waterway is a mode of transport where there are no seaports. Smaller vessels, boats or feeder vessels carry goods to the main cargo ship or to the road transport. Geographical areas with only access to small rivers or lakes make use of inland waterways. It is cost effective, since it serves rural or other areas where there is less access to road.

4. **Special Vessels:** Special vessels are used by the defence for the movement of critical equipments.

5. **Boats:** Boats serve as an intermediate or intermodal transport for carrying goods to be loaded on another transport system like a truck or a ship.

6. **Feeder Vessels** are vessels or boats that carry goods to the larger cargo ship or a mother vessel.

7. **Barges:** Barges are small flat-bottomed long boats used in rivers and canals to carry heavy goods like scrap metals. Usually barges are without power supply and are towed by bigger towboats.

5.2.2 International Transportation

(i) **Airways** or **Air Cargo** is the fastest mode of transport, but at the same time, they can be very expensive. Airways serve international logistics systems and help in the transportation of goods, products, and human resources and are a very fast mode of transport and very responsive. This is also the most expensive mode and it is somewhat limited by the availability of appropriate airport facilities. Air transport is a vital component of many international logistics networks, essential to managing and controlling the flow of goods, energy, information and other resources like products, services, and people, from the source of production to the marketplace. Cargo airlines (or airfreight carriers) are airlines dedicated to the transport of goods by air. Some passenger airlines provide dedicated services to cargo services also through their **Air India Express Cargo Carriers** dedicated for cargo transport via airways. All urgent dispatches make use of Air Cargo Service, even though the cost of freight is high.

(ii) **Seaways:** Seaways or Cargo Shipping is one of the slowest modes of transport, but at the same time, it is cost efficient, where the materials and goods are to be transported in metric tonnes. Bulk goods like food grains, scrap metals, clothes in bales etc. are transported. There are many shipping carriers like container ships, barges, special vessels, boats, feeder vessels etc.

(iii) **Container Ships:** These are ships that carry containerised goods for the purpose of imports or exports. Each container transported is weighed in terms of metric tonnes, for example, a 20' metric tonne of rice or 40' metric tonne of cereals. The terms FCL and LCL are generally used to indicate either a Full Container Load (example, 20′ FCL) or Less than Container Load (20′ LCL). The cost varies according to the load volume of the container.

5.2.3 Multimodal Transport / Intermodal

Multimodal transport or intermodal transport is a combination of a variety of transportation systems. It has a significant impact on cost effectiveness. The advantages of different modes of transport can be utilised for reaching the goals of time, cost and place utility.

For example, containerisation of goods for international logistics helps in transporting goods on container lines to the shipping cargo without the need to unpack or repack. The containers with the goods are transported to the destination port.

5.2.4 Other Modes of Transport

1. **Pipelines**: Pipelines are generally used to transport crude oil, water and natural gas over land. Countries or states that share borders with each other can take the advantage of using pipelines. For example, the GAIL Dabhol-Bangalore Natural Gas Pipeline which connects Ratnagiri and Bangalore, supplies natural gas to Toyota-Kirloskar Auto Parts Pvt. Ltd. and Karnataka Power Corporation Ltd.

2. **Electronic and Communications Transport**: This is the fastest mode of transport that is very cost efficient. It can be used for the transmission of data, electrical energy, telecommunication signals etc.

3. **Ropeway Conveyors and Cable Cars:** Rope conveyors are actually gondola lifts (aerial lifts) which are used to carry goods between two stations (can be a hill station with terrains and mountains). Gondola lifts are also known as **télécabines.** These lifts are suspended by steel cables and moved by engines. In contrast, cable cars are also a ropeway system suspended with cables that may or may not use a motor.

Modes of Transportation

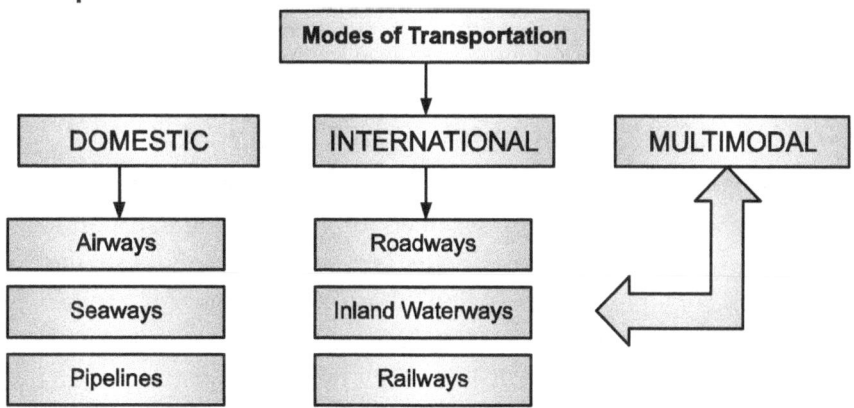

Fig. 5.2: Classification of Transportation

5.2.5 Choice of Mode of Transport

Goodwill can only be earned when business firms deliver goods and satisfactory services to customers. When selecting the means of transportation, the nature of goods, needs of customers, cost, time for delivery (speed), reliability, capacity, access, and security ought to be considered. The whole physical distribution system is affected by the selection of the means of transport. Hence, the proper means of transport should be selected keeping all these factors in mind.

1. **Cost:** The cheapest means for transporting raw materials or finished goods is through waterways. While road transport is relatively costly, airway transport is the costliest.

2. **Speed:** Speed, that is, the time taken by the means of transport in transporting goods, is very important. The shorter the time taken to transport goods or people to a destination is vital. Slow speed takes a longer time. Transportation by airways is the fastest way whereas by humans and animals is the slowest way. Transportation by waterways, though very cheap, is very slow and time-consuming.

3. **Accessibility or Availability:** All means of transportation have no same accessibility. Many countries have no availability of pipelines and waterways. In such situations road transport is the best among available means.

4. **Capacity:** In the carrying of capacity loads the railways and waterways are the best means of transportation as they can transport huge and heavy loads. While transport by road can only accommodate medium loads, airways can carry only limited loads and are the costliest means.

5. **Reliability:** The task of carrying goods to the destination at the right time regularly is called reliability. Transportation by pipelines is the best reliable means whereas road transport, railway, humans and animals are supposed to be good or reliable means of transport.

5.3 Role of Information Technology in Transportation

Information technology plays an important role in the role of transportation within a supply chain. Software systems specially designed for mapping the transportation routes are the most commonly used. Softwares take inputs such as the size of the shipments, customer location, desired delivery times, transportation infrastructure, distances between two delivery points, vehicle capacity. These inputs are transformed into various optimisation options for cost effectiveness and timely delivery. It is an important tool for the purpose of decision-making.

Fleet Utilisation: Softwares also aid in fleet utilisation, by considering the shipment sizes and aligning it with container capacity, sequence of delivery, the sequence of loading and unloading of containers.

GPS (Global Positioning Systems) applications aid in tracking the exact location of the vehicle en route. It helps to understand whether the shipment will be delivered as per schedules or there will be a delay in the shipments due to some reason.

Internet/Websites: Internet or the websites are used to track the shipments details by the customers. A tracking number or a consignment number is allotted for every shipment and it can be used to track the delivery using this number.

5.4 Risk Management in Transportation

Transportation also carries certain risks and it can affect the supply chain and therefore consideration of the alternatives is very important. When one level in the supply chain experiences delays and problems, it affects the abilities of downstream members of the supply chain to serve their customers. There are three types of problems that can cause a risk in transportation.

1. **Disruptions in links to the connecting nodes:** Any unforeseen circumstances like equipment failures, natural disasters and inclement weather, work stoppages, and government intervention, curfews, roadblocks or congestions can delay the shipments. It affects the economy on a large scale.

2. **Risk due to hazards/hazardous materials:** Hazardous material is capable of posing an unreasonable risk to health, safety, and property when transported, which includes hazardous waste. Hazardous materials may pose varying degrees of risk in transportation, depending on the type of substance. In such cases, risk management must include proper trainings to the transporters, proper labelling and packaging of the hazardous materials; shipments in containers must have the containers marked with indications of hazardous materials. In addition, routes should be planned in such a way, that the transportation has a very low probability of risks of accidents etc. In case of exposures, emergency training must be provided to the personnel directly involved in transportation.

3. **Delay in shipments:** Problems or congestion on the nodes, for example an airport, a seaport or a distribution centre can lead to delay in shipments. The business firm needs to take into consideration the different alternate routes available while designing the routes, so that in case of any problems, the route can be diverted.

5.5 Distribution Analysis Control and Management

The choice of distribution channels can greatly influence the success or failure of a business. It is therefore very crucial that the channel members are scrutinised and analysed for an effective supply chain management. Using a distribution channel for marketing the products have different options for reaching the customers within the domestic territories as well as the international customers or prospects outside the region. The channel partners make it possible to reach customers who are within their reach and thus save time and efforts for dealing with the customers. Besides, the channel partners give feedback on customer demand and requirements of the products. It is therefore important to motivate, support and manage channel partners for the growth of business.

5.5.1 Importance of Channels of Distribution

1. **Reach**: Distribution channels help you to reach customers who are located in their territories. In case of companies planning to export their products, distributors and dealers in the other countries help gain access to their local customers. Thus, a company need not establish its presence from scratch.

2. **Cost:** The distributors are responsible for marketing, demand generation, inventory holding, delivering the products, and after sales service support to the customers. This reduces cost of administration and the company is able to manage a large number of customers effectively.

3. **Customer Base:** Working with channel members, that is, the distributors allows you to deal with a huge number of customers belonging to the distributor; thus, it eliminates additional cost of sales and marketing.

4. **Market Knowledge:** Distributors help you to enter new markets quickly and effectively, since they provide you with the current market information. This eliminates the market research activity or other marketing programs. In export business, distributors help you with the knowledge of local customs, government regulations, language and communications support which maybe a barrier to entry.

5. **Internet:** Internet offers customers globally the convenience of making inquiries or placing orders 24 × 7. It also helps to conduct a product review/feedback. Social networking sites are another important tool for marketing and distribution.

5.5.2 Distribution Analysis/Evaluation

Distribution analysis can be performed prior to the distribution activity or distribution can be evaluated for the measure of performance. Distribution analysis is the assessment of how and where the products reach the customers. It also studies the distribution strategies for effective management of the channels of distribution.

(i)   Identification of the length of the channel/intermediaries

(ii) Identification of the method/strategy of distribution

(iii) Distribution control

(iv) Distribution management

(v)   Distribution assessment/Standards of performance

5.5.3 Identification of the Length of the Channel/Intermediaries

1. **Direct Channel/Level 0:** Selling a product directly to the consumers enables an organisation to have a strong control over price, promotion and advertisements. However, it can incur additional set-up costs including hiring and maintaining a large sales team, logistics expenses, and services being provided to the end user. A contact with customers with locations other than the retail outlets can be through the sales team, mails, radio, television, internet etc.

2. **Distributor/Wholesalers as intermediaries:** Large quantities/bulk products are usually sold through an authorised distributor. It reduces the complexities and costs, but the manufacturer loses some of its control over the process and also loses the direct relation/contact with the consumer that can give valuable feedback and two-way communication.

3. **Combination of both:** Manufacturers can use a combination of direct selling and selling through a distributor/wholesaler. For example, manufacturers can sell directly to customers within the geographic area of the manufacturing unit. Further, it can expand its products to other places which is located within the reach of the distributors or which are located far from the manufacturer. Thus, the organisation can have cost benefits as well as take the advantage of the distributor's customer base for selling its products.

Factors for Analysing the Distribution Network

1. **Product:** The type of product, for example, perishable goods, consumer goods or industrial goods will have different distribution network needs. For FMCG goods or perishable goods high-speed transport system should be used, and for gas and petroleum the use of pipeline is advisable.

2. **Market structure:** The type of competition between similar industries.

3. **Cost:** Capital requirements of the company, raw material requirement, costs of transportation or cost of services by third party/outsourcing.

4. **Competitor's channels**: Assessing your organisation against the similar companies with high performance and the type of channels of distribution employed by them.

5. **Marketing environment**: The micro and macro environment.

5.5.4 Identification of the Method/Strategy of Distribution

1. Distribution Strategy

Distribution strategy involves the method or the intensity employed after deciding the appropriate channel of distribution. The intensity varies according to the type of product, geographical location of the customers, and the cost trade-offs. Distribution strategy or the patterns can be classified as:

(a) **Intensive Distribution:** This is a very competent strategy for the distribution of products. The main goal of the manufacturer/ distributor is to gain a maximum reach by using all available outlets. For example, soft drinks are available in almost every outlet. The main goal of the manufacturer is to distribute their brands through multiple outlets to ensure their easy availability to the customer. Intensive distribution is usually required where customers have a range of acceptable brands to choose from. In other words, if one brand is not available, a customer will simply choose another. Any possible outlet where the customer is expected to visit is also an outlet for the soft drink.

(b) **Selective Distribution:** In selective distribution, the customers usually prefer a particular brand or price and will look for outlets that supply the same. Selective distribution involves a producer using a limited number of outlets in a geographical area to sell his products. An advantage of this approach is that the producer can choose the most appropriate or best-performing outlet. This alternative is the middle path approach to distribution. Here, the firm selects some outlets to distribute its products. This alternative helps focus the selling effort of manufacturing firms on a few outlets rather than dissipating it over countless marginal ones. It also enables the firm to establish a good working relationship with channel members. Selective distribution can help the manufacturer gain optimum market coverage and more control but at a lesser cost than intensive distribution. Both existing and new firms are known to use this alternative.

(c) **Exclusive Distribution:** Exclusive distribution is an extreme form of selective distribution in which only one wholesaler, retailer or distributor is used in a specific geographical area. Typical examples are branded outlets for Zara Designer clothes for women, LG electronics, Bajaj automobiles etc. By granting exclusive distribution rights, the manufacturer hopes to have control over the intermediary's price, promotion, credit inventory and service policies. The firm also hopes to get the benefit of aggressive selling by such outlets. When the firm distributes its brand through just one or two major outlets in the market, who exclusively deal in it and not all competing brands, it is said that the firm is using an exclusive distribution strategy. This is a common form of distribution in products and brands that seek a high prestigious image.

2. **Analysis/ Selection of Agents**

    (i) **Carrying and Forwarding Agent (C&FA):** The primary requirement of a C&FA should be that he is a transporter with good warehousing facilities. The C&FA is normally selected to operate in territories or a state in which he is located.

The responsibilities of a C&FA include receipt of goods, storage and care, order receipts from sales people, order processing, dispatch with correct documentation, record keeping, sales and stock reports, collection of sales proceeds from distributors and managing secondary transport for dispatches. The criteria for selection of a C&FA are summarised at Table 5.1 (a) below.

Table 5.1 (a): Parameters for Selecting C&FA

Parameter of Selection	Criteria for Selection
Location of the party	In or close to a main market of the company
Location of the warehouse	Close to the major market
	Outside octroi limits
	Should have good road/transport access
	Labour availability
	Utilities support
	Connected by phone
Past experience	As a C&FA for a similar company
	As a transporter should have access to a good warehouse
History of past experience	Should have handled similar but non-competing companies
	Ability to maintain confidentiality of transactions
Financial strength	To handle all operating expenses till reimbursement
	Insurance
IT capability	Adequate own hardware
	Trained staff to handle simple programmes and reporting formats
Flexibility	In operating hours daily
	To handle peak loads
Transportation facilities	Reliability
	Consistency in source of vehicles
	Additional volumes to be handled at short notice
Attitude, commitment	To be of the highest order/positive
	Willing to expand the business
	Disciplined

(ii) Selecting A Distributor

A distributor is also known as a redistribution stockist. He buys the company products from the company/C&FA and redistributes (sells) it to all the wholesalers, retailers and institutions from where the final consumer or end users buy it or where it may get consumed (in an institution). The distributor 'invests' in the product and ensures that it reaches closest to the point where the end user buys the product and hence has a major responsibility within the distribution network. He is therefore, selected based on a larger number of parameters as can be seen in table 5.1 (b) below.

Table 5.1 (b): Parameters for Selecting a Distributor

Parameter of Selection	Criteria for Selection
Size of the channel partner	Current business portfolio Financial strength/asset ownership including personal assets of partners
Own sales force	Number of sales people Qualifications, background, experience
Current business	Products handled, volume handled Should be of similar products but non-competitive Product quality, compatibility and complimentary
Reputation	Leadership in the market Integrity, fairness in dealings
Market coverage	Territory/intensity, regularity, reliability, relationship, productivity, beat plan adherence Value of institutional business handled if any
Credit extended in the market	Percentage of outlets Percentage of current business Bad debts if any
Stock distribution	Ready stocks or order booking
Infrastructure availability	Warehouse, distribution vans, hardware/personal computers/connectivity
Sales performance	On current business, awards, prizes, certificates won performance
Management of business	Educational background, qualifications of partners, direct involvement in business
Market working	Efforts on merchandising displays
Handling sales promotions	Past experience
Inventory management	Adherence to stock norms recommended by the company

For companies like FMCG and pharmaceuticals only some of the channel partners like C&FA's and distribution can be recruited. The other channel members like wholesalers, retailers and chemists already exists in the market and automatically become part of the network. The effort is only in persuading them to stock and sell the company products.

A distribution channel encompasses several relationships that assist channel members in carrying out various channel functions. Suppliers tie up with various intermediaries in the distribution channel as they help suppliers or manufacturers achieve the objectives of making products available to end customer cost effectively. An analysis of the performance of channel partners by suppliers becomes necessary to evaluate the channel's effectiveness, while designing or structuring a distribution channel. A distribution channel can be assessed in terms of Key Performance Areas (KPAs) such as channel effectiveness, channel efficiency, channel productivity, channel equity and channel profitability.

5.5.5 Distribution Control

Control refers to the power or influence exerted by one channel over the behaviour of other channel members. For example, a well-known retailer may want the manufacturer to modify the design of the product or perhaps be required to carry lesser inventory. Both parties may attempt to exert their power in an attempt to influence the other's behaviour. The ability of either of the parties to achieve this outcome will depend upon the amount of power that each can bring to bear. The performance of a channel largely depends upon the authority/leadership provided to them. This is essential for proper coordination of activities within a distribution network to reach the organisational goals. The leadership can be passive, authoritative, or dictatorial.

Given the restrictions inherent in channel leadership, the final question is "who should lead the channel?

(i)   Wholesaler: In early years, the wholesaler linked the producer and the customer. As such, the wholesaler led most channels.

(ii) A second trend is the apparent strategy of both manufacturers and retailers to exert power through size. In a type of business cold war, manufacturers and retailers are constantly trying to match each other in this respect. The result has been some serious warfare to gain channel superiority.

(iii) The manufacturer should lead if the design and redesign of the channel is best done by the manufacturer and if control of the product, that is, merchandising, repair, etc. is critical.

(iv) The wholesaler should lead where the manufacturers and retailers have remained small in size, large in number, relatively scattered geographically, financially weak, and lacking in marketing expertise.

(v)   The retailer should lead when product development and demand stimulation are relatively unimportant and when personal attention to the customer is important.

Control by Vertical Integration of Channels

In Vertical Marketing Systems (VMS), one of the channel members owns the channel or exerts a substantial influence or control over the activities of the members along the channel. This 'channel leader' oversees the functions of channel members and ensures that everyone performs only those functions at which they are good.

A VMS consists of a manufacturer(s), distributor(s) and retailer(s) pooling their individual strengths together to achieve a competitive advantage. VMSs are a common mode of channel arrangement adopted by companies to get over the intense competition and changing market conditions.

Types of Vertical Marketing Systems (VMS)

A company can develop a vertical marketing system by many ways. The different integration approaches vary in terms of the level of investment, profitability, extent of control, the need to reduce risks, and the bargaining power of the other channel members. The commonly used types of vertical channel systems are the corporate system, administered type of system and the contractual system.

1. Corporate VMS

In a corporate VMS, one company owns and operates the other channel members at different channel levels. A company develops a corporate VMS, when it intends to source nearly all of its internal requirements through the corporate VMS. A corporate system is preferable when the company is confident of protecting its key processes or trade secrets maintaining accuracy and high quality in the channel activities. When the manufacturer owns or performs operations at the wholesaler or retailer level, the vertical marketing system is said to be forward integrated. When a retailer or wholesaler plans to operate or control the manufacturing aspects, a backward-integrated system develops.

Key variables influencing the decision on development of corporate vertical marketing system are:

(a) **The costs involved in implementing the system:** The possible profits must not be offset by the costs involved in implementation of the corporate system.

(b) **Price competition:** The intensity of price competition influences the decision of a channel member on adopting a corporate VMS. In a corporate VMS, the cost of integrating channel functions may result in an increase in the price of the end products. If the intensity of price competition between manufacturers of various products is high, the increase in price will lead to a significant loss of market share, offsetting the gains of adopting the corporate VMS.

(c) **Manufacturing capacities:** Increasing the manufacturing capacities must not lead to significant resource constraints.

(d) **Value addition:** Vertical integration leads to a substantial increase in value addition along the chain.

(e) **Availability of raw materials or channel partners:** If there are no upstream or downstream channel members who can perform the required functions, the company can develop a corporate VMS.

(f) **Trade secrets:** If the company uses exclusive processes or procedures that are not used by other companies in the industry, then, a corporate VMS is preferable.

(g) **Product substitutability:** If the product of the company is similar to that of competitors, corporate VMS is preferred.

(h) **Environmental uncertainty:** If the economic, social, or technical environment is rapidly changing and competitor products are frequently introduced, the companies need to adopt a corporate VMS.

(i) **Co-ordination and team selling:** If selling requires effective coordination and team selling efforts on the part of the company representatives and the distributor representatives, a corporate system is essential.

(j) **Transaction size:** If the order size per customer in a given geographical area is significant, the company must obtain benefits of the corporate VMS.

(k) **Performance of channel members:** If it is difficult to measure the productivity or evaluate the performance of the channel members, a corporate system will be more beneficial.

2. Administered VMS

Unlike corporate system, in the administered type of vertical marketing system, no channel member has complete control over other channel members. Managers of companies following the conventional distribution systems often attempt to first develop an administered system to compete against companies in corporate vertical marketing systems. The extent to which one channel member exerts an influence or control over others varies. In an administered VMS, the level of control is greater than in the conventional distribution system but less than that of a corporate system.

This type of vertical marketing system is widely prevalent in the retail sector because of the increase in the bargaining power of retailers over the last decade. Retailers have become more market and more corporate-oriented, with a centralised administration and distribution, increased product range and retail branding. This phenomenon has led to retailers seeking relationships with those suppliers who can contribute to their development. Retailers want suppliers to collaborate with them in product development, new product concepts and designs, quality control and delivery schedules. Overheads need to be minimised while out-of-stock situations are absolutely forbidden. Due to these changes in the procurement needs, the conventional market mechanism functioning between the supplier and the retailer has given way to a preference for a more stable and mutually beneficial relationship. Such a shift has been aided by views that managing relationships in a vertically integrated system can improve the retailer's competitive performance. In highly stable administered systems, retailers also offer financial loans to suppliers in their investment programs and give training in new production technologies.

The administered distribution systems are more long-term oriented due to the prevalence of a strong channel culture and possible competitive advantage for the dominant channel partner. In administered systems, price is not the sole criterion deciding the extent of inter-relationship between suppliers, manufacturers or retailers. The total relationship orientation on a long-term basis is considered. This type of system is widely prevalent in the grocery, apparel and furnishing sectors.

Some of the factors that bring about the need for an administered vertical marketing system are:

(a) **Need for consistent product quality:** When the products are difficult to manufacture and require compliance to stringent norms, it leads to administered vertical marketing system.

(b) **Need to have a flexible delivery response:** Shorter lead times and flexible delivery schedules also give impetus to administered relationships.

(c) **Joint product development:** The administered system is beneficial when there is a need for mutual co-operation between upstream and downstream channel members.

(d) **Specialised delivery systems:** Distribution arrangements have to be consistent and stable in the food processing and fast food sectors due to the nature of the products. McDonald's has set up an administered distribution system in India for sourcing of different materials used in its products.

(e) **Strong manufacturer brands:** Suppliers have to maintain stable relationship with companies that have strong brands to ensure a steady supply of products. The retailer has to initiate an administered system and absorb the resultant costs.

This type of system is advantageous to both the producers/suppliers and the retailers. Producers have the benefit of reaping profits through steady sales and do not have to compete in changing relationships. They can also ensure the maximum product exposure through the retailers because of the nature of the relationship. Wholesalers and retailers are also benefited because they are assured of a steady supply of products of the required quality as per the delivery schedules.

3. Contractual VMS

This is another type of vertical marketing system in which an organisation enters into agreement or contract with other channel members to undertake different channel functions.

Contractual systems consist of independent organisations that integrate their distribution operations through contracts. These organisations try to reap the advantages of a vertically integrated system while operating independently. The success of such inter-organisation contractual arrangements depends on the commitment and cooperation from different channel partners.

Contractual systems operate through different forms of co-operation. The oldest form of co-operation is where organisations combine similar marketing resources to succeed in increasing market coverage or to offer the products to consumers in a better way. Contractual system can be used when the individual firms feel that it is too risky to offer products or services to customers independently.

Contractual VMS is appropriate when a channel member wants to have the maximum flexibility to alter its products and strategies or when it wants to reduce risk through minimal investment in other channel activities. If the system fails to deliver positive results, the channel member can easily exit from contractual vertically integrated system.

In a contractual VMS, the channel members must have a deep knowledge of the legal requirements since all the contractual agreements drafted are enforceable by law. Generally, companies that have high bargaining power or those functioning in highly volatile industries like information technology prefer to adopt a contractual system. All the members in the system must commit themselves, at least partially, to working as a team to achieve certain common goals. This is because organisations enter into such a system with different objectives like expanding the market demand for their products. This objective holds true for products in the maturity stage of the product life cycle. Industry level promotion where companies not only promote their products but those of other channel members is one form of this approach. It is widely seen in the food products industry.

Retailer-sponsored Co-operative Organisations (RCOs) and Wholesaler-sponsored Volunteer Organisations (WVOs) are two of the best-known forms of contractual vertical marketing systems. RCOs are formed when groups of independent retailers combine and support a single wholesaler. The wholesaler caters to the different needs of the retailer groups and the retailers get benefits in the form of rebates or price discounts from the wholesaler. The channel power is in the hands of the retailers. In a WVO, the wholesaler takes on the onus of establishing a voluntary group of retailers. The wholesaler meets the needs of the retailers far more economically and effectively than the dealers could manage on their own. RCOs and WVOs operate in a similar manner, except for the difference in sponsorship and channel power.

One of the most widely used and successful forms of a contractual system is franchising.

Costs and Benefits of Vertical Marketing Systems

Channel members must be aware of the costs and benefits of vertical marketing system. The costs or benefits accrued depend on the channel power, channel level, and the objective of the participating channel member.

Benefits

Vertical integration is one of the most sought after strategies, whenever a company plans to diversify. The company must consider the benefits of vertical integration from the following perspectives.

1. **Internal benefits:** Internal benefits include improved profitability, better control on the product quality, and increased efficiency in inventory management.

2. **Competitive benefits:** Competitive benefits may include the increased ability to respond to changing market needs. Better economic control, improved marketing expertise, decreased costs leading to better competitive advantage, stability in operations, and reduction in risks arising from competitor's actions.

3. **Differentiation benefits:** The vertically integrated system enables the channel members to differentiate their offerings in terms of better product availability, lower costs, or improved service.

Costs

Vertical integration is always associated with the additional costs associated with administrating the processes. Administrative overheads form a significant portion of these costs. They involve costs associated with setting up and maintaining the system. A company must estimate the costs that it might incur due to opportunism of the channel members, volatility of the markets and industry instability along with the administrative overheads. There is a possibility of operational inflexibility. The heavy investment along the entire channel makes it difficult to modify processes, policies, and strategies quickly to counter external conditions. Since the company has to manage the different functions in the channel, it might not get the opportunity to gain expertise in a particular functional area of the distribution channel.

5.5.6 Distribution Management

Distribution management includes all the processes and activities involved to deliver a product right from the manufacturer to the end user or the point-of-sale. It starts with the design of the distribution network. It also includes channels management, and distribution activities like warehousing, delivery to retailers or the distribution centres, optimal inventory management, secure packaging, efficient customer support and reverse logistics.

(I) MANAGEMENT OF CHANNELS:

(i) **Selection of Channel Member:** Companies need to concentrate on strengthening core competencies and outsource other activities, for succeeding in the market place. With a careful selection of channel members, the distribution channel function can be outsourced. This is very important for any company as the channel members represent the company in the market. Replacing existing channel members is difficult. Therefore, firms have to be cautious while recruiting, to ensure that an ideal channel member can be selected. An ideal channel member will be the one who will serve the right customer at the right time with the right attitude. Hence, a careful recruiting and selection procedure is essential for selecting channel members suiting the company's requirements.

Once companies appreciate the significance of recruitment and selection of proper channel members, they should consider the following guidelines for effective recruitment.

- To assess the exact role to be played by the channel members or the nature of the job they have to perform.
- To analyse the qualifications of the channel member in terms of the firm's requirements.
- The authority to be delegated to channel members.
- Changes that may occur in the future with regard to the role played by channel members.

Recruiting a channel member should be a continuous process for the following reasons:

- Channel members may leave the organisation.
- The organisation might feel the need to change existing channel members.

There can be various reasons emphasising the need for continuous recruitment of channel members. For example, a revision in the company's product policy may call for new types of channel members. Change in customers' tastes and preferences will influence the company to look for the new channel members if the existing channel members are unable to cater to the changed conditions.

(ii) **Channel Motivation:** To motivate intermediaries the firm can use positive actions, such as offering higher margins to the intermediary, special deals, premiums and allowances for advertising or display. On the other hand, negative actions may be necessary, such as threatening to cut back on margin, or hold back delivery of product.

(iii) **Channel conflict:** Channel conflict can arise when one intermediary's actions prevent another intermediary from achieving his or her objectives. Vertical channel conflict occurs between the levels within a channel and horizontal channel conflict occurs between intermediaries at the same level within a channel.

Sources of Conflict

There are many reasons why conflicts arise in distribution channels. Learning about conflicts is important in conflict analysis. The primary reason for arising of channel conflicts is faulty channel design. The different sources of conflicts can be classified into those arising from attitudinal differences and those arising from structural differences among channel members. Structural differences arise mainly due to goal divergence or incompatibility among channel members, tendency towards autonomy and greater control by channel members and competition for scarce channel resources (financial, technological support), especially from manufacturers in multi-channel systems. Attitudinal differences arise from differences in perception, channel roles and channel communications. Conflicts can also arise because of unexpected changes in the competitive environment, consumers and markets, differences in economic and ideological objectives among channel members. In addition to external changes, market channel strategies adopted by channel members also contribute to channel conflicts.

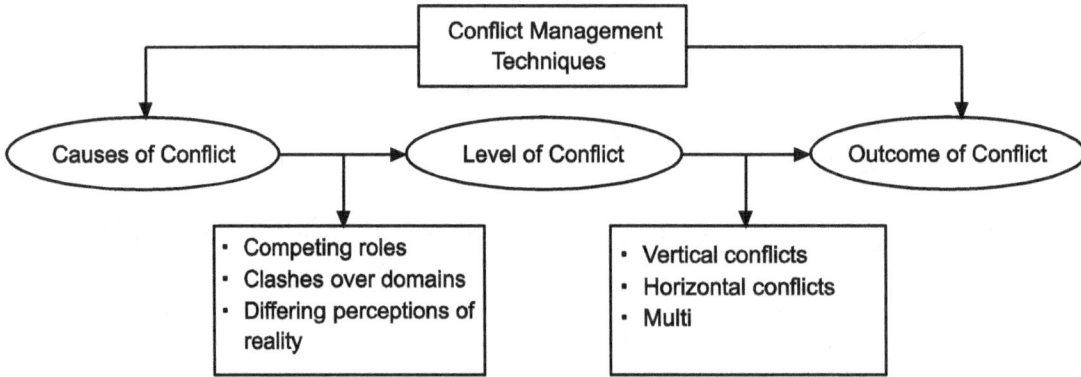

Fig. 5.3: Channel Conflict Model

Some prevalent sources of conflicts in distribution channels are goal incompatibility, differing perceptions of reality and clashes over domain.

1. **Goal Incompatibility**

    Channel conflicts may arise due to incompatibility of goals and objectives among channel members. Differences in policies and procedures of a channel member may be problematic and impede the progress of other channel members. This divergence of goals may lead to one channel member acting in a way that is detrimental to goal achievement for another channel member. This may occur without the former being aware of its impact on the latter.

    Goals may be different within an organisation. The goals decided by top management may vary from goals at the tactical level; those are set because of day-to-day operational policies. Hence, it is necessary to ensure that operational goals are tuned with other goals of the organisation.

Another reason for goal incompatibility is difficulty in measurement of goals. It becomes impossible for channel members to compare the compatibility of their mutual goals and measure the extent of performance of other channel members. Such lack of awareness gives rise to a sense of doubt and conflict.

The difference in goals also arises due to the inherent conditions in the channel. Each channel member faces certain constraints at their level in the distribution channel. As the constraints are restricted to particular levels in the channel, members at each level will develop individual goals in accordance with these constraints. These goals will differ from the goals of other channel members. Goal conflict is widely prevalent in principal-agent relationships, where the principal depends on and directs the agent to perform channel functions on his behalf. Conflict arises in this relationship when the agent performs against the principal's interests. Again, the reason is difference in goals and objectives of the agent from that of the principal. Goal conflicts in an agency relationship can be reduced by designing contracts that ensure mutual benefit for both the principal and agent. The contract must consider the functions and structure of ownership arrangements within the channel and the compensation/incentives on achieving required performance levels for channel members as a part of the agency relationship. Thus, the solution to reducing conflicts in an agency relationship is to ensure that the agent's goals align with the principal's goals.

2. Differing Perceptions of Reality

This is another prominent source of conflicts in distribution channels. It is perception of reality that enables channel members to anticipate future events and their consequences. This, in turn, induces channel members to develop alternative courses of action and estimate the probable results. The perception of reality also has an influence on the goals and values of channel members. However, perceptions of reality can be different. Different perceptions of channel members may be due to:

- One channel member wrongly perceiving the role of another channel member regarding marketing channel functions and flows.
- Lack of proper communication flow among channel members. This affects the way reality is perceived by them.
- Information influencing the decision-making process. This affects the behaviour of channel members.

Thus, conflicts arise among channel members, when channel members have different approaches to interpreting information, decisions made and goals set.

3. **Clashes Over Domains**

   Conflicts in marketing channels arise from the domain definition and the extent to which other channel members accept it. The domain of channel members consists of product range, population and territories served and functions to be performed. Differences in domain automatically give rise to conflicts among channel members.

4. **Product Range**

   Handling a large number of products results in reduction in loyalty among channel members. Distributors cannot show the same level of loyalty towards the products of all manufacturers. This variation in loyalty gives rise to conflicts of interest between manufacturers and distributors.

5. **Population and Territory Coverage**

   Conflict over customer accounts and territory coverage are unavoidable when there are many channel members serving a particular consumer segment. Channel members may cater to certain accounts and other channel members may compete for the same accounts. Hence, manufacturers or suppliers must specify territories for channel members.

   The same is true in franchising, where market territory expansion is a major source of conflicts. The franchiser's strategy of market penetration with the help of new franchisees may reduce the sales of existing franchisees. This is because a franchisee attracts customers from beyond the assigned territories too. With an entry of new franchisee in the region, customers beyond the actual territory may shift to the new franchisee due to proximity of location. Hence, even though the franchiser does not infringe the contract, franchisees may become dissatisfied.

   Franchise conflicts related to customer and territory coverage are greater in business format franchising than in product format franchising. This is because in the business format, the franchisee does not have the flexibility to modify the business model in line with the changing local conditions. Hence, the loss of potential customer becomes a major source of conflict. Conflicts in product format franchising are lower because the franchisee has the flexibility to modify the business model. The franchisor only gives the rights to market products and is not concerned with the mode of business operations.

Performance of Channel Functions

   Sometimes, channel members may feel that they are being asked to perform functions incompatible with their organisational goals. This happens when channel members prefer to perform only channel functions that help them achieve individual goals. As these goals are not common to all channel members, it gives rise to functional conflicts. For instance, manufacturers have a strategic outlook towards marketing their products, while marketing channels focus on operational aspects. To avoid inconvenience of operations, retailers may not train their personnel to identify whether a product returned is genuinely faulty, and then refund customers. Due to this, manufacturers will encounter losses when many products are returned and marketing channels have to be given replacement. Thus, difference in roles among channel members causes conflict.

Types of Conflicts

Channel conflicts can be categorised into different types depending on timing and levels of the channel. They are pre-contractual and post-contractual conflicts, vertical, horizontal and multi-channel conflicts.

Pre-contractual and Post-contractual Conflicts

Channel conflicts may occur at two different points of time in the channel relationship. It could be before a relationship develops or after it commences between channel members. These conflicts arise whenever channel members enter into new relationships.

Pre-contractual conflicts arise when the principal decides to offer a contract to an agent. The major issues are whether a particular agent has the characteristics a principal wants and what strategy should the principal employ to find this out. These problems occur during recruitment of new salespeople or marketing personnel, selection of dealers for their distribution channels and choosing advertising agencies.

Post-contractual conflicts happen after the relationship between channel members begins. The causes are generally unforeseen events, which must be identified and dealt with immediately. One major issue that appears in post-contractual conflicts is the method of evaluation of channels, so that their actions confine to the principal's goals. For instance, differences may arise between the principal and channels while designing compensation programmes.

Thus, at both stages of the channel relationship, conflict identification and management is necessary to ensure proper channel co-ordination. Channel members must take all necessary precautions to identify possible sources of conflicts and devise mechanisms to prevent them.

Channel Level Conflicts

Conflicts can take place at different levels of the marketing channel system – between manufacturer and retailer, wholesaler and retailers, between two wholesalers or retailers at the same level and so on. Channel level conflicts are classified as vertical, horizontal and multi-level channel conflicts.

(i) **Vertical Channel Conflicts:** Vertical channel conflicts arise between channel members operating at different levels within the same channel structure. Conflict between manufacturer and distributors when the manufacturer tries to enforce pricing and service policies on the distributor. This is a type of vertical channel conflict.

(ii) **Horizontal Channel Conflicts:** Horizontal type of channel conflicts arises between channel members operating at the same level within the channel structure. For example, a conflict between two franchisees over clash of domains is an example of horizontal channel conflict.

(iii) **Multi-Channel Conflicts:** Multi-channel conflict occurs when the manufacturer establishes two or more channels catering to the same market. For example, conflicts arise between the manufacturer and wholesalers, when the manufacturer tries to bypass wholesalers by resorting to newer channels like the internet marketing or direct mail.

Conflicts are generally perceived as dysfunctional. However, a complete elimination of conflict among channel members is not recommended because channel members may become complacent in developing mutually beneficial relationships with other channel members and will not compete effectively. Innovation may also be lost. Hence, a certain level of conflict is required as a constructive mechanism in channel relationships.

Techniques to Resolve Channel Conflicts

Conflicts between two channel members can be resolved either by one channel member modifying/changing its organisational goals or by conceding some amount of autonomy/ resources to the other channel member. Conflict resolution processes can be made into effect through mutual agreement or by the use of channel power.

Conflict resolution mechanisms can be divided into two categories – in the first (systematic mechanism), the conflict resolution mechanism is based on the policies that channel leaders implement to resolve channel conflicts in a streamlined manner. These conflict resolution mechanisms are aimed at increasing the level of understanding among various channel members. Some systematic mechanisms include joint memberships in trade organisations, exchange of personnel between two or more channels, distributor councils and various programmes such as co-optation. The second category of conflict resolution mechanism is based on behavioural and attitudinal responses channel leaders offering to solve conflicts in a distribution channel. These responses of channel members are problem solving, persuasion, bargaining and political strategies.

Some strategies implemented under both categories are –

1. **Negotiation (Bargaining):** Channel members use negotiation or bargaining as a tool for resolving conflicts. Negotiations usually take place over price, cash credit, discounts, delivery, inventory levels and other elements in the marketing mix. In negotiations, goal differences are considered as fixed and conflict resolution mechanisms do not mean development of common goals. The outcome of negotiations varies depending on the number of channel members and the extent of balance of power among them.

During negotiations, channel members participate in low risk behaviour, where information exchange is kept to the minimal to reduce the financial, social and physical costs incurred. Sometimes channel members, during negotiation, behave rigidly. Threats, promises and conditional commitments are common features of negotiation process.

The negotiation process is very important especially in marketing channels, because its efficiency has a direct impact on the selling and purchasing costs among channel members.

2. **Initial Bids:** During bargaining, channel members with greater power than their partners make more demanding initial bids. Similarly, weak bargainers put forward less demanding bids or conditions.

3. **Extent of Flexibility:** Channel members with greater power do not yield much from their initial bargaining conditions compared to channel members who have less power.

4. **Time of Negotiation:** More powerful channel members are able to obtain an acceptable agreement faster than less powerful channel members are.

5. **Communication Content:** Channel members with greater power frequently make use of commanding language and actions during negotiations with other channel members.

6. **Negotiation Outcome:** Channel members with more power reach agreements that give them a larger share of total profits of the channel group.

7. **Persuasive Mechanism:** Persuasive conflict resolution is another method used by channel leaders to resolve conflicts. The objective is to move both parties (channel members) towards a common set of goals. In this method, each channel member tries to influence and change the view of other channel member with regard to the conflicting issues. The basic approach used in persuasive conflict resolution mechanism is to highlight the importance of mutually beneficial common goals over individual goals and also reduce differences present in individual goals of each channel member. However, in this method, channel members involve in high-risk behaviour by sharing important information to arrive at a common goal. This is in contrast to the low-risk behaviour observed during negotiations. This type of conflict resolution mechanism is often exercised between franchisers and franchisees. For instance, franchisers may have to persuade franchisees to maintain product quality levels consistently across franchises to project a uniform business image.

Problem-Solving Strategies

This method is also used as a conflict resolution mechanism to settle conflicts among distribution channels. Here, both parties share common objectives, but differ on the decision-making criteria. Open transfer of information about goals and objectives takes place and both parties try to sort out differences by exploring alternative solutions. Unlike in negotiations, co-operation and co-ordination exist among channel members. Channel members are ready to modify certain conditions to arrive at a mutually acceptable solution.

Political Strategies

This is another conflict resolution tool, similar to bargaining. In this case, channel members who have disagreed over each other's objectives agree to a third party becoming involved. This party acts as an ally to the channel members. This method is resorted to only when all other interpersonal methods of solving conflicts fail to work. Political-based conflict resolution strategies make the use of diplomacy, mediators and arbitrators to solve conflicts.

1. **Diplomacy:** It is an approach where each side deputes a person or group to meet its counterparts to resolve the conflict.

2. **Mediation:** In this case, a third party tries to settle conflicts between channel members, either by urging them to continue negotiations till a solution is reached or takes into consideration recommendations made by the mediator.

3. **Arbitration:** In arbitration, the two parties present their agreements to one or more arbitrators, referees or a private judge and accept the verdict delivered. Usually, channel members have a clause in their contracts stipulating the use of arbitration in case of conflicts between them. There are many arbitration centres all over the world, where organisations can take their disputes.

4. **Co-optation:** Co-optation is an information intensive mechanism, which involves free information transfer between aggrieved parties. Co-optation is a mechanism where a new member from outside the organisation is appointed and is involved in the decisions and policies of top management. A channel member makes an effort to win the support of other channel members by including them in its advisory council or board of directors.

Co-optation allows the concept of sharing responsibility so that channel members from different levels can become prominent in the entire distribution system and are committed to the programmes and policies of one another. In this method, one channel member may have to make concessions on its policies and plans to seek the support of the newly elected member from other channel organisations. Co-optation reduces conflicts as long as the channel member treats the new individual member seriously and listens to them. This mechanism is risky because of the physical, economic and financial cost involved.

Exchange of personnel between two or more channels is also viewed as an effective conflict resolving mechanism. This enables participants to visit each other's facilities and facilitates better understanding of each other's point of view. Another frequently used method is the encouragement of joint membership in and between trade organisations. For example, if manufacturers and retailers are associated with each other's trade associations, they become aware of each other's limitations and problems, apart from approach to business. In addition to these strategies, channel members can reduce the frequency and intensity of conflict by adopting following practices during routine channel functions.

Personal Relationships

Channel members must develop personal relationships to reduce the intensity of conflicts and discuss various conflict issues rationally.

- **Error Clarification:** Whenever a channel member errs, it must be brought to the notice of the other channel partner, so that new problems due to lack of awareness of the reciprocating firm do not arise.

- **Distribution Indicators:** Channel members must develop distribution indicators to alert those affected. The indicators can be inventory levels, value of sales or order volumes.

- **Meetings:** The sales personnel of manufacturers must be frequently in contact with sales personnel of other channel intermediaries so that they can share views and prevent arising of conflicts.

- **Appreciate each channel member's requirements:** By visiting the manufacturer's plant and observing activities like ordering procedures and quality management activities, the channel member can gain a clear picture of potential difficulties in getting a product delivered on time. Likewise, by making joint visits to trade fairs and sharing information, both parties can enjoy a harmonious working relationship.

- **Communication:** The communication process within the channel structure and between channel members should be streamlined. Continuous sharing of information through networks can ensure this. It is generally observed that attitudinal differences occur due to improper communication and information processing among channel members. Hence, by designing communication programmes that increase exchange of information about goals, expectations and future plans among channel members, the quantum of conflict will be considerably reduced.

(II) PHYSICAL DISTRIBUTION MANAGEMENT:

The physical distribution involves the following activities:

(i) **Order processing:** Order is received; the order is processed by following a set of procedures for receiving, handling and filling of orders within the timeframe and accuracy. Order processing can be conventional or it may make use of EDI system (Electronic Data Interchange System) for exchanging order requisitions, proforma invoices, bills etc.

(ii) Inventory control: It satisfies the order fulfilment as demanded by the customers. Orders can be JIT (Just in Time) to save the inventory holding costs, or inventory may be stocked as per the market demand.

(iii) Inventory location and warehousing: Inventory size, inventory storage, inventory location and inventory transportation plays an important role in efficient distribution management. One important element of storage of inventory is warehousing facility. Warehousing can also be used for packaging, cross-docking, break-bulk and re-shipments.

(iv) Materials handling: Selecting appropriate equipments for the physical handling of goods, safety of products, protective packaging, security from theft and pilferage are the main functions of materials management.

(v) Transportation: Selection and management of the transport system for the delivery of products to the predefined location. It includes domestic transports like rail, trucks, and boats etc., international transports like airways, ships and pipelines. Transportations can also be a multi-modal system where different modes of transports may be used for increasing efficiency and cost-effectiveness.

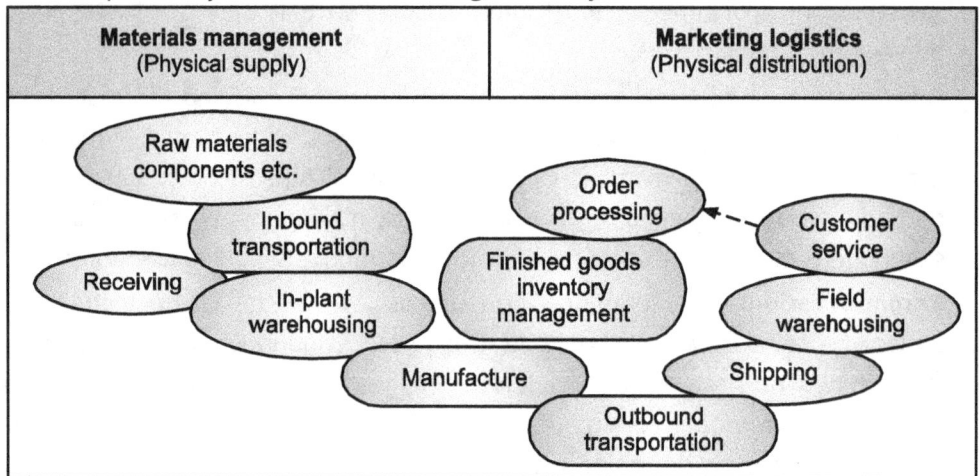

Fig 5.4: Activities in a Physical Distribution System

5.5.7 Standards of Performance of Distribution and Analysis/ Distribution Evaluation/Distribution Assessment

Performance evaluation/appraisal of a marketing channel can take place based on various perspectives. The evaluation assesses the marketing channel's financial performance and looks into societal contributions made by individual members of the channel. From the societal perspective, the performance of marketing channels is assessed by measurement of overall channel performance in terms of the channel's efficiency, effectiveness and equity. To evaluate at a micro-level, an individual channel member's financial performance is determined by studying the channel tasks performed by the member. Channel effectiveness is another parameter that measures channel performance and its ability to satisfy customer needs. It focuses on issues like lot size, delivery time, location convenience and assortment breadth.

Channel equity refers to the distribution of opportunities available to all customers in evaluation of the marketing channels of a region. The primary purpose of distribution is to get the company products within arm's reach of desire. Any channel evaluation system has to keep this in mind and find out how well the distribution channel is serving this primary purpose.

The criteria for evaluation of the channel members vary with their categories and are as follows –

Table 5.2: Criteria for Evaluation

Criteria for evaluation	Popular performance measures
Sales target achievement	• Primary sales • Secondary sales • Achievement of sales target • Sales growth by period • Market share achieved
Inventory management	• Average level of inventory maintained • Inventory turnover (inventory to sales ratio) • Inventory of slow moving stocks • Storage quality
Selling resources	• Number of sales people • Target achievement by each sales person
Market coverage	• Calls per day • Productive calls per day • Extension of credit • Support to new product launches • Support to promotions
Back office support	• Use of PCs • Trained manpower • Reports, records

Channel Performance at a Macro Level

A marketing channel's performance is measured in terms of its ability to meet the manufacturer's business objectives. Performance at macro-level is evaluated in terms of contributions made by the marketing channel to the society. Major elements that will decide the success of an intermediary are channel efficiency, productivity, effectiveness, equity and profitability.

Channel efficiency is a channel performance dimension that determines the ability of intermediaries to perform necessary channel functions with minimal costs. Productivity deals with the extent to which the total channel investment in the form of inputs have been optimised to yield maximum outputs. Productivity and efficiency deal with maximising outputs for a given level of inputs while keeping down costs irrespective of problems faced during the distribution process. The channel's performance is also measured by the intermediary's assistance to suppliers in meeting their objectives. The intermediary's contribution towards the supplier's efficiency and productivity is determined by the extent of contribution to the suppliers' profit and sales.

Channel Performance at a Micro Level

Channel performance at micro-level involves a closer look at the performance of individual intermediaries of a marketing channel. Each intermediary should help the manufacturer achieve the objectives of goal attainment, pattern maintenance, integration and adaptation.

Goal attainment refers to achieving the firm's goals by maximising outputs given the cost constraints and company-specific obstacles.

Pattern maintenance involves co-ordination of processes and functions among organisational units to help the smooth functioning of system.

Integration indicates the co-ordination among the components of a channel or an organisation to meet common objectives and maintain the single unit entity. Adaptation is the modification of resources required to meet system objectives.

An organisation must be able to achieve all four objectives to facilitate smooth functioning of the system.

5.6 Controlling the Distributor and Retailer

By selecting and appointing distributors and retailers, the distribution network offers the benefit of the local market scenario, along with the access to their existing customer base and the sales force team. To realise those benefits, you must control distributor performance through tight management and focused, directed support.

Control on Products

The distributor/retailer should be capable of marketing the type of products being manufactured by the firm. It is expected by the manufacturer that the distributor or the retailer should give commitment and priority to market the products and not those other competitors. To ensure this commitment, a contract can be signed mutually for selling only the company's products. On the other hand, if independent distributors carry products that are competitive with your own, you can secure their commitment by offering sales incentives that reward their loyalty.

Training on Products/Knowledge of Products

The selection of the distribution team must be based on the sound knowledge of your products, markets and the needs of the customers. Ideally, they should have experience and a base of existing customers in your sector. You can meet their expectations for support by providing sales and market training in the form of product knowledge and information on sales and marketing techniques. To simplify access to product and market knowledge, you can set up secure website pages where distributors can download product guides, training material and market data.

Communications

Provide clear guidelines on communications programs, key messages and the use of brand elements such as logos. Distributors/retailers communicate your marketing messages to the customers within their reach. An organisation can support the communications by providing funds for advertising campaigns, supplying direct marketing material and customer-facing publications or running joint marketing campaigns.

Service

Distributors represent the company when they deal with customers. It is therefore essential that they deliver the highest standards of customer service. Poor quality of service will damage the company's reputation. The organisation must provide a set of customer service standards that set out the expectations for the way distributors deal with customers. The organisation must be specific about issues such as dealing with customer complaints or providing advice and guidance to customers.

International Distribution Control

Multinationals need to do a better job of selecting and working with local distributors. In particular, they must understand that distributors are implementers of marketing strategy, rather than marketing departments in the country-market. The result will be better working relationships, fewer plateaus and crises and more consistent growth in market share and sales revenues. Once corporations understand that they can control their international operations through better relationship structures rather than simply through ownership, they might also find longer-term roles for local distributors within a regionalised approach to global strategy.

An established organisation further tries to look for new international markets and thus makes a foray into an emerging market. The first step to the entry in an international market is by appointing a local independent distributor. Initially the sales take off, and there is high revenue generation and the market entry is considered as a smart move. After sometime, there is stagnation in the market as the distributor has run out of new ideas and starts underperforming. As a result, the organisation tries to save itself by setting up its own distribution and sales force. A transition from indirect to direct sales is usually costly and disruptive. It can also create new problems that come to the surface only in the long term; executives may discover a few years later that they have gone too far in correcting a number of situations like this, saddling the multinational with a dense and inefficient network of national distributors. It is therefore very important to control the global network of distributors at the initial stages of market entry.

Managing the Life Cycle of the International Distributor

Make a partnership agreement for a limited period, for example, 2 years or 5 years

1. **Select distributors:** An entry into new international market should be the result of a strategic decision based on an objective market assessment. Focus first on identifying the country, then finding a distributor. "Being market-led rather than distributor-led often results in selecting a better distributor because of a more systematic and thorough assessment of potential partners."

2. **Look for distributors capable of developing markets rather than those with a few obvious customer contacts.** The choice of distributors and the terms of the relationships should serve the multinational's long-term goals. "The most obvious distributor is not necessarily the best partner for the long term. The closeness of the market fit can be a liability as well as an asset, because the distributors represent the market's status quo, and we are selling a replacement technology and attempting to change the market. Choose a company-fit distributor. A partner with a culture and a strategy we feel comfortable with, in terms of the investment they will make, the training they will give their people, and the support we provide them.

3. **Treat the local distributors as long-term partners:** Structure the relationships so that distributors become marketing partners willing to invest in long-term market development. One traditional way of doing this is to grant national exclusivity to a distributor, although such an agreement can become unproductive if conflicts of interest arise once entry is established. A more effective solution is to create an agreement with strong incentives for appropriate goals, such as customer acquisition or new product sales. After all, the local distributor is the de facto marketing arm of the multinational in its country.

4. **Support market entry by committing money, managers, and proven marketing ideas.** To retain strategic control, multinationals must commit adequate corporate resources. This is especially true during market entry, when corporations are least certain about their prospects in new countries.

    Traditionally, multinationals have demonstrated commitment by sending in technical and sales personnel or offering training to distributor employees. Such support is good, of course, but more experienced corporations now go further and do things earlier. In markets regarded as strategically important, they have started to take minority equity stakes in autonomous distribution companies. Although this increases exposure without achieving control, it opens the door to cooperative marketing based on shared information, thus increasing the advantage and effectiveness of both the multinational and the local partner.

    Sometimes multinationals invest in distributors in ways that do not lead to co-ownership but that demonstrate solid commitments to the relationships.

5. **Maintain control over marketing strategy right from start.** An independent distributor should be allowed to adapt a multinational's strategy to local conditions. However, multinationals should convene and lead planning sessions and exercise authority about which products to sell, how to position them, and budgeting. If corporations provide solid leadership for marketing, they will be in a position to exploit the full potential of a global marketing network.

   Multinationals committed to maintaining early control over marketing strategy find that it is important to have employees on-site. Some send a few employees to work full-time at the local distributor's offices. Others establish country or regional managers who can keep a close watch on both distributor performance and customer needs.

6. **Distributors must provide with market and financial data.** A multinational's ability to exploit its competitive advantages in an emerging market depends heavily on the quality of information it obtains from the market. In many countries, the distribution organisations are the only sources of such information. A contract with a distributor must therefore require detailed market and financial performance data.

   Not having these data can lead to serious problems. The reaction to a request for market and financial data reveals a lot about a distributor. Most distributors, of course, regard data like customer identification and price levels as key sources of power in their relationships with suppliers. Several multinational executives said that the willingness of potential distributors to provide such information was a prime indicator of whether successful relationships could be achieved.

7. **Build links among national distributors at the earliest opportunity.** Although a multinational's primary focus after entering a new country is establishing a customer base there, the company should create links among its national distributors as soon as possible. The links may take the form of a regional corporate office or an independent network such as a distributor council. The transfer of ideas within local markets can improve performance and result in greater consistency in the execution of international strategies.

Points to Remember

- Transportation refers to the movement of goods, raw material and finished products between different facilities in a supply chain.
- Strategic Decisions for Transportation include
  1. Facility
  2. Inventory
  3. Transportation
- A transportation management system is an organised system that may use information technology for the effective transportation operations. Transportation system is an important component of the supply chain.

- Cross-docking is a logistics practice where the goods are unloaded from an incoming transport system like a truck or semi-trailer and then directly loading these goods onto outbound transport system with very little or nil storage.
- The technique by which the retailer does not keep goods in stock but instead transfers customer orders and shipment details to the manufacturer, another retailer, or a wholesaler, who then ships the goods directly to the customer, is known as drop-shipping.
- There are three basic modes of transport that a company can choose from –
   1. **Domestic:** Includes Roadways, Railways, and Inland Waterways.
   2. **International:** Airways, Seaway, Oil Pipelines
   3. **Multimodal:** Transports using multiple modes like Roadways and Seaway in a combination.
- This is a very competent strategy for the distribution of products. The main goal of the manufacturer/ distributor is to gain a maximum reach by using all available outlets.
- In selective distribution, the customers usually prefer a particular brand or price and will look for outlets that supply the same.
- Exclusive distribution is an extreme form of selective distribution in which only one wholesaler, retailer or distributor is used in a specific geographical area.
- In a corporate VMS, one company owns and operates the other channel members at different channel levels.
- Unlike corporate system, in the administered type of vertical marketing system, no channel member has complete control over other channel members.
- Contractual VMS is another type of vertical marketing system in which an organisation enters into agreement or contract with other channel members to undertake different channel functions.

Questions for Discussion

1. Define transportation and state the importance of transportation.
2. Discuss the various modes of transportation.
3. Explain distribution analysis control and management.
4. Elaborate on the controlling of the distributor and retailer.

■■■

Q.1 Define Physical Distribution System (PDS). Elaborate the Elements of Total Cost in PDS. **[15]**

Q.2 What do you mean by Distribution Channel? Discuss the Factors in Selection of Distribution Channel. **[15]**

Q.3 Define Logistics Integration. Explain the Functional Areas of Logistic Integration. **[15]**

Q.4 Explain in detail Remuneration of Sales Person. **[15]**

Q.5 Explain the term Physical Distribution Management. Explain the Techniques in Controlling Distributors and Retailers. **[15]**

Q.6 Write Short Notes (Any Four): **[20]**

(a) Transportation

(b) Distribution Objectives

(c) Standards of Performance of Distribution

(d) Strategies of Channels of Distribution

(e) Logistics Management

(f) Motivational Tools for Intermediaries.

■■■

Notes

www.ingramcontent.com/pod-product-compliance
Lightning Source LLC
Chambersburg PA
CBHW080727020726
47503CB00010B/2818